THE LOST CODEX
OF THE CHRISTIAN HERETICS

KYLA MERWIN

THE LOST CODEX
OF THE CHRISTIAN HERETICS

Cover Design
Teddy Raines, Tula Design

Copy Editor
JeanMarie Morrison

Published by KMC Media Co.
Portland, Oregon
www.kmc-media.com/books
Printed in the U.S.A.

ISBN: 978-0-9910689-2-0
978-0-9910689-3-7 (EBook)

Publisher's Note
This is a work of historical fiction. Certain locations, agencies and historical incidents are included, but names, characters and other incidents are either the product of the author's imagination or are used fictitiously.

For the Heroes in My Life

Bob Morris
Raymond Merwin
Ken Merwin
Sam Merwin
Jim Prather
Gary Winz
Amr Abdel Karim
Mike Cheney
Ronald Del Carlo
John Spence

With special thanks to
Christopher Dent
for encouragement during the manuscript's tender beginnings.

And finally to Elaine Pagels, whose seminal work, *The Gnostic Gospels*,
inspired this book and shed light on a dark time.

Thank you.

Historical Note

In 1945, outside a remote village in upper Egypt, peasant farmers unearthed a large clay jar sealed at the top with a shallow bowl. They feared a *jinn* would be released and wreak havoc on them if they opened it. Their hopes for treasure ultimately overcame their fear, and the eldest brother raised his mattock and smashed the jar.

To his extreme disappointment, only 13 leather-bound papyrus texts lay in the crumbled clay. These texts were traded for oranges and cigarettes, and sold on the Black Market in Cairo. It took over 30 years for all of the precious manuscripts to be recovered, translated and published for the world. They are called *The Gnostic Gospels*.

The story that follows is a fictional account of the recovery and translation of those texts. Though based on historical figures and events, what is written here is entirely fictional, except for the literal translations of the Gnostic manuscripts – the words of the heretics.

"Anthony, and others like him,
sought the shape of his own soul,
hoping to accept the terrors and ecstasies
of direct and unremitting encounters with himself,
and, having mastered himself,
to discover his relationship with the Infinite God."

– Elaine Pagels, *Adam, Eve, and the Serpent*

– THE CHARACTERS –

Katherine Howard Spencer • Owner of an antique store in New York, wife to Nick Spencer

Nick Spencer • Attorney in New York City

Etienne Desonia • French archeologist in Egypt, college friend of Katherine and Nick

Hugo Nelson • New York billionaire

Eugene • Manager of Katherine's antique store

Cato Nafarah • Agent of the Egyptian Department of Antiquities, hunting Etienne

Omar Kassab • Agent of the Egyptian Department of Antiquities, under Nafarah

Jahib • One-eyed bandit who brings a manuscript to Etienne

Zafar • Store owner in Qina, friend of Bahij

Father Antonio • Catholic priest, based in Tenerife, Africa

Dara • Etienne's live-in housekeeper

Miss Donatta • Italian art collector living in Cairo

Muhanna Ali al-Samara • Discoverer of the Gnostic manuscripts, from al-Qasr

Uhm Alia • Muhanna's mother

Abdul • Muhanna's brother

Abu al-Hamd • Member of the al-Sayyid clan, blood rivals to the al-Samara clan

Talib Nagi • Director of the Coptic Museum in Cairo

Shadif • Collector who deals with Etienne, suspected to be involved in the Muslim Brotherhood

Henri Poirier • French archeologist, Etienne's rival

Father Mhand • Coptic priest from the village of al-Qasr

Taya • Caretaker of the Coptic church in al-Qasr, and of Father Mhand

Rasul Taj • Owner of an antique store in Garden City, Cairo

Table of Contents

Prologue A Jar in the Sand...i

1 The September Feeling..1

2 A Call From the Past..8

3 A Tangled Strand of Pearls...24

4 Two Aspects of Isis...34

5 A Deal Gone Sideways...45

6 The Man Who God Forgot...69

7 Flight of the Intrepids..87

8 Divine Intervention..102

9 Wars of Words...116

10 A New Deal...137

11 A Bridge in Time...152

12 Gardens of the Past...171

13 Friends and Enemies...187

14 Caves of Deceit...210

15 Memories in the Distance..232

16 Pillars of the Soul..250

17 A Great Ruckus of Chickens and Men..264

18 The Search for God and Glory...281

19 What Lies Within the Truth...303

20 The Price To Pay...322

21 A Heart's Weight...338

22 Capture and Consequence...353

23 The Long Road Back...377

24 Caves of the Heart...398

25 A Raging Storm...413

26 The Way, The Truth and the Life..424

27 The Key...434

Epilogue Journeys Onward..444

Prologue

A JAR IN THE SAND

And follow that which is inspired in thee from thy Lord.
Lo! Allah is Aware of what ye do.

— Verse 2, The Koran, SURAH XXXIII, *The Clans*

Outskirts of Nag Hammadi, Egypt 1945

The sun blistered down upon the day, drawing every drop of life from the hard-baked ground. Muhanna Ali al-Samara and his two brothers rode solemnly alongside each other, their camels impervious to the heat and the urgency of the day. Three of their cousins joined them in a motley collection of six: strangers to, outcasts of, and enemies in, the land nearby their own. Three extra camels, for packing out riches, plodded in tow behind them. There was strength in numbers today. The al-Samaras had ventured far from home, though close in terms of miles, into the hostile territory of the Inland Empire, ruled by the ruthless al-Yassid clan.

From the distant horizon, with heat rising in sheets from the sand, they appeared as shadows, wavering figures riding above the ground, six phantoms emerging from the abyss. Their turbans and robes rippled in the breeze. Each had a soft-colored scarf worn around his neck, to serve as a prayer cloth on which to kneel before Allah in devotion and gratitude. The silhouettes they created were haunting, tribal, primordial even, as if risen from the roots of the earth and driven by the singular need for survival.

From high atop the cliffs of Jabal al-Tarif, Abu al-Yassid watched the travelers approach, as the Nile flowed by in the background. At first he thought they were from his own village, returning from a supply trip in the nearby city of Nag Hammadi.

Abu's eyes narrowed in a combination of rage and delight, however, as the shapes came closer and his view became startlingly clear. The leaders of the al-Samara clan, his sworn enemies, had roamed far beyond their limits and had sealed their fate with their arrogance.

Abu calculated the time it would take to return to his village of Hamrah Dum and back again to the cliffs. He had ridden far today, much further than his normal survey of the crops under his family's control. He didn't expect to see anything of interest when he set out; he'd merely been inspired to wander. *Allah had willed it*, to be sure. Now, suddenly and urgently, he needed to rally his clansmen. A dozen of their strongest could swoop down upon the unaware al-Samaras and kill them within the span of a minute, reveling in their blood, and leaving their bodies to rot in the sun.

Abu gazed into the sky, feeling the sun on his face. *A good day,* he thought. *Allah smiles upon me.* The heart of the enemy clan had stumbled directly onto the tip of his sword. By the setting of this day's sun, Abu would deliver a glorious victory to his family. The head of the snake would die in the sand and, with it, the violent feud that had cut through the generations before him. Abu's desire for vengeance, weaned from youth on hatred, was made stronger, more virulent, and perhaps – in the absence of a carefree childhood – more bitter. The youngest al-Yassid turned his camel away from the cliff and raced homeward.

Muhanna and his brethren approached the cliffs with caution. Until recently, they had not been this far from their village in many, many years. Not since a quieter time, a time when rivalries had not become so bloody, a time when the sources of their injuries could still be remembered. It had taken much urging, insistence, anger even, for Muhanna Ali to convince his brothers and cousins of this errand.

But Allah had spoken clearly to Muhanna and he would go. The idea had flashed bright and clear in front of him while he was tilling a skinny row of corn stalks. *Go to the cliff of the tombs, where the birds thrive, there to find the seeds of a better life.*

To *fellahin*, village farmers, life rose and fell from the land, and those with fertile ground would prosper. Those without would struggle. The land of Muhanna's family, sharecropped for an absent landlord and taxed by the government, was sandy scrabble. It took much work, much water, and much prayer to eke out a living from year to year, generation to generation, with no hope for permanent land ownership or the prosperity that came with it.

Muhanna thought of his hard-working father, Amr al-Samara, just two weeks dead and cold in the ground. The cowardly al-Yassids, a pack of them, had laid in wait for the unsuspecting farmer. They planted a decoy in the fields, a man whose sole job was to bang two sticks together, and then skitter through the fields from one location to the next.

Woken in the night by strange noises, Amr, the head of the al-Samara family, rose to survey the perimeter of his farm. Concerned about the irrigation system – which was the lifeblood of his crops and his sheep, and easy prey to spiteful sabotage – Amr strode the land in the dark cold hours before morning.

It was then and there he met his death, as the al-Yassids sprung up behind him, sliced his throat and defiled his dying body with their spit and urine. Muhanna found his father when the sun came up, and he – the coldest, most shrewd and cunning of his family – knelt in the dirt and wept.

I will have bloody, merciless revenge, swore Muhanna, with his face to the heavens as he had many times before. And the weight of it bore down on him. So too, did the weight of his family fall upon him. The survival of the al-Samara clan rested on Muhanna's thin, hard shoulders.

Now, in an unexpected gift from Allah, Muhanna had a vision to improve the land and the lot of his family. It would be *he*, Muhanna, eldest of the sons of Amr al-Samara, who would raise the clan to prosperity. It would be *he* who would earn the praise and respect of his dead father and of the God he worshipped.

In his vision, Muhanna saw, and realized it to be true, rich fertile soil at the base of the giant cliffs. The Cliffs of Jabal al-Tarif rose high into the eastern sky, and were pockmarked with tombs, a sacred cemetery of ancients, long since forgotten. In the shade of these abandoned tombs, many species of birds gathered, along with rodents and reptiles, beetles and bugs, each prey or predator to the other.

Nesting along the Nile or roosting in the empty tombs, birds traveled these skies and scoured the sand for food. They ate ravenously, leaving behind their droppings to mix with the sand. These droppings, in turn, created a thick, rich fertilizer called *sabakh*. When mixed with ordinary soil, *sabakh* produced a thriving environment for the growing of corn, wheat and fava beans – the crops of the al-Samara.

Muhanna brought his brothers and cousins together to collect as much of the thick soil as they could carry, day after day for nearly a week. They carried their treasured soil in cloth bags, counterbalanced and strung with rope over their camels. *One more trip,* Muhanna had insisted, *and we'll have enough.* The others were anxious to avoid this area, a zone considered neutral by authorities, but ruled by their al-Yassid enemies nonetheless. But Muhanna had been sent here by Allah and his confidence – and iron fist – ruled the day.

On this last day, Muhanna chose a large pair of boulders sitting like sentinels at the base of the honeycombed cliffs. It was evident that these two boulders had once formed one, and had broken apart in their fall from the side of the mountain. It was here they would dig today. Then their work would be done and they could celebrate their good fortune and the grace bestowed upon them.

They had dug for only an hour before Muhanna's youngest brother, Abdul, called out. "Muhanna! Come quickly!" Muhanna raised his head from his work and held out his sharp digging tool, prepared for any attack of man or beast. "Over here, come look!" cried Abdul, who was kneeling in the sand. Muhanna and the others circled around the kneeling man. "Look what I found!"

Sitting deep in the sand, partly exposed in the hole Abdul had dug, was a large, red earthenware jar. Four handles, loops near the top, could be seen jutting out from the ground. Abdul and a few of the others began to work furiously to raise the jar out of its sandy grave.

"We've found treasure!" exclaimed Khalifah, Muhanna's middle brother. He brushed sand from the rough surface of the jar. Three feet long and a foot in diameter, the jar was heavy, and sealed at the top with a shallow bowl embedded in thick black pitch. When Khalifah shook the jar from side to side, they heard a soft, slushing sound.

"It's a *jinn!*" cried Muhanna's cousin, Jabaz. "Put it back! Put it back!" He looked around wide-eyed, fearful they'd stumbled upon an evil spirit that, if released, would follow them for the rest of their days, playing nasty tricks on them. The circle widened as several of the men stepped backward.

"Don't be a silly woman," mocked Khalifah, who was neither smart nor kind. "We are in the shadow of ancient graves." He pointed his gaze to the cliffs. "This is clearly a treasure, buried long ago, and dislodged when these stones fell from the cliffs." He turned to Muhanna, who was still holding his digging tool. "Use your mattock, Muhanna. Break it open."

iv

"No!" cried the fearful cousin, Jabaz. "I say put it back. *Now*." Excited murmurs rose and fell among the gathered men, some agreeing with Jabaz, others eager to reveal what was hidden inside.

Muhanna considered the jar for a moment, the happenstance of its discovery, and its significance to his mission. *This was not in his vision. Was this a distraction? A test of devotion to his purpose? Or was this the real treasure Allah wanted him to find? In this jar would he find the seeds of his family's fortune? Or would he find only trouble?*

"Stand back," ordered Muhanna. A hush fell on the gathering as Muhanna knelt down and ran his hand along the pottery. It did indeed look very old. It was faded and chipped, brittle from the hot sand. Yet the stone was cool against his touch. It looked innocent, docile, not the likely home of a *jinn*.

Muhanna rose and stood with authority over the treasure. A breeze came up suddenly, blowing his robes behind him, causing the tail of his turban to rise and flutter in the wind. "*Allahu Akbar*," he whispered, raising his mattock high over his head. "God is great." As if guided by fate, or pushed by the powerful hand of God Himself, the mattock dropped through the air and fell upon the jar, shattering it into countless jagged pieces.

It seemed as though Muhanna's heart stopped beating for a moment, as he and the others peered into the shards of red stone. Just then, as the wind began to howl through the cliffs and echo through the empty tombs, something stirred from within the jar.

Muhanna dropped his mattock to the ground as he and his company involuntarily stepped away from the broken jar. A few dropped to their knees in fear. Great dismay covered their upturned faces as they watched a plume of gold rise from the remnants of clay. The mysterious form twisted and sparkled as it stretched into the sky. For a few dazzling seconds it lingered, glittering in the bright sunlight. Then, in a breath, it was gone.

In the near distance, ten riders on camels watched the frightening scene at the boulders. Their eyes were riveted on a shimmering funnel of gold. They pulled up their camels sharply and watched in fear and awe. Their camels shifted nervously as the men looked back and forth between each other, wordlessly. As the gold plume rose into the sky, they saw their enemies kneeling at its feet.

Abu al-Yassid drew his face into a dark scowl. *What evil magic was at hand? Did the al-Samara command it? Or did this shimmering spirit rule them?* It mattered not. Abu would not tarry with such a thing in the wind. The al-Yassid leader turned his camel toward home, hiding his rage in the dark creases of his heart. Vengeance would come another day.

As the golden plume dissipated and the wind calmed to a mild breeze, Muhanna approached the broken jar and peered inside. There, amidst the clay and dust, he found no gold, no silver, no coins or gems. There was only a pile of books, bound in leather, with golden scraps of papyrus dancing in the air. The treasure of Muhanna Ali al-Samara, and his coveted new prosperity, lay in the sand in a disappointing heap of paper and broken pottery.

1

THE SEPTEMBER FEELING

She who reconciles the ill-matched threads of her life
and weaves them gratefully into a single cloth,
it's she who clears the loudmouths from the hall
and clears it for a different celebration,
where the one guest is you.

– Rainer Maria Rilke, *Love Poems to God*

New York City, September 1947

Katherine would remember the day clearly – every detail of it – as the day defeat turned into opportunity. She would look back on it as a departure into something that was both unexpected and inevitable, a relief and a dread. She would remember the exact moment it began. But how she would get from that precise moment, to where she would arrive, she would never completely understand.

As a personal rule, Katherine hated September. It made her restless. It was quieter than summer, dimmer. The sun didn't stay as long in the sky. The leaves were turning gold and red, carpeting the ground in color and light. The sky was a raw and stunning shade of blue. Lovers strolled through Central Park, hand-in-hand. Children were rushing back to school with new clothes and knapsacks full of hopes and happy expectations. Katherine hated every single bit of it.

She only felt the crisp bite in the air, the chill unmistakably calling in autumn. It was the Breath that says: *You are not what you thought you were. Fall now. Let go and become something else.*

Thirty one Septembers had marked the years for Katherine Spencer, each one disappearing softly into the years that came after. Each year inheriting the deepening scars that accumulated and melted into each other. Springing from every loss, belonging specifically to none, the September Feeling, the Fall, was reduced so precisely it could descend, in its whole, any day of the year, any time of the day.

It was a restless feeling, like a leaf used up: released, let go of, separated from the whole. It was a falling, a dying, and it seemed to happen every year. Katherine would feel the need to reinvent herself – in September. And it began just so, on a Thursday, in 1947.

World War II had ended with the A-bomb, two years prior. The American economy was flourishing, and the spirit of the people along with it. There was an air of optimism and relief in the city so tangible one could feel it. *The Diary of Anne Frank* was just published, to the horror and fascination of the world. The British proposal to divide Palestine was rejected by Arabs and Jews, and the matter turned over to the United Nations. Al Capone was dead, the United States pushed an airplane to supersonic speeds, and the Yankees were set to play the Brooklyn Dodgers in the World Series, where a man named Jackie Robinson was breaking the color barrier of the nation's favorite pastime. These were the things that intrigued the country. But not Katherine Spencer.

Katherine was looking in the bathroom mirror, finishing her make-up, dawdling before she caught the train uptown into the city. She picked a fleck of lint off her sweater. Her lips: bright red and precise. Shoulder pads: square and solid. The lines in her stockings: perfectly straight, following all the right curves. A renegade lock of hair popped out of her chignon, and she tucked it back into place. Everything was in order.

And yet … Katherine squinted at her reflection and pursed her lips in the expression that she had come to believe was charming about herself. Something wasn't quite right. *Can a woman look at her face so often,* she wondered, *see mostly what she wants to see, become so accustomed to the look of herself, that she doesn't notice the changes, until one day she doesn't recognize herself at all?*

"Good morning, darling." Nick kissed her on the cheek, and adjusted his suspenders as he stepped next to her in front of the mirror. She watched him work proficiently on his bow tie until it was a perfect yellow butterfly at his neck. He smoothed his starched collar into place. His blonde hair was already combed, parted smartly down the middle; every hair in line.

"My God, we're a swanky couple, aren't we?" said Nick, in his clipped British accent.

2

"Look at that," said Katherine into the mirror. "You're absolutely right." *How easy it is,* she thought with some degree of irony, *to view the bright shining smile in the mirror as if it was your own. Easier still, to flash that custodial smile – that keeper of secrets – at someone else.*

Nick wrapped his arm protectively around his wife's shoulders and kissed her on the forehead. "The bank papers are due today, aren't they?"

"Mmmm," Katherine murmured in response, tilting her head in the mirror, with no expression at all on her face.

"Are you quite all right?" asked Nick, quietly concerned. It was not in his nature to draw out the emotions of any situation. He would much prefer to observe a spectacle than risk being caught up in it.

"Of course," replied Katherine. "It's the right thing to do. Absolutely."

"You're a brave girl, Katherine. I'm terribly proud of you."

"Mmmm."

"Really," said Nick. "Think of all the time you'll have to devote to other things."

Like what? wondered Katherine. *Sitting around getting bored and old?* "Have a good day, darling," she said, kissing her husband on the cheek. "I'll see you tonight. 'Round six?"

"About that. Maybe seven. I have a late meeting. Good luck today." Nick didn't even look twice into the mirror before he said good-bye. "Love you, darling." Then she heard nothing more than his predictable rustling in the hallway – tweed jacket, wool overcoat, scarf, hat, gloves, keys, door, footsteps, door – and he was gone.

I have to go, too, she thought. *I have a ruined business to sell. I have bills to ignore, customers to abandon, one last payroll to worry about, antiques to pack up and ship elsewhere.* She moved down the quiet hallway to the foyer.

Without warning the front door opened and Nick popped back in. For the briefest of moments Katherine felt a wave of relief. It was as if in this one gesture all bad things could be – would be – swept away.

3

"How about I take my girl out to dinner tonight?" Nick flashed his most dazzling smile.

He knows I'm unhappy, thought Katherine. *And he doesn't know what to do about it. Not entirely helpful, but terribly sweet.* "That would be lovely, darling. Thank you."

"Anywhere you want to go."

"Paris?" A frown passed briefly across her husband's face. Katherine shifted her wieght slightly. "San Francisco?"

"For you, San Francisco." Nick beamed at her. "But just this once."

"Love you, darling." Katherine moved to her husband and held onto him. He let her linger there, content to feel her, fragile and warm and nestled into him. The moment was brief, and stung them both, in its sweetness and its vulnerability. Such moments came rarely, and for a reason. They could break you, and Katherine knew it.

Nick finally kissed her good-bye and closed the door softly as he went out. She watched him from the front window as he walked briskly, with purpose and intent, up the street. *What personal sorrows does he take with him when he leaves this house?* wondered Katherine. *What happens in his heart when the smile he gives to me, given a reprieve, falls from his face? What hides inside my husband that I haven't offered room or time enough to understand?*

Katherine stood in the foyer, entirely unable to move. Maybe a minute passed, maybe less. Then, without thinking about it, but doing it every day exactly the same, she took a cursory inventory of her purse: lipstick, pocketbook, linen handkerchief, compact, keys. She rubbed her fingers across the bronze military star she'd hung on a chain. *Heroic or meritorious achievement.* Katherine sighed, and then she snapped her purse shut and gave herself one last look-over in the hall mirror.

God, I'm old, she thought. *At 31, I'm ancient.* She frowned at her expression. She pursed her lips, immediately decided she liked the look of it, and that she wasn't that old after all. Katherine put on her winter coat and walked out the door, carrying weightier concerns, and no idea what was to come.

By mid-morning, Katherine was sitting in her small, cluttered office at the back of her store, putting off a solemn stack of paperwork.

Failure was staring down on her. Downstream of one signature, everything would be different. Like everything was different when she signed her application to Oxford – the application everyone said she was crazy for filing. The one that would open up a new world of opportunities for her. The one that would shape and direct who she would become as a woman and a person of the world. The one that would more than likely be rejected out-of-hand. The one that no one on God's earth could have stopped her from submitting. The one that represented, in retrospect, a page of destiny.

The year was 1933 and her brother, Ben, was leaving. He could go wherever it suited him, do as he pleased. He rode, as always, on a blessed tide. Katherine, by contrast, was expected to stay close to home, get married, raise children, be small. Katherine's mother seemed intent, desperate even, to hold her daughter to the same slate of low expectations as her own. As least it was so in Katherine's mind. But such things weren't the stuff of her dreams back then. So in 1933, when Ben trotted off to England, Katherine followed, to shape her own fate.

On this day in September of 1947, however, the page of destiny that lay before her was quite the opposite as her application to Oxford. It would cast a shadow upon everything she said or did or felt from the moment the ink hit the page. This page was not ushering in endless possibilities. It was a paper issuing her absolute defeat.

For just a moment Katherine felt the old familiar heat of panic rising behind her eyes. But, no, she was resolved. She had left panic behind months ago. She had then become desperate. This antique store, *The Silver Butterfly*, was the one thing in life that had ever been truly hers, just hers. And it was bankrupt. If Katherine had thought to question her passion for things bought and sold off the shelf, she might have found a vacancy there, a bankruptcy of her spirit. But Katherine had been driven past logic to make her store a spectacular success.

All that her dead brother had left behind in the world – a bronze star and a life insurance policy – had been gifted to Katherine. She turned it into a dream, and fifty-thousand dollars of inventory. Her fine taste and circle of affluent friends launched the store – and her confidence – into fantastic realms and for several years she rode a wave of success. Bit by bit, however, she reached beyond her means, and purchased more products than she could sell.

Eventually, Katherine's unique collection of collectibles began to collect dust on the equally unique shelves. She had all the right ideas, the drive, the brains and, God knows, the education. And still she spent more money than she brought in, month after month after

5

month. When she started this business, she and Nick had agreed that the Silver Butterfly would have to stand on its own, and not be subsidized by their personal savings.

An empty bank account, combined with her husband's practical advice and prudent fiscal sensibilities, as well as one last desperate and disastrous gamble on a rare coin collection, and Katherine was finally forced to admit defeat. She was selling every single precious thing she owned, sweeping the remnants off the floor, and going home to be a good wife. She just never thought or dreamed or dared to imagine that such a miserable fate would ever happen to her.

She found herself wondering if there was – at this final hour – another way, a way to save her store and redeem herself in the eyes of her husband, her clients, and the small world of friends and acquaintances that spun around her. She closed her eyes and rested her head in her hands. *God help me,* she thought, in a prayer that called out to no one but herself.

Eventually, Katherine turned her attention back to the documents in front of her. When Ben had died, Katherine had been furious – with God, with Ben, with a world that continued when hers had stopped. She was sickened by the violence and hatred and destruction of the war. But when she saw the newsreels of the Nazi death camps, she knew in her heart that God was dead. She hadn't prayed since.

Katherine stared blankly at the tidy stack of papers prepared for her signature. *I'll be a housewife. I'll spend long, dull, monotonous days doing nothing more important than waiting for Nick to come home. Which will be the big hour of the day, because then I'll have someone to talk to, who of course won't want to talk to me because he's been exhausted by colleagues and clients all day. I'll fuss over him like a lonely, obedient puppy. I'll chat on and on about the most mundane topics, like the neighbor's dog and the price of butter. But at least it'll be the cocktail hour so I'll be able to pour us martinis.*

Over dinner, we'll share a bottle of wine that I'll drink most of, and finish off while doing up the dishes. (Which will be the second big highlight of my day, because I won't have had a real meal all day, tending to eat onion and mustard sandwiches standing over the sink in the absence of any discerning company.) Then of course we'll retire to our easy chairs with a brandy or two before bedtime, to catch up on the Evening *Post and any gossip I can drum up in the absence of intelligent conversation, which will of course, have entirely escaped me.*

6

One dull day will turn into one numb night after another after another until I'm drinking martinis before Nick gets home (which will be later and later the more continually bored and boring I become). I'll madly brush my teeth to hide the smell of gin when I kiss him hello. He'll walk through the door and I'll begin pretending that I've had a delightful day and how was yours, dear?

Then I'll start brunching with ladies who like to sip champagne from mid-morning to mid-afternoon at The Club, which I'll join for the company and the gossip of equally irrelevant, useless, boring women. Then they'll trot off to pick up their perfect little children from their perfect little schools and take them to their perfect little homes while I stop by the grocer for another bottle of champagne.

Pretty soon I'll have a case of the bubbly poison stashed in the back of the pantry for little mid-morning pick-me-ups. Before you know it, I'll be drinking it for breakfast the moment Nick walks out the door, which won't be one minute too soon, and I won't stop until everyone knows I'm a raging drunk because I'll have let myself fall to pieces, with chipped fingernails and dirty hair, slurring my words into the telephone and ranting to my few remaining friends about the slow milk delivery service...

The telephone rang out of nowhere, bringing Katherine back to herself. The strange, dark voice in her head vanished completely. *Good Lord, I have a terrible imagination,* thought Katherine, reaching for the phone. *It pulls on me.*

The call was probably Nick wanting to check up on her. Maybe it would be an unwitting customer, hoping that she still had that one perfect and precise, old and polished, immaculately preserved *whatever it was* they needed to make their Park Avenue home complete. She would never have guessed that it would be the operator, connecting an overseas call from Cairo. The next voice she heard on the crackling line was French, and buttery soft, and familiar. It was a voice that belonged to a past that had never completely let go of her.

2

A CALL FROM THE PAST

As a bee seeks nectar from all kinds of flowers
Seek teachings everywhere.
Like the deer who finds a quiet place to graze,
Seek seclusion to digest all you have learned.
Like a madman, beyond all limits, go wherever you please
And live like the lion, completely free of all fear.

– Ancient Sanskrit Saying

The telephone line crackled in Katherine's ear as he spoke. "*Bon jour*, Katherine. *C'est moi*. Etienne."

Katherine's face flushed hot in an instant and her heart pounded so fiercely in her chest that it hurt. "Etienne." She said it so softly he didn't hear her.

"Katherine?"

"Etienne," she said again, loudly. "You truly are a cad. Why haven't we heard from you once in all this time?"

"*Cheri*, at least do me the courtesy of not acting as though you picked up the telephone everyday to talk to me."

"How long has it been, Etienne? Six years, now? Seven?" Katherine knew exactly how long it had been. And she knew that the sun had been warm that day. And the leaves had been brittle underfoot. And that there had been no breeze.

"Ten. It's been ten years," said Etienne.

"Well, tell me everything. Where are you? How have you been? What have you been doing for the past decade?" She heard her old lover clear his throat on the other end of the line. "And what in God's green earth are you doing in Egypt?"

Etienne paced along the deck outside his house, dragging a long telephone cord behind him. The sun was setting in Cairo, coloring the sky with shades of gold and pink. He vaguely noticed the view of the city beyond his balcony, like anyone who fails to notice the simple, most dear or most lovely things they see every day: the fragrant blossoms of an orange tree in the yard, the person across the breakfast table, a four-thousand-year-old pyramid made of two million, perfectly-cut, blocks of stone.

"I'm calling on a matter of some urgency, Katherine," said Etienne.

"Really?"

"Katherine, of all the people in all the world, only you can help me."

"I find that hard to believe, Etienne."

"It's true *cherí*. Please hear me out."

"Alright, tell me, what is it that *only me*, of all the people on earth, can do for you?

"I need to reach Hugo Nelson."

Katherine almost laughed. *"The* Hugo Nelson. Hugo Amsterdam Nelson?" Hugo Nelson was wealthy almost beyond measure. He owned an unrivaled art collection, a fair chunk of Wall Street, two newspapers, several politicians, and favors from the powerful and the not-so-powerful.

"Oui, cherí. Hugo Nelson. And I need to do more than find him. I need to make a deal with him."

"Really?" asked Katherine. *Had I expected something different from Etienne?* she wondered. *An explanation. An apology perhaps.* "Etienne," Katherine sighed on her end of the line, as if she was a patient mother explaining the painfully obvious to an unreasonable child. "Mr. Nelson is nearly as reclusive as he is powerful. He's very hard to reach."

"But he knows *you*, Katherine."

"Barely."

"Barely is enough." Etienne thought of buttering Katherine up, making her feel special, as though she was unique and rare in all the world. But in Katherine's case it would be useless. Because it was true.

"It's impossible, Etienne. At least for me. Why aren't you asking Nick? Nick knows him far better than I do."

"Because Nick would never agree to what I'm proposing. Yes, use him to get to Nelson, but *you'll* have to do the bargaining."

"For your information, Etienne, husbands and wives don't *use* each other. They support each other. With *love*, I might add. And *honesty*, I might further add."

"But of course." Etienne propped a bare foot on the railing of his deck.

"Only you wouldn't know that, would you?" snapped Katherine, surprising even herself. "Or have you been happily married all this time?"

"I would be delighted to talk with you about all my lovers, Katherine. But perhaps some other time."

"How thrilling for me. I can hardly wait."

"Katherine, there is 100,000 dollars in this deal for you. Or is *The Silver Butterfly* so prosperous that you don't care about money?" Etienne cringed for a split second. He knew she was struggling. The world of antiquities, the world they both lived in, swirled in secrets and discoveries. Etienne had made it his business, and a lucrative career, to be a scholar of secrets.

"Aren't you even going to ask how Nick is?" responded Katherine. She paused. "How Ben is? How *I* am, for that matter?"

"How is Nick? And Ben? You – I can tell – are as delightful as ever."

"Nick is fine. Ben is dead."

"What?"

"Ben is dead."

"Oh Katherine. *Je suis vraiment désolé.* I am so sorry. So terribly sorry. Jesus. I didn't know." *How could I not know that?* wondered Etienne.

"It's okay. It's fine. Really. Forget I brought it up."

"*No*. Katherine, tell me what happened."

"Well, a war happened."

Etienne had already heard, had seen first-hand, too many young men lost in the war against the Nazis. He didn't ask for more details, but waited for Katherine to continue, to speak to him of her brother's death, however she could.

Katherine was silent for what seemed like a long time, until Etienne was about to ask if she was all right. When she spoke, it was in another voice. "Is this legal, Etienne? This deal you want me to make with Hugo Nelson."

So that's how this will go, thought Etienne. "Let me just say something else first. I know how important Ben was to you. He was my friend. And an amazing man. I couldn't be sorrier to hear that he was killed. If I can do anything--"

"You know, there's really nothing you can do or say. It was awful. It was sad. We miss him terribly, of course. But really, there's nothing more to be said about it."

"Can you tell me what happened?"

"No." *I will not forget you, Ben.*

"Katherine..."

"Really." Katherine softened. "Some other time."

"*Oui*, Katherine. *Oui*."

"For now, tell me more about Hugo Nelson. Please."

Etienne paused for a few moments and then, not knowing how else to reach her, he began to speak. "Hugo Nelson has smuggled something out of Egypt," he said. "And I want it back." Katherine waited. "It's a book."

"A book," she stated flatly.

"More than a book, really," replied Etienne. "It's a codex, a compilation of several manuscripts, from the earliest years of Christianity, bound together in one collection."

"How do you know Nelson has it?"

"*Cherí*, you know as well as anyone, the world of art and artifacts is not so big that secrets can be easily kept."

"A world occupied by a relatively small cadre of beautiful, excessive people?" Katherine teased, her tone lightening. In an intentional and well-practiced way, Katherine cleared a path to put the darker conversation behind them.

"You could say that," replied Etienne.

"And are *you* one of those beautiful, excessive people, Etienne?"

"I'm more of what you'd consider on the *fringe* of those people."

"A scrapper, of sorts?"

"You could say that."

"And you want Hugo Nelson's codex of manuscripts?"

"Yes."

"Why? Please tell me *why* you want to take a artifact from a man who apparently wanted it so badly, and is so obsessive, rich and powerful, that he stole it right out of Egypt?"

"I didn't say I wanted to *take* it. I said I wanted to *trade* it."

"So what is it, anyway, this book – this codex – you want so badly?"

"Katherine, I cannot explain this all to you on the telephone. Just say you will help me."

"I will *not* help you, Etienne. Not until I know what this 'codex' is."

Etienne knew he would have to go to the beginning to explain. But no, that would be too far. That would take them back to Oxford. He paused. How much should he say? How much could he trust her? So much had happened between them. Did all of the good get swallowed whole? He spoke, risking everything before he could stop himself.

"I have spent the last decade traveling through Egypt searching for artifacts from an early Christian sect called *Gnostics*."

"Gnostics?" replied Katherine. "Why haven't I ever heard of Christian Gnostics?" She heard Etienne sigh 3,500 miles away.

"Very little is known about them," began Etienne. "The Gnostics were a splinter group of Christians in the first 200 years after the Crucifixion. Their worship and their writings were considered heretical, and their writings were nearly all destroyed in the fourth century. Virtually everything we know about the Gnostics we get from what the orthodox Christians – their enemies – wrote about them."

"What do *you* know about them?"

"Well … first of all, the Gnostics claimed *knowing* God," said Etienne. "On a deep and intimate level. They claimed that the Divine was inside of everybody. And, believe me – to the great concern of the Church – they claimed that people did not need a priest or deacon or bishop to reach God. God was available, right then and there, to everyone: the beggar and the prince, the Arab and the Jew, the pagan and the priest."

"I can see why they were considered heretics."

"Yes." Etienne continued, wondering what Katherine was doing at that moment, where she was sitting, what she was wearing, all the time hoping that he could still intrigue her as he once could. "Therefore their writings were destroyed, the members were murdered, and their teachings were lost forever…"

Etienne paused. "Until now. *Mon cherí*, there has recently been a discovery in Egypt of enormous magnitude. A cache of Gnostic documents have been found in the desert. They are 1,600 years old, preserved in the hot dry desert sand for all these years, waiting to be found. Or, you might say, to be *revealed*."

"Revealed?" asked Katherine skeptically. "Revealed by *whom*?"

"Katherine, I believe that these books are the lost gospels – books and documents too provocative, too daring, to be included in the orthodox Bible. The Gnostic Gospels have been unearthed, *by whatever hand*, nearly two thousand years after they were written."

"And Hugo Nelson has them?"

"Nelson has one codex, one 'book of books,' if you will."

"Do you have the others, Etienne?"

Etienne had always loved it when Katherine used his name in sentences like that, even when she didn't need to, just to hear the sound of it out loud. Etienne answered as if he could not care less. He was not the same person he was ten years before.

"I have one, here in Egypt," said Etienne. "Sold to me by some villagers. The other 11 are missing, presumably scattered around the Black Market in Cairo. For that matter, they could be sitting on somebody's book shelf collecting dust."

"But you'll find them, won't you?"

"Every single one," said Etienne.

"I don't understand why ancient Christian documents were hidden in Egypt. The whole Middle East is predominately Muslim, yes?"

"Good question. In the early years following the Crucifixion, the Christian movement spread from Palestine throughout the Roman Empire. The original disciples spread out, mostly on foot, telling their various stories. By the end of the third century, there were Christians from southern England, to the eastern Mediterranean, in north Africa, Egypt and through all of western Europe. Even as far east as India.

"As they traveled, their stories were passed from generation to generation, until they were finally written down. Some of these stories became what we call the Canonical Gospels – Matthew, Mark, Luke and John – and were included in the Bible. Others were not.

"I am convinced that the codex Nelson has is part of an ancient library – 13 codices in all, including the one I have. I believe that this library is the only – and the complete – doctrine of a group of early Christians, long ago lost to history.

Etienne almost knew too much about the Gnostics: ideologies, cultural nuances, their alphabet, names, places they lived, places they died. From the insignificant to the mind-boggling, Etienne had learned – digging his hands raw in the dry desert sand, putting the pieces together one fragment at a time – virtually everything about them that was known to living man. Knowing too much, wanting too badly, he knew he could misspeak, misstep. To be concise, to be persuasive, would be difficult.

"The word Gnostic means *knowing*," he began, carefully. "Knowing from *experience*, instead of from faith. The Gnostic Christians had rejected several guiding principals of the Orthodox tradition – particularly the need for a Pope. They claimed direct,

14

personal experience of God, superseding the faith of mere believers. This system completely circumvented the hierarchy of the Church. Needless to say, such a digression undermined and infuriated the ruling order. The Gnostics were labeled heretics, and all their traditions and writings were destroyed."

"How do you know all this, Etienne?"

"I paid attention in school," said Etienne, grinning into the phone. No response from Katherine. He cleared his throat. "It was a major part of my research into early Christianity. The more I learned, the more intrigued I became. The message of the Gnostics is... well, it's tremendously compelling, let me put it that way. At any rate, I've been searching for the lost gospels for almost a decade."

"And you think you've found them?"

"Katherine, if I can get a hold of those manuscripts, we will have direct access to the words of the Gnostics. Finally, after nearly two thousand years, the heretics will speak for themselves."

So this, mused Katherine, *a pile of old books, is what Etienne, after ten long years, is calling about.*

"Of all the writings of the Gnostics, known or imagined, Nelson has the most compelling manuscript of them all. And it is hidden within the other manuscripts collected in the codex that he smuggled out of Egypt.

"What manuscript is that?"

"A secret book, all but forgotten, that says that God is inside of us all, and that is where we will find the path."

"What path?"

"The direct path to God ... and to eternal life."

Static crackled over the international phone line. Katherine raised her voice. "Oh rubbish. There is no such thing as everlasting life, Etienne. You know it and I know it."

"Are you sure, *Katerina*? So sure, *cherí*, that of all the mysteries in all the Universe that you, personally, know the limits of humankind?"

"I'm hanging up now..."

Etienne did not miss a beat. "I have the Knife of the Asps."

For a moment Katherine was stone silent. "You do not."

"I do."

"It must be a fake. I know you. You would *never* give up one of the world's most rare and precious artifacts. You wouldn't. Besides that knife is more rumor, speculation and myth than it is a reality."

"The knife is real, Katherine. And I have it."

In Katherine's silence Etienne could picture her face, upturned, anxious to hear the details, wanting as she always did, the whole story from start to finish. And, as always, he wanted to give her all the things she longed for. He wanted as much to punish her for not taking what he could offer.

"It was said," began Etienne, "that Marc Antony presented the extraordinary jeweled dagger to Cleopatra as a gift of his devotion. When, much later, news reached Egypt from Rome of Antony's politically strategic marriage to Octavia, Cleopatra returned the knife to the man who had spurned her. When Antony came again to Cleopatra's Egypt, he carried the long, slender dagger on his belt. After his final defeat to his rival Octavian, at Actium, and subsequent retreat to Alexandria, he drove that same knife into his own heart. The Knife of the Asps came to represent the enduring love of Antony and Cleopatra –"

"And their final gestures of revenge against Rome," murmured Katherine.

"Well," Etienne replied, breaking the spell he had cast with some amount of pleasure and some amount of pain. "How much of that story is actually true, we will never know. We do know what is false: Antony used his war sword to kill himself. And quite sloppily at that. The length of the sword made an awkward angle for such a task and Antony bled and suffered long before his body was found and taken to Cleopatra, in her own temple prison, to weep over."

"But there *was* such a dagger..."

"Forged in Rome," replied Etienne. "And brought to Egypt 30 years before Christ was born."

"I've read about the legendary Knife of the Asps, made from solid gold..."

16

"I can tell you for a fact that this is true," said Etienne. "And it rests in a matching gold sheath, which is etched in the most delicate, intricate detail you can imagine."

"Tell me…"

"Katherine, you have to see it to believe it. There is nothing on earth to match the handle of the blade. Two golden asps – symbols of Egyptian royalty – entwine themselves around the slender crossbar and up the hilt. The head of one snake is cut out of one solid, flawless emerald. The other snake's head is cut entirely from one ruby. A ruby so rare, the likes of it may not have been seen before or since."

"That dagger would be priceless," whispered Katherine.

"Yes, it is," replied Etienne. "And it is mine."

Katherine's heart started to pound, the murmur of a hope, a dream, rising inside her. "Okay, let's just say that what you have truly is the Knife of the Asps. What makes you think Hugo Nelson will trade for it?"

"Because the Knife of the Asps is among the most coveted artifacts in the world. Naturally he'll want it. More, he'll *insist* on having it. Owning the Knife of the Asps is like having the Hope Diamond or The Holy Grail. Once Hugo Nelson learns of it, he will *have* to possess it."

Strange and different things drive men like Hugo Nelson, agreed Katherine silently. *Things I understand.* "Etienne, how did you ever come into possession of the knife? And how do you know it's real?"

Etienne paused. Katherine thought she heard a sigh, a longing, on the other end of the line.

"That is a story that I will tell you, some day – all of it. But not today."

"Tell me."

"No, it's a long story, Katherine."

"I have all day." Somewhere, so deep inside of her that it seemed like a phantom dream, Katherine felt as though only a day or two had passed in all those darkening years.

"Some other time, really."

"Why don't you just tell me now, so I can stop pestering you? And then we'll talk more about Hugo Nelson, and this deal you want me to put together." She thought of Nick, who she loved so dearly, who knew her and defined her in so many ways. But right now she wanted to hear Etienne's voice. She wanted to hear it in her ears, her blood, her bones.

Etienne had forgotten her frank persistence, and he loved the remembering of it. "*Cherí*, you must trust me. This is not something I will speak of over the telephone. But someday we will sit together and I will tell you. I promise."

Hearing, and believing, his impossible promise, Katherine relented. "And you are willing to trade the Knife of the Asps for one of these Gnostic manuscripts?" she asked.

"Yes."

"It's not a fair bargain, Etienne."

"I know."

"Then why are you doing it?"

"Well," he said. "This won't be the first time I've made an inequitable trade." Etienne wanted the manuscript for reasons far beyond money. But Etienne didn't speak of that to Katherine, either.

"How will we do it? I mean, both the Knife of the Asps and the book will have to leave one country and enter the other – illegally. They will have to be hidden and, God help us, safe. A thousand things could go wrong."

"We'll make the transfer by ocean liner," explained Etienne. "The beauty of this plan is its simplicity, and its audacity. Katherine, you'll negotiate the trade with Nelson. Then ship the manuscript to me in Cairo, in care of *Miss Donatta*, in Garden City. Write that down. You'll need to create a suitcase with a false bottom, two inches deep. The manuscript will have to be packed with extreme care. It's 1,600 years old, and extremely fragile."

"Yes," interrupted Katherine. "I got that."

"When it's ready, send me a telegram saying, 'The weather in New York is clear. Come visit us.' If you use any other word but 'clear,' I'll know the deal is off. Have you got that?" Static was all Etienne heard in response. "Katherine?"

18

"I've got it, Etienne."

"Ship the codex the day you send the telegram. On that same day, I'll ship the dagger to you, smuggled in a crate of Egyptian antiques."

"This will take a fair amount of trust between us, won't it?" said Katherine.

"If we succeed, Katherine," said Etienne, skirting the question, "Nelson will get one of the most rare artifacts in the world, I'll get one of the manuscripts I've been trying to find for over a decade, and you, *mon petite cherí*, will get a tax-free commission of 100,000 dollars." Etienne liked to imagine the two shipments passing each other in vast silence on the Atlantic Ocean – both innocent of, and relying upon, each other.

Katherine also knew that by striking this bargain, she would be a woman changed, compromised, unlawful. She would be sweeping away the last remnants of the person she had once been, like dust from a collection of unwanted, unlucky antiques.

She glanced out the window, watching a leaf make its lonely way, in somersaults, to the ground. Katherine knew she could wind up in jail for long, horrible years if she took Etienne's offer and got caught. But it was so easy to be lured by the prize.

"I'll do it," she said. Katherine knew she should have said no. And she *would* have said no, had anyone else been asking but Etienne.

If Katherine thought to consider that God was not an ever-looming threat, unsatisfied, hungry for another pound of her flesh, she might have seen the wisdom of Etienne's words: *that the Divine was inside her*. But Katherine wasn't listening to anything but the voice of her own hunger. She was determined to fix all her problems in the most expedient way possible. And Etienne just offered her a personal, private gift of salvation. She swept the bank papers off her desk and into the trashcan.

Before she rung off Katherine asked one more time, "Are you sure about the Knife, Etienne? Are you sure you want to give up that incredible treasure?

Etienne surveyed the vast city beyond his balcony, feeling entirely separate from everything and everyone that surrounded him. A combination of loneliness and determination rested its full weight on his heart, and distracted his thoughts.

"Etienne? Are you *sure?*"

"*Oui*, I am sure." He cleared his throat and, promising to call back in a month's time, hung up the telephone. Etienne sat quietly, with the phone in his lap, letting his thoughts carry him to other times and places.

Etienne was at home the night he learned of the Gnostic Library. Two strangers, traders from the south, had visited his house the previous winter, and had sold him a collection of papyrus documents known in earlier times as a codex. They claimed it had been discovered in the desert near the town of Nag Hammadi, 600 miles south of Cairo. They claimed it was one of 13 books found, intact, near a burial site. They promised to return with the rest, which they would sell for a 'fair' price. Then they disappeared.

With great excitement, Etienne spent the next month translating the papyrus codex he received, making pages and pages of notes. And still, the villagers hadn't returned.

Tired of waiting, Etienne took his codex to the Coptic Museum in Old Cairo, to show the museum's curator, his friend, Talib Nagi. He was hoping Nagi would have heard news of other, similar documents. Nagi might also have some clues as to the fate of the strange villagers who'd gone missing.

Nagi got very excited at the sight of the papyrus book. He said it was the second such book he had seen. Unfortunately, the Coptic Museum was too poorly funded to be in a position to buy it. So the man who owned the codex smuggled it into America instead, and sold it to an American financier named Hugo Nelson. To his great credit, Nagi had the presence of mind to take a photograph of the first page. He and Etienne carefully examined that page together under a magnifying glass. What they read was this:

These are the hidden sayings that the living Jesus spoke
and Judas Thomas the Twin recorded. And Jesus said,
'whoever discovers the interpretations of these sayings
shall not taste death.'

Etienne could hardly breathe. The scattered pieces of his decade-long search were falling into place. Etienne knew that fragments of a Greek document were found in the 1890s, establishing the existence of a gospel attributed to Thomas, with words identical to these. But the Greek text was in pieces, incomplete and largely illegible. Etienne was reading from a page of the *Gospel of Thomas*, and Hugo Nelson had it – in its entirety. *Just an old book*, thought Etienne. *No one had any idea...*

Unlike the canonical gospels of the New Testament, this text was considered hidden, or secret. Etienne speculated that the Gnostics were protecting their teachings from their enemies. Also, they may have cloistered their initiates in a manner that gave them privilege and mystery. More likely, they were simply hiding them from destruction at the hands of those without *gnosis*, without the *knowledge of God*.

In Gnostic tradition, a twin was not a sibling, but a person whose learning had made him or her equal with Jesus. The Gnostics believed that through prayer and meditation, the Divine could be found in the Self. That they were, in fact, the same. And that no one needed a savior to find God. Jesus was a guide. Not the son of God who found his way to man. But the son of man who found his way to God. Jesus was a model, to teach humanity, to show the path to spiritual understanding. And when a disciple attained *gnosis*, or enlightenment, Jesus was no longer his spiritual master. The two became equal, identical, like twins.

Etienne wondered if Hugo Nelson knew any of this. And if he did, would he be at all willing to sell the codex? Nelson, he assumed, didn't care in the least that the contents of this book might create a revolution in the study, and practice, of Christianity. But Etienne did. And Etienne was fascinated to discover those sayings. And more: the interpretations of those sayings.

Etienne had also heard that there were other people interested in the Gnostic Gospels. Talib Nagi told him about a group of religious fanatics bent on finding and destroying the manuscripts. With news of the discovery traveling rapidly through academic circles, it wasn't long before the curiosity of the religious community was aroused.

No one knew – but many could guess – what might happen if the masses suddenly embraced the idea that the Divine resided within themselves. If no intermediary was needed, if each and every person could have direct contact with God, what would be the purpose of institutionalized religion?

Indeed, the Gnostics professed that their spiritual practice was *superior* to that of the Orthodox Church. They claimed to have personal first-hand knowledge of God, knowledge from *experience*, while the followers of the church merely *believed* what was told to them.

Etienne suspected that *The Gospel of Thomas,* and the other 12 books in the Gnostic Library, could offer written proof that there was more to the story of Christ and salvation than the Bible had ever told. Etienne's mind wandered further and further back in time, imagining the culture that created Christianity.

He was scanning history for clues, like he scavenged the desert for artifacts; like he searched for the Truth in the dry and prickly landscapes of his heart. His thoughts were like a razor cutting across time and space, always looking inward to see the reflections of the past.

It was not the disciples, he recalled, or any witnesses to Christ's life, who actually wrote the canonical gospels. They were written by unknown authors, 35 to100 years after Jesus walked the earth, penned from an oral tradition. Etienne knew that when the Bible was created, the early rulers of the Church manipulated its contents to support their hierarchy of unquestionable power.

Such decisions were made in 367 A.D., when Athanasius, the great Arch Bishop of Alexandria, issued a decree called, *The Lenten Letter* – one of the most powerful and bloody documents of all time. This letter listed all the documents that were to be recognized in the Old and New Testaments of the Bible. It was this letter that determined what was, and what was not, the Word of God. It determined what was heresy and what was truth, and how religion would be practiced.

In these early years of Christianity, there was no separation between church and state. The people's religion was not just what they practiced or how they worshipped, it was how they lived their lives. Soon after *The Lenten Letter* came out, all known Gnostic Gospels were destroyed. Gnostic practitioners – hundreds of them, young and old – were put to the sword. In the gathering pools of fear and blood, Gnosticism disappeared.

Sixteen hundred years later, in Egypt in 1947, it was rumored that zealots were sent directly from Rome to destroy the recently discovered Gnostic texts. As a scientist, Etienne rejected rumor and gossip, and gave his attention to the tangible and the measurable.

But as an archaeologist, and a person who made a living by procuring artifacts from obscure places and people, Etienne paid close attention to such talk. Many great discoveries, in science and in human nature, began as nothing more than whispers and wild speculation. And Etienne knew that.

Etienne also knew that, in this quest for the gospels, he would eventually cross paths, and purposes, with Cato Nafarah. Nafarah was a field agent for the Egyptian Department of Antiquities. This agency was charged with the daunting mission of protecting Egypt's cultural heritage, which was not only a matter of national pride, but one of economics and tourism as well.

Nafarah, who had been passed over too many times for promotion, had been hounding Etienne for years. He had convinced himself that Etienne was breaking Egyptian law and selling artifacts to private collectors. Which, in fact, on occasion, when absolutely necessary, he was.

But Etienne was determined that not Cato Nafarah, nor religious zealots, nor Hugo Nelson would keep those manuscripts from him. He had been searching the Egyptian countryside – from the rich delta to the barren desert, from the crowded markets to the sparse villages – without rest for ten years, gleaning meager leads from scraps and stories.

Never in his wildest dreams did he imagine that an entire Gnostic library would be found, intact. These books could offer a new perspective on the primordial war between light and darkness, good and evil. These books could possibly even reveal spells, or chants, or secret paths through one's interior leading directly to God. *Maybe*, thought Etienne, *they will even reveal something – some miraculous thing – that will save me.*

3

A TANGLED STRAND OF PEARLS

But perhaps God needs the longing,
wherever else it should dwell,
Which with kisses and tears and sighs
fills mysterious spaces of air –
And perhaps is invisible soil from which
roots of stars grow and swell...

— Nelly Sachs, Nobel Laureate, from Israel

Etienne should have known that calling Katherine after all those years would only lead to trouble. But he wanted that trouble. He wanted to stir up that pot. He wanted it all to unfold just as it did. Even if he didn't know it at the time. In the face of such a grand and daring quest, it was easy to pretend this was not about love.

Back in Oxford and later, in Paris, Etienne measured his days in accordance with Katherine – where she was, what she was doing at the time, what she would think of him. If she was absent, he considered what he would tell her when he saw her next. Etienne gravitated toward Katherine, in his thoughts and in all his waking dreams. He got to wondering if it was a sickness of some sort, or a fickle obsession that would pass, some day, onto someone else.

Etienne came to understand that this was the natural inclination of his spirit to right itself. *All that makes up a man,* he concluded, *rises to the imperative that is caused by an inconsolable longing, the quiet, incessant ache that only one person can calm. A man will lean naturally toward that which makes him right. This is what happens,* thought Etienne when he hung up the telephone, *when a man misses a woman. It is what happens between Katherine and me.*

It wasn't long after Katherine hung up the telephone that she panicked. Nick was going to be furious. Beyond furious. Worse. This madcap scheme was an invitation straight into prison.

24

But then she thought about Hugo Nelson and his circle of power and influence. Certainly Etienne had been right: when Nelson learned about the magnificent Knife of the Asps, he would move heaven and earth to have it ... and to protect his source in the process. Katherine felt a new wave of confidence rush over her.

She thought back on the unexpected conversation that had changed the course of her plans. She found she was remembering not so much Etienne's words, or his pursuit, but rather his voice. It dismantled the façades of her heart as easily and softly as a wisp of the wind. And it made her lose her rational mind entirely.

Katherine was fiercely loyal to Nick, but she caught herself repeatedly imagining the embrace of her former lover – as though it was just yesterday that they shared coffee in the morning, art and architecture in the day, and their bodies in the night. She tried to remember exactly what it felt like to be kissed by Etienne, and found that she couldn't, and the not-remembering intensified her longing. She wanted freedom, and the Etienne she knew at Oxford, and a wild summer in Paris in 1936.

Maybe it's the me I knew at Oxford that I really long for, mused Katherine. *Maybe if I can hold onto a strong enough piece of that time, that place, some forgotten part of me will wake up and everything will be different. Maybe everything will become simple, and clear. I wonder, was it ever clear? Or was it just more irresponsible?*

At that time in her life, Katherine couldn't separate Etienne from Nick, or from her brother Ben, or even from her father. They all were, and remained, inextricably linked to each other, and to forces beyond her understanding.

Katherine followed Ben to Oxford. She would have followed her twin brother anywhere. Even though it was ridiculous. Even though it was rare in those days for a woman to attend Oxford. She wasn't going to be stopped. Katherine worshipped Ben. He was more than her closest friend and confidant. He was the only person who understood the things that drove her.

It was Ben who watched her shrink and harden after their father left, because it was Ben who paid attention. It was always Ben, with his easy smile, his perfect confidence, and his enviable ability to rise beyond the petty strivings of ordinary mortals. It was always Ben. Katherine's mother was far too busy and distracted by her sorrows.

Katherine's roaming thoughts led her further into the past than she had wished to go. But suddenly she was there, in 1928. She found herself back in a dark time on a road she longed – and feared – to travel.

Katherine watched her mother wandering through their old house with a dust cloth, as though she could wipe away her husband's memory, and her pain. It never worked of course, and her mother died young and still loving Katherine's father. She suffered his absence every single day of the rest of her life, since the day he backed out of their driveway on his way to somewhere else. She suffered every day she road the train into the city to type and take dictation.

In one startling moment, Katherine's mother had fallen from a position of social grace to the role of an abandoned, husband-less wife. Her crown was taken from her and she stood alone, deposed, cast out of the Kingdom of Happily-Ever-After. She felt the shame of desertion. She endured the pity she saw in the eyes of the privileged ladies in the Well-Married Society. She resented going to work every day. She refused to feel oh-so-fortunate that she found a position as a secretary instead of a housekeeper. But greater than these sufferings, greater than the humiliation of being held up to the scrutiny of marriage and found lacking, was the great cavern of longing in her heart.

She missed her husband's voice, his hands, his face, the smell of him, the warmth of his skin, the quiet confidence that, at the end of the day, he would come home. She missed the man she married, the man she walked to down the isle to greet, pledging a lifetime of love and devotion. She missed the man whose children she bore and raised, and for whom she would always long. She missed him every time she absently walked to the window and stood there looking out at nothing, and every day she cried, and every night she slept alone, and every morning she woke up in a bed that was far too big for one.

Seven years after her husband left, when her children were away at college, Katherine's mother took to her bed and died. The doctor called it tuberculosis, but Katherine knew full well that her mother had simply given up on living.

But not me, thought Katherine. Katherine had suffered on that first day, over what she never could have imagined would happen. She threw herself into her mother's arms to be assured that her daddy would be right back, and that every thing would be okay. But her mother couldn't offer her anything. She just stared over Katherine's shoulder, out the window. They stood there together, in their collective shame, mother and child, both left.

Ben understood, in some deep, unexpected way – in a way that he should not have had to understand – that his mother and sister were now damaged women, and that he was their keeper and their protector. He was eleven. Later that night, when Katherine went to bed, it was Ben who came to the door of her room and said, "Good night, Doll." Just like her father had said it every night for all the previous eleven years of her life. Katherine turned her face away from the wall, toward Ben, and knew in that moment that he would never desert her.

Until his death, that held true. Ben was the one who taught her things. He bandaged her scraped knees and read her bedtime stories. He cleaned up after her and scolded her for her mistakes. He checked her homework, made sure she ate right, and thoroughly scrutinized all her dates. It was Ben who held her when she lost her dog and her way, when she lost a friend, or lost her mind. It was always Ben.

So Katherine stopped suffering over her absent father, and let her mother do it for all of them. Ben became her hero and her savior. He had always been as close to her as she was to herself. They were two of one mind. They knew each other's thoughts and joys and fears with few, if any, words passing between them.

In all the ways that they were different, Katherine began to imitate the qualities of her brother, qualities that didn't come naturally for her. She thought Ben was about the smartest, cleverest kid she knew, so she studied when everyone else was playing, and rose to the top of her class in school. She laughed and played with single-minded vigor, secretly wondering all the while how Ben found such extraordinary delight in ordinary things.

She tried, like her twin, to be resilient, but she never became as self-sufficient or self-contained as her brother. Perhaps she didn't want to be. Perhaps if she had, he would abandon her too, and leave her to her own resources – to strength and indifference and fortitude. So she muscled her way into Oxford, holding on to Ben, and to a life she was supposed to have grown out of.

Just like that, Katherine's mind propelled her to 1936, Oxford, and all its wonderful, innocent, mayhem. Like a portrait in her mind, Katherine recalled the pale brick buildings, Gothic structures reaching to the skies, announcing to the world that this was a greater, uncommon place to be. In her mind, she crossed the bridges of stone arching over the quiet, meandering Thames.

She saw green, the startling green, of the lush happy springtime. Far away from where she sat, Katherine turned her face to the thick, quiet snow that fell on the college in winters of white, hushing the land and its inhabitants. These were the places and the seasons that marked her first steps of independence, of separation from her youth.

Looking back at all that happened from the day her father left, to Oxford, to Etienne's phone call, Katherine saw relationships that were so convoluted she could never untangle them. She could never lay them out neatly in her mind like a strand of pearls, each one leading in natural, logical succession to the next. No, her relationships were not that simple. And she was far too close to see where the damage began.

New York City, October 1947

Katherine shivered. The evening was crystal clear and ice cold, with New York's city lights out-dazzling the stars. A breeze swept up for brief, chilling moments, causing all the women in their thin evening gowns and wraps to huddle in close to their escorts. The men all wore black tuxedos and bow ties under their heavy overcoats.

Why does men's clothing always seem so much more reasonable? wondered Katherine. A crowd of closely linked couples moved quickly and with great aplomb up the grand staircase to the Metropolitan Museum of Art. *And I'm dressed like all these other ridiculous women,* thought Katherine to no one but herself, *cold to the bone.*

The gala opening of the Louis XIV exhibit – on loan from *The Louvre* in Paris – attracted everybody who was anybody in art, politics and power. Even – it was widely rumored – Hugo Nelson, who rarely subjected himself to the masses, but chose instead to surround himself in small gatherings of the most wealthy, extravagant people he could find. But this night, it was said, there was to be an unveiling. An unveiling that tempted even New York's most reclusive eccentric from his huge, mysterious estate.

Hugo Nelson could buy, trade, borrow, or steal just about anything on earth he wanted. Except the love of one woman. Patrice LaMere was a fiery, young actress who Hugo had first seen in the early days, after the war, on an Off-Off-Broadway stage. He had fallen instantly in love with the red-haired siren, though she entirely rejected him. He could have easily handed her all her star-struck hopes and dreams with the snap of his fingers. He could offer her jewelry,

28

prestige, clothing, world travel, a beautiful home, and servants catering to all her whims. And still she would have none of him. The more he pursued her, the more cruel she became in her rebuffs. The crueler she behaved, the more incessant became his pursuit.

It was Patrice LaMere who would be unveiled this night at the Met. Hugo could see every detail in his mind's eye: her handsome, young escort, with his slicked back hair, his tailored tuxedo, and his dashing smile, sliding the black stole from her shoulders. Her creamy white skin, warm beneath her mink stole, shivering for just a moment at the rush of cool air on her bare skin.

Hugo would see this, if it drew him out of his home, if it made him endure the mindless chitchat and stares of the nameless, faceless throngs, if it killed him with jealousy. He would see Patrice LaMere that night.

At least that was the story on the street.

Nick and Katherine made their way through the crowds, sipping champagne while Katherine stopped to show Nick all the details that he would have missed without her: the use of light and shadow in the baroque paintings, the elaborate carvings in the gilded furniture, the silk and beadwork in the royal clothing.

Nick was paying more attention to finding Hugo Nelson than to anything that concerned a dead French king. He had promised Katherine a reintroduction, and wasn't entirely sure he could negotiate it. He wasn't sure if Nelson would even be there.

"Nick, relax," said Katherine, taking another glass of champagne from a passing waiter. "You look so unhappy."

"I'll relax after we've met with Nelson."

"We'll find him." Katherine reassured her husband with a squeeze of his arm. "But let's get to it, shall we? I know you won't be able to enjoy yourself until we get this over with."

"I already regret getting involved in this scheme," said Nick. "Etienne is not trustworthy, you know." As every seasoned husband and wife would, they let that comment pass without elaboration. "Katherine, you could go to prison for this. Forever. There's nothing I could do to help you, if you get caught."

"I won't get caught," whispered Katherine.

"There isn't a jury in the world that wouldn't send you straight to Sing Sing. I couldn't defend you against smuggling, not at this point. The country is still too tender from the war. Secrets and proprietorship are matters of state security. Nothing could save you."

"Not even you, Nick Spencer, brilliant attorney at law, savior of the persecuted and the downtrodden?" Katherine beamed at her husband.

"I could perhaps offer you up as guilty by reason of insanity," he offered. "Besides I defend the rich and the sinful, not the persecuted and downtrodden. But I can also think of a hundred other people I'd rather have you dealing with than Etienne Desonia."

"So, tell me Nick, if this is all so distasteful to you, why *did* you get involved? Why didn't you just let me trot off by myself to this gala, and track down Hugo Nelson on my own?"

"For one thing, you're my responsibility." Katherine scowled at him over her shoulder as they stood before a painting of the King Louis that reached nearly fifteen feet high. "For two," continued Nick in his typical, British, self-deprecating tone, "something always draws me straight into my own undoing. I can see it coming. I can tell myself all the things I *should* do. I know perfectly well what's right and what's wrong.

"Then something happens. A tumbler clicks over in my head and I can no longer hear the voice of reason. I march straight away from my own good judgement toward ... you." He smiled at his wife. Nick was making fun, but he also knew that this sort of self-sabotage was true, and had cost him dearly before. And, for certain, it would again.

"You just can't help yourself can you?" Katherine laid her head on his shoulder for a moment and let him kiss the top of her head. He smelled good. And she felt safe, and excited.

"Look, Nick, there's Hugo Nelson, over there." She pointed across the room with a slight nod of her head. Gazing through the elegant entourage that swirled nearby, Nick eventually caught Nelson's eye. Nick also caught notice of two inconspicuous, but formidable, bodyguards hovering in the background. They were dressed perfectly for the occasion: dark, subtle, silent. *It's the look on their faces that always gives them away*, thought Nick, *that serious expression, ready for anything, anxious for a kill*. Nick smiled and ushered Katherine smoothly in Nelson's direction.

"Spencer, how are you, old fellow?" Hugo extended his hand to Nick as the couple approached. "It's always good to see you. Reminds me of old times."

Nick shifted slightly, but looked toward Katherine. "Nelson, you remember my wife, Katherine."

Katherine extended her hand. Nelson shook it with casual indifference. "I believe we ran into each other recently in the lobby of the Shubert Theatre… a few months ago, didn't we?" said Katherine.

"Yes, didn't we," replied Nelson coolly.

"It was a presentation of A *Streetcar Named Desire*, I believe," added Nick. Nelson glared at Nick, angry to be reminded of another of Patrice LaMere's performances, from which his exotic gift of tropical flowers, imported for the occasion from Polynesia, was returned. "I don't believe I've seen that particular play," replied Nelson. "The theatre typically bores me to tears."

"Is that right?" said Nick. "My mistake, then. Perhaps it was at the opera we last met."

"Now that is possible," said Nelson. "But only if it was Verdi. American composers are entirely too provincial for my taste."

"And just when the Americans are gloating about their military prowess over the Italians," replied Nick.

Katherine wasn't at all pleased with the conversation. Mostly because she wasn't part of it. Clearing her throat, she gazed at Nelson over her champagne flute. Her long black glove led his eyes from the glass to her décolletage as she sipped her drink. "Mr. Nelson." She spoke very softly, to get his undivided attention. "I have something you want."

Nelson cocked an eyebrow at her, revealing his surprise and his curiosity.

Katherine cast a brilliant smile at him. "You just don't know it yet." Then she turned and walked away. Katherine's gown was cut to a deep V in the back and the long strand of pearls she wore grazed her bare skin as she walked away.

Nelson watched Katherine approach a distinguished gentleman in a perfectly-tailored, designer tuxedo. When she caught the man's eye, just by moving across the room, he moved to her immediately and embraced her in his arms. That left Nick to explain to Nelson that

31

Katherine's was a call he should take in the morning; that what she had to offer was something no one else in the world could.

Nelson watched Katherine, who was chatting happily with Robert Wagner, the powerful New York senator, as if she had nothing more important on her mind than the bubbles in her champagne.

Wagner was an old friend of Katherine's father. He'd held every important post in the Democratic party in New York, and was raising a son – just older than Katherine – to follow in his illustrious footsteps. Senator Wagner was a good Catholic, an extraordinary civil servant, a champion of the children and the arts, and was approaching 70. He doted on Katherine like the favorite godchild she was.

Wagner had helped Katherine's mother secure a good position in a government office when she needed a job. He continued to stay close to the shattered family, providing an epoxy of sorts, and a window into the world of happy families. He also provided a vague, perhaps unwilling, link to Katherine's father. Katherine's mother had held desperately to that link, that connection of mostly static and dead air, listening intently for any scrap of news, while trying to appear nonchalant.

In her own mask of nonchalance, Katherine looked over only once at Nelson to return his gaze. They looked at each other across the room as people dashed around, lofting champagne flutes, making conversation they intended to be titillating.

In that moment, through a constantly moving sea of people, Katherine and Nelson recognized something in each other, something intangible and elusive, something compelling, something bordering, perhaps, on desperate.

The defining difference between Katherine and Hugo Nelson was that Nelson was rich. Not just rich, but rich-rich. He had been driven from birth, from a time when he was dirt-poor and growing up in the streets. He succeeded through his wits, his audacity, a sort of mania, and an abundance of man-made luck. Over the years Nelson had become powerful, eccentric, used to having his way unquestioningly, and, perhaps, evil.

But Katherine had no idea about all that. She grew up in a working middle class family, reading *Life Magazine*, *The Evening Post* and newspaper stories about the glamorous lives of people like Hugo Nelson. The kind of life she wanted. This deal was more to her than money. It was more to her than helping Etienne, even. It was her invitation to the Table of The Successful.

This deal would make her a player, in the eyes of Hugo Nelson, society, and the New York's high-end business community. This would be the realization of a dream for Katherine, an accomplishment, a ratification of all her efforts in life. Katherine was born – or came to it early in life by circumstance – to have a hunger in her.

4

Two Aspects of Isis

Such things could be risked by a queen
who was also an Amazon and an artist in love,
since what she did was right because she did it;
and not by a patriotic citizeness whose dignity
was determined by the judgement of her fellow citizens.

— Emil Ludwig, on Cleopatra and Octavia

New York, November 1947

Nick Spencer sat behind his desk, looking out onto Wall Street, absently clicking a pencil against his ink blotter. Every detail of Nick's office was as carefully chosen and orderly as his life. Shelves upon shelves of law books, bound in burgundy leather, were stacked nearly floor to ceiling covering two walls of his office. Behind him – selected by Katherine – were several paintings. Of what he couldn't say, if he wasn't looking directly at them. The carpets were Persian and the curtains were a respectable, if indulgent, hunter green, in silk damask.

Nick worked at a sturdy mahogany desk from his high-back, leather chair. For his clients, he provided two matching, smaller chairs. An overstuffed chair and sofa were tucked into one corner, emitting a aura of warmth and safety for those clients who saw Nick as a friend and a confidant. For his more reckless or troubled clients, there was a small wet-bar in the opposite corner. The window on the south wall looked out over New York's financial district, reminding him and his wealthy clients of the clout and prestige of *Doughty, Spencer, and Muir, Attorneys at Law*. It was all just as it should be.

Years before, Katherine had stood by Nick's side and picked out every single element of his office with him, thread by thread. She had taken one look at his bare surroundings and masterminded the

34

creation of a dignified office worthy of an Oxford-educated attorney. Then she turned her mind back to other matters: all concerning herself.

Why do I love her with such an obsession? wondered Nick. *Maybe there is something compelling about someone who is absolutely certain that they operate at the center of the Known Universe. Maybe it's because* everybody *loves her. Maybe it's because for all that love she never once let herself feel any of it. Never once that I know of, at any rate. Not from me, her mother, or Etienne. Maybe from her brother. Maybe.*

I can't say I blame her, really. She's lived all her life feeling that she was not safe, that she required the protection of men. It must always be there, in the back of her mind, that at any point she could be overpowered; she could be hurt, penetrated, scorned, abandoned.

These are the kind of thoughts that can dance you like a puppet, thought Nick, who knew what it was like to live with monsters – events perpetually on the outskirts of his mind, silent, but constantly there. *It always takes something big, something rather startling, to cause a person to call out those dragons from their caves and confront them on the open plains of your heart. And something big did happen, to all of us, didn't it? Etienne called.*

It was time. Nick was to meet Katherine uptown at *The Silver Butterfly*. He took a few hours away from his high-rent clients to be with his wife on the day the crate arrived from Egypt. He couldn't keep himself away and just let her report back to him. No, he had to be there. He was involved in this himself, much more deeply than he ever would have imagined.

Eugene was there too, naturally. Even though she really couldn't afford his wages, she kept him employed, partly because he worshipped her. Nick harbored a veiled resentment of Eugene, even though it was pointless. Eugene loved other men the way Nick loved Katherine: completely and in every way. Eugene just happened to think that Katherine was the rarest, most exciting, and most allusive of creatures. *Of course,* mused Nick as he watched them, *everyone does.*

"The Egyptian shipment. Finally." Eugene came to stand by Katherine's side, a crow bar dangling from his hand. "You must be very pleased." He looked guilelessly over at his boss.

Katherine was standing on the loading dock behind her store. The wooden doors were flung open and waiting silently for the delivery truck that would bring the crate from the customs authority.

Katherine stared at the empty alley with a far away look. The delivery would be a simple wooden box – five feet long, three feet wide and four feet deep. *Odd that such a shape could hold all of someone's hopes and dreams,* thought Katherine. If putting the sum of a life's ambitions into one crate seemed foolish, if staking the happiness of all the days to come on one business deal seemed even more foolish, Katherine didn't care. *Let us each have our own measure of fate, and our own measure of courage.*

It made her feel on the verge of greatness that she considered such a risk worth taking, when others would choose a more carefully measured, sensible course. All the great people of history took tremendous risks, by Katherine's reasoning. And this was the gamble she was willing to take in her journey to the life she wanted – to her own realm of power and a kind of security she'd never known.

Life eternal, thought Katherine. *Not for me – the living beyond death. To most people, eternal life is propagating with children, carrying on the family line, breeding generation after generation. To the ancient Egyptians it was to rule the universe, a god embodied, forever. To Antony and Cleopatra it was to never surrender to their conquerors. For me, I care only about the here and now. And it's right around the corner, inside that box.* Katherine allowed herself a smile.

"Well, look at you," remarked Eugene. "Pandora couldn't have been more excited."

"And look what happened to her," muttered Nick, coming up from behind to join them.

"Congratulations," continued Eugene, ignoring Nick. "I'm very much looking forward to seeing what's in this shipment."

"Eugene, you have no idea," smiled Katherine. She looked up at him, tilting her head to one side, saying nothing more.

Eugene's round, brown eyes were accented by jet black hair, receding almost imperceptibly, which he combed straight back off his face. His black mustache was precisely trimmed, thin and meticulous. Short and slender, Eugene was the sovereign keeper of Katherine's daily operations. He helped control the inventory, sweep the floors, display the windows and make the bank deposits. He made an art of flattering and dazzling their wealthy Upper East Side patrons, all of whom adored him and asked him advice on everything from their marriages to their marigolds. His knowledge of antiques and world history was remarkable. But Eugene, it turned out, couldn't sell anything to anybody.

Katherine touched Eugene's arm. "There's something I have to tell you." Eugene studied her carefully for a moment. "It will make you mad," she said. "Then it will make you very pleased, I think."

"I absolutely *hate* it when you do this." Eugene crossed his arms, the heavy crow bar resting easily in the crook of his elbow. "What? *What?*"

"I lied to you."

The combination of curiosity and fear, mixed with self-righteous disapproval, was more compelling than Eugene could bear. He had always found himself on the other side of judgement. "It's okay," he said. "Just tell me... *what?*"

"There is something in this crate that is ... not exactly... on the manifest."

"*Oh, no*, Katherine. You didn't!"

She looked straight back at him. "I did."

Eugene turned and walked ten feet away from her. "I cannot believe that you... you..." he lowered his voice, and turned back to face her. "You smuggled something out of Egypt?"

"The Customs officials passed *right over* its secret cache." She smiled and sat herself on top of an old steamer trunk. She casually crossed her long legs. Alligator pumps framed the high arches of her feet. The seams of her silk stockings were, as always, perfectly aligned and only that one loose strand of hair compromised her perfect chignon. "Although passing through Customs was considerably easier than putting this deal together, I can tell you that." She brushed back her hair.

"Why Katherine? Why did you do it? Did you know what you were doing? Did you know the risks you were taking?" Eugene lowered his voice to a near whisper. "Prison being among them, I might add?"

"Of course I knew the risks." Now there was no smile lighting her face. "Frankly, I needed this deal. We've been operating in the red for many, many months, and –"

Eugene pointed his gaze at Nick. "Did *you* know about this?"

"I did. But this is Katherine's party, old boy."

Eugene turned back to Katherine, pointing the crow bar at her accusingly. "I am, quite honestly, horrified with you right now." Katherine crossed her arms defiantly and Eugene let the crow bar drop to his side. "Okay, tell me how you did it."

"I was working for a client overseas." Katherine distracted herself from Eugene's eyes by examining her fingernails. "And a collector here in the states. A delicate series of negotiations, attention to the most miniscule of details, and weeks of waiting, finally, *finally* culminate in this delivery."

She stepped off her perch to gaze down the alleyway, still empty of traffic. "How long can it take to get from the Port of New York to uptown Manhattan, for crying out loud?" She looked at Nick who simply shrugged and shook his head.

"Who is this collector?" pressed Eugene.

Katherine eyes narrowed for the briefest of moments. Eugene held his ground, not wavering, even the tiniest bit. Katherine sighed. "Hugo Nelson," she said, looking vaguely over her shoulder at Nick. Nick stood nearby, hands in his pockets, leaning nonchalantly against a rack of shelves. *No culpability here,* Nick thought to himself, *just the supportive, benevolent husband in Katherine's shadow, the one lucky man to whom she gives her love.*

"Hugo Nelson?" Eugene's jaw dropped. "How could you do all this – without me knowing about it?" asked Eugene.

"I couldn't involve you at all." She gazed seriously at him. "I wasn't going to put you in danger."

Eugene just waited, his hands on his hips. The folds of his pleated pants rested on the tops of his black and white spectator shoes. His thin tie, perfectly knotted, hung stick-straight against his starched white shirt. The letters *EDC* were monogrammed on his shirt cuffs. He was a man of precision and patience. He had to be. All the odds in life were stacked against him.

Katherine continued, "Mr. Nelson held virtually all of his communications with me through intermediaries. I rarely ever saw him in person."

"How did you ever get involved with him in the first place?"

"Nick knows him, from the war. The first time I met him was in London in 1943. And then again last summer at the theater. Nick re-introduced us last month at the opening of a new exhibit at the Met. I had heard that he was in possession of an ancient manuscript that had been smuggled out of Egypt. I had a customer who wanted that manuscript: someone who was willing to trade an artifact significantly more valuable for it." She paused. "Nelson took the trade. He wanted it so badly, we negotiated an additional fee for my brokering services. The cash will be paid upon delivery of the artifact. The artifact is in that crate."

Nick thought he should add something to help out his wife. "Nelson is always looking for exceptionally rare artifacts to unmistakably, permanently, establish the pre-eminence of his art collection. He is rather unreasonable about it, quite frankly."

"You *know* Hugo Nelson?" asked Eugene. "*Personally*? And he knows you?"

"I met Nelson in France, during the war," explained Nick. "He was an odd duck. Smart, oh, he was incredibly smart. But there was something not quite right about him. He emerged from the war a millionaire. While the rest of us were getting irretrievably damaged by the horrors of it all, Nelson was getting rich. Rumor was that he was secretly working for the Nazis, feeding them information in trade for Jewish art and gold."

"I don't believe it," breathed Eugene, sincerely taking every word to heart.

"I knew for a fact that he was capable of it," continued Nick, "because I was in British Intelligence during the war. He and I had several encounters, most of them miserable. But we never caught him at spying, though we followed him very carefully. He was assigned to European Allied Headquarters as a supply clerk. A nothing, a nobody. He turned his nothingness into a fortune. And destroyed all sorts of lives along the way."

"What was he like back then?" pressed Eugene.

"Well, he was a charismatic man. Not particularly handsome, but he had an elusive air about him – part humor, part indifference – that drew people like magnets. Not because he was nice. No. He was something else altogether. You could just tell he was dangerous. You could tell he knew things he shouldn't know. He was a hard man to resist."

"Fascinating," exclaimed Eugene. "I had no idea…"

"I contacted Mr. Nelson the day after the Museum gala," interrupted Katherine. "I had a proposition." She paused, momentarily wandering in her mind to somewhere no one else could go. "It took me weeks to convince him, through intermediaries, mostly. More than a month of waiting, mostly. I suspect he made me wait just because he knew he could. Then one day, in a rare personal appearance, he walked into the store. He just asked me one question before he turned around and left."

"Good God!" Eugene's eyes grew enormous. "What did he say?"

Katherine continued. "He stood just inside the door and said, 'What are you willing to risk for this, Katherine?' I just stared at him as though I was frozen to the floor. 'Everything,' I said. It was out of my mouth before I knew what I was saying. Then he walked out the door without looking back. That afternoon, his assistant called and said that we had a deal."

"What exactly was the deal?" asked Eugene.

"If I could procure this one particular artifact for Nelson, he would give me the manuscript and 200,000 dollars. Half of which I will keep; half will go to my client in Egypt."

"Can I also assume that supplying Hugo Nelson's diverse and eclectic obsession of antiques would insure a prosperous future for the store?"

"It would help insure a prosperous future for you, too, Eugene. Your days of dusting shelves are over."

"And what did you know about smuggling artifacts, for heaven's sake?" he asked.

"Nothing. Then." Katherine's voice flattened into a monotone. "Now I know it's a dangerous game, winner take all. And, in this case," she announced, brightening, "I win."

"How in the world did you do it?" asked Eugene.

"Once the deal was settled with Nelson, I hid the manuscript in a suitcase and shipped it to my client in Cairo, on the White Star Line. On the same day my client shipped a package to me, for Nelson."

"Just like that?" said Eugene.

"It was easier than I thought. With the war over, Customs doesn't seem to care as much about what is going out, as what is coming in. I said a silent blessing over the manuscript and turned my thoughts to the incoming shipment. It was *that* shipment that made me nervous. The crate coming to America is the one that could get me into trouble." *But*, said Katherine to herself, *this has as much to do with Etienne as it does my business. And I want, with everything inside of me, to lay my eyes upon the Knife of the Asps.*

Katherine admired Cleopatra VII of Egypt. She had read that this Egyptian queen, of Greek descent, was exceptionally intelligent, spoke 11 languages and ran the most prosperous empire on earth. She was the lover of Julius Caesar, and later his protégé, Marc Antony. *Thrilling*, thought Katherine, *the idea of having lovers without judgement. To have a lover before marriage was sin enough. To have two lovers and their children and never marry – that was astonishing.* Katherine sighed. *But Cleopatra was a queen, and I ...*

Just then they all heard a rumbling in the alley. A large delivery truck was backing over bumps and potholes in the dirt alley, belching smoke and slowly making its way to the loading dock of The Silver Butterfly. Katherine's heart started to race.

In a flurry of lifting and hauling, huffing and puffing, the crate sat at her feet and a sweaty delivery man was holding out a clipboard holding the manifest and Proof of Delivery for her to sign.

Katherine took the pen, flipped through the documents, and stopped dead in her tracks. She looked around and found four faces staring expectantly at her: Nick, Eugene and the two delivery men. She had a sudden and intense fear that a squad of policemen was right outside the doors, just waiting for her signature before they jumped out and clamped her in irons.

Before she could stop herself, her signature was on the page and the delivery truck was rumbling back down the alley. She was alone with her prize.

Katherine moved to the crate and ran her hand along its rough surface. "Let's open it, shall we?" she looked up at Nick and Eugene, beaming.

"Maybe you could tell me something first," insisted Eugene. "Because I'm not opening that crate until you tell me what's in it ... that is 'not exactly on the manifest'."

Katherine paused. Eugene waited. She suppressed a grin and spoke in quiet, slow voice. "It's the Knife of the Asps."

Eugene stared at her. "The Knife of the Asps," he repeated. He began to pace the floor. "The Knife of the Asps." He stopped pacing long enough to stare at Katherine, then continued tracing and retracing his steps, first in one direction, then the other. He finally spoke. "Let's break into this thing."

"I thought you'd never ask." Katherine flashed a smile at Eugene. It was the kind of smile her husband had seen a thousand times. The kind of smile he couldn't wait to see again.

Together they loomed over the wooden box labeled, 'British Protectorate of Egypt.' The word, CLEARED, was stamped on the side in bright red ink – the exact color of Katherine's lipstick.

They stood staring at the box, not as if they were afraid to open it, but rather savoring the satisfaction of it. Eugene finally drove the tip of the crow bar into the narrow slit between the crate and its lid. The nails squeaked with resistance in equal proportion to their mounting anticipation. Eugene slid off the heavy lid to reveal layers of straw carefully packed around an array of pottery and statues.

It was as if time itself had been captured and stored in this box. The room suddenly became very quiet. Katherine's face took on a look of wonder and excitement. *She looks so young in this moment,* mused Nick. *She looks happy.*

Nick wandered into the background and watched Katherine and Eugene as they began lifting out the artifacts, one by one. "These we'll sell, for a commission," explained Katherine, silently thanking Etienne for sending such a splendid collection.

From the crate, Katherine and Eugene lifted out vases and jewelry, statues and goblets. They drew out silver and pottery, and stone artifacts carved out of pure, black onyx, jade, pink granite and blue lapis. Eugene touched each piece reverently before ticking them off the bill of lading. Katherine cast the inventory aside with increasing carelessness.

"I'm looking for a statue of Isis," Katherine explained, her eyes catching a scowl on Eugene's face.

Eugene searched the manifest for such a statue. It was something Katherine had done earlier, a dozen times. There she was: *Statue, Egyptian, alabaster and gold, 1750 B.C., Isis,* listed innocuously among the other legitimate artifacts of the collection. Eugene returned his attention to the crate.

As Katherine and Eugene made their way through the box of Egyptian treasures, the fragile pieces were becoming scattered all around them on the floor. "Good God," intervened Nick. "Can't you be more tidy about all this?" They ignored him. Nick took it upon himself to collect each piece from the floor and place it on an empty shelf that Eugene had prepared specifically for this shipment.

Eugene's hands finally touched the delicate outline of a carved figure, laying in the very bottom of the crate. "Katherine," he whispered. Eugene reached deep into the wooden box. He carefully lifted out an alabaster statue, draped in strands of packing straw. It measured three feet in height, and one in diameter, with gold inlay weaving a collared necklace across her shoulders. The same gold inlay decorated the statue's headdress, which represented the disk of the sun. Isis stood on a round marble platform carved with the images of three lions. Eugene held the artifact above the crate.

Katherine looked up. "That's it!" A smile that cloaked a smirk of triumph crossed her face. She set aside the bowl she was holding. Katherine took the heavy statue and gingerly set it on the floor. She knelt by the beautiful figure, like a worshipper at a shrine.

Nick thought it terribly odd to see this woman, his wife, in her black wool skirt and heels, perfectly put together, kneeling on a cold cement floor. *What is it that causes such a disparity?* he wondered. *Worse, what is it that brings us all to our knees eventually?* Nick hoped that he would never see such a day. And he knew, just the same, that he most certainly would.

"Isis was the Goddess of two worlds," murmured Katherine, looking up at Nick. "She invoked the powers of both heaven and earth." Katherine admired Isis for many moments. The elegant statue stood solitary on the warehouse floor, a shipping crate for a temple, and shreds of straw to worship at her delicate, alabaster feet. "She was also known as the Lady of Rage," added Katherine. "They say she created nightmares by the thousands with her black words." Katherine took a deep breath, and laid the statue on its side. "Hand me the crow bar."

"What?" Eugene looked at her with a hard scowl.

"I need the crowbar, please."

Saying nothing, he reached back, and slid the crow bar across the cement floor. It rattled through the silence and the absurdity.

"Watch this." Katherine traced her finger along the base of the statue, where the round platform merged with the long, bare legs of the goddess. There, a thread-thin glue line, barely perceptible, ran the perimeter of the statue's base. Firmly grasping the crow bar near its hook, Katherine gently tapped along the glue line. One more rap and the bottom popped off neatly and rattled to the floor.

Katherine looked into the hollowed-out shell of the statue. Frowning, she shook the statue. Then she reached her hand inside. She looked again. Katherine stared up at her husband, totally helpless, and he stared back at her for one long, desperate moment. The look on her face carved itself into Nick's memory, where it would always remain, as clear as the moment it happened.

Katherine stood and hovered over the statue for some time, ever so slightly shaking her head, as if in confusion. Finally she reached down without a word, took the statue in both hands, and flung it with all her might against the wall. Isis shattered with all her dreams into a thousand pieces on the floor.

5

A DEAL GONE SIDEWAYS

Beware your heart's desire, for it shall surely be yours.

– author unknown

Katherine lit up a Lucky Strike. *Damn Etienne anyway*, she thought. For the fifth time that day she rang up the overseas operator and rattled off Etienne's telephone number. Then Katherine put her head on her desk and listened to the connection ring in her ear. Finally the operator cut in. "There's no answer on the other end, ma'am."

"I know that," snapped Katherine, sitting up. "Let it ring."

"Yes, ma'am."

If she calls me ma'am again, I'm going to scream, grumbled Katherine to herself. They sat there in silence, the telephone operator and Katherine, waiting for someone to pick up the phone, knowing it wasn't going to happen. They were both, in truth, waiting for Katherine to give up. She thought to count the number of rings: let it ring to a hundred, or to a lucky number, and then ring off. But Katherine didn't have a lucky number over four, so she just stared out the window, wondering where Etienne was. "I'll try back later," she finally said.

"Thank you, ma'am."

The line went dead. Katherine slammed the receiver down in its cradle, hard. She picked it up and slammed it down again. A terrible feeling began to grow inside her. It was fury, accumulating upon itself, billowing like a thunderhead. Covering her face with her hands, she tried to stave off the voices of panic, raw and familiar, raining down on her. *I can think my way out of this. There's an answer there's an answer there's an answer…*

Katherine glared at the telephone. Finally, she shoved the whole thing off her desk and watched it rattle to the floor. The receiver fell off, and she still sat there, staring as if in a trance, while the drone of the dial tone turned to a steady, alarming beep.

Nick finally tiptoed into her office and put the phone back together. "Are you alright, darling?" he asked. Katherine looked up at him, stared incredulously, and then put her head down on her desk.

"Eugene is going through all the other artifacts from Etienne," continued Nick. "He was so upset about the statue, he couldn't bring himself to sweep it into the waste basket. He said you could do it yourself. I told him I'd do it, but he's still in a very foul mood about the whole thing."

"I'll make it up to him."

"You know," began Nick, using his best attorney voice, which was the voice that most particularly annoyed Katherine. "You might feel some sense of relief, Katherine, that the dagger wasn't in that crate. What you were doing was extremely dangerous. Who could fancy that you, Katherine Howard Spencer, would *ever* be in the business of smuggling?"

Katherine lifted her head and stared at Nick. "Etienne cheated me," she said, her voice low and mad. "He now has that ridiculous manuscript he was entirely obsessed about, and I have nothing. Worse, now I have to answer to Hugo Nelson, empty-handed. Forget for a minute the 100,000 dollars that was supposed to come to me for all my efforts. Hugo Nelson will probably kill me. *Kill me.* And you're standing there asking me if I'm *alright*?" Katherine got up and started pacing her office. "No, I'm not alright. I'm not the least little bit alright!"

Nick calmly watched her, saying nothing. Katherine plunked herself back down in her chair. *Is Etienne angry? Could he possibly be nurturing some terrible grudge? I just cannot believe that Etienne would actually go to all this trouble to cheat me. Still... where is the dagger? Where is the goddamned dagger?*

Katherine considered her lover and her husband through the lens of time. She still found it hard to understand how it was she ever chose between Nick and Etienne. Each was as different to her as he was important. They had been inseparable at Oxford, the three of them and her brother Ben. They would not have survived the rigors of that school without each other. She in particular, one of the few women at the prestigious university, driven there for reasons she herself did not entirely understand. There were times, back at Oxford, that she wished she hadn't loved either Nick or Etienne, felt as though she shouldn't have loved both, and wanted to have loved only one. But which one?

Nick was sweet, and more handsome than he ever realized: tall stature, naturally athletic, with unfailingly excellent posture, bred into him through his proper British heritage. He parted his blond hair straight down the middle and combed it off his face, making his sea-green eyes seem soft and enormous. Nick had an easy smile that hid an almost imperceptible, but constant, sense of tension. A person might never know that Nick was carefully gauging everyone around him, so that he could anticipate their needs and respond to them in advance.

Every thread of Nick's clothing was carefully selected, color-coordinated, and looking fresh, as though he just put them on. He held up his trousers with fashionable suspenders, always with a bow tie to match. Nick also had a subtle habit of using both his hands to adjust the glasses on his face, pausing, and then crinkling his brow in singular concentration. Katherine had watched him do this a thousand times, whenever he was reading, absorbing unfamiliar information, or trying to explain something. It was as if to help himself, and everyone around him, see more clearly. *I've come to love that gesture,* thought Katherine. *It's a secret, an intimacy that only I see, that only I have noticed and understood. If that isn't love, what is?*

Still, I remember, and can almost touch, a different Nick. I remember him though a veil, spontaneous and engaged. It's like a dream I can see, and then it's gone, like a fish slipping through my bare hands. The war changed him in ways I can't understand, can barely name. Still, we understand each other. We forgive each other, the way people do who want to stay married. If that isn't love, what is?

Katherine often found herself searching her husband's face, however, looking for something more. Perhaps she was looking to recover the way they used to be as a couple, before time and disappointment interrupted them. Somehow she just couldn't find the best of Nick any more. It never occurred to her to wonder where the best of herself had gone.

And then there was Etienne. *How did I ever say no to him? Etienne was nothing I would ever want in a husband, but everything I ever wanted in a man.* His irreverent smile and crystal blue eyes set off his dark, unruly curls, giving him the look of a mirthful pirate. He had a deep, throaty voice that dripped from his mouth with a smooth French accent. "Ooo la la," he would always say, just to tease her. "Ooo la la la la." But Etienne could no sooner be attached to one woman than a bee could be tied to a single flower. The nectar drawn, the creature must fly on or perish. Despite how wildly she loved him, and their time together in Paris, she said good-bye, leaving him before he left her.

When Katherine thought of those things, she remembered fully and clearly why she chose who she did. Still, she was drawn from time to time, back to her memories of Etienne, and to the question that could never be answered: *What if I had chosen differently?*

Nick and Etienne had been an enviable pair, a pair that everyone seemed to circle around. Nick and Etienne were friends held together through respect and rivalry, envy and adoration. The two very striking, very different young men seemed to find a comfort and a home in each other's vacancies. Katherine knew that this friendship would endure much, including the dulling rays of time, the breadth of the Atlantic Ocean, the Second World War, and her.

"Darling, are you listening?"

Katherine rubbed her eyes. *Lord, how long has Nick been talking?* "Of course I'm listening," she said.

"I say, it's not that terribly bad. You'll see."

"I'm going to Cairo." Katherine was almost as surprised as Nick was to hear herself say it.

"Now, don't get carried away," said Nick.

"I have no idea how badly Nelson will react to this," she said. "But I'm not going to sit here without the dagger and wait for him to show up. I can't. I'll send him a telegram saying the shipment is being held up in Customs. No, that's a bad idea. I'll ring him up on the telephone and tell him the shipment was delayed in... Alexandria."

"Katherine -"

"My best hope is to get to Egypt, recover the dagger, bring it back to America, and settle my dealings with Nelson as quickly and as smoothly as possible."

"You should just drop the whole nasty business," Nick insisted. "I'll straighten things out with Nelson."

"Nick. Don't you get it? I shipped off Nelson's manuscript and I have *nothing* to give him for it! Nothing! I'm going to Cairo."

"All by yourself?"

"That's right."

"I don't bloody think so."

"Watch me." *And don't think I didn't catch your sarcasm, Nick. I'm not going to spend one more miserable day sitting in this store, worrying. I'm going to Egypt to find Etienne. And when I do, I'm going to wrap my fingers around his little French neck.*

"Damn it, Katherine!" Nick slammed her office door shut in a rare display of emotion. "You don't know the language. You don't know the land. You don't even know how to find the dagger once you get there."

"I think you're over-reacting," stated Katherine.

"I damned bloody well am not! Don't you know it's not safe for you over there? The Muslims don't regard women the same way we do. Worse yet, you're an infidel to them."

"A what?"

"An *infidel* – a person without faith. Fundamental Islamists despise the infidels, westerners, like you and me. They will die for their religious convictions. And they will kill for them. They don't even want their *own government* to be secular."

Katherine just stared blankly at her husband.

Nick sat across from his wife and laid his hands on top of hers. "Katherine, most Muslims don't want a separation between church and state, like we have. And we have for good reasons, by the way. They want the government to be Muslim and all the laws of the land to follow Islamic tradition. This is exactly what I'm talking about, Katherine. You don't know what you'd be getting yourself into."

She met his arguments with silence. Katherine learned long ago that silence cannot be argued with. It was an unfair thing to do, and she knew it. But Nick wasn't stopping. She had also learned, long ago, that Nick could be carried quite a long way on the momentum of his convictions.

"Do you know, Katherine, that just by showing up, you'll be considered an enemy to many of the people? You'll have to cover your head at all times, and your arms. Do you know that? Not to mention the conflict brewing over there between the Arabs and the Jews. And

America is picking sides. Add to all that the fact that the British Crown, the Egyptian nationalists, and the monarchists, are all jockeying for power over there. It's a bloody mess! You simply cannot go!"

"You said I couldn't run my own business, either."

"Well..?"

Katherine pulled her hands away. *Well, there you go. With one little word, you've put my failure into the bright, glaring spotlight.* Of all the people in all the world that Katherine thought would never throw defeat in her face, it was Nick Spencer. She expected her husband to keep certain secrets, secrets of failure and loss, of mistakes made. If she could not deny these things to him, how could she possibly deny them to herself? "I'm going to Cairo."

"Katherine, darling, stop for a minute. You can't keep pushing yourself so recklessly. It's over. I'm sorry about that, but, frankly, you've been running crazy ever since we lost Ben, doing everything anyone tells you not to do. It's time to slow down. We don't need the money. I can fix things with Nelson. Really I can. Don't go to Egypt."

Nick was right, of course. That Katherine was genuinely scared to go to Egypt alone didn't matter. It was another little secret she would pretend not to know. She was scared and she was going anyway. And she absolutely wasn't going to let her husband bail her out of this problem. She would fix it herself. "I'm going," she snapped. "Besides, *we* didn't lose Ben. I did."

They stared at each other across her desk for what seemed like an interminable time. Nick knew the silent despair that roiled inside his wife, causing her to make such alarming decisions and unkind statements. Still, it took enormous restraint in these moments to keep his own thoughts in check.

A loud knock came through the door. Startled, mostly relieved, Katherine and Nick suspended their anger and their regret, like a soap bubble in the air, willing to let it to drop back and burst down upon them in its own time.

Eugene poked his head inside Katherine's office without waiting for an invitation. "Katherine, there are people here." Eugene looked over his shoulder and then stepped into the office, closing the door behind him. "It's someone from the Customs office, and he's with a man from the Egyptian Department of Antiquities." Eugene was uncommonly pale.

50

"Well, send them in," said Katherine. "But, Eugene, take your time."

"They must be after the dagger," said Nick. "Unless they know about the manuscript – God, do you suppose they intercepted the manuscript?"

"I don't know," Katherine whispered. *God help me,* she thought, *could this day get any worse?*

Nick settled into the chair across from Katherine's desk, crossing his legs and cleaning his eyeglasses with a handkerchief. Nick was picking a fleck of lint off his pants, casual as could be, just as their visitors stepped into the room. Only a tiny furrow on his brow, if one were to look close enough, betrayed his discomfort.

"Katherine Spencer, this is Mr. Patrick Morris, from the Customs Authority," Eugene announced stiffly. Morris stepped into the room. He had bushy eyebrows, showing hints of gray, and a soft, pensive face, like somebody who had known too many people he had to forgive. "And may I present Mr. Omar Kassab," added Eugene, "from Egypt."

The Egyptian brushed past Morris and Eugene. Katherine stood up and shook Kassab's hand across her desk. "Mr. Kassab, it's a pleasure to meet you." She then extended her hand to the Customs officer. "Mr. Morris. Please let me introduce my husband, Nick Spencer." Nick rose and shook Morris' hand and then turned to Kassab.

Katherine could feel the red-hot moment of tension as Nick and Kassab squared off. They seemed to be silently testing each other's mettle and nerve in those few short seconds, as they locked hands and eyes. Nick then shot a blinding smile at Kassab and let go of his hand.

Kassab was small and rumpled and nasty-looking. *He looks as though he just got off the airplane in the same wrinkled brown suit he wore for the past three days and two nights,* thought Katherine. Kassab had jet black hair, wavy, heavily greased and combed back off his face. He spoke with a thick accent that was both compelling and frightening.

Nick sat back in his chair. He crossed his legs again, and cast a bored look over at Kassab, looking entirely relaxed. *How does he do that?* wondered Katherine. Nick's eyes, however, recorded every detail of the Customs agent and the ominous man from Egypt.

Kassab, meanwhile was scrutinizing every detail of Katherine's office. It was large enough, but over-crowded with books and boxes, magazines and mosaics, statues, carvings and sculptures. All the things she couldn't – or wouldn't – sell. A framed picture of Nick was perched on her desk, a dusty globe sat on the corner, and a silver paperweight in the shape of a butterfly held down a stack of unpaid bills.

Katherine looked down at the paperweight for a moment and took a deep breath. The word *Believe* was engraved on the sterling silver surface. It gave her a moment of courage and she silently thanked Ben in heaven, who gave her the paperweight as a gift when she entered Oxford.

"Would you like me to stay?" asked Eugene, pursing his lips. "I can stay..."

"No. Thank you, Eugene. I'm sure our guests won't be staying all that long," Katherine said as coolly as she could manage. Eugene turned to go, casting a narrow glance at Kassab. "And Eugene," she added hastily, "please leave the door open."

Katherine sat back in her chair in what she hoped was a graceful gesture, and turned to Kassab and Morris. She did not invite them to sit. "It is not often we receive visitors from the Egyptian government," she said. "How can I help you?" She directed her questions to Kassab, because it was not out of the ordinary in the antique business to deal with American Customs.

Kassab spoke slowly, with the considered precision of someone who knows he is the most important person in the room. "Please understand, Mrs. Spencer, this is not a casual visit." He looked down at the globe sitting on her desk. A flick of his finger sent it spinning. "Are you, perhaps, planning a trip?" he asked.

"I was just talking to Katherine about Palestine," said Nick, halting the spin of the globe in its stand. "As you certainly know, there is tremendous conflict growing in Palestine, as thousands and thousands of Jews – displaced by the war – are migrating back home, to Jerusalem.

"The Arabs, of course, do not want to give up their holy city. Nor do they want to give up the land where they were raised, and have worked for generations. Naturally. Thousands of Jewish immigrants live in America, of course, so we tend to be quite sympathetic to their plight. Not without compassion for the Arabs, of course. It's the Arabs; after all, who control the vast oil reserves in the Middle East.

Not that oil has anything to do with anything, of course. It's a humanitarian issue that's at stake. Quite a terrible situation, really. Could take years to sort out."

Katherine smiled inside. *Only Nick could get away with such a thing. He was so naïve-looking. So guileless.* But Kassab listened with thin patience. He began to stroll around Katherine's office, picking up various objects, turning them over and over without really looking at them. He would then carelessly put them down where they didn't belong, as though they were an afterthought in his hand.

I'm going to ignore that, thought Katherine. She leaned forward and crossed her fingers under her chin, casually resting her elbows on her desk while Nick talked on. *Moments come upon me from time to time. Moments when audacity rises above everything else – insecurity, intimidation, fear, jealousy. There is a certain fire in boldness that burns, in a flash, all the fearful aspects of my heart.* Katherine blew a small, secret kiss to her husband.

Nick grinned. Then things got ugly.

Kassab came to stand directly behind Nick, putting a firm hand on his shoulder. Kassab cleared his throat and, that easily, took command of the room. "I am quite aware of the situation, Mr. Spencer. I am Muslim. Now then, why don't you tell me instead about the Knife of the Asps?"

Nick shrugged off Kassab's hand and looked over at Katherine, a portrait of innocence. "What?" Nick and Katherine asked in unison.

Morris stepped in. "We have it on good authority that the Egyptian Knife of the Asps was smuggled into America, you see, in a shipment of pottery delivered to *this* address. And it was shipped by uh, one, Etienne Desonia. The Egyptians claim that Desonia is a criminal, with a history of dealings and transactions, uh, outside the scope of the law."

"Well, I'm not at all surprised," said Katherine, trying to hide a new anxiety welling up inside her. The flood of doubt returned, to quench – in their never ending battle – the fire of boldness. "Etienne was quite a scoundrel as I remember, from our days together at Oxford." She looked at Nick and then back to Kassab. "But I can assure you, every single thing he shipped to me was entirely legal."

"And I can assure *you*," Kassab responded, "that Desonia is notorious in the Egyptian government for his repeated acts of piracy against the country. We are convinced, Mrs. Spencer, that the Knife of the Asps was in the shipment you received this morning."

"But Customs already checked that shipment. Mr. Morris, you should know that better than any one."

"Indeed," replied Morris. "But in the event we've overlooked something, you see, we would care to search your store. If you don't mind."

"I do mind," said Katherine firmly.

Morris dug through his coat pockets, red in the face, fumbling. He eventually withdrew a wrinkled document and held it out. *Fine,* thought Katherine, *a search warrant.* If Katherine felt any momentary relief that the Knife of the Asps wasn't in the shipment, it was entirely overridden by another emotion: fury. At Etienne, at Morris and particularly at Kassab, who had so callously imposed himself upon her store, her privacy, and her illusion of control.

Kassab and Morris spent hours searching. They ransacked Katherine's office, the store room, the shelves and every closet, drawer, box, cubby hole, nook and cranny they could find. They made a dreadful mess of things while Katherine stood by, her arms crossed, her eyes narrowed. She followed their movements with the long-suffering indignation of a hen guarding her beloved, doomed eggs. Nick stood at a distance, while Eugene followed them around, straightening as he went, as best he could.

Nick was angry. Though he looked as though his only concern was his wife's dignity, he was quietly stewing about Etienne, blaming him for the entire mess. *When is this going to end?* he wondered. *Today? After the Customs Authority leaves, empty-handed? Will Katherine willingly drop the whole mess and let us get back to our lives?... Not bloody likely. Now I'm going to have to go with her all the damn way to Egypt.*

Eugene passed by Nick, stopping only to complain briefly in his ear. "God, that woman causes me grief!" said Eugene.

You have no idea, brooded Nick.

Morris came to stand by Katherine. "Well," he said. "That's just about it." Katherine scowled at him. Morris dabbed his forehead with the handkerchief from his pocket, and breathed an enormous sigh of relief.

But Kassab was seething. "We'll go through the shipment one more time," he announced.

"What the hell for?" snapped Katherine. Even Morris sighed.

"We've been assuming that the contraband has been taken from the shipment and hidden in this building," said Kassab. "But perhaps... perhaps... it is still hidden within the shipment itself."

"Oh, for crying out loud," said Katherine.

"This time, we're going to be more careful," stated Kassab. "And we're going to compare the artifacts against the manifest. Which is *where*, exactly?"

Eugene produced the crumpled manifest, and Kassab and Morris carefully re-examined each artifact from the crate. It was not long before Morris, crinkling his brow, approached Katherine.

"There's an alabaster statue of Isis listed here, you see?" said Morris, while they all stood still in the store room. "Where is that statue?"

"Behind you," replied Katherine. "In the waste basket."

"What happened here?" asked Kassab suspiciously hovering over the shards of white stone.

"It broke. Obviously during shipment. Unless one of your Customs agents was careless," said Katherine, looking at Morris. "Not that it really matters. It was a cheap replica."

"Alabaster does not break into this many pieces during a shipping accident," observed Kassab.

Katherine sighed. "What you are seeing is evidence of a temper tantrum," she confessed.

"My wife was angry that the statue was broken," Nick chimed in. "She finished off the statue with a crow bar."

"Confiscate those pieces," ordered Kassab. "It might be interesting to piece back what we can."

Will this ever end? thought Katherine. *They're going to find a hollow center, shaped just like a knife. And a glue line on the base.*

And then I'm done for. Katherine started to shake. Deep inside she felt a trembling that she thought would take her to her knees. Her

55

face was hot, so suddenly, she feared she would throw up on the spot. The room began to fall out of focus. She felt dizzy, and unbelievably, unbearably, tired. Katherine took hold of the back of her chair to steady herself.

Nick saw her distress and silently touched her hand. As quickly as it overtook her, Katherine's fear reached its pinnacle and began to subside. Again, the battle with fear. *Was it pretense? Optimism? Blind hope? Better wits?* She couldn't say. But the voice of reason suddenly seemed very loud.

It's entirely unlikely, she told herself, *that they'll be able to piece the statue back together. I really did a job on poor alabaster Isis. What can they possibly find? Nothing. Nothing.* Katherine took a deep breath and focused on the room around her. *Please just leave*, she willed, as she stared at Kassab and Morris. *Leave now.*

Finally, finished with their second search, and having meticulously boxed the alabaster remnants to take with them, Morris and Kassab prepared to leave the store. Kassab put on a thin overcoat and buttoned it with slow precision. Equally as unhurried, he came to stand directly in front of Katherine and Nick. Nick took his wife's hand and calmly squeezed it, giving her the last infusion of confidence she needed to make it through the nerve-wracking inspection.

"You are instructed not to leave town – all three of you – until I've resolved this matter," said Kassab in an eerily quiet, casual voice. "Rest assured, you have drawn the attention of the Egyptian government. We are not at all forgiving in these matters."

"Frankly Mr. Kassab, I'm tired of you trying to intimidate me," retorted Katherine, her resentment finding a voice as Kassab's departure became imminent. "You can suit yourself. Watch me all you want. I'm not going anywhere but home."

"I *will* find the Knife of the Asps," Kassab added coldly, changing his tone entirely. "You can tell that to Etienne Desonia when you speak with him."

"Our transaction is complete," she said. "I have no reason to be speaking with Monsieur Desonia any time soon."

"You can also tell him that you'll both be spending time in prison... very shortly."

"Considering this shipment is entirely legal and flawlessly documented," she snapped back, "I have to tell you you're mistaken. And I take great exception to your threat."

Katherine moved to the door, indicating the end of their visit.

Morris, his face flushed, shook her hand and then Nick's. Then he took his heavy wool coat and scarf off the coat rack near the door. The Customs man hastily bundled himself up against the late afternoon chill. Kassab stood by, looking out the window, his thoughts already elsewhere. Nick reached out, in a gesture of truce, to shake Kassab's hand. "Where can we reach you, if we do hear anything about this knife of yours?"

"You cannot." Kassab ignored Nick's outstretched hand and simply stared at him for a long, miserable moment. Nick smoothly moved his hands into his pants pockets. Kassab pulled on his leather gloves and walked out the door.

Morris, finding himself without his associate, made haste to bid his good-byes. "We'll be in touch," he assured Katherine. "It's my hope to settle this matter as quickly as possible." He looked carefully at her, as if he wanted badly for her to be innocent. "I'm hoping for the best," he added, as he walked out the door into the frigid afternoon.

"Very well then," said Katherine, and closed the door behind him. She stood at the window long after Kassab and Morris had shaken hands and parted ways.

Am I brilliant? Or am I blessed? thought Katherine. *I should be on my way to jail right now. But the storm has passed, and things have turned out for the good after all. I should learn to stay calm in the eye of such storms. But I suppose I don't have that kind of trust – the kind that is the luxury of people who always expect good things to happen. But I'm not one of those people. And this was another one of those times.*

"Dreadful chaps," muttered Nick after Morris and Kassab left. "Seems the Egyptian fellow knows Etienne quite well."

"I, for one," said Eugene, "hope I never see Omar Kassab again, as long as I live."

"I was bloody relieved, I can tell you," said Nick, "when the Customs Authority showed up and there was no knife."

"We'll have to sneak out of the store somehow," said Katherine, joining her husband and Eugene. "Kassab is probably watching us, from very close by."

"Well, *you* at least," added Nick.

"Then we can get ourselves together as fast as possible – to leave for Cairo." Katherine ventured the statement as if it was a foregone conclusion.

Eugene turned to them. "You're going to Cairo?"

"We're going to Cairo," sighed Nick, putting an arm around Katherine's shoulder.

She leaned into him and he kissed her forehead. Katherine smiled. *Things are starting to come together perfectly.* "We're going to Cairo," she said.

"Well," offered Eugene. "No matter what happens there, so long as you keep yourselves out of jail, you'll have something to come back to."

"How's that?" Nick asked.

"I've been cataloguing the artifacts from the crate. There are some extraordinary pieces in there. I'm convinced that we can launch the store to a whole new level. Just to start, the commission on these pieces will put us into the black.

"Then, I was thinking, with the end of the war, trade is easier, and people's curiosity toward the foreign and the exotic is escalating. If we can set up a distribution agreement with this friend of yours in Egypt – assuming he doesn't get himself arrested, *and* he has continued access to this quality of merchandise – we can supply more exotic antiques than any other importer in New York City. As for Hugo Nelson," he added bitterly, "he'll just have to find someone else to do his nasty smuggling."

"Well said," Nick replied with an uncomfortable, distant smile.

Katherine looked at her husband closely for a moment. "The next big problem of the day," she said, distracting herself, "is *how* to get out of the store, home, packed, and on a flight to Egypt – all without running into Kassab."

"Idlewild has a daily flight to the UK," offered Nick. "We can get at least that far by tomorrow night."

"What about Morris?" asked Eugene.

"I'm not the least bit worried about him," stated Katherine, looking around the room for a disguise of some sort. "He's probably half way home by now, looking forward to martinis and pot roast with his boring wife." She stood in the middle of the room, hands on her hips, looking around, until her eyes rested on Eugene.

"Eugene?" she began in her sweetest tone. "Would you please come with me and Nick into my office?"

Eugene walked with Nick and Katherine back to her office and stood at the door, his arms crossed firmly across his chest. A deep frown was carved on his face. "Now what?" he asked.

"Would you mind taking off your clothes?" asked Katherine. Eugene and Nick looked at each other and frowned. "I have a plan," she added.

"Whenever you have a plan," Eugene replied, "I have a problem."

Katherine looked fondly at Eugene, and squeezed his hand. *When he says certain things, familiar things that he knows simply because we've spent so much time together, because we have a history, I feel ... seen. It's rare to feel that way. The way it used to be with Ben – that beautiful wonderful feeling of being known.*

"I have no right to ask," she began. "I know I haven't. But ... I need to borrow your clothes," explained Katherine. "So I can get out of here."

"I don't believe they'll fit," said Nick.

"This is not a fashion show," she insisted. "It only has to pass from a distance. Kassab is not going to be standing right outside, just waiting to nab me the moment I walk out the door." She paused for a moment. "Is he?"

"Not likely," admitted Nick. "It's far too cold outside for his thin Egyptian blood. Did you notice the coat he was wearing? No. He's definitely not loitering outside the door. Not in this weather. He'll need to find some place warm – if he's waiting for you at all. Which he most likely is."

"So, Katherine," Eugene interjected unhappily. "If you're wearing *my* clothes, I don't suppose I need to ask whose clothes I'll be wearing."

"You'll be wearing mine," said Katherine, with some amount of solemnity. "We're about the same size, more or less," she added.

"That's just great, Katherine. Thanks. As if you haven't ruined my day enough already."

"What the hell did *I* do?"

"Oh, I don't know, Katherine. Smuggle an Egyptian artifact into the country? Smash a beautiful alabaster statue? Lie to the Customs Authority? Nothing, really. And now you're setting me up. All in a day's work, I'm sure."

"Eugene, I know you're upset about the statue, but truly, it was only a replica."

"I'm not upset about the statue, Katherine." Eugene stood toe to toe with his boss. "You worked on that shipment for weeks and weeks and never once mentioned the Knife of the Asps to me. Never mind that it was illegal and unethical, you could at least have told me about it."

"I know you think you're right, Eugene. But you're not. What would you be thinking of me if you were sitting behind bars right now?"

"You should have told me." Eugene stared at Katherine for a moment and she stared straight back. *Pound for pound,* thought Eugene, *she's tougher than any man I know. She's driven in ways I never see in other women, and seldom see in other men. So many times I've watched her point a long, red fingernail in someone's direction, and stare straight through their skin. Still, I wonder what sorrows she is holding back with that great force of energy that swirls constantly around her?*

"You're right," Katherine said, walking around to the chair behind her desk. "Not about the Knife, but this disguise. It isn't fair. I'll think of another way to get out of the building."

"You're wrong," countered Eugene. "About the Knife ... *and* the disguise. It's the best way."

"Eugene," began Katherine. "I haven't any right to ask you –"

"To tell you the truth," sighed Eugene, "I've always dreamed about wearing your clothes. I'm particularly keen on those alligator pumps. Besides," he quipped, "you wreck my day every day. Just by being so beautiful."

Katherine shook her head in gratitude. *How does loyalty overcome betrayal? That I lied to Eugene, and lost in my bargain, should have changed things. Winners are forgiven. But not me. Of all the things I could have done, for Eugene, lying is the most intolerable. I wonder if I could ever deliver a gesture like that, a gesture of such grace?*

"No harm can really come of it," offered Nick. "Kassab simply can't arrest a man for wearing women's clothes."

"That's right," said Eugene. "Kassab will probably follow me for a few minutes before he even tries to stop me. In the mean time, you can leave the store wearing my clothes."

"Kassab won't even detain Eugene," Nick added. "He has no real jurisdiction here. He just wants the Knife of the Asps. As soon as he realizes his mistake, he'll turn around and head back to the store. We'll wait until five o'clock, when the streets are most crowded. By the time Kassab discovers his mistake, and returns, we'll be gone."

"But if he does ... detain me," stammered Eugene. "You'll find me, right? You'll come and get me. Right?"

"Of course," said Nick, reassuringly.

"Absolutely," added Katherine.

Eugene began undressing.

The sidewalks were beginning to fill with people as the five o'clock hour approached. With November upon them, it was already dark, and it seemed later than it actually was. The darkness heightened the sense that their actions were clandestine and dangerous. "I'm actually beginning to enjoy this," said Eugene, not convincing anybody.

Eugene's hair and face were shielded by Katherine's wide brimmed hat. The skirt fit well enough, with a row of safety pins expanding the waistband. Her overcoat was loose and bulky enough to cover any flaws in his attire. He also put on Katherine's silk stockings, causing even Nick to smile. Katherine's gloves presented the first obstacle. They were far too tight.

"Allow me," said Nick, cutting them with scissors from cuff to palm.

"They won't stay on," complained Eugene.

"Yes, they will." Nick took a roll of black tape from Katherine's desk, and wrapped it several times around Eugene's wrists. "The coat should hide this,"he added. "Just keep your hands in a loose fist. Like this."

"Right. Got it," nodded Eugene, imitating Nick's gesture.

The next problem was Katherine's shoes. "They're killing my feet," said Eugene wobbling around the office.

Katherine, on the other hand, reveled in a moment of divine justice. "You men have no idea how miserable high heels and hose can be," she said. "Try wearing them every day."

"Frankly, I don't want to know," said Nick, embarrassed at the sight of it all.

"Can you bear them?" Katherine asked Eugene, touching his arm gently. "It's important."

Eugene drew in a deep breathe and sighed. They then went to work on the details of Katherine's disguise. Eugene folded under his pant legs to shorten them, securing the hem with safety pins and tape. The waistline, gaping a full six inches beyond Katherine's figure, had to be cinched up tightly, so they didn't fall right off her.

"The belt's too big," she complained. "I ran out of little holes..."

"No worries," said Nick, pulling the belt off his wife. Taking the sharp tip of a letter opener, Nick poked a few extra holes in the leather. "Sorry 'bout that, old boy," he said to Eugene. "I'll buy you another one."

"That's Dior, if you'll notice," replied Eugene, pale in the face.

Katherine tucked in Eugene's crisp white shirt, and Nick knotted the necktie for her, something she had never had the interest to learn. She then trotted off to the bathroom to check out her costume, posed a few times, liked the look, and returned to her office.

"You look rather stunning, my dear," offered Nick. "If I do say so myself. Considering you're dressed like a man, that is." Eugene raised his eyebrows. "Never mind," Nick muttered, rolling his eyes.

"You look just like Kate Hepburn, my dear," said Eugene. "Which makes me think we should do something with all that hair."

Katherine fastened her hair in a clip on top of her head, and covered it under Eugene's hat. "How's that?" she asked.

"Fabulous," said Eugene. "Here." He handed her his soft flannel scarf, and helped her wrap it high around her face. Finally, Eugene belted his long, black wool coat around her waist, and her disguise was complete.

Katherine took everything from her purse and shoved it into Eugene's coat pocket, except the small bronze star. That, in a moment of privacy, she hung around her neck. Then she practiced walking around the room like she thought a man would. "This isn't working," she complained. "I look like a penguin."

She does, thought Nick, *particularly in Eugene's black and white shoes. But that's not the sort of thing a man tells his wife.* "People just can't change how they walk," he offered. "How they look, yes. Their clothes, hair, even their voice, if they try hard enough. But how they walk – that's harder. Don't worry about it, darling. Just concentrate on getting to the car. It's only a few blocks away. Once we're there, we're home free."

Katherine and Eugene walked in circles around each other, nervous, occasionally looking up and seeing an odd caricature of their own image. Nick was pressed against the storefront window, amidst a display of brocade and cherry-wood furniture that he didn't really notice.

"I think the crowds are pretty much at their peak," he announced. "No sign of Kassab or Morris." Nick turned to Eugene. "Now's the time, old chap."

Katherine took a subway token from her desk and pressed it into Eugene's hand. "Take the first train you see. To anywhere."

"Alright then," said Eugene, making his way to the front of the store. "Here I go."

"Meet us at the Waldorf Astoria at seven p.m.," instructed Katherine. "I must see your face – to know you're alright."

"Katherine, really, I'll be fine. I'll just ring you up."

"You think I'm going to let you keep my favorite purse?" insisted Katherine with a smile. "The bar at the Waldorf. Seven p.m. Please don't be a second late."

"Not if I can help it." Eugene took a deep breath, squeezed Katherine's hand and, just like that, stepped out into the heavy foot traffic.

Bless him, bless him, bless him, said Katherine silently to the winds of fate. *For the love of God, please keep that man safe.*

Eugene walked fast, occasionally looking over his shoulder, but moving at a steady – if a bit wobbly – pace. He was swinging Katherine's purse wildly by his side as he made his way west, toward the subway station.

Huddled down low and peeping over the edge of the storefront window, Katherine and Nick watched Kassab step out of *The Boulangerie*, the French bakery across the street.

"Oh, good Lord!" exclaimed Katherine. "I didn't think he'd be so close!"

"He must have circled back through the alley," said Nick, "and entered the bakery from the back door. I bet he's been waiting there ever since he left here an hour ago."

They could see Kassab's breath in the cold November air. He was hunched over, looking miserably cold, his hands jammed deep into his pockets. His bones seemed to resist every step down the sidewalk, as he hurried along, working against blood that threatened to freeze him solid. *He must want desperately to return home,* thought Nick, knowing the feeling well, *to the heat of the desert, and the comfort of the familiar.*

Kassab was a good half-block behind Eugene, and Nick and Katherine forced themselves to stay another few minutes. Katherine started pacing the main gallery of the store, clunking around in Eugene's fancy shoes. Nick sat there, wondering what the hell they had all gotten into.

"Kassab must be around the corner by now," said Nick. He looked at his wife. "It's time to go."

"One second," said Katherine. "I have one more thing to collect."

Nick followed her as she dashed into her office. She had a pile of books, periodicals and magazines stacked in a corner. She rummaged through the pile and picked out the April 7, 1947 issue of *Life Magazine*, with two Sunday School pupils on the cover: a boy and a girl, clean-cut, certain, on their way, the girl carrying a Bible. Nick wondered why she picked that particular issue. *Certainly*, he thought, *it must have had something to do with Ben.*

"I hid a piece of parchment – the first sheet of Nelson's manuscript – between these pages," Katherine whispered, showing Nick.

"You *what?*" asked Nick, astonished. He was looking at a centuries-old piece of papyrus with faded black ink, crumbling at the edges. The page was pale golden-yellow, with etchings from an extinct language: beautiful, symmetrical, precise, as if it was penned by an architect of letters.

"Insurance," Katherine said. "Page One of whatever book this is that Etienne is so set to have." She turned and gathered up a few books and magazines, the day's newspaper, and a stack of unpaid bills from underneath the silver paperweight. "The one place Morris and Kassab didn't bother to look," she added. "*Life Magazine.*" She placed the magazine inside the newspaper, stacked it all up, and shoved the whole mess into Eugene's briefcase.

My God, that woman stuns me, thought Nick, somewhere between anger and adoration. Together they left *The Silver Butterfly* and walked in the opposite direction of Eugene and Kassab.

"This may be my last night on earth as a free person," said Katherine.

"You're being melodramatic," replied Nick dryly. But he checked them into the Waldorf, one of New York's most expensive hotels, without complaint. A few quick stops along the way, and Katherine was dressed in a simple wool skirt and sweater, stockings and flat-heeled black shoes. Katherine beamed as Nick led her through the lobby to the *Bull and Bear*. There they would wait for Eugene.

They settled into the bar and ordered martinis. The *Bull and Bear* was wildly popular, a hot spot for the after-hours business crowd. It could be said that as many deals were closed over cocktails at the *Bull and Bear* as in any office during business hours. For years it had been an all-men's club, but during the war they opened their doors to the fairer sex.

Katherine loved the whole place: the Art Deco architecture of the hotel, the lavishly appointed lobby, the small elegant rooms, the buzzing crowd in the bar.

Two martinis into the evening and twenty long minutes past seven, Eugene finally rushed into the bar. He nodded to a few men at a nearby table, and threw himself dramatically on a stool next to Katherine. "You have no idea what I've been through!" he exclaimed.

Eugene carried a large bag from Bergdorf's with Katherine's clothes folded neatly inside. He wore a crisp white shirt and casual slacks with tassled loafers. He slapped the Bergdorf's bill on the bar.

"Gin and tonic, please," Eugene called out to the bartender. "Make it a double."

Katherine and Nick smiled at each other. "My dear, the depth of my love for you knows no bounds," gasped Eugene. "I can only say this: I want a big fat raise."

"Done," said Katherine. "Assuming I'm not in jail by this time tomorrow. Or dead."

"That's not funny," snapped Nick, looking around the bar. "Let's go into the dining room," he whispered. "I'd feel better with some semblance of privacy." As they moved to the dining room, Nick took Katherine's arm and whispered in her ear. "He is such a dandy, Katherine. How do you take it?"

"You're just jealous," replied Katherine, smiling.

Nick ushered his wife to their table. "Right," he said, sarcastically. But it was true. Besides being brilliant, supposedly, and being Katherine's best friend, Eugene was the one person his wife came to rely most upon every day. They were intimate in ways that were easy, without expectation. They shared an affinity that was not the luxury of a couple in marriage.

Eugene unfolded his napkin neatly in his lap. "I had no way of knowing whether or not I was being followed," he began. "Oh – bouillabaisse, please, grilled asparagus, and, oh ... let me think ... filet minion. Rare. And another gin and tonic, please." He held up two fingers saying, *make it a double*, without really saying it. "I only knew that I *had* to get to the train station. So I walked as fast as I could, considering the snow, ice, and those ridiculous shoes."

66

"Do not complain to me," said Katherine, after she and Nick had also ordered dinner. "It's not that easy is it? Women don't dress for comfort, Eugene. They dress for men." She took a sip of the champagne they ordered at the table. "And try keeping the seam of your hose straight while you're at it."

Leave it to Katherine, thought Nick warmly, *to turn the conversation to herself.* "Go on, Eugene," he said. Katherine just shrugged her shoulders, and took another sip of champagne.

"I felt like I was running," said Eugene, "and that everyone was watching me." Truth was – with Katherine's scarf covering most of his face, including his moustache – Eugene blended in completely, as invisible and faceless as the rushing five o'clock crowd around him. But no one wanted to tell him that. In New York, it was easy to feel special, extraordinary, just by being there. But it was even easier to feel completely anonymous, even lonely, because of the crowds.

"I passed a play bill announcing the premier of *Finnian's Rainbow,*" he said. "And I remember thinking, I hope I live to see that play. I *love* that story… Still, it was two more blocks to the subway. I didn't *dare* look back. If Kassab was behind me, and I turned to look, the ruse would be up. I would be caught, and Kassab would return to the *Butterfly.*"

"Oh, my God," said Katherine.

"I kept thinking, if Kassab did lay a cold hand on my shoulder, stopping me in the street, there was nothing he could do, or would do, to hurt me. Right? Am I right?"

"You're right," Nick responded, dryly.

"Right," said Eugene. "So I just kept walking. Just a little further and I'd be there."

"Eugene, you are so amazing!" gushed Katherine.

They are truly enjoying this, thought Nick. *They're acting like children.* The waiter brought Eugene another gin and tonic. *That makes three,* counted Nick. *And no sign of slowing down.*

"Finally, I reached the steps to the subway," continued Eugene. "I couldn't help it. I stole a glance over my shoulder. Did I see Kassab in that one quick second?" He shrugged. "I couldn't tell. Had Kassab seen me? Probably. I had to get to the platform. And on the first train to anywhere."

Katherine hunched over her *Veuve Clicquot* and listened intently.

"I couldn't help myself; I turned again, *and there he was,* some ways behind me – practically running to catch up. I turned and ran, almost constantly looking over my shoulder – afraid to look, but more afraid not to."

"I can't believe this," whispered Katherine.

"I tripped several times in those horrible shoes. Fortunately, Kassab was disoriented in the station. Crowds were pushing and shoving. Trains were screeching through the tunnels. It was mayhem, as usual. I dropped a token into the pay slot and moved through the turnstile to the nearest car. I knew just how much time I had before the doors would close me in. And shut the Egyptian out."

Oh so what, thought Nick. He sighed. *I should appreciate Eugene more. But, well, I don't.* Nick listened to Eugene in the background of his jealousy.

"Kassab must've seen me step into the subway car," said Eugene, "which was completely crowded with people, by the way. He ran the last many yards that separated us. I could just see on his face the determination that he *had* to get on that train. He reached the doors, breathless, just as they were closing. He pounded the doors and windows. But, *you know,* the trains stop for no one." Eugene put his hand on top of Katherine's. "As the train moved away from the platform, I took off your hat, and turned to the window."

"You did not!" exclaimed Katherine.

"*I did.* Kassab's entire face turned from surprise to rage in a few short seconds. Then he turned his back and walked away."

"What an extraordinary story!" exclaimed Katherine. "Eugene, I cannot thank you enough." She covered his hand with her own.

"I'm afraid for you, Katherine," said Eugene. "If you do get to Egypt, he'll surely be looking for you."

Nick sat still and quiet through Eugene's dramatic story, the silent observer, the one no one paid any mind to. Nick was always the one who sat in the background, knowing more than anyone ever imagined. He knew, for one thing, that Kassab would deeply resent the humiliation of being tricked, that his anger would sit inside him, hard. Defeat was cold, but anger was hot. It would burn into him. This, Nick knew.

6

THE MAN WHO GOD FORGOT

God speaks with each of us as He makes us,
then walks with us silently out of the night.
These are the words we dimly hear:
You, sent out beyond your recall,
Go to the limits of your longing. Embody me.
Flare up like flame and make big shadows I can move in.
Let everything happen to you: beauty and terror.
Just keep going. No feeling is final.
Don't let yourself lose Me.

– Rainer Maria Rilke

Cairo, November 1947

Etienne drove west, toward the pyramids. His Willys MB Jeep rumbled through the streets, a throwback to WWII military generals and their attachés crusading across the landscape. He steered across the Nile River, out of Cairo and onto the rough roadway to an arranged meeting with the enigmatic Shadif.

Shadif was a shrewd black-marketeer, far wealthier than he ever appeared, and far more sinister that even Etienne would have believed. But Shadif almost always wanted something that Etienne had, or could get. And Etienne almost always had a new and more compelling expedition in the works that needed funding.

Shadif owned an entire building in Giza City, which housed his extended family. The home was remarkably opulent on the inside compared to the run-down, cement block exterior. Shadif had carefully planned it that way. Giza City was a ram shackle town that supported, and was supported by, foreign tourists to the Sphinx and great pyramids of Cheops, Chephren, and Mycerinus. The dirt streets were filled with stray dogs, carts, and garbage. Children, carrying sticks and balls, ran barefoot through it all. Less fortunate children stood on street corners, selling cheap trinkets and tokens of the relic monuments.

It was on just such a street that Etienne visited the notorious trader. Etienne sat in comfort and luxury on the shaded rooftop terrace of Shadif's home. Together they drank fresh-squeezed limeade and nibbled on light snacks, while Shadif's man-servant hovered in the background.

On the street below, a busy market place was humming with people who shopped the open-air stores for carpets, eggs, vegetables, live chickens, linens, pots and pans and just about every article of clothing a local family could want. It also offered more than enough trinkets, papyrus, and pyramid paperweights to attract swarms of tourists every day.

Etienne and Shadif tuned out the noise of the street below and began the delicate, intricate dance of bargaining. Shadif was a lean, hard man who wore the traditional robe, or *jallabiya,* and turban of the Muslims. He picked at a plate of olives and cheese while they talked, and easily drank a quart of limeade, with frightening amounts of sugar.

Etienne sat at the table, turning a colorful charm-bracelet over and over in his fingers. "It's an astonishing find," said Etienne. "Like nothing you've ever seen before." He did not relinquish the stones to Shadif, but held them to the light, strewn between his fingers.

The bracelet, woven of braided silver, held seven different charms. Each charm was made of a different precious stone. Each stone was cut into a distinct geometrical shape. The stones in the bracelet were significant, nearly as large as grapes, each suspended by a tiny gold cap and loop of silver.

Nearest to the clasp hung a dazzling garnet, cut into a precise, richly colored cube of red. Next in the chain came a tigers eye, formed into perfectly round ball, shimmering with glimpses of gold and brown, culminating in an 'eye' of gold. Then followed a yellow topaz, cut in the shape of a pyramid, as clear and brilliant as a beam of sun. A jade stone, in an oblong shape, came next. It reflected no light, but drew the eye into a deep, seemingly bottomless pool of green – the kind of green that Etienne thought could surely hold all the mysteries of the ages.

A light blue aquamarine came next, cut in a round design, like a diamond solitaire, capturing the eye in brilliance and light. It reminded Etienne of all things pure and young and fresh to the world.

Then followed a stone of lapis lazuli, in a marquis cut, a stone so thoroughly and purely blue, it was breathtaking. The seventh stone was an amethyst, cut into an asymmetrical shape with many facets, absolutely flawless in its cut and clarity. The purple seemed to radiate with energy, calling to Etienne to hold it, to covet it, to require its beauty and its tranquility with all his heart.

Such was the unique beauty and allure of these jewels. These bracelets came to be known as the *Path of the Hearts* to mystics, archaeologists and artisans. Only a few had ever been found. And only in Egypt.

"An astonishing find, you say?" Shadif scoffed. "If I had an English pound or 10 Egyptian piasters for every time I heard that, I'd be a rich man."

"You are a rich man, Shadif," said Etienne. He moved the stones through his hand, pausing to touch each one, as though he was traveling the beads of a rosary.

Shadif laughed and contemplated an olive. "Not rich enough, I'm afraid." He popped the olive into his mouth, chomped at it expertly, and spit the seed over the balcony.

"You have an empire at your feet, Shadif," said Etienne. "Land in the delta, a beautiful wife, power, art, properties. What more could you ask for?"

"I could ask for a moment's peace!" said Shadif. "I could ask for relief from the pesky, meddling government. I could ask for a wife who didn't have a thousand demands of me." He sighed. "Thank Allah for her sweet gifts, all of the them, none-the-less."

Etienne listened patiently, not taking his eyes off Shadif.

"I could ask for the damned Brits to get out of this country," continued Shadif, his humor suddenly gone. "That's what I could ask for. Or," added Shadif, his cheerfulness returning, "I could just settle for a little, teeny bracelet, at a *fair price* – for once."

Etienne draped the bracelet over a crisp linen napkin on the table. "But to part with such rare beauty," he said with a smile, "such exquisite, biting splendor. It would surely break my heart."

Shadif took up the bracelet and examined it closely. He then pulled a small jeweler's loupe out of his pocket and, fitting it snugly to his eye, examined each stone one by one. Eventually, he put both the bracelet and the magnifying loupe down on the table. "Would 15,000 English pounds mend your broken heart, Etienne?" he asked.

"No amount of money can mend such a thing, my friend."

"How did you become so attached to this little scrap of a thing?" asked Shadif, carelessly picking up the bracelet. "Look, the settings are all scratched up."

"Those are ancient symbols, Shadif, if you care to look again." Etienne took a lighter tone. "You see, what one man sees as a little trinket, another may see as the blood of his life."

Again Shadif picked up the loupe and the bracelet, crinkling his entire face as he scrutinized the charms. "A man's passion can be the weapon of his destruction," he warned Etienne. "I fear for you my friend."

"Can you help me, then?" Etienne asked, lightly. "Release me from this insatiable passion?"

"I would be less than a friend if I did not at least try."

"What is the *least*, then, that you can do?" Etienne asked.

Shadif sighed. "Now you ask me to think with my head and not my heart. What a pity."

"My apologies, *ostaz* Shadif."

"I say that 25,000 English pounds should mend your broken heart."

Etienne cocked an eyebrow. "I say that my heart is more sorely broken than that," he replied coolly. Shadif narrowed his eyes and glared at Etienne with a disturbing intensity. Etienne did not stir under Shadif's ferocity, but rather, added, "To think, I must live a lifetime, by the minutes, remembering what is lost to me…"

Shadif laughed loud and long. "For your eloquence I offer you 40,000 English pounds!" But he stopped laughing and calmed to a slow, lethal tone. "But do not ask more of me my friend, lest you stretch the limits of our friendship."

"We could not call it a friendship," Etienne suggested, "unless it stretched us from time to time, now could we?"

Shadif's man-servant approached them, agitated. "There is a man here to see you, *ostaz*. His name is Monsieur Henri Poirier. Some sort of government official. He insists on seeing you, this minute."

Etienne snatched the bracelet from the table and put it in his pocket, just as Henri Poirier pushed his way onto the terrace. Henri was a small man and heavy around the middle. Working his way through the house, up the many stairs and onto the secured rooftop was no small feat. Beads of sweat had accumulated on his forehead and in the creases of his neck.

Henri lifted his white, straw fedora and delicately dabbed at the perspiration with his handkerchief. Collecting himself, he stood ramrod straight and smoothed out his enormous moustache. "Shadif Raghib al Sachur," he said, bowing deeply. "It is my honor to meet you at last." He then reached out to shake Etienne's hand. Etienne declined. "Etienne Desonia, so good to see you again."

"I wish I could say likewise," responded Etienne.

"You have me at a loss, Monsieur..." said Shadif.

"Allow me to present myself: Henri Charles Poirier, Professor Emeritus of Religious Antiquities at the University of Paris, currently serving as Ambassador to the Royal Egyptian Academy of Archaeology, representing the great nation of France. At your service."

Etienne rolled his eyes.

"To what do we owe the pleasure of your esteemed company Monsieur Poirier?" asked Shadif.

Henri settled in with a glass of wine from the servant and picked through the olives as he talked. "Well, I was in the area... And, well, I heard that a certain artifact was loose on the Black Market here in Cairo..." Shadif shifted in his seat. "Oops, did I say *Black Market?*" Henri laughed. "So sorry, I realize that can be an uncomfortable phrase to some people. At any rate, a magnificent piece of jewelry was stolen – presumably by workers or the usual, seedy hangers-on – from an archaeological dig. *My* archaeological dig, to be precise, at the Kula pyramid."

"What does all this have to do with me?" asked Shadif.

"The stolen jewelry is a bracelet," replied Henri. "One of seven known to exist, all identical, known as the *Path of the Hearts*. It belongs to the Egyptian people, of course. And the Department of Antiquities is extremely interested in recovering it. Of course."

"I still do not see how any of this concerns me," said Shadif calmly. But he glared at Etienne, displeasure cemented into the hard lines on his face.

Merde, thought Etienne. The traders who sold him the bracelet had claimed it was a family heirloom. Though he hadn't necessarily believed that, Etienne surely hadn't expected, or even imagined in his mind's darkest ramblings, that it had been stolen from Henri Poirier. But this was not the first time some irate archaeologist or government official had arrived on Etienne's doorstep when something precious had gone missing. Nor was it likely to be the last.

"How very interesting, Henri," interjected Etienne. "And you came all the way from southern Egypt to Cairo, to this very place in fact, because of some mythical, imaginary bracelet?"

"You know it is not imaginary, Etienne," said Henri. "And you know why I am here."

Etienne crossed his legs. "No, I'm afraid I do not Monsieur Poirier – of the Royal Museum of *whatever*. But please, tell us, why *are* you here? Certainly this is not where you belong. No cross on a map, no dusty library, no lecture hall full of enthusiastic, naïve students, no servants or scholars to dirty their hands for you..."

Henri laughed. "My dear boy, you astonish me!"

"You, Henri, you... astonish *me*!" Etienne was unable to find the words to say exactly how he felt. Which was just as well.

"I beg your pardon, Monsieur Shadif," said Henri. "We air our differences at your table. My profound apologies."

"Perhaps you can explain..." said Shadif.

"Yes," said Henri. "I can explain everything. Let me begin by saying that this bracelet, the *Path of the Hearts*, is known to be for sale in Cairo."

"You are not in Cairo, Monsieur Poirier," interrupted Shadif. "You are in my home. Uninvited."

"The bracelet belongs only in a museum," insisted Henri. "It is an artifact of the state, and a symbol of the great history of the Egyptian people."

"Such an artifact must be worth a great deal to a museum, Monsieur Poirier," said Etienne.

"Indeed, it would," said Henri.

"What interest is it of yours, I might wonder?" asked Etienne. "Are you a scientist now? Or a detective?"

"My interest is purely in preserving a cultural icon, an artifact of supreme significance to the people of Egypt," said Henri.

"An artifact of supreme significance to your tenure, I imagine. Or is it your salary you're concerned with?"

"The Path of Hearts belongs in a museum!"

"Then let a museum buy it," said Etienne, matching the tone of his words to the ice-cold hatred that lay inside him. It was a terrible feeling, hard and familiar. Though he had lived with it for many years, long periods of time would pass while it lay quiet and still, just beyond feeling. Until he thought of Henri Poirier. Then, like a startled snake, it would coil and strike. As poison in his blood, the hatred would consume him.

"Only a scoundrel of the worst kind would barter such a priceless artifact for English pounds, I'll tell you that!" retorted Henri.

"Only a scoundrel of the worst kind would take that which does not rightfully belong to him, is that what you are saying?"

"I am saying, Etienne, that you are in over your handsome head. That these are affairs of state, and your scheme will unravel – leaving you to hang by its threads!"

"And I am saying, Monsieur Poirier, of the Royal Academy of plagiarism and obscurity, that, as you taught me, all the words in the world mean nothing against the proof of possession."

"I am saying to you, Etienne, for the last time, *hand over the bracelet!*"

"Bracelet?" asked Etienne. "Oh, *pardon moi*, I thought we were talking about something else entirely."

"I promise you, Monsieur Shadif, if you purchase a jeweled bracelet from this scoundrel, or anyone else, you will be arrested immediately by the authorities. Your lands, your property, your business – everything will be taken from you."

"The long arm of the Egyptian government has embraced even the likes of you, Henri?" Etienne asked.

"They wait even now outside this building," he said.

Etienne and Shadif couldn't help but look out over the side of the rooftop onto the street below. Two dark-suited men could be seen standing under the shaded awning of a storefront, occasionally looking up in their direction.

"*Bon soir Monsieurs*," said Henri as he parted, downing the last of his wine in one indelicate gulp. "And Etienne, do not doubt that you are being carefully watched."

God, thought Etienne. *I get tired of hearing that.*

Etienne left the Giza plateau uneasy and unfinished. He drove his jeep east, toward Cairo. The great pyramids rose up behind him, and the setting sun had turned the western sky a deep, brilliant orange. The monuments and the clap-trap town nearby looked wholly unreal in the dusky sky, like a scene on a painted picture postcard.

But Etienne had his mind on other things. Over and over his thoughts churned up memories of Henri Poirier. The hatred bubbled and grew inside him, until it threatened to engulf him.

Etienne drove fast, as if to leave his demons behind. They would chase him down, though, feeding on the desperation, and would not go away. On and on Etienne drove, until the sun abandoned the day and lonely night took its place in the hours.

Two hundred miles later, Etienne found himself far into the eastern desert, well past Cairo, on the road to Suez. Tired, weary from the rage, Etienne let his darker thoughts rest, and allowed an armistice for the time being. He turned his jeep toward home. He turned his thoughts to Shadif.

Etienne knew that Shadif would eventually buy the bracelet, for an amount closer to 50,000 English pounds. Etienne suspected that Shadif would be quite delighted, in fact, to put one over on the Egyptian monarchy that he so greatly despised.

But Etienne would revisit that deal later, when the government wasn't so rabid on the subject. In the mean time, Etienne had a Gnostic Library to recover.

Looking back, Etienne tried to trace the beginning of his solitary quest. It didn't start with the telephone call to Katherine. It didn't even start in 1945 with the discovery of 1,600 year-old manuscripts in the Egyptian desert. No, it started much, much earlier than that. Before he dropped out of his doctoral studies at the University of Paris, before the horrible episodes of World War II, before he left France forever and took up residence in Egypt.

It began in Oxford in 1936, when he took the woman that his best friend loved and made her his own. He lost her of course, but perhaps that was right. It had caused Etienne to wonder over the years if there wasn't some sort of Divine hand directing things, kicking up storms that knocked people about like tumble weeds, for reasons inconceivable to mortal man. It seemed ridiculous to Etienne, though, that the Divine Master of the Universe, the Lord of All Things and All Time, would bother to interfere with his love life.

Still, he wondered, because he believed that it was his right and his destiny to have Katherine. He believed that his love for her took him beyond the rules of human decency, that he deserved to have her – no matter how much pain it caused Nick Spencer.

And he never stopped believing that, though for many years he made himself forget her, and them. For many years he filled every second of his time, so that he wouldn't have to return to her in his mind. He hated the thought of Katherine doing things without him: simple things, like having coffee and sharing the Sunday paper, buying shoes, reading in quiet, laughing the way she sometimes did – from deep inside. Those visions sat inside him, coiled and silent, for a decade of time.

In that time Etienne feasted himself on everything but love, and the terrible weakness that comes with it. He woke up every morning with one or another beautiful woman, money at his disposal, success in his profession, and the accolades of his peers. He was dead empty.

One morning, during the war, Etienne had woken up next to a woman named Beth, a British army nurse, who he was seeing whenever he returned from desert warfare to the city of Cairo. She was perfect: pretty, kind, smart, loving, devoted. He looked at her in the rumpled bed, her blonde hair splayed around her shoulders and face, and he watched the innocence of her sleep and the beauty she wasn't aware of. And Etienne didn't feel a thing.

It was at times like those that he would think of Katherine; he would let himself remember her, through the misty veils of pain. Then being with Beth would make him sad, and it wasn't fair – to Beth or to any of the women Etienne had tried to spend his heart upon.

Etienne, in his longing and his confusion, turned to solitude. Surely he could find his own heart in the realms of loneliness. Surely a moment of Grace would descend upon him and he would find a new kind of peace. Surely he would emerge, through the fires of isolation, a changed man.

Etienne, instead, got colder and colder inside. Once he let himself remember, he began to long. He began to hunger for the feeling of being full, of being in love and loving to be alive. To wake in the morning and not feel the cloak of dread fall upon him.

The more Etienne tried to find some semblance of peace, the more it alluded him, and he wandered for years, in and out of the arms of women, in periods of enormous solitude, and through the rough and bloody terrain of war. The man who God forgot. The forsaken one. Then one night, in Cairo, he wandered into a bar, and met a man named Demitri.

Over whiskey and cigarettes, Demetri spoke of a renegade band of early aesthetics, who defied the institutions of religion and found their own path to salvation. He spoke of a group of wanderers who created heaven on earth, where ever they were. Who focused on their personal relationship with their Maker. Who tended to the matters of themselves, each other, and all life on earth. Who did not separate themselves from their Creator, and were, in effect, never alone.

Never alone, thought Etienne. *I simply cannot imagine it.*

"You *are* God," Demetri had said. "Don't you see that?"

Etienne felt a deep stirring in him that reverberated so strongly he could feel it inside the cavity of his chest, and in all his joints and muscles. For one brief splitting second the weight and the glory of it almost hurt. "There is a secret, inner path," said Demetri, mysteriously, "to peace and fulfillment."

Etienne woke the next morning with a raging headache, a foggy memory, an upset stomach, and one crystal clear purpose: to discover the secrets of the Gnostic Christians. He thought he would find these secrets in books – in the writings of this strange sect of ancient wanderers. *If* he could find such books. Indeed, if the books, or the wanderers, had ever even existed.

Armed with new inspiration, Etienne re-focused his career as an archaeologist, relic hunter, excavator for hire. As a member of the French Resistance, Etienne had made it an occupation – and the perfect undercover identity – to be a digger of artifacts. He took his livelihood from ancient history, from the dead past – some sort of godless creature wandering through forgotten and desolate places.

But he knew how to turn a profit from such adventures. In this way, he funded many expeditions after the war in his search for traces of the Gnostics, looking for clues to the secret, inner path to the Divine, to Enlightenment. A way to God. A way back to himself.

It was late into the night after his visit with Shadif, and subsequent race into the desert, when Etienne returned to his home, exhausted, in the low hills of Cairo. There, in the dark, he found someone waiting for him. But it was not his housekeeper, Dara, who was always waiting there, warm and welcoming. This was Dara's weekend to be with her family, and Etienne was looking forward to the solitude, to a couple of stiff brandies and a long night of dreamless sleep. Instead, he found Cato Nafarah.

Nafarah was a tall, angular man, attractive more through dress and stature than inherent good looks. He was brought up in a well-to-do and strict Muslim household, educated in London, and restored home to make his mark upon Egyptian society. He had been posted at the Egyptian Department of Antiquities through the influence of his father and his father's acquaintances. Eventually – through great determination, hard work, self-direction and a keen knowledge of anthropology – Nafarah rose to a field position in the sprawling bureaucracy. A senior position, however, in a comfortable office with a respectable salary still eluded him.

He dressed like his counterparts in the West, having been deeply influenced during his studies abroad. But Nafarah had great difficulty reconciling his admiration of the modern advancements of the West – in technology, literature, art, music and industry – with his deep, holy love for Egypt and the Islamic way of life.

Unable to marry the two in his heart, Nafarah harbored profound resentments toward the people of Europe and America and, in particular, anyone who dared usurp that which was sacred to Egypt. These scoundrels were often foreign archaeologists, swarming to Egypt like locusts, hungry to establish their reputations and their fortunes.

But just as frequently they were local villagers, who – as in eons gone by – raided tombs and grave sites, selling the spoils in backroom deals for the price of stolen gold. But the greatest usurper of all, in Nafarah's mind, was Etienne Desonia of France.

Nafarah was determined to arrest Etienne with the kind of single-mindedness and longevity that leads a person to obsession. The individual steps of that obsession, each one building upon the others, led Nafarah to Etienne's home that night, with a warrant for his arrest.

"I know about the Knife of the Asps," murmured Nafarah in a low voice, as he stepped from the shadows of Etienne's porch.

"What?" stammered Etienne, startled out of his exhaustion. "What *the hell* are you doing here?" His fury then rose up in him in an instant. "Leave my home. Right now!"

"You'll be coming with me tonight," replied Nafarah calmly.

"No. I won't." Etienne flashed for a moment upon the jeweled charm bracelet he was trying to sell to Shadif. In his weariness, Etienne had unintentionally left the *Path of the Hearts* in his jeep, tucked safely into a secret compartment under the driver's seat. For this oversight, he was suddenly, deeply grateful.

"Smuggling is a capitol crime in Egypt, as I'm sure you know. You've tested the law before, Etienne, but this time you've gone far too far."

"I'm sure I don't know what you mean," snapped Etienne. "Now, if you don't mind, I've had a long goddamn day, and I'd like to get some sleep." Etienne tried to push past Nafarah and into the relative safety of his home.

"But I do mind," replied Nafarah, raising a pistol. "And where you're going, I'm afraid sleep doesn't come easily."

"Well then, you barbaric, stuffed-shirt of a man. Tell me what it is you think you know that gives you the right to shove a gun in my face. I'll deny it, naturally. And you'll have no proof. As always. We'll spend 10 hours downtown going 'round and 'round in circles, getting nowhere. Then you'll have to let me go. As usual."

Nafarah bristled, but didn't move his gun one inch.

"*God,*" continued Etienne. "Don't you ever get tired of being wrong? Why don't we just shake hands and go our separate ways? I forgive you. Now lower that gun and let me pass."

Nafarah smiled, his white teeth flashing ominously in the dark. "What I know will be your undoing, Etienne. *What I know* is this: you stole a jeweled knife, hid it inside an alabaster statue, and smuggled it out of Egypt. You shipped it from Cairo to Alexandria and from there

80

to America. Specifically, to New York City. Specifically, to a retail store called The Silver Butterfly. Even more specifically, the statue was of Isis, and it was a fake. But the knife was real. How you came upon it, I cannot guess. But you have stolen the Knife of the Asps. And you will rot for it."

"As usual, Nafarah, you are wrong," replied Etienne, with a deepening sense of dread. Nafarah knew a startling amount of information, including the point of delivery, which would lead him directly to Katherine Spencer.

Etienne thought he had known the most intense loneliness. No. For hours into the morning he paced a dark and gloomy cell. The cement box that held him reeked of urine and waste. It had no window, no exterior ventilation, and no light other that that coming from a long, empty corridor. He felt as though he was at the far end of Hell. For hours, as he paced the darkness, he worried incessantly about Katherine. When he wasn't imagining her dark fate, he thought about one other person: the potter.

Etienne had paid – and paid handsomely – to have the original statue of Isis replicated, carved hollow, and mounted on a special pedestal. In order for the statue to pass Customs, the potter had to measure the exact dimensions of the knife, hollow the statue to fit the knife precisely, insert it, and seal the base. He was the only person other than Etienne to lay eyes on that knife since the war. The potter did his work meticulously. Then he packed the hidden dagger into a crate loaded with pottery and other artifacts that Etienne provided. The crate was then loaded onto a cargo ship traveling north on The Nile.

Apparently the potter then went straight to the Egyptian government to collect another fee: the fee of betrayal. But the shipment had already left harbor before the potter made it through the bureaucratic labyrinth of the government. He likely asked them for money, reasoned Etienne, which would have slowed things considerably. And which he was likely denied. The Egyptian government didn't work that way. Bribes were generally initiated *by* the government, to get information, before the bird was in the cage, as it were. The potter probably didn't know that. *Sorry little bird,* thought Etienne. *But not sorry enough.*

But that still left Etienne in miserable shape for five days, with meager food and water, avoiding questions to the best of his ability and adamantly denying any knowledge of the Knife of the Asps. In between what Nafarah called 'friendly conversations,' which left

Etienne sore and bruised, Etienne had time to do only one thing: think. He had a burning desire to spend those many hours plotting his revenge against the potter. But his thoughts were constantly drawn back to Katherine.

Nafarah would have found Katherine's address on the bill of lading. If they discovered the smuggled dagger at her store, they would return it to Egypt as an artifact of the state, and throw Katherine in jail for who knows how long. Etienne had been so sure that nothing could go wrong. And now it looked like they both might lose the best of their lives, living behind bars.

Still, Etienne was hoping against all odds that they somehow wouldn't find the Knife and that they wouldn't smash every single precious artifact in the crate looking for it. Or that Katherine had already passed the dagger on to Hugo Nelson before they got to her.

It was then that it occurred to Etienne that he had a bargaining tool: he had a Gnostic manuscript. If Katherine had done her part, the *Gospel of Thomas* would be in Garden City that very moment. Nafarah would want that manuscript, badly. That there were more codices on the loose would make Etienne even more valuable to the government. Perhaps he could win his freedom, and Katherine's, by offering up the codices he had. And Nafarah was shrewd enough to know that if anyone could find the others, it would be Etienne.

Etienne recalled the night he bought the manuscript – on one of Cairo's rare, rainy nights. It was a night when nothing seemed real.

Etienne was relaxing in the company of Dara, his housekeeper and companion. They were on the terrace of Etienne's home, sipping brandy and talking about nothing. Dara's company was soft and easy. Which was sometimes pleasing to a man, although never totally satisfying. They chatted and drank and watched a winter rain pour over the city. When an urgent banging came through the door, Dara rose to answer it.

'Please relax, *cherí*,' said Etienne, touching her arm. Etienne did not normally receive visitors, and almost never unexpected ones late in the evening. So he moved cautiously to the door, in bare feet, carrying his brandy snifter. He opened the door to find two men, shrouded in dark, hooded cloaks.

'Etienne Desonia?' One man stepped forward, and drew back his hood, revealing a patch over his left eye. Etienne immediately set his brandy on a table in the foyer.

Birds of Paradise, dramatic flowers of orange and purple, were arranged in large vase on the table. Dara added fresh flowers weekly, at Etienne's request, to keep it lush and abundant. Tucked discriminately into the vase, Etienne hid a long, razor-sharp stiletto. Next to the flowers sat a solid gold miniature of a cobra, staring fiercely under its hooded crown with round emerald eyes. Next to the golden snake, was a fish tank, home to several tropical fish, radiating in splashes of orange and blue and red. Colored glass stones were scattered at the bottom of the aquarium, more than an inch thick, in all the colors of the rainbow.

Etienne let his hand linger on the table. "Yes, I am Monsieur Desonia. What can I do for you?"

"I am Jahib, of the village of Nag Hammadi," the one-eyed man rasped in the strong regional dialect of the Inland Empire. The man nudged his partner and whispered something to him in Arabic. The second man stepped forward, reaching into his tunic. Etienne slowly moved his hand toward the stiletto.

"This is Zafar," said Jahib, watching Etienne carefully. Zafar withdrew a thick leather manuscript from his tunic, and held it out.

Etienne took the manuscript from Zafar, warily, keeping an eye on both men. It was clear they were not common visitors to Cairo. Their dress was worn and plain, and typical of the remote villages sprinkled along the Nile throughout Egypt. Their shifting demeanor revealed an anxiousness and discomfort in the city. Naturally, Etienne mistrusted them both. But the book, a codex of various different manuscripts, he found very curious. Very, very curious.

Etienne looked carefully at the codex, while keeping a sharp eye on Zafar and Jahib. The book was made of animal hide, a soft leather turned brittle and hard. The binding was remarkable. It was the oldest example Etienne had ever seen of papyrus bound into a book rather than rolled into lengthy scrolls. With extreme care, he lifted the worn cover to reveal page after page of fragile papyrus, crumbling at the edges. Etienne was immediately able to decipher the writing as Coptic. Long extinct, the ancient Coptic language was once widely used in Egypt, before the introduction of Arabic, particularly in religious writings.

"Where did you get this?" asked Etienne.

Zafar was more well-spoken than the one-eyed Jahib. "I am a trader of old and used items. I have a respectable business in Nag Hammadi. It is my job to travel to the surrounding villages to gather trinkets and tokens to sell in my store."

This Etienne doubted. *More likely this man makes his living out of looting artifacts.* But that was fine by Etienne. He did the same thing, only on a slightly larger scale. "Why are you bringing this book to me?" asked Etienne. "It looks like it belongs in a museum."

"We were assured," answered Zafar, shifting nervously, "that you would find a... more suitable ... home for it."

"By whom were you assured such a thing?"

"That I cannot say." Zafar firmly crossed his arms over his chest. Etienne shrugged and handed back the book. "No, no!" replied Zafar, pushing away Etienne's outstretched hand. "I can tell you only that he goes by the name of Shadif. He has worked with me in the past on some ... trades. He gave me your name."

Shadif. Sometimes Etienne hated to hear that name. What Etienne couldn't figure out was why, if the wealthy collector wanted this codex, he didn't just buy it directly from these villagers? Shadif must not have thought it was valuable. Or, if it was, that it would eventually make its way back to him. It was not like Shadif to hand out unrequited favors. "This book must have come from an archeological site," stated Etienne. "Which means it is illegal for you to bring it here."

"No, no!" insisted Zafar. "It came from a family I know. It is a *family* matter. They have asked me to sell it for them."

"I see."

"You interested in that book?" pressed the man with one eye. "It is very old."

"It seems to be very old, indeed," said Etienne, turning his attention back to the codex.

"You will have to pay a good price to have such an old, important book." Jahib moved in closer, his one eye fixed on Etienne.

"That it is old, I can clearly see. That it is important, I do not know." The two villagers, expert bargainers, said nothing for a full minute, letting the time fill only with a silent battle of nerves. He who spoke first, lost.

"I will pay you 80 Egyptian pounds." Etienne finally broke the silence, not interested in quibbling. The book was obviously much more valuable than the villagers could possibly have imagined.

Zafar and Jahib looked at each other. "300 Egyptian pounds," said the one-eyed man. "No less."

"150. No more."

"Done," announced Zafar, apparently very pleased with their good fortune. "You are a wise man, Monsieur Desonia. You recognize a good deal when you see it."

Etienne pulled out his wallet and slowly counted 150 Egyptian pounds into the rough, dirty palm of Zafar. While Zafar stared only at the bills being dropped one by one into his hand, Jahib was taking a careful look into Etienne's wallet. He was probably thinking that they should have asked for more money. Etienne must have seemed very rich to these men of the desert.

"Thank you, thank you." Zafar was bowing a hasty exit, perhaps fearing that Etienne would change his mind.

Jahib started to follow, but as Zafar descended the last stair below him, Jahib turned back to Etienne. "I have many more books like that one," he rasped in a low voice. "Twelve more. You will see me again."

Before Etienne could speak again, they disappeared into the rainy night. That was the last Etienne saw of them, and that was almost a year ago. Etienne had not yet found the store that Zafar claimed to own in Nag Hammadi. Of the dozens and dozens of people Etienne had asked, no one knew – or admitted to knowing – the raspy one-eyed Jahib. Shadif had sworn to Etienne that he did not know how to contact the two strange men. They occasionally came to Shadif, but they kept their secrets to themselves.

On day five, Etienne began to tell Nafarah the story. He didn't tell Nafarah about the manuscript that Katherine was smuggling into Egypt. And he left out as many details as possible, including the stiletto in his foyer, the names of the villagers and the bit about Shadif. But Etienne told Nafarah all the rest.

Nafarah listened, without saying a word, without taking any notes, without any expression on his face at all, while Etienne relayed the story.

As Etienne was finishing the abbreviated tale, a knock came on the wooden door of his cell. A nervous-looking man came into the room, announcing an urgent a cable from America. Nafarah took a small flashlight from his inside lapel and shone it on the telegram in the dark cell. He read the message in silence:

PACKAGE NOT SECURED STOP

SUSPECT ESCAPED STOP

PLEASE ADVISE STOP KASSAB END

Straining his eyes, Etienne read the black lettering through the telegram as Nafarah's light illuminated the yellow paper into an opaque film. Reading backwards, all Etienne had time to make out was:

PACKAGE NOT SECURED STOP

Nafarah crinkled up the communiqué, shoved it in his pocket, and stormed out of the room. Etienne was left in solitude, not knowing if it was day or night, or how many days had passed altogether, or how long he would be left alone. What he *did* know, was that the Knife of the Asps was missing.

It was several hours later when Nafarah returned to Etienne's cell. Nafarah offered an unequivocal deal: The Knife of the Asps *and* the Gnostic library, all 13 manuscripts, in return for their freedom. When these were in his hands, all charges would be dropped against both Katherine and Etienne. Etienne accepted. Nafarah narrowed his steel gray eyes and said, "I will be watching you, Etienne Desonia. I will be watching you very, very closely." Etienne was tremendously annoyed at that last comment, but relieved beyond measure that his plan had worked, and he could win Katherine's freedom.

When Etienne was released, he went straight home and began to ring up the overseas operator. He didn't even stop to retrieve Katherine's shipment, containing the *Gospel of Thomas,* which was waiting for him in Garden City. Etienne was desperate to locate Katherine, to make things up to her, to assure her that the Egyptian government was going to drop their charges, and to find out what the hell happened to the dagger. He called twenty times in two days, trying to find her or some news of her arrest. He didn't know that she would find him first.

7

FLIGHT OF THE INTREPIDS

Let me not pray to be sheltered from dangers,
but to be fearless in facing them.
Let me not beg for the stilling of my pain,
but for the heart to conquer it.

– Rabindranath Tagore

Katherine and Nick arrived at Idlewild airport before dawn the next day. The sky was barely beginning to show signs of light. Though it wasn't quite dark, the morning was more gray than blue, stranger, softer than night. It was that in-between time, that not-quite-real time: the time of ghosts and shadows, dreams and secrets.

For all her bravado, when Katherine approached the four-prop Pan American Super Constellation, her enthusiasm waned. Its nose looked like that of a dolphin with a long metal body, wings sprouting from the massive engines and a three-finned tail. Surely this thing could not stay aloft across the Atlantic Ocean. She stopped cold at the top of the stairs that led to the entrance of the aircraft.

"I don't feel good."

And so it begins. "We don't *have* to go," Nick said gently into her ear. The wind blew across the tarmac. He pulled up the collar on his overcoat and held tight to his fedora. "We can just ring up Hugo Nelson and explain –"

"My Aunt Fanny," said Katherine. And she stepped through the doorway.

They settled into their seats, just a few rows from the front of the plane, close enough so that Katherine could see the exit door from where she sat and count the number of steps it would take to get there. Two clocks embedded in the bulkhead announced times for the locations of their departure and destination: currently 7:14 a.m. in New York and 12:14 p.m. in London. As the passengers clattered about, settling themselves in, Katherine pressed herself up against the small square window, quiet.

The stewardesses bustled back and forth along the length of the aircraft, tending to pre-flight details, handing out pillows, tucking things away and chatting amicably, and still Katherine remained motionless. After a fair amount of fussing and formality, the airplane finally bumped down the runway and revved its engines to their extremes for take-off.

Katherine abruptly raised her head and clutched Nick's hand with such ferocity he winced. "It's a miracle these planes ever make it across the Atlantic," she blurted. "And I know it." It was a reflection of this common fear that nobody else in the entire cabin said a word until the plane was well off the ground and had relaxed its steep pitch into the sky.

"How can something as heavy as an airplane," asked Katherine, "loaded with people and luggage and petrol, suspend itself in the sky? That's what I want to know."

"*Speed*, Katherine," whispered Nick. "We're going 150 miles an hour. We're not suspended at all; we're actually *flying*."

Katherine, in her mind, sat there and held the plane in the air through sheer will. The only part of air flight she enjoyed was landing, when a combination of fear and exhilaration rushed like a hot serum through her body. In the shortest of time, the wheels met the ground, the massive props ground to a stop and the plane rolled to a safe, tidy stop. But that was many long hours and another day away.

The airplane was still gliding above New York City. The morning traffic, the great buildings stacked neatly around each other, the solitary Statue of Liberty – all sparkled in the morning sun like little toys in a giant window display. The great blue expanse of the Atlantic Ocean appeared before them, and they left land behind them for another 4,000 miles.

The captain's voice crackled over the intercom, announcing their altitude and flight time to London: 20 thousand feet and 14 hours. Katherine sat back in her chair and sighed.

This was only the beginning of their long journey to Cairo. Nick had planned a circuitous route, to fend off Kassab and anyone else who might be trying to follow them. With no word from Katherine about the Knife of the Asps, Hugo Nelson would surely be on a rampage of his own. From New York, they'd stop in Iceland to refuel, then they'd fly on to London. From London, they would switch planes – to the un-pressurized, less luxurious DC-3 – and fly to Tenerife, off the western coast of Africa. From this island paradise, they would fly directly into Cairo.

A pretty stewardess, exuding efficiency, was making her way through the cabin with refreshments. She wore a tight and trim uniform: front-pleated grey skirt, crisp white collared blouse, grey gaberdine blazer, and a swanky, embellished cap. She also wore short black curls, a pasted-on smile and perfect ruby-red lips.

When a pocket of turbulence jostled the plane, Katherine grabbed Nick's hand again. Her face was hot and pale. "What was that?"

"It's alright," Nick assured her. "It's just turbulence. Think of it as *bumpy air,* darling. The plane was built to fly in bumpy air." The plane settled itself into a smooth, droning glide.

"I don't think so," stated Katherine. "Look at the stewardess. She looks really worried."

"She looks fine. Why don't you read one of your magazines?"

That made Katherine smile. She had a collection of magazines tucked into an oversized, alligator purse. One of them carried the pirated page of Nelson's manuscript. "I'll have a big glass of ice," said Katherine to the stewardess as she walked by. "As big as you've got." Katherine rummaged through her bag and pulled out a pint of Wild Turkey and a pack of cigarettes.

"Katherine, it's *morning,*" said Nick.

She looked at him without a smile. "You think I don't know that?" Katherine lit up her Lucky Strike, and leaned across Nick toward the aisle. "Could you tell me, Miss," said Katherine. "Miss. Why are we turning? I distinctly feel the plane turning."

"Just a course correction, ma'am," said the stewardess, returning with a tumbler filled with clinking ice cubes. "Everything is fine."

"Course correction?" Katherine turned to Nick. "Great. We got lost already." She took a short sip and then a long draw on her glass of whiskey. As the warmth and comfort of the cocktail took hold, she looked at her watch. *Thirteen hours and fifteen minutes to go.* Katherine sat back in her seat and stared out the window at the vacant sky. She stayed that way for a long time, relaxing for the first time in days. Nick looked over at her often, her head resting against the little window. He knew she was afraid. And he knew that she was also dreaming of far away places, secretly wishing she could get there on her own wings.

It was another day and night, many long tedious hours, two layovers, three magazines, four meals, countless snacks and a great deal of shuffling around before they began their flight south from London, over the Mediterranean, toward the Canary Islands.

It wasn't easy to catch up to them, but Kassab had the will of the Egyptian government behind him. Through some diplomatic string pulling, he learned the Spencers' flight itinerary and caught up with them, silently, in Britain. When Kassab left the subway station, tricked by a mere storekeeper, he was raging. *What man with any dignity would dress himself up as a woman? For any reason?* Kassab's own sense of dignity could not allow this defeat. He may have been tricked, but the Americans had clearly cheated.

More determined than ever, Kassab sat in the very back of the humming DC-3 and planned his revenge against the Spencers. They were straying into his domain and the game would not go so easily for them in Egypt. There were things there beyond their imagining. Things he had seen. Things he had done. Their naïveté and their arrogance would be their undoing. Kassab smiled grimly, wishing only the cheating storekeeper was also on the airplane.

Katherine stared out the window in a remote silence for much of the trip. From high above the earth, she searched the sky for the hidden key that would help her make sense of her life. She was sure that *some one thing* was missing that could put all the tumblers in place and redirect her to a better course.

Days and months and years had combined themselves into a slate of colorless beige in her mind. Painted from a lesser palate, her life seemed mottled and tinged, and splattered upon by arbitrary moments of fate. Though not particularly boring, her days had become predictable. Predictable in all the sorrows and contentments they offered, in every mannerism, move and mood of her husband, in a future carefully planned and orchestrated, the way she was taught would make her happy. Predictable days leaning into the slow, inevitable spiral to a disappointing life.

Not any more, swore Katherine silently, as she kept company with the endless sky.

Nick had a book in his lap, but he wasn't reading it. He was drifting through his own private world of hopes and plans. It was a compelling world to be drawn into, with limits imposed only by his own imagination. He was drawn to a different place, far from where he was, far away from Katherine. Not because he didn't love her. Quite the opposite. He loved her madly, but he couldn't seem to make her happy. And he was getting tired of trying. Rather, he was getting tired of failing. And he was tired of feeling bad about it.

A short series of bumps and pitches jolted them out of their individual reveries, as the plane was thrown from side to side. Katherine sat up in her seat and, naturally, dug her fingernails into Nick's arm. She looked behind her to find the stewardess.

"Oh, no." She turned back around and sunk low in her seat. "Oh God, no."

"What's wrong?" asked Nick, as the plane settled into calmer sky.

"Kassab!" Katherine exclaimed under her breath. Nick looked to the back of the airplane. "Don't look!"

"Katherine, are you *sure*?" asked Nick, not wanting to believe that they'd been followed. Katherine looked at Nick, as she had come to do over the years, with tortured patience, saying nothing. "Well, why hasn't he walked right up here, then, and confronted us?" reasoned Nick, restraining a great impulse to look toward the back of the airplane.

"How the hell should I know!" snapped Katherine. Her eyes darted around the cabin, as if she could find a way out.

Nick's mind began a wild search, looking hard, as he had learned to do in the military, for a solution that wasn't obvious. This time, at 10,000 feet, there wasn't one. "Let's just calm down," he said, adjusting his glasses. "Let's reason this out, shall we. What's he going to do? Arrest us in Tenerife? How can he? You don't have the dagger."

"Yes, dear, but there's that little matter of the papyrus."

"He has no jurisdiction in Tenerife, at any rate," offered Nick.

"So he's just following us, you think? To Cairo?" asked Katherine. Nick nodded. "What will happen when we get to Cairo?"

"Now that could be nasty business. Legally, he can detain us for months, just for questioning.

"Is that true?" asked Katherine. "We're Americans for God's sake."

"Yes, it's true, legally. And *illegally*, he could do pretty much anything he wants."

"You're scaring me."

Nick wanted to say, *I told you so.* He wanted to say, *See Katherine? You should have listened to me. You insisted on getting into this mess. You insisted on going to Egypt.* But he knew that Katherine wasn't the only one to blame. "It's possible Kassab is just using us to rout out Étienne," he said. "I gather the Egyptian government is more interested in him than they are us."

"So, how do we get rid of Kassab in Tenerife?"

"Well," began Nick. "Let's get you off the airplane and safely through Customs before Kassab has time to make any sort of fuss."

"How?" asked Katherine.

Nick thought for a moment. "You go first, with the papyrus hidden in your magazines. I'll delay Kassab on the airplane, somehow. You get through Customs as quickly as you can, and then leave the airport. Take a taxi into Tenerife."

"To where?"

"Tell the driver you want to go to *El Capitaine*, in Santa Cruz. He'll know the place, surely."

"How do *you* know the place?" asked Katherine.

"I was in Tenerife for a short stint during the war."

"You were? How come I didn't know about it?"

Nick said nothing. He had picked the *El Capitaine* because he would never forget it. He had gotten himself into a fair share of trouble in that pub. He was compelled in some way to take Katherine there, to explain what had happened, to free himself of the burden of too many lies.

"I know." Katherine interrupted Nick's thoughts. "War secrets. To tell you the truth, I don't want to know."

92

"Katherine, pay attention," said Nick. "This is important. If the Customs officials find the papyrus in your magazine, simply tell them that you're an antique dealer. And that you came across this single piece of papyrus in a recent shipment, apparently tucked in by mistake. Stick as close as possible to the truth, understand? Tell them you're personally taking the page to the Egyptian Museum in Cairo. You're just a concerned art dealer trying to get the papyrus to its rightful owner. Flash your calling card from the store. Be confident. Look them straight in the eyes. That should get you through Customs without any problems."

"Alright," said Katherine. "I've got it."

"You'll be long gone with the papyrus before Kassab ever gets off the plane," continued Nick. "Once I'm through Customs, I'll meet you at *El Capitaine*. We'll lay low for awhile, depending on how much commotion Kassab causes at the airport. If need be, we'll take a train up the coast, and a steamer to Alexandria."

"But that will take *forever*," complained Katherine.

"Better forever than in jail."

"Well put." Katherine sighed and relinquished the point. "Then how are you going to delay Kassab while I'm doing all this?"

"I don't know yet," said Nick.

Just then another stewardess walked by. Her name was Ingrid. She was tall and slender, a stick of a woman, who moved with a military precision. Her long blonde hair was pulled back tightly off her face into an enormous bun at the nape of her neck.

"Could I have a large glass, please?" asked Katherine, pulling out her bottle of whiskey. "With just a splash of water." Ingrid nodded, far too polite to scowl. Then Katherine turned to Nick and in a casual tone, as though she hadn't a care in the world, said, "Wake me when we get there, dear, will you?"

Katherine sat back and stared out the window at a gathering of ominous clouds over the restless sea. Finally, her whiskey untouched, Katherine closed her eyes and drifted off to sleep.

Nick had loved Katherine since the moment he met her. He'd never known any one remotely like her. The women he knew were perfectly proper and reserved and appropriately... British. Katherine was a whirlwind. She did whatever she wanted, swore like a sailor, was smart as a whip, and never apologized for herself. He loved her completely. He had no desire to look elsewhere. But elsewhere had come looking for him.

People like Nick never asked for more in life their fair share. And he took whatever life offered up to him, unquestioningly, for good or for bad. He'd taken it on the chin before, plenty of times, and didn't say a word. So when life offered up a rare reward of sorts, who was Nick to say no? In the haze of beer and war, in the distance of time and place, with death just waiting to catch him unawares, he wasn't compelled to deny himself the pleasure. However momentary or wrong he knew it to be.

Nick later wondered how many mistakes, in the history of time, people made when they'd had too many cocktails. How many of those mistakes just passed by, unnoticed. And how many of those mistakes damaged people's lives forever? Ruined marriages? Destroyed families? Toppled empires?

The mess he had gotten into seemed entirely unfair to Nick, who had led a pristine life thus far. He worked hard, loved deeply, fought well. Nick would not have called himself a drinking man, and he was loyal to Katherine with all his heart. But once, just this one time, circumstances converged, and he made a mistake that would unravel the threads of his perfectly respectful life.

Nick had had a bad damn day. At the height of World War II, two officers from British Intelligence – a corporal named Robert Gibbs and Lieutenant Nick Spencer – were sent to Tenerife on a special mission. Though Tenerife was neutral during the war, HQ suspected a spy cell was operating there, feeding information from allied forces through an underground communications network to the Nazis. Their mission was to uncover the cell and arrest its members. If the spies resisted, they were to be shot on the spot. Nick's job was to locate the traitors. The rest was up to Gibbs.

Gibbs was one of those fellows raised in the shadow of WWII as it built momentum in Europe during his formative years. He saw the newsreels as a youngster of the militarization of Germany, their occupation of Austria, the Blitz Krieg of Poland. Young Gibbs knew it would be his duty to fight some day. Which elevated his naturally impetuous gusto toward life into sheer recklessness. Gibbs raced headlong into everything he did. He denied himself no indulgence, laughed heartily, and took from life what he wanted. He was passionate and effective and dogged in his work, and equally so in his pursuit of his pleasures.

Nick often wondered if Gibbs knew, somehow, that he would not live beyond the war years. Gibbs had only so much time on this earth and he used up every single bit of what life offered before he was taken. Back at HQ in London, Nick stayed on the periphery of Gibbs' activities and watched him from a detached, bemused distance. *He is young,* Nick had once thought, with some degree of envy. *He has his whole life in front of him to sober up and take life seriously. Those days for me are over. Thankfully.* But in Tenerife, with just the two of them together, Nick got caught up in the reckless frenzy of Corporal Robert Gibbs.

They drank themselves silly in the *El Capitaine* bar. They had one lead on the suspected Nazi spies – a man who swore he was a witness to the espionage. That man had abruptly disappeared. Nick had spent the entire day tracking him from every possible angle: friends, neighbors, family members, business associates, drinking buddies. He went through his mail, his closets, his garbage. He searched the streets, the bars, the beach, the plaza. Nick finally found him in the morgue. Their Tenerife operation was a bust. Furious, unaccustomed to failure of this magnitude, Nick was resigned to drink half the beer in town before he went back to London with the bad news.

Hugo Nelson was also at *El Capitaine* that night. They hardly knew each other. But Nelson, too, got caught up in the revelries. He drank and swore and sang songs with Nick and Gibbs, buying several rounds 'for the Allies.' Nelson seemed to bring an authenticity to the night that it would not have otherwise had: a validation, a seal of approval, a confirmation of their efforts and their purpose.

Nelson brought something else with him that night: women. They were beautiful and giggling and drinking champagne, and they clung to Nelson like magnets. But he was happy to share. Nick would come to regret that night. He would regret it dearly.

Katherine didn't sleep very long or very deeply. She woke with a start after only a few minutes, and looked at Nick, totally dazed, as if she'd come from somewhere far away. She rubbed her eyes, downed her whiskey in a few long swallows, and tapped the passenger sitting in front of her.

The big, burly man – who had been intermittently snoring and grunting for the previous several hours – was finally on Katherine's last nerve. An enormous Stetson cowboy hat sat low over his round, ruddy face. He fussed in his seat and let out an enormous snort.

"Excuse me," said Katherine, poking him harder with her finger. "Can I offer you a handkerchief?"

The man in the Stetson woke up startled and grunted in her direction. "Huh? What's that?" He had a slow drawl to his words that made him sound soft, despite his size.

"The entire plane is rattling," explained Katherine. "Perhaps you need something to clear your nasal passages?" Katherine offered her pint of Wild Turkey to him.

The big man laughed loud and long. He took a healthy swig of the burning liquid, and he and Katherine were friends from that moment on. They chatted for hours as if they had absolutely everything in common, with no reason to doubt their life-long acquaintance. Together the two of them drew all the surrounding passengers into their conversation, passing around Katherine's whiskey like distracted soldiers in a foxhole.

They made their acquaintance with a small, fidgeting man sitting next to the man in the Stetson. He was an accountant, from Ireland, who had never flown before. Though he and Katherine had a great deal to commiserate about, Nick heard Katherine assuring the Irish traveler that airplane flight was safer than crossing the street. "Airplanes were meant to fly in bumpy air," she said. Nick watched his wife admiringly, over the top of his book, while he sat quietly in the background of her commotion. *Maybe she'll pass the bottle to Kassab back there, and invite him to the party.*

Across the aisle Katherine met a chubby lady in a green and pink floral print dress. Bernice was nice, and full of happy chitchat, the type of person Nick liked to meet at cocktail parties full of strangers. Bernice clutched a handbag the size of a small suitcase on her lap, when it wasn't wedged in between her stout legs on the floor. The man next to her, presumably her husband, pretended to sleep through the entire flight, apparently not the chatty type at all.

"Look!" exclaimed Bernice, pointing across the isle and past Katherine. Out the window they could suddenly see land. A small clump of terra firma rose up from the great blue ocean. White caps looked like dabs of frosting on the water.

"According to local legend," said the man in the Stetson in a mysterious tone, "the Canary Islands are the highest peaks of the lost island of Atlantis."

"Really?" asked Katherine. "I'd like to believe that." She paused for a moment. "I'd like to believe that Atlantis was real. That for eons of time – before we even started calculating time – an advanced civilization lived there." Katherine wondered if perhaps the Atlanteans could fly. If they lived where there was no crime and no war. Where there was no sorrow too deep to bear.

She turned to Nick. "From up here, it's not hard to imagine that one big, giant wave could wash over that small patch of land, covering it forever. Just like that."

Nick smiled and took Katherine's hand in his. Soon they would be landing.

When the British Airways DC-3 touched down on the small African island of Tenerife, it was a typically dry and sweltering, yellow afternoon. Ripples of heat rose off the tar runway. This was a sleepy African port of call, which ran on a rhythm of its own.

Hoards of transient travelers and new technology had come to this little corner of the globe since the war ended. But no rush of modern civilization could veer these island inhabitants from the steady metronome of their schedules or their traditions.

One of the common attitudes of this culture was the notion that if you were not from Tenerife, you were, and would always be, an outsider. And the only thing worse than an outsider, at least to the local authorities, was an outsider with a badge.

The local constable, Rambaba, who was in charge of airport security, did not need to remind himself of this unspoken truth. It always crossed his mind, though, whenever an international flight arrived in his domain. Rambaba took a slow drag on a fat cigar. From his tiny office in the airport terminal, he watched the shiny airplane taxi down the runway. His belly, a full six inches over his belt, pressed against the desk. A receding hairline exposed his damp and rosy forehead.

You just cannot be that fat and not sweat all the time, thought Phan, Rambaba's young deputy. Across the desk from his formidable boss, Phan sat stiffly in his crisp white uniform. He was a skinny kid with surprisingly soft features and brown, innocent doe eyes. Phan moved his hand along the thin red sash that crossed his chest, running his fingers in a delicate caress from his shoulder to his waist and back up again. Phan was eyeing the ornate box that held Rambaba's cigars. Phan cleared his throat. "Another gift, Constable?" he asked, cocking a thin eyebrow.

Rambaba leveled a keen eye on Phan. He puffed on his cigar, watching a stream of blue smoke travel through a shaft of sunlight. "My indifference to Signor Hayes, and his business here, keeps him trading in Tenerife."

Constable Rambaba enjoyed many gifts offered by frequent business travelers, seeking to ingratiate themselves with the local authorities. The Constable rarely delved too deeply into the affairs of these men. He just wanted peace and quiet. And his indifference provided just that – and kept him in expensive cigars and good company as well.

"A convenient arrangement for you," commented Phan, still thinking about how a fine cigar like that might taste. "And them, of course," he hastily added.

With extreme precision, and all the time in the world, Constable Rambaba stubbed out his cigar. Phan had recently been transferred to the Constable's office, only a few weeks prior. He was too naïve yet to fully understand the protocol of this office. And he was young. He would have to learn. "Make no mistake, Phan," said the Constable. "Tenerife is my domain. The law is *here*, with me. No one crosses it." His eyes narrowed, almost disappearing in the round dough of his cheeks. "No one."

Phan squirmed in his chair. "Yes sir. Of course sir," he said. He drew in a deep breath and gazed at the exit door to avoid the eyes of Rambaba. "I guess I'll go on a little walk-about."

"You do that." Constable Rambaba turned away from his deputy and stared again out the window.

As the sun reached its peak on this ordinary day in his well-ordered life, the Constable saw the DC-3 jerk to a stop on the tarmac. He grimaced. This flight was from London, in the United Kingdom. He did not trust the British. And he did not want this technological beast or its foreign occupants to disrupt the languid tranquillity of his day.

Rambaba leaned back in his chair, put his feet on his desk, and re-lit his cigar. He would have gazpacho tonight. *Yes, cool gazpacho, and a nice, cold glass of beer. And perhaps the company of Miss Patra. Three more hours...* Rambaba laid out his entire evening in the blue curls of his cigar.

What he couldn't see was the tall, dark-haired man, wearing a crisp, olive-green suit, standing just inside the terminal doors. Slowly, deftly, this man turned a gold coin over and under, between his fingers, as he stood fixed to this one particular spot. His hard eyes were focused on the plane landing from London, waiting, patiently waiting.

As the plane taxied toward the terminal, Ingrid, the blonde stewardess, announced their arrival. It was one o'clock in the afternoon and 85 degrees in Tenerife. Katherine was still talking with the man in the Stetson, whose name she finally learned was Buck.

Turns out Buck was right proud of his name, his heritage and the great state of Texas. He was also inordinately proud of his family's secret recipe for spicy barbecue sauce. Seems barbecue was a big deal in Texas. *Must be all those cows running around on the open plains,* thought Katherine. She wondered vaguely if they didn't have cows roaming the streets of Houston. But she didn't have time to ponder the finer points of Texas culture.

What she did learn that piqued her interest was that Buck envisioned the family sauce on every table from California to New Jersey, from West Africa to India. Indeed, Buck traveled frequently through Tenerife, and was friends with the Constable stationed at the airport.

"I bring him gifts from America from time to time," Buck was saying.

"Barbecue sauce?" asked Katherine.

Buck laughed out loud. "Caviar mostly. Little appliances. Gadgets. Cigars. Things like that."

"Really?" said Katherine. "Isn't that nice of you?" She squeezed Nick's hand. "This is a good omen," she whispered.

Nick didn't believe in omens, good or bad, and he suddenly didn't much care for their plan. As the plane taxied to an uneven stop, a dark panic began to rise up on the outskirts of his mind. "I know it was my idea," he whispered to Katherine. "But I don't like this: my wife leaving the plane on her own, in a foreign country, with illegal contraband in her handbag. I don't like it."

Katherine threw Nick her best I-can-take-care-of-myself-thank-you-very-much-you-overbearing-mother-hen look. Nick sighed. They were out of time and options.

"I'll meet you at *El Capitaine*," whispered Katherine, as if she was arranging a clandestine love affair. "I'll take the first taxi I see."

Katherine was holding tight to her handbag. Everything in it was important to her, including her passport, make-up, the page of papyrus, and a complimentary bottle of spicy barbecue sauce. Ingrid was opening the front door, as an efficient ground crew in starched blue uniforms rolled out the tall, mobile stair-steps to meet the airplane. Buck had heaved all 250 pounds of himself out of his seat and was breathing heavily as he wrested his briefcase from beneath the seat in front of him.

Buck said his good-byes, wrapping Katherine in an embrace that took the wind out of her. Then he made his way to the exit, tipping his enormous Stetson to Ingrid. "It's time for me to go," announced Katherine. She turned to Nick and kissed him quickly on the cheek. "For luck," she said.

They both looked inadvertently over their shoulders at Kassab. They Egyptian sat at the back of the airplane, his legs crossed casually, reading a newspaper. He seemed to have all the time in the world, and an unsettling sense of confidence.

"Now, you're okay?" Nick looked his wife over in that instant as if he was memorizing her face, afraid that he wasn't ever going to see it again. "You know just what to do?" She threw him her best smile, and headed for the cabin door. One quick glance back at Nick, and she was gone.

If I could put a protective coat of armor around that woman every time she walked away from me, said Nick to himself, *I would.*

The passengers were busy collecting their belongings. Kassab had risen from his seat and was leaning over two other passengers to look out the small window of the plane. *He's watching Katherine,* thought Nick. He tried to do the same, but was blocked from view of the window across the aisle. Besides, he had a more pressing matter to attend to. The front-most passengers were funneling themselves into the aisle and out the door.

Bernice was sufficiently blocking the rest of the plane on her own, for which Nick was extremely grateful. She gathered up a brown paper bag of food snacks, a faux-mink wrap and her enormous white purse. Nick smiled, feeling very warmly toward her and sorry for what he was about to do. He liked the chubby lady, though what she thought she would do with a fur wrap in 85 degrees of humidity, he had no idea.

Still, Bernice had repeatedly offered him treats from her brown grocery bag during the flight. She had a soft way about her, generous and jolly. Nick wouldn't have been entirely surprised if she pulled a puppy out of that bag of hers, complete with a diamond-studded collar and a bone from the butcher shop.

Just as Bernice looked as though she was ready to make her way up the narrow aisle, Nick threw up. Or at least he pretended to, gagging and spitting into a little white bag from the seat pocket. He clutched his stomach and stumbled into the aisle. He intentionally knocked Bernice off her feet and back into her chair. Everyone on the airplane stopped to stare. "Oh, God!" exclaimed Nick. "I'm so sorry!" He took out his handkerchief and began to dab the corners of his mouth.

Ingrid pushed her way down the isle and came to Nick's aid. "Sir, are you alright?"

"I think it was something I ate," he said, looking as bleary-eyed as he could, leaning heavily against Bernice.

"Here's another bag," offered Ingrid, delicately taking hold of the one in Nick's hand. The passengers around Nick scrambled to help by handing him more little white bags. Except for those few who were holding tightly to their own, just in case.

"I'll get some hot towels," said Ingrid, rushing back to the galley. *You do that*, thought Nick. *And take your time*. He noticed that, in the commotion, the clasp on Bernice's purse had come unfastened. *Perfect*. "I'm alright now," Nick said, starting to stand up straight. "Quite alright... whoa!" He wobbled back and forth across the aisle.

Nick reached toward the armrest to steady himself but his eyes were fixed on the strap of Bernice's purse. He knew he'd only get one chance. As he staggered away from her side of the aisle, he grabbed the strap and fell with it, and the various contents of the purse, onto the floor. *No puppy*, he noticed. *But enough stuff to spend quite a little while picking up before anyone else can leave this airplane.*

Nick dared to look back at Kassab. He saw him fuming, trapped at the back of the airplane behind a wall of curious on-lookers. Nick looked away, knowing that if Kassab could kill him with his eyes, he would surely be dead.

8

DIVINE INTERVENTION

I don't steal money, I don't hit anyone. What will you charge me with?
I have felt the swaying of the elephant's shoulders;
And now you want me to climb on a jackass? Try to be serious.

       – Mirabai, 15th century aesthetic and poet from India

Katherine crossed the scorching tarmac, trying to hold her alligator handbag casually by her side, letting it swing ever so slightly. Nearing the terminal doors, the small crowd of passengers who had managed to leave the airplane was slowing down, forming a funnel of hot, cranky people. Katherine noticed a man she hadn't seen on the flight, standing just outside the terminal doors.

He stood out against the weary crowd, a statue of composure, in no great hurry it seemed, to be going anywhere. *Handsome,* thought Katherine, impressed that anyone could manage to look crisp and elegant in the island humidity. He was tall and fit and wore a dark, olive-green suit, custom-tailored to hang perfectly on his frame. His brown skin and dark eyes made him look mysterious and alluring. That someone would look so well put together assuaged Katherine's fears about entering a strange and remote culture.

As she waited impatiently in line, the heat began to bear down on her. *Get on with it,* she thought, waiting for everyone to get around to getting inside. The sun was soaking right into her bones, weighing her down, melting the muscles that held her up. Sweat was gathering on her brow and the nape of her neck, and she was increasingly anxious about getting through Customs.

Katherine took a few deep breaths and focused her mind on a nice, cool martini at *El Capitaine.* She forgot entirely about the man in the suit, until she felt a cool hand on her arm.

"Mrs. Spencer," he stated calmly, his dark eyes revealing no emotion. "I am Cato Nafarah. With the Egyptian government." He took her arm with a grasp so tight that it made her wince. "Please come with me." He started to lead Katherine away from the terminal.

Katherine's face flushed with fear. In a red hot second she imagined all manner of suffering and isolation: a dank, smelly room, a bare light bulb, some unknown source of dripping water, gruesome devices to extract information. "Hey, wait a minute," she managed to say. "That hurts!"

Nafarah moved his hand to the back of her neck. "Please don't be foolish," he said calmly, applying pressure to a point that made Katherine want to drop to her knees. "Keep your voice down, stay calm, and everything will be just fine."

"Let go of me!" Katherine growled between clenched teeth.

"I suggest you keep your mouth shut, Mrs. Spencer. As this very moment, my associate, Mr. Kassab, has your husband under arrest. If you cause a scene out here, the time you saw him last will be the last you ever see him." Nafarah dug his fingers into her neck, driving knives of pain down her spine. "Do you understand?"

In that moment Katherine nearly burst into tears, feeling the threat of hysteria pushing to the surface. *It wasn't supposed to happen this way,* she thought in a panic. "Please don't hurt Nick," she whispered, her eyes spilling tears. "Please."

"Do *not* cry, Mrs. Spencer. You're starting to draw attention to yourself."

"Okay, okay," murmured Katherine, trying through searing tears to regain her composure.

They began to move toward the end of the terminal building and around the corner, out of sight from the crowd on the tarmac. Suddenly, through the vortex of pain and shock that swirled inside her, Katherine realized that Nafarah was trying to get her quietly away from the tarmac.

"Allow me to carry your bag for you, Mrs. Spencer," he said, in a quiet, authoritative tone. He took hold of the straps on Katherine's handbag. "Let go now."

He's going to take my purse, and Etienne's papyrus, just like that. Katherine yelled with a ferocity that surprised even her. "Help!"

She grabbed hold of Nafarah's hand with all her might, and started pulling him back toward to terminal doors. "Help me!" she screamed, digging her red nails into the top of Nafarah's hand.

Caught off guard, Nafarah's steely expression turned to one of confusion and then frustration and finally pain, as he struggled to release himself from Katherine's grasp. He dug in his heels and pulled against her.

Katherine leveraged all her weight against Nafarah, and held on for all her life. "He's trying to steal my purse!" The crowd waiting to enter the terminal began to notice and gather around the spectacle.

"Hey ole buddy," they heard a man drawl. "I think ya oughta to let the lady go."

Thank God, thought Katherine. Buck was standing there, calm as could be, resting his thumbs on his big silver belt buckle. Katherine let go of Nafarah's hand and they both tumbled ungracefully to the tarmac.

Buck helped Katherine to her feet, unabashedly dusting her off. Next Buck, without a single word, picked the Egyptian from the tarmac and leveled him with one meaty right hook to the jaw. Nafarah sunk slowly back to the tarmac in a tidy, olive-colored heap.

Stumbling away from the fight, Katherine reeled backwards and tripped right into the arms of one of the onlookers. Regaining her balance, she turned to apologize and found herself looking into the eyes of authority.

Between guilt and gratitude, Katherine made the sign of the cross and bobbed to her knee. *Bless me Father, for I have sinned.* Out loud she mumbled, "I'm sorry, Father."

"Not at all," replied the priest. Standing in a long black robe, the man was an imposing figure – slight and lean, but commanding recognition and respect.

It had long been to Katherine's dismay that the rituals of her Catholic upbringing had stayed with her through the years. *Bless us, oh Lord, and these thy gifts…* These words ran through her head every time she sat down to a meal, which was almost always fish on Fridays, like it or not.

Today, though, Katherine was glad to be in the company of a priest. She used to think that everyone in the clergy was harsh, judgmental and threatening. In this particular moment, however, this particular man represented everything she thought was strong and honorable and reassuring. In a strange land, far from home, his presence gave her comfort. She took back, in that one instant, everything mean she had ever said about nuns and priests. Which was plenty.

"Are you alright?" asked the priest.

"I need to find my husband," she stated, looking toward the airplane.

"I'm Father Antonio," he said warmly. "And who might you be?"

"Katherine Spencer," she dutifully replied. "But I need to find my husband."

Father Antonio held onto her hands, staring directly into her eyes for a long moment. He finally cocked his head to one side. "You're safe now."

"You alright, honey?" Buck stepped up beside them, satisfied that Nafarah wasn't going anywhere, at least not for a while.

"Yes, yes. I'm fine. Thank you. But I need to find Nick." The Texan looked confused. "We got separated," stammered Katherine.

"Well then," offered Father Antonio. "He's probably inside the terminal, looking for you. Not to worry."

"But I am worried."

"Just who the Sam Hill is *this* man?" demanded Buck, pointing to Nafarah with a nod of his Stetson.

"I don't know," said Katherine, starting to shake. "He was trying to steal my handbag."

Buck and Father Antonio looked down at Katherine's oversized purse. Just then a sharp whistle came across the tarmac. "Well, that would be the Constable," said Buck authoritatively. "Everything's gonna be a-okay. Don't cha worry."

Nafarah stirred on the ground, groaning in a vain attempt to sit up. He squinted into the hot sun and fell back on the tarmac. Buck turned back to hover in pride over the man who had accosted his new friend from New York City.

"You should leave immediately," Father Antonio whispered in Katherine's ear. "Will you allow me to escort you?"

"Yes. Yes please," said Katherine. The gathering crowd had increased in size as travelers inside the terminal had caught wind of the commotion. More and more of them were stepping outside into the heat and excitement, unable to see a commotion and willingly sit apart from it.

They want to participate, thought Katherine. *To be a part of the out-of-the-ordinary. Even after the bloody, terrible years of the war – when people had seen too much and lost too much – a scuffle between strangers on an airport tarmac was irresistible.*

"These are strange times in Tenerife," whispered Father Antonio as he led Katherine through the crowd.

Still helping Bernice pick up her belongings, Nick glanced out the plane's small window toward the terminal, and the hot black tarmac that stretched before it. There was some commotion going on out there. He got up and looked closer, leaning over Bernice's husband, who had sat back and tried to ignore the whole miserable episode. Katherine's slender figure came into view through the tiny window.

Nick stood up and cleared his throat. "You know," he said. "I'm feeling quite well all of a sudden." He looked around. Bernice was still on her knees, poor thing, collecting the last of her treasures from underneath a nearby seat. He touched her on the shoulder. "I am so very sorry," he said. "Truly, I am."

Then he collected his overcoat and fedora, and climbed right over the top of her. Bernice looked up, pursed her lips, and snapped her handbag closed.

Nick muscled his way up the aisle, leaving the astonished passengers behind. Ingrid stood befuddled, looking out the door with a steaming hot towel in her hand. Before Bernice could collect herself and clear the isle, Nick was half way across the tarmac.

By the time Nick got to the terminal, Buck was pulling some fellow from the ground by the lapels. Nick pushed his way through the lingering crowd.

The man groaned and held his hand to his jaw. Buck had one hand on the man's collar, and was scratching beneath his Stetson with the other. His eyes met up with Nick's. Katherine was nowhere to be found. Nick saw the local police scurrying across toward them. "Where's my wife?" he asked.

"Well, for cryin' out loud in a bucket," replied the big Texan. "She was just here."

A brisk shot of a whistle in his ear, and Buck nearly dropped the man he was holding back to the ground. "Jeez-us Ka-ryst almighty!" He turned to the noise. The Constable arrived in a flushed and angry sweat, with his scrawny deputy clipping along close behind. "Rambaba, you old goat!" bellowed Buck. "You nearly scared the hell right outta me!"

"What is happening here?" demanded Rambaba, surveying the situation.

"This fellow's a thief!" Buck nodded his Stetson to the man in question, who stood wobbly and dazed, supported by Buck's hefty arm.

"That *fellow* is an agent of the Egyptian Government!" Everyone wheeled around to see Kassab, dark and brooding, waving a badge in Rambaba's face. "As am I."

Kassab took the dazed man under his arm. "This is Cato Nafarah, with the Egyptian Department of Antiquities." Kassab was practically screaming. "There is going to be great retribution over this!"

Rambaba was neither impressed, intimidated, nor threatened. He was annoyed. Not only had his day been disrupted by a scuffle, it was totally derailed by two foreign officials intruding into his personal domain. The inhabitants of Tenerife were aligned politically with Morocco, and felt no love for Egypt. But an agent of *any* foreign government meddling around in Tenerife was particularly bothersome to Rambaba.

"Well, in that case,' the Constable said stiffly to Kassab, "you will both need to go downtown for questioning. Your testimony in this matter will be most valuable."

"We have no time for this," snapped Kassab. "We have important government business here."

"Unfortunately, you have no jurisdiction here," replied the Constable.

"Matters of Egyptian security *are* my jurisdiction," snapped Kassab, "regardless of where the offense takes place."

"As far as I can tell, " Rambaba stated flatly, "your colleague here is the one causing the offense. Here, in my jurisdiction."

"You must release us both, immediately," commanded Kassab, fuming.

"I cannot." Constable Rambaba shrugged his shoulders. "You will stay in my custody until this matter is straightened out." With one snap of Rambaba's fingers, the deputy stepped forward and clamped a pair of handcuffs on Nafarah. Then he moved to Kassab and did the same.

"Take these men to the precinct," Rambaba ordered his deputy, taking the Egyptians' badges and passports from their suit coats. "I'll sort out their stories later."

"You will regret this," hissed Nafarah. "I promise you that."

"You two." Rambaba pointed a meaty finger at Buck and Nick. "You two are coming with me."

"But wait," protested Nick.

"It is done," stated the Constable. Even the boisterous Texan dared not offer a contrary word.

Katherine let the chaos on the tarmac fall behind her as the priest guided her indoors. He was strong; she could tell that by the way he took her arm. And lean, with a kind of personal strength that could only come from great discipline.

Katherine wondered briefly what an Italian priest was doing in Tenerife. But she didn't linger on the point. She was safe, however momentary or tenuous that safety was.

Inside the terminal, Father Antonio guided her to the Customs station – a rickety table more representative of a bridge game than a Customs Authority. But the three men standing there – with suspicion carved into their faces, and their arms crossed uncompromisingly across their chests – made it very clear that this was no neighborhood social affair.

It was all the more to Katherine's surprise then, when they smiled as they saw her coming. She smiled back, tentative, awkward.

"Blessings!" Father Antonio waved at them warmly. He reached out his hands to each one. "Are you all well today?"

"Yes, Father," the first one answered.

Father Antonio turned to the tallest of the three, who stood bulky and hunched, towering over the small table. "Renne, hello. How is your wife? Is she well?"

"She is well, Father," he answered. "I think she is getting better, a little every day."

"Very good to hear." The priest took hold of Renne's hands. "I am praying for her, rest assured."

"Thank you, Father."

Katherine watched all this unfold standing in the shadow of the good priest. *How unbelievably lucky can I get in one day?* In her lifetime Katherine had come to question dumb luck, and to wonder if miracles actually did happen, even to people like her.

Still nervous about the papyrus hidden in one of her magazines, Katherine reached for a cigarette, then checked herself. *Absolutely no smoking in front of a priest. At least not in Baltimore, where I was raised. Lightening might strike.*

"Do you have your passport, my dear?" Father Antonio turned from the table and addressed Katherine in a serious tone. "They will need to see your passport."

"Of course." Katherine rummaged through her purse. "It's right here." She held out the little blue booklet that held her picture and the many little boxes waiting for international stamps.

One man at Customs took her passport while the one called Renne took her purse. He pulled out the magazines and set them aside, for a better look inside her enormous handbag. Meanwhile Father Antonio was distracting Katherine with polite conversation.

"How long are you staying in Tenerife, Katherine?" he asked.

"Oh, I'm not," she said, looking over his shoulder at Renne. "I'm traveling on to Cairo today, with my husband. Our plane leaves in a few hours ... days, I mean. We're taking a short excursion into Santa Cruz before we go on to Egypt."

"How did you get separated?"

"Uh ... I don't know." Katherine flinched at the lies. For the briefest of moments she wondered why it was so easy to deceive the people who were the most kind to her.

Father Antonio seemed concerned. "Where is your husband now?"

"I don't know." Katherine looked back across the terminal, faltering. "He should have caught up by now."

Renne, the Customs man, had surveyed everything in her handbag, and was turning his attention to the magazines, when Katherine heard Nick's voice. "Katherine!"

She spun around. "Nick!" *Thank God. Thank God.*

Her husband, with Buck right next to him, was being led across the terminal by a hugely round, red-faced man in a uniform.

Katherine turned her attention back to Renne. He was flipping through the first in the small stack of magazines she'd brought with her. *If he makes it to the* Life *magazine, where the papyrus is hidden, that's it. My trip to recover the Knife of the Asps will be over, here and now, just like that. I'll most certainly go to jail. Or worse, be sent back to America, to face Hugo Nelson.*

"Father," she said. "That's my husband, coming across the room. Are we finished here, please?"

The priest looked her over carefully. *He can't* really *see directly inside of me,* Katherine told herself. *Or take an inventory of all the sins in my heart. I don't care what the nuns said.* She tried to look as innocent and unhappy as could be: a woman lost and accosted, wanting only to rejoin her husband.

Father Antonio looked over at Renne and paused a moment as the man picked up the incriminating magazine. Katherine held her breath, while her heart pounded like thunder in her chest. She felt a sudden urge to scream out, *It's not my fault! It's not my fault!*

"You're finished there, aren't you Renne?" said the priest, in a casual, authoritative tone.

Renne paused, the magazine limp in his hand, the stolen papyrus just pages away from his fingertips. His brow was deeply crinkled, his eyes darting between his colleagues, the priest and Katherine. "Uh..."

The priest reached over and, with the easy expression of one who wields ultimate authority, picked up Katherine's alligator handbag. *Priests are good at that expression,* thought Katherine. *The one that tells you they have God's ear, and are therefore in charge of everything and everyone. No questions. No back talk.*

"Thank you, Renne," said Father Antonio. "You're doing a fine job. Your wife would be very proud of you."

With nothing left to do but acquiesce to the priest, or make a big scene to the contrary, Renne nodded. "Yes, I'm all finished here," he said. He then put the *Life* magazine with all the others, back into Katherine's purse.

Just then, Nick rushed up, scooping Katherine into his arms. "Are you alright, darling?"

Katherine suddenly felt weak down to the bones in her toes. "I'm fine," she said. "Really." Katherine felt her chin start to quiver. "I'm just a little tired."

"Don't worry, darling," said Nick, kissing her forehead. "We'll be in Cairo before you know it."

"Well, then." Father Antonio smiled broadly. "I see you are in good hands. My blessings to you." Without waiting for an answer, he turned and walked away. *I will never see him again,* thought Katherine as she watched the priest disappear into the crowd. *And I didn't even say thank you.*

Nick and Katherine were then ushered in a big huff into the Constable's office. Buck came along too, having assigned himself as supervisor of what he called this 'whole crazy damn mess'. He felt responsible, as though being familiar with Tenerife, and pals with the Constable, gave him a certain amount of ownership in the affairs of American travelers, and new friends.

They all sat in the Constable's tiny, sweltering office, trying to explain what happened, while Rambaba sat impatiently behind his desk in a big heap of flesh and sweat. He took a slow drag on a fat cigar.

"I saw this man trying to grab Mrs. Spencer's handbag," said Buck. "But she was giving him a mighty fight, I'll tell you that." He beamed at Katherine.

"And who's this man to you, Mrs. Spencer?" asked the Constable, jotting down notes.

"Nobody. I've never seen him before in my life," said Katherine. "He just came up to me and took a hold of my purse. It all happened so fast. The next thing I knew, I was inside the terminal."

"And you," Rambaba pointed his cigar at Nick. "Where were you all this time?"

"I was delayed on the airplane."

"How's that?"

"Well, there was this woman, I don't think I caught her name. At any rate, she happened to spill her purse in the aisle, and I stopped to help her pick everything up. Things had rolled all over the place, underneath chairs, down the aisle. It took quite awhile to get her all collected up and on her way."

"And your wife just took off without you?"

"I thought he was right behind me," offered Katherine.

"Let me get this straight," said Rambaba. "You left an airplane in a foreign land, crossed a tarmac, were accosted, rescued – apparently by Buck here – and then went through Customs without *ever noticing* your husband was not with you?"

"Right about the time the man grabbed me," replied Katherine, "I noticed Nick wasn't with me."

"I thought he grabbed your purse, not you," said Rambaba, his eyes narrowing.

"Well, yes…" stammered Katherine. "He did."

"Go on," said the Constable.

"Well, then Buck came along, and then the priest."

"What priest?"

"Father Antonio. He took me through Customs. He said it would be best if I didn't linger on the tarmac."

112

"And why do you suppose that was?" asked Rambaba.

"I have no idea."

"And it didn't occur to you to find your husband?"

"It all happened so quickly..." Katherine shook her head, looking around the room for answers.

The Constable didn't wait for an explanation. "This man who grabbed you, uh, I mean who grabbed your purse, he's apparently from Egypt." They all just looked at him, blankly. "Well?" said the Constable. "What is your business in Egypt?"

"Visiting a friend," said Katherine.

"Just traveling," said Nick, at the same moment.

The Constable looked back and forth between Katherine and Nick, scowling. "And you have no idea why this, uh..." He picked up one of the passports on his desk. "This ... Cato Nafarah – an agent from the Egyptian Department of Antiquities – wanted your handbag?"

"I don't know what he wanted," Katherine explained for the second time, thinking that lying was still the best strategy under the circumstances. Telling him that Nafarah was after a priceless dagger that she didn't have didn't make any sense. She was also prepared to lie about the papyrus, should Rambaba find it. Just like Nick had instructed her. She even thought to drop Hugo Nelson's name, tell Rambaba that she was in the employ of the powerful American financier.

That should impress him, she thought. She was wrong about that last part, but he never found the papyrus. Rambaba eventually just got tired of them.

Just as Buck was explaining that he had traveled with Katherine and Nick from America, and could vouch for their character, a knock came at the door. "Come in!" grumbled the Constable. Standing in the doorway was Rambaba's deputy, Phan. His crisp white uniform was wrinkled and starting to come untucked. The smart red sash he wore was crooked, and in Katherine's mind, he looked sad and anxious, like he wanted badly to be somewhere, anywhere, else.

He looks more suited to a school yard than a security office, she thought. Phan stood in the doorway for a few minutes, stiff as a post, before Rambaba even acknowledged him with a grunt and a glance in his direction.

"The Egyptians are secured, sir," Phan said. "We're checking out their stories now. Should take a couple more hours before we hear back from Egypt. In the mean time, they're locked up downtown."

Rambaba said nothing to Phan, but turned his attention back to Nick and Katherine. "You have tickets on the next flight to Cairo?" he asked.

"Indeed, sir!" said Nick. "And we'd like to be on it. I don't like the idea of someone stalking my wife. You understand."

The Constable glared back and forth between them. Just then Buck interrupted. "I don't guess those two Egyptian fellows will be released in time to catch that same flight... will they?"

Rambaba's eyes narrowed, nearly nearly swallowed whole by his round face. Buck reached over and helped himself to one of Rambaba's expensive cigars. *The Lord giveth and the Lord taketh away*, thought Katherine. "No, I don't suppose they will," said Rambaba, following Buck's movements with his eyes.

"Could take a day or two just to sort out the details," suggested Buck. "Those boys seemed mighty wily to me." Buck took a razor-sharp cutter from Rambaba's desktop, and clipped off the end of his cigar. He let it lay where it fell, on a stack of papers. "Got a light?" he asked.

Rambaba lit Buck's cigar, leaning his face away from the smoke, and snapped his lighter closed. "And what are *you* waiting for?" the Constable snapped at Phan. The deputy had been standing there quietly, eyeing the cigars on the Constable's desk.

"Uh, nothing sir," said Phan, with disappointment in his small voice. "Just waiting for further instructions."

Constable Rambaba slowly rolled his own cigar around the inside of an ashtray, leaving behind an ash the size of his thumb. "Get out of my office," he finally said. Phan left without another word. Everyone stared after the young deputy in silence.

Except for Rambaba. "You as well," he said, waving his cigar at Nick and Katherine, swirling smoke through the shafts of sunlight in the room. "I'll take care of the Egyptians."

"Thank you sir," said Nick, ushering his wife quickly out of the office, with Buck following close behind them.

"Well, I'll say this for the Constable," said Buck. "He sure can be ornery when he gets his dander up. Doesn't like any one who questions his authority, not one Goddamn bit." He blushed and tipped his hat. "Sorry, ma'am."

Katherine smiled back at him. There was more to Buck the-Texas-Barbecue-Man than she would have guessed. But whatever reasons he wielded so much quiet power in Tenerife, she decided she didn't want to know.

9

WARS OF WORDS

To learn the scriptures is easy, to live them, hard.
The search for the Real is no simple matter.
Deep in my looking, the last words vanished.
Joyous and silent, the waking that met me there.

– Lal Dad, 14th century wanderer and poet, from Kashmir

10,000 feet above Africa

Katherine was completely spent by the time they boarded their flight to Egypt. It was evening, and they wouldn't arrive in Cairo until late into the night. Katherine was looking forward to a stiff shot of whiskey and a long, dreamless nap. She could hardly keep her eyes open. When she saw a familiar face in a black cassock and white collar walking down the aisle toward her, she stirred, wide awake in a wave of guilt. Her lies were unraveling.

Oddly though, she also felt a small degree of comfort, as if this man was some sort of divinely appointed father protector. As if, somehow, his destiny had been intertwined with hers. *Besides*, she told herself, *he's a priest. He has to forgive me.*

"Hello," said Father Antonio. The tone of his voice implied more of a question than a greeting.

"Hello," said Katherine.

"You've scratched your plans to visit Santa Cruz?" asked the priest.

"Yes," said Katherine, her face flushed. "We decided to go straight on to Cairo instead."

116

"Well, that's my good fortune isn't it?" said Father Antonio, as he settled himself into a seat across the aisle. "I'm traveling to Cairo myself this evening." The warmth of his smile and unassuming manner smoothed out the awkwardness of their unexpected second encounter. "Church business."

Katherine introduced Father Antonio to Nick as the man who helped her through Customs. Nick reached over and shook the priest's hand. "Jolly good then," he said warmly, though he would have preferred to spend the flight into Cairo without company. "It gives me the opportunity to thank you for helping my wife. I am in your debt."

Father Antonio spread his hands in a humble gesture. "It was my pleasure. And the right thing to do."

Pondering misty concepts of destiny, Katherine drifted off to sleep, leaving Nick alone to keep company with the priest. Raised in a family that largely ignored religion, Nick hadn't the slightest notion of what to say or how to act. But the priest was in a mood for chitchat.

"I truly detest these night flights," said Father Antonio. "But from Tenerife, we've no other choice in the matter."

Priests are allowed to detest things? "Makes for a long day," said Nick.

"Indeed."

"We're both so grateful that you were at the airport this afternoon," said Nick, annoyed that he had no more imagination than to repeat himself.

"Indeed. Happy to help out."

"Now that I think of it," added Nick. "What brought you to the airport so early in the afternoon? For an evening flight, I mean?"

"Ah," said Father Antonio. "My devotions, naturally."

As if I know what that means, thought Nick, a nodding smile stamped on his face. "Naturally."

"Where are you staying in Cairo?" asked the priest, pressing for more conversation.

"Don't know yet, frankly. We left in a bit of a rush from America," explained Nick. "We're looking up an old friend."

"Well then," said the priest. "Perhaps I could suggest the Shepheard's Hotel. It's magnificent, in the heart of everything, near the Nile, shops, museums. You will love it, I promise you. Any taxi driver can take you straight there."

"Thank you."

"It's a bit pricey, of course. So if you're worried at all about that, I can recommend the Grand Hotel. Clean, friendly, still close to everything. But more modest."

"Is that where you stay in Cairo?" asked Nick.

"Yes, it is. Myself and my brothers of the Church. We are meeting in Cairo – four of us – to discuss the growing conflict in Palestine. And how we can be of help."

"They've got quite a mess over there, haven't they?"

"Quite," said the Father. "The conflict in the Arab lands is very serious, and the Church is trying to calm the growing rift. The United States and Britain are supporting the Jews, but the Arabs won't stand long for that. Palestine is their home land. It is holy to them. They will not give it up. And no one can deny that the Middle East is strategically important to the West, to the European nations, and to Russia. In military bases and in oil."

"You know a great deal about world politics," remarked Nick.

"Does that surprise you?" asked Father Antonio.

"Well, yes. I suppose it does."

"Priests don't just sit in church day in and day out, reading the Bible, praying, and concerning themselves only with matters from 2,000 years ago." Father Antonio laughed. "Though, indeed, we do a lot of that."

"I see," said Nick.

"The Church is very concerned about what happens in the world."

"Tenerife is quite a ways from the Middle East, isn't it?" asked Nick, wondering why a priest from the west coast of Africa was so involved in the Palestinian question.

"Not so far, my son. Our world is not so big."

118

"Where are you from, originally?" asked Nick.

"Oh, a small village in Italy, very near to Rome, called Fiumicino. On the western coast. Very beautiful." The priest sighed. In his face Nick saw a sudden longing, a deep, immense sadness. Then it was gone.

"Did you grow up there?" asked Nick.

"Oh, yes," said Father Antonio. "I've lived there all my life, except for four years of seminary in Rome. And, of course, my recent appointment to Tenerife."

"Sounds lovely," Nick said.

"You've no idea," said Father Antonio. "Things do not move as fast in Fiumicino as they do in America. Or even Rome. We are a small village. I've known the people there my entire life. I baptized them, christened them, gave them first communion and every communion thereafter, married them, counseled them, and was there to deliver last rites when they passed on to the glory of Heaven."

"Sounds like you miss it quite a lot."

"It is God's command that I go to Tenerife. I miss the church where I grew up, of course. But God asks, and I go."

"You grew up ... in a church?"

"Does that sound strange to you?"

"Well," Nick admitted. "Yes. It does."

"My mother took me to church every day of my young life. Every day. I loved it there. It was so quiet, so completely sacred. Mother and I would sit there and pray under the colored stained-glass. It was very serious business. It was the house of God and the people treated it that way."

"When did you decide to become a priest?" asked Nick.

Father Antonio laughed. "This is not something one decides. One is called to the priesthood. For me, it was at a very young age. I knew, I just *knew*, all of a sudden in this one instant, that it was my destiny to share the Word of God. It made my mother very pleased, I think. But it went far beyond anything familial, or mortal. It was a Divine calling. She understood that."

Nick watched Father Antonio become enraptured with his memories. "There was something rare about my mother," he continued. "She was as close to God as any living person I have ever known. She literally glowed from it, from inside, as though she was in constant, silent communion with her Divine Maker. Of course she knew the Holy Bible backwards and forwards, but she had more than knowledge of the Word, she had ... something that may be difficult for you to understand. She had in her, the Holy Spirit."

You're right, thought Nick. *I have no idea what that means.* "Is she pleased with your post in Tenerife," asked Nick. "And your work in the Middle East?"

"I hope so." Father Antonio fell silent. "She's been called back to God."

Now what does that *mean?* wondered Nick in a moment of silence. "Oh," he said. "I'm sorry to hear."

"That is the way it sometimes is, my son. He calls the best among us back to Him early. Too soon."

I should be here for a damn long time then, thought Nick.

The priest was not all that much older than Nick, maybe 40, and it was strange to hear himself called *my son.* Even his own father hadn't used those particular words, that Nick could recall at any rate. He thought to comment on it, but rather let silence fall between them, in respect for Father Antonio's loss. After a while Nick offered up a change of subject.

"So, Father, let me ask you a question, if I may. It's a ... religious ... question."

The priest laughed. "That is what I do best."

"Right," said Nick. "So... what do you know about a group of Christians called the Gnostics?"

"Why are you asking?" Father Antonio seemed startled.

"Well, I guess because you're the only priest I know. Who happens to be sitting next to me on an airplane. With two hours still to go to Cairo."

"No, I mean, what is your interest in the Gnostics?" asked Father Antonio.

120

"Purely academic," replied Nick. "Something I came across, related to work."

"Well, there is very little to know, as far as I understand," replied Father Antonio. "Let's see... the Gnostics were one of many independent off-shoots of the Catholic Church, 200 years after the time of Christ. Like many heretics of their age, they wanted to take control, and put the Word of God into their own hands. They went so far as to manufacture their own truths and place them *before* the words of the Apostles themselves! They refused to be governed by the authority of the Church. Like many other radicals, their beliefs had no substance. They defied God by scorning the Church, and consequently disappeared from the face of the earth."

"Is that right?"

"Worse." Father Antonio continued in an instructive tone of voice. "The Gnostics taught people that they could find their *own way* to God, and to salvation. But the position of the Church, as dictated by Jesus directly to his disciple Peter, is the understanding that there is only one Church, One God, One Law. Jesus is the *one* savior. Through Him *alone* can we enter the kingdom of God. Anything outside of the one true Church delivers people from the hands of our Savior, straight into the pits of Damnation. This is all anyone really needs to know."

Nick imagined the priest at his pulpit, consumed with his passion, rousing his flock into a fervor. "When people lay aside their egos," continued the priest, "and put their lives into the hands of Jesus, our Savior, everything else falls away. Fear, greed, hate, arrogance. These were the accouterments of the Gnostics."

"The Church seems to have created a hierarchy of incontrovertible power," suggested Nick.

"That is the way it is," stated the priest.

"Doesn't that then subjugate all of human kind to powerlessness and futility?" asked Nick. "Won't your religion, your world view, always require helpless people needing the church?"

"A Doubting Thomas, are you?" laughed Father Antonio. "Such questioning must surely make you a good barrister."

"Still, I am curious. Is there nothing on earth people can ever do to save themselves? Or help themselves?"

"And Jesus sayeth unto him, I am the way, the truth, and the light. John 14, verse 6," quoted the priest. *"No one cometh unto the Father, but by me."*

Katherine had woken during the conversation and was now glaring at her husband in silence. She believed, in the deep recesses of her mind, that Nick would burn in the firey pits of Hell forever for arguing with a priest.

But Nick was not about to be diverted from his point. There was a new anger and a power in his voice that was intoxicating. Nick continued, emboldened by the drug of self-expression. Outside of the courtroom, Nick was the model of reserved British decorum. A quiet part of Nick that had been polite and enduring for decades, was now finding a voice. A loud one.

"Seems to me as though you have just removed personal authority from the individual," Nick argued. "And in one fell swoop created a mass of mindless, hopeless, helpless sheep. *And* you have set a standard for political and social domination. Is *that* the intention of your Savior? It seems rather that you have just propagated a doctrine that serves, above all else, *the Church.*"

"You would have them save *themselves?"* Father Antonio argued. "That would be like the blind leading the blind! The Holy Bible says there is One Word. It doesn't tell people to run around and find their own path to God. No! God loves us too much for that. So He has given us a map. All we have to do is obey. And anyone who has the arrogance to think that he can rise above God's law is destined, my dear boy, to wander lost in this world, void of love and light and direction. And remember this: The Church is God. And God is the Church."

Nick was about to respond when Katherine – in an unusually quite tone – said, "Nick. Don't you want to drop this?"

Nick looked at his wife with an uncommon fire in his eye. It almost startled her. "Yes," he snapped. "I do." Nick turned to the priest. "My apologies." Then he rose to find the restroom.

Katherine watched her husband disappear in the front of the plane. She sat in an uncomfortable silence with the priest. Part of her wanted to blurt out an apology for Nick. "Nick has a brilliant mind," she said finally, quietly. The priest did not respond but smiled at her knowingly. *Your husband is wrong,* Katherine heard the priest saying in her imagination. *And he is going to burn in the fiery pits of Hell forever.*

122

When Nick returned, visibly uncomfortable, Father Antonio rose and patted him on the shoulder. "Excuse me, will you? I think I'll take a little break myself."

Nick was talking to Katherine long before the priest was out of earshot. "The priest's argument is the voice of fear," he said. "The voice of fear and domination that has been imposed upon the world for nearly 2,000 years. I'm starting to believe that the Gnostics were obliterated because they were feared and hated by the hierarchy of the church, who set *themselves* up as divine authority to rule over everyone."

"What makes you say that?" asked Katherine. "What makes you think that the Gnostics didn't disappear just because their movement was just too small and too radical."

"Isn't the *one thing* the early Christian leaders would fear more than anything," speculated Nick, "was that the common man might find his *own* way to God? Don't you think that is why they destroyed the Gnostic writings? Isn't the message of the so-called right thinking church that if something is different, it's bad, and it must be destroyed? Can you count, Katherine, do you know the number of people, the many cultures, who have suffered under the banner of holy righteousness, all in the name of God, just because they were *different?*"

"The Church does not destroy people. It saves them," retorted Katherine, harkening back to voices from her youth.

"No. Religious institutions have tromped across the globe since the beginnings of Christianity, bending people to their will. And this is the precedent they've set for the future. A precedent of hate, prejudice, judgment and fear."

"Alright, Nick. I see your point. So let's just drop this, shall we?"

"While we're at it, let's talk about The Spanish Inquisition, The Crusades, The Salem Witch Trials, Joan of Arc. The list of Christian brutality and oppression goes on and on and on."

"Nick!" Katherine grabbed her husband on the arm. "Stop it!"

He shook loose his arm. "Is it so awful, so sinful, to disagree?" Nick asked. "If the priest is absolutely right, he has nothing to fear from exploring a different opinion, now does he?"

"Nick, I don't think you heard him. All he was saying is that if you believe in God, you will be forgiven for your sins, and saved. Can't you just leave it at that?"

"No, he wasn't. Just listen to yourself for a second, Katherine," pressed Nick. "You don't believe in all that rubbish any more than I do. How come, sitting in front of a priest you're all of a sudden pretending to be a good Catholic lamb, content in the flock. Why is that?"

"I'm not pretending. I'm just trying to be the tiniest bit respectful. You might give it a try."

"No. You're pretending. And you're good at it, Katherine. About a lot of things."

Katherine ignored his last comment. "What makes you think you know what I believe in?"

"Because I've heard you ridicule Catholicism countless times, that's how."

"Does that mean I don't believe in God?" Katherine snapped. "No. It doesn't."

"You certainly don't believe in hell-fire and damnation. And that's the real truth for you. Whether you're sitting by a priest, in a church, in a restaurant or in a water closet. And you know that, Katherine. You know it. And you, of all people, should have the courage to live it. Wherever you are."

"Don't lecture me Nick!" Katherine snapped. "You have judged for yourself and decided what's right, haven't you? If you stop lecturing and listen for one second, you could hear. You have thoughts from your head, and others quite different, from your heart. There are childhood thoughts and angry thoughts and grown up, logical thoughts. And they're all different. And yet they're all true. And sometimes they rattle around in your head – my head – all at the same time!"

Katherine was close to tears now, torn between what she learned as a child and what she knew as an adult, forced to face the contradictions, and hurting somewhere deep inside because Nick had called her integrity into question.

They both looked up to find the priest standing over them, watching, a moral intruder and judge to their conflict.

"Miss Katherine," offered Father Antonio. "You hold many opposing thoughts in your mind, all at the same time." The priest reached across Nick and gently laid his hand on Katherine's. "It will rip you apart, child, if you do not find some peace within yourself."

Nick glared at the priest. He *did* understand the battle between faith and intellect that Katherine was trying to resolve.

"Perhaps the three of us can put away our conflicts for now," offered Father Antonio, "and just allow the differences – between each other and within ourselves."

"Well, Father," said Nick. "That sounds quite reasonable, seeing as I've managed to upset both of you." Even though Father Antonio got in the last jab, Nick smiled broadly and easily.

"I offer you my apologies," said the priest. "The path I've chosen is a difficult one. It is not for everyone."

"It's my fault, Father. I got carried away. Please, accept my apology." Nick contained his scorn behind a smile, swallowed his pride, and silently wondered why he cared so vehemently about the unspoken voice of a small, long-forgotten, band of Christians.

"Enough said, then," responded Father Antonio.

Nick put his arm around Katherine and she rested her head on his shoulder. Instant forgiveness. More than forgiveness: confidence that they'd work this out. As they'd worked out most everything in the nearly 15 years they'd been together. Katherine was also showing Father Antonio that, in the end, she and Nick were united. Nick kissed her forehead and said a little prayer of thanks to the God he didn't believe in.

Cairo, Egypt

They landed without further incident in Cairo, said stiff, polite good-byes to Father Antonio, and made their way through Customs without so much as a sideways glance. *Maybe the worst is behind us,* Nick mused hopefully, knowing in his heart it wasn't true.

Bone weary, Nick found a little booth where he could exchange American dollars for Egyptian pounds. They left with thick stacks of strangely-color money and a pocketful of golden coins, the value of which they would have to calculate in their heads every time they made a purchase.

I love this part, thought Katherine, following Nick into the warm night air. It was a short-lived sentiment.

Three different cab drivers descended upon them as they left the terminal. Each one calling to them in turn, offering a ride into the city. "Best price. You come with me, yes?" "This way, this way." "You from America? I love America." On it went, until Nick and Katherine were paralyzed with indecision. They followed the one driver who, talking cheerfully, simply grabbed their bags from their hands and headed for his car.

The cab ride from the airport to their hotel turned into a frightful excursion. Through some combination of terror and exhaustion, Katherine didn't say a word the whole time. Rather, she held onto the door handle with one hand, and to Nick with the other, until her knuckles hurt. The driver, who spoke fairly good English, raced along the roadway at a startling clip. Traffic became increasingly congested as they reached the city core, but that didn't seem to bother Harvey one little bit. Or slow him down much, either.

The driver's real name was Harbeh, but realizing that they were overwhelmed American tourists he suggested that they call him Harvey instead. *He's done this before,* thought Nick. *Many times.* The more gracious the cabbie was, and the easier he made their startling entrée into the city – the bigger the tip. And the more likely he could hire them for their entire stay, at the day rate.

The beat-up cab he drove – with its loose springs, torn seats, scrapes and dents – attested to his experience as one of the thousands of competing cabbies in Cairo. It attested to the highly-coveted passengers, the inflated rates, the tips, the streets where he sometimes got lost, the long, sweltering days, wrestling fares from other drivers, dodging cars and people and goats, and the constant sound of beeping horns that never left his head, even when he slept.

At the Shepheard's hotel Katherine handed Harvey a bundle of Egyptian pounds as she leapt out if the cab, thankful to be alive. She handed another several bills to the doorman who collected their luggage. That doorman would come to know Katherine, watch for her at the end of days, smile and say her name when he held the door for her. He was a tall black man, from the Sudan, with red shot through his eyes.

126

Does he consider himself lucky? wondered Katherine at the man's quiet graciousness. *Or does he consider himself doomed, out of step with his true destiny? Maybe he's a son of kings, cast into service by unlucky fate. Perhaps he comes from a long line of poverty and has raised himself to higher ground.* Katherine would never know.

What Katherine did know was that he had a young daughter who used a cane, because she saw them together one day as they left the hotel hand-in-hand. The girl called him "Papa Mine," and he responded with a smile that put the sun to shame.

Of the doorman, Katherine also knew that the way he carried himself – with calm and constant dignity – somehow made her feel humble.

Settled into their hotel room for the night, Katherine sat at a small dressing table and ran a brush through her hair. "My lord, what a day. I can hardly believe all that happened since we left New York."

"We were lucky today," replied Nick. "Extremely lucky."

"And I can't believe you picked a fight with a priest. And me, for that matter."

"I can't apologize to you for being right, Katherine. I won't do it."

A sudden silence marked the space between them.

"Though I will say I never should have gotten into it with Father Antonio." Nick rubbed his tired eyes. "I ought to have known better."

"You know you're impossible to measure up to."

I hate to hear that, thought Nick. As a young man he had often wondered why it was so easy for him to be good, to be steady. His whole family was always the best, clearest, smartest. Nick wondered back then if there was anything really interesting inside of him, interesting enough to make him bad once in awhile.

"I understand the voices in your head, darling. And I'm sorry." Nick wrapped his arms around her and pulled her close, knowing she would let go first.

"I had no idea there was such a place on earth," exclaimed Katherine the next day. She was jostled backed and forth, lurched forward and back, and bounced up and down, as her cab nearly scraped every single car in its proximity. Traffic seemed to be one great big pinball game of speed, agility and raw audacity. Harvey had shown up first thing in the morning and took her and Nick in his speeding taxi through the busy downtown core, past the slums and into the suburbs of Cairo.

Katherine rolled down the back seat window and held up her camera. There were cars, people, goats, carts and bicycles all sharing the streets at the same time in a system organized only on mayhem and courage. Horns and bells and shouts mixed with the engines of busses and cars, creating an urgent and undulating concerto blaring in the streets.

Through the lens of her camera, Katherine framed a young man on a bike. He looked to be about 16, and was delivering pita bread to some unknown destination. The bread was piled precariously high on a long pallet which the boy balanced on his head. He made his way slowly through the stream of erratic, rushing automobiles, chiming a little bell as he went. The look she captured in his face was one of calm concentration – of a young man doing honest, rightful work to earn his daily wages – a beautiful portrait of balance and grace in a chaotic world.

Suddenly Katherine heard something new above the cars and horns and people. A lovely, compelling call, a moan of sorts, came across the air. "What is that?" she asked the taxi driver.

"The *muezzin*," he replied. "A holy man. He climbs the minaret, the tower on the nearby mosque. See – over there." Harvey pointed out the window. Rising a block away, above the other buildings, Katherine and Nick could just barely see a spire, tapering to a point, with a spiral staircase leading to its pinnacle.

"That is the el-Hussein Mosque," said Harvey. "One of the holiest places in the city."

"What does el-Hussein mean?" asked Katherine.

"El-Hussein is the son of the holy prophet, Muhanna," explained Harvey. "And he is buried in that mosque. It is a very holy place to be. Many go to worship there."

"And the *muezzin*, what does he do?" asked Katherine.

"The *muezzin* climbs to the minaret to call the people to prayer. At all the mosques in all of Islam, this happens, five times a day."

"Where is Islam, exactly?" asked Katherine.

The driver scowled at her, confused. "It is everywhere. It is everywhere Muslims are. In Egypt, and India, Saudi Arabia, Libya, all around us. Even as far away as Asia. All over the world."

"Oh." Katherine sat back in her seat. "I guess I didn't know that."

They sat in silence the rest of the way as the clustered city gave way to shops and homes in the expansive suburban area of Cairo. Harvey parked the cab in the circular driveway of a sprawling home that overlooked the city.

Nick counted out Egyptian pounds to pay the driver. "Stay here for a few minutes, will you?" he asked, handing Harvey another 10-pound note. "We may be needing your services again in very short order." Nick had no idea what they might find at Etienne's house, or how they might be received.

Katherine rang the doorbell and then immediately began pounding on the door. Her heart was racing as she saw a figure approach through the oval glass in the door. Closer and larger the image grew.

Then the door opened and there stood Etienne Desonia, in the flesh, looking virtually the same as he did the last time they parted, ten years before. As much as she'd anticipated this, she was still startled to see his face.

He stared at her a long moment, saying nothing. "Katherine!" He grabbed her to him and wrapped his arms around her, nearly knocking her off her feet. When he felt her stiffen in his arms, he stepped back, grinned widely and sized her up. To Etienne, she looked a little bit older, tired, and unnervingly beautiful.

"So, Etienne, where the hell is my goddamn Knife?" snapped Katherine.

"What?"

Katherine pushed her way past him and he watched her engulf his foyer in her anger and her beauty. "I want the dagger, Etienne. I want it back and I want it now." To Etienne's eyes, Katherine was stunning. She was tall and slender, but slightly smaller than he remembered her, thinner maybe, depleted somehow. Her perfectly-coiffed brown hair was rolled off her face in the fashion of the time and fell to her shoulders. Her eyes were on fire and dazzled him to the bone. They were translucent green, clear, as if lit from behind. Though he seemed to remember them the hue of deep jade, he still felt as if he could swim right into her eyes and live there.

Etienne took that entire bundle of feelings – hating himself for having them – and tucked them back where they belonged, in a dark little torture chamber at the bottom of his heart.

Etienne turned to Katherine. "Not, *Hello Etienne*. Not, *How are you, Etienne?* Not, *Good to see you, Etienne?* Must the first words of out your mouth be angry?"

Most women Etienne knew, and Nick for that matter, wouldn't dare be caught saying a swear word. But not Katherine Spencer. She spent too much time in college with unruly boys like Etienne, Nick and her brother, Ben. She didn't give much of a damn about being proper, or to concern herself with what other people might think of her. She just did whatever it was she wanted to do.

Of course, she paid the price for it in polite society. She had few friends, as most women in her circle were busy rearing children. These women wouldn't cuss to save their lives, and never dreamed of something as audacious and pedestrian as owning a business.

Etienne knew Katherine regretted her impetuousness from time to time. And he knew she simply could not stop herself. He might have smiled at her if he wasn't so annoyed with her, and so thoroughly confused.

And there stands Nick, right beside her, thought Etienne, silently. *As though his presence validates and legitimizes every outrageous thing she has ever done or ever will do. I hate that about them. Especially Nick. He, at least, should know better.*

"Etienne, don't play with me. Just hand over the Knife," demanded Katherine.

"Katherine, Nick, please come in," said Etienne, warmer than he felt at the moment. "And tell me what the devil you're talking about."

Nick at least had the good manners to shake Etienne's hand. "Good to see you again, old boy," Nick said. He kept talking as they
130

made their way into the living room. "Sorry it's under such difficult circumstances, of course. This whole business has been rather nasty from the start, though, hasn't it? I do hope we can get it all straightened out. We've got a sticky situation back in the States."

"With Hugo Nelson, I assume." Etienne having adjusted to their unexpected appearance, was starting to put the pieces together in his mind.

"Damn right with Hugo Nelson," snapped Katherine. "You can't imagine how angry he's going to be. Or to what lengths he'll go to get what he traded for. Cheating Hugo Nelson was stupid, Etienne. It was plain damn stupid. And cheating me... cheating me was just plain damn mean."

"I didn't cheat Hugo Nelson, Katherine. Or you for that matter. If you'll please do me the courtesy of calming yourself down for a minute..."

Jesus, Etienne, thought Nick, rolling his eyes. *Telling her to calm down is just going to make her madder.*

"Just give me the damned Knife!" yelled Katherine.

"I don't *have* the damned Knife!" Etienne yelled back.

None of them knew quite what to say next. If Katherine didn't have the Knife, and Etienne didn't have the Knife, *where,* they all wondered, *was the damned Knife?*

"Let's think this through," said Etienne, offering them a seat in his living room, pouring them coffee. "And before you get all huffy with me again, Katherine, let me tell you, you have no idea what I've been through the past seven days. The last two, in fact, trying – around the clock – to find *you.*"

Katherine crossed her legs and lit a cigarette. Nick found a nearby ashtray and put it on the end table next to her chair.

"The knife was in the crate when it pulled out of port in Cairo," said Etienne. "I personally supervised the packing and loading of the knife and the crate. They were never out of my sight."

"So it must have been intercepted somewhere between Cairo and New York," offered Nick. "But who knew it was there?"

A distant look crossed Etienne's face for just a moment. "The potter," he said. "He was the only one."

"Who's the potter?" asked Katherine.

"I hired a local craftsman, a potter from Khan el-Khalili, to replicate the statue of Isis, carve the hiding place, create the removable base and seal the dagger inside. He's the only one who knew."

"Do you suppose he somehow intercepted the shipment, in Alexandria, perhaps?" speculated Nick. "And stole the dagger back?"

"No," said Etienne. "I'm certain he did not."

"How do you know for sure?" asked Katherine.

"Because he was the one who turned me into the Department of Antiquities, here in Cairo, that's why. Where I spent five miserable days denying any knowledge of the Knife. Not that they believed me for one second, of course."

"Holy Jesus," said Nick. "That explains the ..." his voice trailed off. Etienne shifted uncomfortably for a moment. On his face and arms, Etienne still wore a few, fading bruises of Cato Nafarah's friendly conversations.

"The question is," said Etienne, changing the subject, "what happened to the Knife between here and New York? Perhaps the potter, failing to extract money from the government for his information, then sold that same information to someone else. Perhaps he knew someone who trades on the Black Market. And that person could have boarded the ship in Alexandria and stolen the knife. Or perhaps someone else took it after it arrived in New York."

"Do you know this potter, Etienne?" asked Katherine. "Can you find him again?"

A distant smile crossed Etienne's bruised and clouded face. "Finding things, including people, is what I do."

"You're sure the potter is the key, then, to where the Knife is?" asked Nick.

"Well, let's think about that for a moment," said Etienne. "Who else knew? Me, you, Katherine, and Hugo Nelson, right? Who else?"

Etienne and Nick turned to Katherine. "No one," she said. "Really. I didn't tell a soul."

"Then the potter is our only lead," said Etienne. He stood up. He had telephone calls to make. "Where are you staying?"

"The Shepheard's, downtown," said Nick.

"I'll meet you there in the morning, for breakfast," said Etienne. "Nine o'clock. In the mean time, I'll make some calls. This potter has a reputation – not always a good one – at the great bizarre of Khan el-Khalili. We'll go there together, tomorrow, to squeeze him out."

Katherine stubbed out her cigarette. "Why can't we just go *now*?" she asked.

"Patience," said Etienne, smiling at her. "We'll catch this little bird. We just have to put out some sugar. And let him come to us."

"What the hell does that mean?" asked Katherine.

"You'll see," said Etienne. "Tomorrow."

Katherine scowled at him. "Trust me," said Etienne. "Now then, shall I give you a ride back into town?"

"Not at all," said Nick. "We've got a taxi waiting outside."

Katherine left uneasy, not quite ready to go, somehow wanting something else, something unnamable. She and Nick got back into their waiting cab and sped back into the heart of the city.

The next morning, Etienne found himself sitting in the lobby of The Shepheard's, the grandest hotel in Cairo, waiting for his tardy friends. The Shepheard's had been occupied by British Intelligence during the war, but over the past two years had been restored to its original opulence and grace. The memory of the military's presence there merely gave it an added air of mystery and importance.

This particular morning, as usual, the lobby was bustling with people. Etienne was sharing a davenport with a gentleman in an immaculately pressed, white linen suit, a leather briefcase at his side. Etienne ignored the man in deference to his mind's own wanderings. Clouds had begun to gather outside and he began to think of rain. Rain always took Etienne to thoughts of Katherine. It was raining when he met her, at Oxford, in a café, many years before.

Oxford, England 1936

He noticed her right away. Even though the café was crowded and noisy, Etienne noticed her. Who was this woman, relaxed like a cat, in her own personal, over-sized, over-stuffed chair? She was reading a book, like many students who frequented this place after classes to study. She sipped hot tea, wrapping ten long, slender fingers around the cup, blowing into it occasionally to feel the hot steam on her face. It seemed to please her. She looked up from time to time, toward the clock on the wall, and then to the front door, and back to her tea. She was waiting for someone.

The last time she looked around the room, however, she didn't look back at her book. She looked straight at Etienne. He returned to his newspaper – the newspaper he hadn't read one single word of in 20 minutes. He'd spent those 20 minutes thinking about the rain, thinking about this woman in the rain, thinking about rushing through the rain to meet her. He wanted to walk with this woman in the rain.

Who was she and where was she from? How he might meet her? He looked up to find his cup of coffee and saw her watching him again. This time he met her gaze. A warm brush of intimacy painted an invisible bridge across the room straight from her to him. Etienne held onto it, captivated.

Just then his best friend, Nick, showed up out of nowhere and kissed the woman on the cheek. Etienne could not quite understand what he was seeing. She was his. And Nick was kissing her. Then Nick walked across the room to Etienne and collected him up like chattel. They walked toward the woman as though it was the most natural thing in the world. Etienne hated that. It made him want to holler out loud. Instead, he smiled as Nick introduced them.

"So *this* is the woman who stole my friend's heart, and time and reason," said Etienne as he shook her hand. She responded as though nothing had ever happened. But of course, nothing *had* happened. It was all in his imagination.

"I say there. Might you pass the ashtray?"

"I'm sorry?" Etienne was startled out of his memories.

The gentleman in the linen suit pointed to the ashtray on the end of the coffee table. "The ashtray, if you don't mind." He held up a burning cigarette.

134

"Oh yes, certainly," said Etienne, obliging.

"Dreadful traffic you've got here in Cairo," said the man, with a highbrow American accent.

"Yes," said Etienne, distracted from the comfort of his private thoughts.

"Maniacal really. Every man, woman and child for himself, it seems to me," said the man.

Etienne found something rather compelling about the man, though he couldn't quite name what it was. "You're from America?" he asked.

The man nodded. "Does it rain often in Cairo?" he asked. "I expected nothing but sun and heat, quite frankly."

"*Oui*. It's rare," said Etienne, thinking again of Katherine. *I never would have made her wait for me while I avoided a storm. I would have walked through a deluge if she were on the other side.* "But don't expect it to last for long. The rain will come and go in the winter months, but usually it comes fast and heavy and leaves very quickly."

Etienne let himself be distracted from his thoughts, most recently his frustration that Katherine couldn't bother herself to be on time. "So you're in Cairo on business?" he asked. "Or pleasure?"

The man gave Etienne a calculating look that caused a chill to run up his spine. "Both, " he said. "Absolutely. Yes, both."

Just then the doors to the lift swung open. The operator held the doors for Katherine and Nick as they made their way to the lobby. They were looking weary and a little overwhelmed. *Cairo can do that to a person,* thought Etienne, standing. "I see my friends have finally arrived," he said to the gentleman. "*Au revoir*. Enjoy your time in Cairo."

"I intend to. Absolutely."

Etienne made his way toward Katherine and Nick, but Katherine walked right past him without even saying hello. Etienne stood beside Nick, and together they watched her cross the lobby.

The gentleman on the davenport stubbed out his cigarette and looked up at Katherine. His legs were crossed casually, as if he hadn't a care in the world.

"What are you doing in Cairo?" asked Katherine.

"Looking for you, my dear," replied Hugo Nelson. "Looking for you."

10

A NEW DEAL

Jesus said, "Do not lie, and do not do what you hate, because all things are disclosed before heaven. For there is nothing hidden that will not be revealed, and there is nothing covered that will remain undisclosed."
— Saying 6, Gospel of Thomas

Hugo Nelson led the group into the elegant restaurant of the Shepheard's Hotel. He had prearranged a secluded table in the far back of the room. As soon as they were all seated, Katherine began her explanation.

"The Knife was not in the shipment," she stated, with nothing better to tell him than the truth. "Nick and I came to Egypt to find it." Nelson watched her with a casual arrogance while she talked at a rapid clip. "And we will. With Etienne's help. I promise you. We already have a lead: the potter who carved the statue to hide the Knife. Etienne thinks —"

Nelson cleared his throat. "You needn't bother, my dear. I have the Knife."

Katherine, Nick and Etienne looked at him in stunned silence. Finally, shaking her head in disbelief, Katherine said, "You *what?*"

"I have the Knife." Nelson placed his napkin across his lap in an elegant gesture, and signaled for the waiter. "Turkish coffee, please."

"How on earth —?" began Etienne.

Nelson looked at him condescendingly. "My dear man, you can't possibly believe that I would leave such a magnificent artifact in the hands of amateurs." Katherine flushed with anger. "Besides," said Nelson. "I just couldn't wait to see it for myself. So I took it."

"But how?" pressed Etienne.

A waiter appeared with coffee, which he poured into four tall, glass cups held in woven frames of copper, with looped handles. He set on each cup on a delicate lace doily. Etienne ordered eggs and fruit for all of them, with fresh bread and jam. Then Nelson gestured the waiter away.

"Why didn't you tell me?" demanded Katherine. "We came all the way to Egypt to look for the damned thing."

"That's what I was counting on." Nelson glanced at Etienne.

"I don't understand," said Katherine, shaking her head.

"It's complicated." Nelson gave her a half smile, half smirk that told her he had no intention of explaining himself.

"So, show us the Knife," said Etienne, crossing his arms over his chest.

Nelson narrowed his eyes. "You don't think I'd be crazy enough to bring it with me, do you?" he replied.

Etienne scanned the room. "Yes, I do."

"You think I just walked into this hotel with a priceless, *illegal* artifact in my briefcase?" The soft tinkling of plates and silverware mixed with light conversation and floated through the restaurant.

"*Oui.*" Etienne's eyes were now riveted on Nelson. Nelson laughed. But when he picked up his briefcase and laid it on the table, between his coffee and a bowl of sugar, nobody moved.

He's bluffing, thought Nick. *He couldn't possibly have the Knife in that briefcase. He wouldn't dare.* Nick sat back in his seat. *It's probably full of money...*

A hush fell on the group as Nelson dialed combination for three separate locks and sprung the latches. He smiled into the briefcase as he lifted the lid with a slow, deliberate relish. Then he moved his gaze to Katherine, who was staring at the case as if only she and it existed in the world. Nelson calmly spun the case around for everyone at the table to see. Forged 2,000 years before, by the finest craftsmen of the Roman Empire, at the height of its glory, as a gift of devotion to the most powerful woman in the world: The Egyptian Knife of the Asps.

Katherine involuntarily covered her heart with her hands. Even in the subdued lighting of the restaurant, the dagger and its sheath were of such startling brilliance that Katherine had to blink several times to believe what she was seeing. She was overcome with its beauty, and the doomed love it represented.

Katherine's eyes were drawn first to the gems that made the heads of two snakes. They were dazzling: a ruby and emerald, both so exquisite, so flawless, that they seemed to have been dug from the deepest mysteries of earth and time. The snakes were wrapped around the hilt of the dagger, their bodies molded from gold, their skin etched in silver and textured with hundreds of perfect little diamonds.

The thin gold blade gleamed brilliantly, reflecting the light from the chandelier above them. In contrast to the handle, it had no markings and not a single flaw. Its lines were perfectly smooth, as though it was formed through fire and light, untouched by hands of mortal man. Resting next the knife, in folds of blue velvet, was the sheath, inlaid with carvings and gems so fine, so precise, as to baffle the imagination.

"You can have it for yourself," announced Nelson, closing the lid and snapping shut the latches. "Frankly, I'm more interested in the codices." He returned the case to the floor.

Katherine and Nick were stunned into silence. But Etienne had seen the Knife, had owned the Knife, and had other concerns on his mind. "*Codices?*" he asked, stressing the plural. His expression turned serious. *If Nelson knows there are more manuscripts, and has decided that he wants the entire collection,* thought Etienne, *things are going to go badly.*

Nelson turned to Etienne. "There are 12 *other* codices floating around on the Black Market. I don't believe the Egyptians realize what they've got a hold of."

"Do *you?*" asked Etienne.

My God, thought Katherine. *Etienne is so sure of himself.*

Nelson stared at Etienne for what seemed a long time. Nobody moved. Nobody said a word. "Thirteen leather-bound manuscripts," Nelson finally said. "Dating from the fourth century A.D., transcriptions of earlier, Greek documents, the earliest known writings that were bound like books, rather than written in scrolls." Nelson paused to add a spoonful of sugar to his coffee and to take a delicate sip. "Early Christian writings," he continued. "Gibberish, mostly. Interesting enough from an archaeological standpoint, however."

Nelson lowered his voice and made a command of his desire. "I want them all."

"Why did you let Katherine ship your codex to me, if you wanted to keep it all along?" asked Etienne.

"Good question," replied Nelson.

"Well?" pressed Etienne.

Nelson studied Etienne for a moment. "You were the missing link."

"I beg your pardon?" said Etienne.

"You are the one person who can deliver the rest of the manuscripts to me."

"You know that about me, do you?"

"I do now. Now, I know a great deal about you."

"Then you know that I'd rather have the codices than the Knife. Which is why I offered the trade in the first place."

"Yes." Nelson allowed himself a laugh. "But you don't know about the million dollars, yet."

"Million dollars?" asked Katherine, lighting a cigarette.

Nelson glanced over at her and then returned his attention to Etienne. "But there is something I must know first," he said, settling in with his coffee. "Tell me about the Knife of the Asps. It's a magnificent piece. I must know: where did you find it?"

"It's a long, boring story," said Etienne, shaking his head. "You really wouldn't care."

"Yes, I would care."

Etienne set his eyes on Nelson. "You only think you would."

"No," said Nelson, with a humorless expression. "I *know* I would. Every single detail."

Etienne sighed.

"Tell us Etienne," said Katherine, touching him on the arm.

"Well, get comfortable then," grumbled Etienne. "It's a long story." Etienne turned his attention solely to Katherine and Nick, as if Nelson wasn't even in the room. "I have, of all people, Adolph Hitler to thank for it."

Katherine and Nick looked at each other, scowls drawn across their faces.

Etienne continued. "I had gone underground in Egypt as part of the French Resistance during the war. We were fighting the *Afrika Korps* – an unstoppable force led by Rommel, Hitler's field marshal in North Africa. I joined a covert team of British SAS Raiders assigned to sabotage their ground operations."

"Good lord, Etienne," said Katherine. "I had no idea you were in the Resistance. We always assumed you were in France. Safe."

"I *was* in France, fighting. Until the Occupation. In 1940, I went to Cairo. By 1942, everyone there was convinced that Rommel's forces would soon occupy Alexandria. Rommel seemed to know every move the British made, before they made it. We nicknamed him, *The Desert Fox*. He was brilliant, unnervingly brilliant. British Intelligence was searching madly through Cairo for someone they called 'Rommel's Spy,' convinced that critical, strategic information was being leaked to the Nazis."

"So you were in Cairo, looking for this spy?"

"No." Etienne paused. *How far do I want to take them? How far into those memories do I want to take myself?*

"Etienne?"

"I was sent on different sorts of missions."

"Different sorts? What kind of 'different sorts'?"

"Well, one in particular, was to blow up a bunker in western Egypt, in a place called the Qattara Depression. This valley was considered impassable. I can tell you, it was Hell. Mountains rise straight up about a thousand feet into the sky. Huge salt-bogs on desert floor swallow vehicles whole, like quicksand. Add to all that, it was heavily guarded by enemy forces – on land and by air."

"Tell me you didn't go there, Etienne," stated Katherine.

Don't you know me? thought Etienne sadly. *Have you forgotten me entirely?* Sighing, he continued. "We believed that a small group of

141

men could make it through on foot, if we carried only explosives and water. And the most minimal food rations. Hunger was the least of our worries. We'd have to pass through 30 miles of scorching heat, sniper fire and strafing from enemy aircraft."

"Why? Why would you do such a crazy thing?"

"Nobody wanted to be there, Katherine. But everyone wanted to stop Hitler. Even if we died in the process." Etienne regretted his words when he saw the look on Katherine's face. But unable to take them back, he moved further into his story. "The bunker was critically important to Rommel's troops. Reports from British Intelligence indicated that the bunker housed weapons, ammunition, maps, food and supplies and – most importantly – vast stores of water. We *had* to go. The real trick would be to find it, in 11,000 square miles of nothing but desert, in the dark."

"Did you? Find it, I mean?" asked Nick.

"With nothing more complicated than a stolen map and a mine sweeper. The bunker was built inside the wall of a cliff. The sweeper picked up the thick metal doors, and we found the entrance veiled under a layer of desert camouflage."

"We who?" asked Katherine. "A group of soldiers?"

"Well, not exactly *a group*."

"Then who, exactly?"

"There were four of us – Wilson, François, Anderson and me. I can tell you, we were under-informed and overly enthusiastic." Etienne looked at Nick. "We miscalculated the amount of explosives we needed. Intelligence really had no idea how much live ammo was in that building. Every last bit of it ignited. We blew the hell out of the bunker, lost all the maps, letters and official communiqués, and killed every living person, plant and animal in a hundred-yard radius. God, we killed Wilson, too. It was awful." Etienne paused for a long time. His companions had the grace and consideration to stay quiet.

"We also exposed a secret tunnel," continued Etienne. "There was a tunnel leading from the bunker deep into the heart of the cliff. When the dust settled, we discovered a chamber at the end of that tunnel. In that chamber were four dead Italian soldiers, killed by the blast, six crates of counterfeit British pounds – billions, which they planned to use to disrupt the British economy, and one padlocked chest. Inside that chest was the Knife of the Asps, complete with papers authenticating it to the year 33 B.C. The money, we turned over to the authorities. The Knife, we kept."

"Then what happened?" asked Katherine, her voice low.

"François and Anderson were killed eventually, in different places and horrible circumstances, before the war finally ended. *How I survived it all,* thought Etienne silently, as he always did when he thought of the war, *and they did not, is beyond my understanding.* "They were good men, with families. They deserved to return home."

"Indeed," said Nick, patting his friend on the shoulder. "They all did."

Etienne looked into Katherine's eyes, feeling as though he had misspoken, had said too much. She stared back at him blankly. "The Knife remained in my possession for the years following the war," continued Etienne. "I came to think of it as a rainy day contingency, an artifact to do something good with one day." The Knife of the Asps had become even more to Etienne, but he would not speak about that. It became a memory, a symbol of those that were lost, of those he missed, of those that were left behind.

"Fascinating," said Nelson, loudly. "That is one helluva story." Etienne regretted that his memories, his personal story, would become part of Nelson's bragging arsenal.

A waiter in a starched white tunic quietly appeared with breakfast, set on dishes of fine bone china. Each person's plate was filled with scrambled eggs, toast and a half tomato, broiled and topped with sprinkles of hard cheese. The group was silent as the waiter meticulously placed down choices of butter, jam and marmalade in silver dishes. A platter piled high with fresh fruit – mango, pineapple, sliced pears, figs – was set in the middle of the table, for sharing. The waiter then bowed and left them to their own company.

"So," began Nelson, looking over his food. "I'll give you a million dollars to recover the other 12 manuscripts and turn them all over to me. In addition, I'll give you back the Knife of the Asps."

"I don't care about your money," replied Etienne. "But you still owe Mrs. Spencer 200,000 dollars. Half of which is mine. We've delivered our end of the bargain." Etienne took a slow sip of his coffee. "I say you pay up, shake hands and bid us all *au revoir.*"

"And the other manuscripts?" smiled Nelson. "What about them?"

"There's nothing stopping me from recovering the whole collection of codices on my own and keeping them for myself."

"Nothing stopping you?" repeated Nelson. "There are hundreds of villages along the Nile in Upper Egypt alone, covering some 500,000 square kilometers, populated by, approximately, oh, say, 15 million people. The majority of those people speak only the rough Arabic dialect of their region, and most despise foreigners, like you and me. Many of them are at war with each other, in violent blood feuds that have lasted for decades. And maybe *five or six* of all those people in Egypt – and in the world for that matter – know where the discovery was made. And of those half dozen people, *only one* knows what happened to the codices after they were found." Nelson paused. "I know who that one person is."

"You know who discovered the codices?" Etienne asked.

"Yes, I do."

"Then why don't you just go get for them for yourself?" asked Etienne.

Hugo shook his head condescendingly. "I don't make a habit of cavorting around foreign countries, digging in the dirt, for ... well, *anything*. No, you'll be far more effective than I could ever be. You're familiar with the people, their customs, modes of transportation, the language. Not to mention, the manuscripts will eventually have to be shipped out of Egypt. I can't be involved in that, of course. I never meddle with affairs of other governments. But, I'm happy to fund your expedition, naturally. With 200,000 dollars. And seeing as how you didn't actually deliver the Knife of the Asps to me directly, this is the only way you're going to get that money."

"You do know you're spending a ludicrous amount of money for some dusty old books," said Etienne.

Nelson sighed. "Money," he said. "It's such a funny thing. When a man finally feels that he has enough – more than enough – he can start to lose interest in money, can start to long for other things."

"Nelson, I've seen one of the manuscripts," said Etienne. "They aren't worth anywhere near a million dollars. Let alone the Knife of the Asps."

"They are to me," stated Nelson flatly.

"Then why all the cloak-and-dagger bullshit?" snapped Etienne. "What did you gain from having us ship artifacts across the

144

Atlantic Ocean – which was extremely dangerous, by the way – just to swap them back again?"

Nelson turned to Katherine. "You started this, my dear, with your offer of a trade. But I needed to test your mettle. Can you play the game?" He looked back at Etienne. "I needed to test both of you."

"Lovely," said Etienne. "But it was still quite a gamble to send the one manuscript you already had back to Egypt, to me."

"Not really."

"Hows' that?"

"Because, my dear fellow, when I want it back, I will simply take it."

There followed a long, uncomfortable silence "What will happen to the manuscripts when you have them all?" Etienne finally asked.

Nelson paused again, sizing up Etienne, carefully formulating his answer. "I'll hire someone to translate them, of course. Then we'll publish them for the whole world to see."

"And who might that be? Your translator, I mean."

"I think that just might be you, old boy," Nelson replied, picking through the platter of fruit. "The manuscripts will be returned to Egypt, eventually – most likely to the Coptic Museum. But it will be my name that is attached, forever, to the discovery and to the collection."

Etienne sat again in silence. Nick and Katherine suffered through the pause. Not Nelson. He was busy making a big production of buttering his toast, carefully spreading the butter, evenly and precisely, over every single grain of bread.

"Are you a religious man, Nelson?" asked Etienne, breaking the silence.

"Catholic," responded Nelson. "Born and raised."

More silence. Katherine shifted nervously in her seat. Nick's eyes darted between Nelson and Etienne.

"Here is the deal," Etienne finally said. "I will require the 200,000 dollars up front. Cash. Converted to Egyptian pounds. That's not negotiable. I'll contact you when I have the manuscripts. You do not contact me. Ever. We'll meet again here, in this restaurant, when the time comes. Alone. If I see any hint of the government, or your personal body guard for that matter…" Etienne nodded at a solitary man having breakfast at a nearby table. "…the deal will be off."

Nick and Katherine turned their heads over their shoulders to look. Big and stocky, with the look of a prizefighter, a man sat calmly eating pancakes. He watched their table, not the least bit embarrassed at the faces staring back at him. His demeanor was matter-of-fact, his expression more smug than self-conscious.

"You'll then give me the Knife of the Asps," continued Etienne. "And the number of a Swiss bank account, holding a million American dollars. When I've verified the authenticity of both, then I'll give you the manuscripts, all thirteen of them. But not before I am confident that the money is there and the Knife hasn't been replaced with a replica. That is the deal."

Nelson tilted his head to the side, considering Etienne's proposal. Etienne sat still as a stone, his eyes fixed on Nelson's face. Nick looked as though he was about to jump out of his skin, the dormant volcano coming to life. Katherine just sat there and watched.

Nelson nodded his head once in Etienne's direction and then stood up. "Done," he said. He drew an elegant gold pen from inside his suit coat and scratched out a phone number on a lace doily.

Nelson then picked up his briefcase and strode out of the room, leaving a perfectly buttered piece of toast on his plate, untouched. His bodyguard dropped his fork mid-bite and followed Nelson out of the restaurant.

Katherine looked over at Etienne. He was hard to read. After nearly 15 years, Nick was virtually transparent to her. But Etienne – he was never easy to understand. Katherine wondered if he was happy with the deal.

"Well, that was interesting," said Nick, breaking the silence at the table.

"How the hell did Nelson get his hands on the Knife of the Asps?" snapped Etienne. "And – if he wanted the manuscripts all along – why didn't he just say so from the beginning?"

"He's extremely eccentric," offered Katherine.

"I agree," offered Nick. "He's probably enjoying this whole mess tremendously. It's a game to him, Etienne."

"Still," said Katherine. "I know enough about Nelson to know that the information and the money will come, as he promised, in his own time."

"He's a nut case," muttered Etienne, picking up his fork and attacking his eggs.

The three friends finished their breakfast in silence, each of them wandering into their own thoughts. Watching Etienne, Katherine marveled at how he'd changed. He'd become shrewd somehow. Almost callous. On the outside, he was still so much the same. It made her think how convoluted things had become over the years. How murky the memories were. How much had happened.

If I could take one, single pearl off the strand that makes up my life, thought Katherine, *and hold it to the light to see it again more clearly, it would be a rainy afternoon in a café at Oxford.*

Oxford, England 1936

He dashed into the café, seeking shelter from a sudden downpour. A little bell on the door rang when he entered, and Katherine looked up. The bell rang every time someone came or left, and thus far she had managed to ignore it completely. Katherine was having tea, waiting for Nick to join her so they could study together before they went to their separate residences for the night. As the downpour continued, Katherine watched this most incredible man come inside, shake the water from his scandalously long hair, survey the room as though he owned it, and settle onto a soft sofa. He picked up a used copy of *The Oxford Daily Mail*.

Across the room, looking up occasionally from her steaming cup, she watched him. Nick was late. Probably waiting out the rain. *Which is ridiculous*, thought Katherine, *this business of trying not to get wet.* A slow stroll through a steady downpour was one of her favorite things. *Besides*, she thought, *people dry.* Her thoughts wandered around her mind, and her eyes wandered around the room.

Katherine found herself drawn to this one man, and she couldn't seem to look away. He was dark and wet and soft, camped as he was on the big sofa, with his newspaper spread all around him. It

147

was as though he thought he could read all the pages at once. Katherine was so intrigued, she found herself wanting to sit closer. She wanted to watch him, up close and unseen, as he roamed through the news of the day. She stared straight at him as he sat reading. She felt invisible somehow, all the way across the hazy room filled with noisy students. It was so easy, so innocent.

Then suddenly, the man looked up from his newspaper, straight across the crowded room, right at her. Startled, her face flushed, she still could not, or would not, look away. So she just sat there, drinking her tea, looking at him. He didn't turn his eyes away either. They both seemed entirely willing to cast aside any semblance of good manners.

Who is this man, she wondered, *watching me watching him?* It took only a few moments for her thoughts to jump straight out of her head and onto that sofa. *She* was the newspaper, laid out to be read and known and digested. It was she who rested without resistance in his hands, as he gingerly turned her, page by page, caressing her between his fingers, naturally, almost absent-mindedly, as he read her and knew her, line by line.

Katherine may have sat like that, thinking those startling thoughts, for a minute or an hour, she did not know. Then, without warning, she saw his eyes widen. A frown crossed his beautiful face and he looked away. With this small gesture, the spell was broken.

Katherine looked away as well, suddenly embarrassed, caught staring. A second later she felt a familiar hand on her shoulder, and Nick bent down to kiss her cheek. He was bone dry. *When had it stopped raining?* Katherine felt like she had just walked out of a movie house to find it had turned dark outside while she was in a make-believe, daylight world.

And then the unthinkable happened. Nick walked straight over to her secret newspaper lover and *shook his hand.* He pointed back to her and the two began to make their way over, talking easily. Katherine panicked in a brief, hot moment. *How can I talk my way out of this?* She thought to pretend she was blind. But that was ridiculous. She thought to say that she was pondering a picture on the wall behind him. But she didn't know if there was a picture on the wall behind him. Frankly, she didn't know of there was a *wall* behind him. The next thing she knew Nick was introducing her to his best friend.

"So *this* is Etienne," Katherine heard herself say.

"What next then?" Nick was talking. "Do we just wait?"

"*Non*," replied Etienne, signaling the waiter for the check. "I don't imagine it'll take long before we hear from Hugo Nelson. In the mean time, we have some work to do."

"What's that?" asked Katherine, shaking away her memories.

"We have a manuscript in Old Cairo to collect, for one thing. As well as one in Garden City."

"You have another one?" asked Nick, louder than he intended. "Besides the one from Nelson?"

"*Oui*. Two villagers brought it to me one night, about a year ago. I haven't heard from either one since. Nor can I find the store one of them claims to own in Nag Hammadi."

"Why didn't you tell Nelson about it?" asked Nick.

"Because I don't want him to know." Etienne threw his linen napkin on the table. "You think I'm going to hand over 13 precious Egyptian manuscripts to that greedy, maniacal, self-obsessed American, so he can do a quick and dirty translation, slap his name on the discovery, and brag about them in front of his ridiculous friends? Not on your life."

Nick's eyes grew big. "But Etienne, you made a deal."

"Deals change."

"But Etienne, really..." began Nick.

"Are you with me, Nick?" Etienne glared at both Katherine and Nick. "Or against me?"

Nick and Katherine shifted in their seats. *I'm with Nick,* thought Katherine. *Etienne must know that. But surely we didn't come this far to walk away. But what if Nick decides to stand on principle about the new deal with Nelson? He is so wonderfully, beautifully, frustratingly ethical. But now he'll have to choose sides, between honesty and Etienne. For Nick, life is only black or white, only one way or the other.*

"I'm with you, of course." Nick smiled easily. "We're mates, aren't we?"

Etienne smiled back, but the two old friends saw misgivings in each other's eyes.

We're back, thought Katherine. *The three of us. Just like it used to be.* For the first time in a long time, she felt almost happy. And then she thought of Ben. *He would have thrown himself square in the middle of all this, stirring up more dust than all of us combined. Mending the rifts between us. He should be here.*

"Well, we can give up the search for the potter," Katherine suggested, willfully pulling herself to other thoughts. "If Nelson has the Knife, who cares about the potter?"

Nick nodded. A distant smile crossed Etienne's stormy face.

"So, Etienne," Nick began. "If the manuscript that Katherine sent is in Garden City, where is the one you received from the villagers?"

"I keep an office at the Coptic Museum in Old Cairo. It's there. We'll go to the Museum, then to Garden City. We also need supplies. We could be on the road for weeks. Months, even."

Nick groaned. "You do know that I work for a living, don't you?"

"What is it about finding 11 manuscripts lost on the Egyptian Black Market that doesn't sound like work to you?" retorted Etienne with the beginnings of a grin.

We're together and we have a plan. Katherine smiled. Somewhere in the back of her mind it occurred to her that she should telegraph Eugene and let him know what was happening. But after several days of turmoil, all Katherine wanted at that moment was to dream.

Outside the hotel, Etienne hailed a taxi. Nick had wandered off to buy cheap book markers from some young Arab boys who were selling trinkets and begging for *baksheesh*, tips. Katherine was talking to the doorman, asking questions, smiling brilliantly, charming him with her unique combination of sincerity and naiveté. It took Etienne a few minutes to round them both up and pile them into a dented cab.

Though Katherine suggested that they give up their search for the potter, Etienne had other ideas about that. Eventually he would find that potter, and have a few words with the man who'd betrayed him. But not today. Today he had other things to do.

The trio left immediately for Old Cairo and the Coptic Museum. "I underestimated Hugo Nelson," said Etienne in the taxi. "I was convinced he'd have little interest in the Gnostic codices once he got hold of the Knife of the Asps." Turns out Nelson knew more about Etienne than Etienne knew about him. Which made Etienne furious. Nelson's obsession to have the manuscripts rivaled his own. "To think that he'll ask me to be the translator on the project is ludicrous," said Etienne, mostly to himself.

"What do you suppose he really plans to do with them once he has them?" asked Katherine.

Etienne looked out the window of the cab at the passing traffic. "I don't know," he said. "But we can't afford to find out."

"Then why'd you make the deal with him in the first place?" asked Nick.

"He knows the man who discovered the manuscripts in the first place," said Etienne. "It's a terrific lead. I was out of ideas, frankly. At a dead end."

Etienne didn't mention that he had also agreed to turn the manuscripts over to Cato Nafarah and the Egyptian government. That deal he did for Katherine, for her protection.

As the taxi drove them into the heart of Cairo, Etienne found himself thinking of Notre Dame, and a day when he couldn't reach Katherine even though she was standing right in front of him ... a day when he first wanted to protect her, even from her own private fears. Etienne could see her still, standing at a window, in the great church in Paris, looking out at a world that was changing too fast around her.

He wanted that day back. To do over. But there was nothing to do now but bury his longing and let the speeding taxi carry him forward, into a dark and misty future.

11

A Bridge in Time

He that cannot forgive others,
breaks the bridge over which he himself must pass
if he would ever reach heaven;
for everyone has need to be forgiven.

– George Herbert, British metaphysical poet

Old Cairo

The Coptic Museum was in the oldest, most conservative part of the city. The Christians in Egypt, called Copts, were made up of a very small minority. Nearly all Egyptians were Muslim, following the teachings of the Prophet Muhammad and the religion of Islam. The Copts and the Muslims had lived as neighbors, however, in relative peace and acceptance, for centuries.

This was due, in part at least, to the Copts' strict and long-held adherence to Jesus' directive to 'render unto Caesar the things that are Caesar's, and unto God the things that are God's.' The Copts, accordingly, submitted to their Muslim rulers, but worshipped God in their own way. The Coptic Church was never controlled by – and never tried to control – the government in Egypt, which greatly accounted for their longevity as one of the oldest institutions of Christianity in the world.

Etienne explained all this to Nick and Katherine as the taxi took them through the narrow, cobbled streets of Old Cairo. As the taxi rolled to a stop, they could see ruins from the Roman period near the entrance to the Coptic Museum. The crumbling stones of once massive columns always reminded Etienne of the great history of Egypt, and the many places she had conquered, and times she'd been conquered in return. Etienne paid the driver and they walked past the ruins, through a tall iron gate and down a long driveway.

The driveway led to a courtyard, flanked by two stone lions. As were most things in this part of town, the Coptic Museum was a modest structure. The trio walked past Tara, a little girl of nine who Etienne had come to know, sitting under an orange tree full of fragrant blossoms. Tara had long black braids and an enormous, heartbreaking smile. She should have been in school. She should have been learning to read and write. She should have been learning history and science, mathematics and literature. Instead, her parents posed her, alone at a table, day after day in that courtyard, with a glass of lemonade. She would sit there for hours, waiting to catch the eye of a tourist and smile.

'Oh! How sweet!' they would exclaim. 'Take her picture!' With permission of the parents first, and *baksheesh*, Tara would smile for the tourists' cameras. All day. Every day. As they walked by, Etienne touched Tara on her little shoulder and passed her a piece of chocolate. This, perhaps, she wouldn't have to share with anyone else.

A greeter stood at the entrance of the museum, collecting fees. "*Salam 'alekum*," said Etienne, shaking Jamil's hand. "Peace upon you."

"*Wa 'alekum es salam*," replied Jamil. "And peace upon you." Jamil was short and wiry. He did not wear the traditional turban and *jallabiya*, or robe, of the Muslims. He was a Copt, and wore cotton pants and a jacket. He looked curiously at Katherine and Nick.

"These are my friends, visiting from America," explained Etienne. "Nick Spencer, and his wife, Katherine."

"*Fursa sa 'ida*," said Jamil, moving to greet them. "Pleased to meet you. And welcome." If Jamil was shocked that Katherine stepped forward and firmly shook his hand, in a gesture considered unusual if not inappropriate for a woman in this culture, he said nothing.

"I left something important in my office," explained Etienne.

"Fine, fine," said Jamil, returning to his post.

"We'll only be a few minutes."

"Fine," repeated Jamil, collecting money from a fresh group of tourists. Not nearly as many travelers found their way to the Coptic Museum as they did to the famous Egyptian Museum. The latter was located near the finest hotels along the Nile, and was home to great and countless artifacts, including colossal statues of the pharaohs and the treasures of young King Tutankhamun. The Coptic collection was sparse in comparison, and of interest mostly to seekers of religious

153

history. Jamil was happy when people arrived in groups, eager to see the Christian artifacts of Egypt.

Katherine, Nick and Etienne made their way to the stairway that led to the second floor and the few offices housed in the museum. Etienne silently nodded to Nick and Katherine to descend into a dark stairwell. Katherine started to protest, but Etienne quickly put his finger to her lips. Without making a sound, Etienne disappeared into the shadowy depths of the museum. Katherine and Nick had no choice but to follow.

There were many long and narrow corridors in the basement of the museum, intertwined in an intricate web of passageways. In the stillness and the dark, their footsteps echoed through the deserted hallways, punctuated eerily by the small flashlight Etienne took from his satchel. The basement was strictly off-limits to everyone but the senior staff at the museum, and Etienne didn't want to alert anyone that they were down there. They crept along in silence. Katherine had come late in life to fear the dark, and was holding Nick's hand, hunched in close to his body.

They finally stopped at an alcove, nearly hidden from view in the dark corridor. Etienne drew a key out of his pocket and unlocked a heavy wooden door. They entered a small room through the arched doorway and Etienne closed the door behind them. Turning on the bare light that hung from the ceiling, he snapped off the flashlight and handed it to Nick. The room was small and cramped, without windows, and littered with crates, boxes and books that had been put in storage and forgotten. Etienne saw Katherine shiver. Or, more accurately, from four feet away, he felt it.

Etienne grabbed a screwdriver from a dusty shelf and walked over to a stack of boxes in the far corner of the room. He moved the boxes off to the side, one by one, and knelt on the floor. Etienne bent over his work while Nick and Katherine hovered nearby.

Carefully inserting the screwdriver between planks in the floor, Etienne was able to loosen one of the floorboards. The plank swung easily on two small hinges, revealing a small, hidden compartment under the floor. Etienne had spent hours creating – and disguising – the secret cubbyhole. From this little space, he drew out a bundle wrapped neatly in a starched white cloth and handed it to Nick. "Careful," he said. "That package is over 1,600 years old."

Nick held it at arm's length, as though it was a baby he didn't know how to hold. Etienne replaced the floorboard and the boxes that covered it. Then he dragged a wooden crate into the center of the room to use as a table. Nick laid the swaddled treasure on the crate with great care. They all crouched around the makeshift table, while Étienne slowly drew back the first heavy fold of cloth. A pair of clean white gloves was tucked inside, and Etienne put them on. "Oil from my skin, the roughness of my hands," he explained, "could crumble a manuscript like this to dust." Katherine blanched, remembering the disintegrating edges of the page she had handled in New York.

Etienne took great care in unwrapping the manuscript, one fold of cloth at a time, while Katherine and Nick looked on. A look of great wonder appeared on Etienne's face, and he looked, for a moment, unburdened by the cares of a tumultuous lifetime. What he revealed from the cloth was startling: about 14 inches long, 12 inches wide and two inches thick, with a worn leather covering. The cover was wrapped around the fragile papyrus leaves and tied with a thin leather strap.

Etienne could hear Katherine and Nick draw in their breath. This was a book that few had laid eyes on since the early Christians buried it in the desert 16 centuries earlier. Etienne opened the cover to show them more.

"Much of this manuscript is bound, like a book. See? Extraordinary, considering their age. Binding was not common practice until the Middle Ages. Rather, scribes penned manuscripts onto scrolls of papyrus. But here we have a series of books, gospels, including the *Dialogue of the Savior* and the *Secret Book of James*, bound together into one codex. Then there are these random few pages of papyrus, a letter, which has been tucked inside the cover. It makes me think that these documents were buried in a hurry, perhaps at the risk of being destroyed."

"What does the letter say?" asked Nick, scanning the meticulous, blocky rows of symbols on the loose page of papyrus.

"This appears to be a treatise from a Gnostic leader called Silvanis," explained Etienne, pointing to loose pages of papyrus inside the cover. "Listen." Then he read the words from the first golden pages, words he'd read a hundred times before:

"End the sleep which weighs heavily upon you. Depart from the oblivion which fills you with darkness... Why do you pursue the darkness, though the light is available to you? ... Wisdom calls you, yet you desire foolishness... a foolish man goes the way of the desire of every passion. He swims in the desires of life and has foundered ... he is a ship which the wind tosses to

and fro, and like a loose horse which has no rider. For this one needed the rider, which is reason *... before everything else ... know yourself."*

"Remarkable." Nick's voice was just a whisper.

"What does it mean?" asked Katherine.

"Silvanis seems to be urging his followers to resist unconsciousness," Etienne explained. "It is said that pursuing *gnosis*, or inner experience of the Divine, is a lonely, difficult process, one that is met with great internal resistance. He is saying that we are all asleep, or unconscious of inner knowledge, until we wake ourselves up, and seek the shape of our own souls."

"Seek the shape of our own souls..?" asked Katherine.

"He goes on to explain," Etienne said, reading:

"Bring in your guide and your teacher. The mind is the guide, but reason is the teacher... Live according to your mind ... Acquire strength, for the mind is strong ... Enlighten your mind ... Light the lamp within you."

Just then they heard a noise. A tiny click. The sound of a door closing. Etienne immediately turned off the overhead light. Katherine gasped as they were plunged into total darkness. Something haunting and dark rose inside her. She wanted to run. She wanted to turn on the lamp, to bring in the blinding light of day. Her breath came in stiff gulps.

"Shhh," said Etienne, touching his hand to her lips in the dark. It pleased him to know just exactly where she was in the pitch black. *It was like leaning into your lover in the dark*, he thought, *and knowing just where to kiss her*. He could not explain how it happened, only that it did. Katherine covered his hand with hers for just a moment, then drew herself away.

"Don't worry," Etienne whispered as softly as he possibly could, pulling off his gloves. "There's a way out of here, but we have to be very, very quiet." They could hear footsteps in the hallway now and muffled voices. Etienne was certain that agents of the Egyptian government had followed them and were planning to confiscate the manuscript.

Etienne moved in the dark to the back wall and slid aside a heavy crate. It moved easily and quietly once he had released a particular latch – another devise he had labored long to create and to disguise. There was a small opening behind the crate that became a tunnel just big enough to crawl through.

Nick went first, with the flashlight. Katherine followed, miserable all the way, bruising her knees and putting runs in her hose. Etienne remained behind just long enough to re-wrap the manuscript in the cloth, tuck it into his satchel, and swing the crate back in front of the small opening. The last thing he heard before entering the tunnel was a loud, repeated pounding on the storage room door.

The three friends scrambled in silence through the tunnel, on their hands and knees, for fifteen minutes. The tunnel took them under the museum courtyard, past the main road and up into a busy marketplace. In the lead, Nick kicked out a small floor grate and they all helped each other up, spilling onto the floor in the back room of a linen shop.

"Greetings, Etienne, you old dog!" The merchant loomed over them, rubbing his hands together. "Always happy to have you stop by."

Etienne smiled up at him weakly. For the price of a tablecloth and some napkins made of the finest Egyptian cotton to be found, they would be on their way.

Katherine and Nick threw themselves in a heap on the soft davenport in Etienne's living room. Etienne's home was spacious and bright and seemed very far away from the crowded, noisy city center. Katherine fell asleep instantly, her body still adjusting to the time change.

Nick absently ran his hands through his hair. *Hugo Nelson isn't going to let Etienne translate the Gnostic library*, he thought. His tired mind took him back to Italy, to a darker time, a time when he knew Hugo Nelson was *absolutely* interfering with the business of other governments.

Nick forced his mind back to the task at hand: finding the eleven manuscripts that were still missing. The task seemed insurmountable. *It could take years,* he thought miserably. *We barely know where to begin. Between government agents, renegade nationalists and land mines left behind from the war, it'll be a wonder if we don't all die out there in the desert. And in the end,* sighed Nick deeply, *we'll still have to deal with Hugo Nelson.* Nick tossed and turned as the afternoon waned and his mind chased itself in circles. *Leave it to Etienne to live on the one and only hill in Cairo,* he thought, as he faded off to sleep.

Etienne, his guests settled for the afternoon, took a bottle of champagne from the icebox and a pack of cigarettes out onto the verandah. There he stayed until the sun started to drop from the sky and memories started to burn through his heart.

Paris 1936

They called her 'Kat' back then, at school. Everybody they knew at Oxford assumed that she and Nick would be together forever. They became inseparable, as if Katherine was showing Ben that she was there, but apart. Ben didn't seem to mind at all. He and Etienne considered her the glue, the light, which held all of them together, though she would say that wasn't so. It was Ben, in her mind, who was the light at the center of their universe.

Ben had an uncanny knack for making himself, and everyone around him, happy. More than inclusion into his blithe world, Ben offered lighthearted humor, a sense of raw fun, occasional glimpses into the forbidden, and straight-ahead episodes into the prankish.

One night he led a group of coeds into the backyard swimming pool of a vacationing professor. The instructor in question was away on a short sabbatical to receive some award or other and had left his classes in the hands of a substitute, which alerted Ben to a unique opportunity. The professor's stately manor was on the perimeter of campus, and left in the hands of a trustworthy caretaker. Ben happened to know that the caretaker regularly spent his Friday evenings at a local pub, playing pool and sipping Brandy Alexanders.

It was the perfect opportunity, in Ben's mind, for a little skinny dipping with friends. They each carried a bottle of cheap wine, which they tossed carefully to Ben, who was the first to scale the stone fence surrounding the property. One after another they popped over to the forbidden side. Clothes all cast aside, corks popping, Ben orchestrated a bacchanal of revelry in the blue-tiled pool. Lit from below, the water emanated an otherworldly light around the group as they sang, smoked and swam into the night, spirits floating above the laws that governed the ordinary.

They barely escaped with their clothes when the caretaker returned and flashed a blinding light on their escapade. Ben spent a month on disciplinary probation, but talked his way out of any formal police charges. In the Bank of Intrigue, however, Ben put another deposit into his long-standing account. Kat and Nick hadn't been invited, of course, though she heard Etienne had been there. Kat responded with a superior indifference, as if she and Ben were the original pranksters of all time, and the others, including Etienne, were mere tagalongs.

Besides, Kat had Nick. Life at Oxford was chalk-full of pressure: classes, homework, cramming for tests, parties, love affairs, grades, all colliding in a rising tide. They were young. They were ambitious. There were high expectations on all of them, much of it self-imposed. Through all of it, Kat and Nick stood together, comfortable, secure, predictable. That such a routine would eventually become boring, Kat could not yet imagine.

Then came the spring of their junior year. They'd spent three school years together. Final exams were raging through everyone's lives, pulling them all into a heightened ability to read, memorize, study and regurgitate. Fear of failure kept them going at a relentless pace. For most of them, any grade less than an A, maybe a B, was a dismal failure. Everyone was half insane. And there were Kat and Nick – so often and so commonly referred to, it was almost like one word, 'KatanNick' – steady through it all. Then the final final was passed and summer stretched ahead of them.

Nick had been offered an internship at a prestigious law firm in London. But Kat didn't want to go to London. She said she wanted to do nothing more than dig her bare toes into the cool, green grass, sleep in, read about all the mythic heroes and gods, from Achilles to Zeus, and watch the summer wilt away. Young, confident, impervious to heart-breaking pain, Kat and Nick decided to take a vacation from each other – to 'recapture themselves,' they said. 'We'll decide how we feel in the fall,' they said. They agreed to not know, and not to worry about not knowing. And so he went. And she stayed.

She and Ben and Etienne kicked around Oxford together for a month. Then, Ben met a girl from Switzerland and decided on a whim to take the train with her to Zermatt to see the Matterhorn. He would be gone several weeks, at least. That left Kat and Etienne to entertain each other, each circling quietly around the other, not knowing who they were together without Nick and Ben to define them. One day, out of the blue, at a lazy picnic on the lawn, Etienne invited Kat to Paris. What made that woman say yes, Etienne would never know. But she put down her copy of *The Iliad* with the page dog-eared halfway through, looked him in the eye and said, "God, yes."

Later she said she felt guilty – guilty that she didn't feel guilty. She and Nick knew they needed to separate, because they had gotten so comfortable with each other they had become indifferent. Ben had also told Kat that Nick was changing her, making her cautious, reserved, *appropriate*. The words scared her. She believed everything Ben said. The closer Kat and Nick became, the more she and Ben fought. Etienne thought she was glad to be rid of them both for a while, to live in a world free from their immediate influence.

Maybe that's why she skipped off with Etienne to Paris in the middle of her sleepy Oxford summer. Etienne didn't know. Neither did he know why she turned her heart over to him, or how much of her heart he really possessed. He *did* know what made her not want to leave Paris at the end of that summer. He knew instinctively that the blooming, the unfolding of her spirit, could never again be completely contained. When summer ended, Katherine knew what she would find back at Oxford and she didn't want to go. She still loved Nick, Etienne assumed, but she simultaneously was paralyzed by a sinking feeling – a near panic – of returning to a predictable life.

In the mean time, though, Kat and Etienne spent their summer in Paris, laughing, exploring, eating and over-drinking. The wine was heady, the art and architecture were extraordinary and the company was intoxicating. Kat was wild and free and unrestrained for perhaps the first time in a life that kept her confined – if only subtly – to a straight, narrow corridor of behavior. She took her camera with her everywhere she went, beaming from behind the lens at everything she put to film.

One evening Kat crossed a line – a razor-thin, invisible line that the two had danced near and around for a month. From *Le pont d'Iena* bridge, higher than was comforting, the Eiffel Tower rose above them, the Seine flowed beneath and expanse of Paris stretched into the distance. They talked about the day behind them and the days ahead like they talked about everything: carefully. They were careful not to commit themselves to the future. They were always careful to say enough, but never too much, because neither one knew what was going to happen. They were expressing their interest, but not their promises.

As they talked that evening, on the bridge, Kat lifted her wrist to breathe in her new French perfume. Then, in a simple, graceful motion, she extended her wrist to Etienne. It was an elegant and un-self-conscious gesture typical of Kat. But not without calculation. She wanted Etienne to kiss her. Etienne smiled at her with all the tenderness he could demonstrate, outrageously grateful that she made the overture. He took her hand and bestowed a light kiss on the delicate flesh of her wrist. Then he kissed her forearm, then the tender pocket inside her elbow. Then she was in his arms.

There she was and there she stayed, in Etienne's arms, through the rest of Paris and on every bridge thereafter they could find. They kissed like that all August, and the real world slipped away. It was as though they were detached from everyone else, circling only around each other. They didn't know where the rest of the world was. They didn't care.

Kat and Etienne stayed in a flat owned by Etienne's parents on the Rive Gauche where all of Paris was at their disposal. In the mornings they ate warm, buttery croissants that flaked on their fingers. They drank steaming hot espresso in tiny ceramic cups. They shared crepes filled with chocolate and raspberries after late night suppers at open-air restaurants. They hiked the distant landscapes surrounding Paris where they would stop and recover lunch from their knapsacks – meat and cheese, a baguette, a few apples or grapes, red wine. They drank champagne in the mornings, and fed each other strawberries and cold watermelon, while the sun streaked through the window and the sheets fell off the bed.

They toured *The Louvre* day after day: the Mona Lisa, room after room of furniture and tapestries, marble statues and more paintings than most people could see and forget in ten lifetimes. Kat lingered for a long time over an elegant white marble statue of Artemis, the Roman goddess of the hunt. She returned to see that particular statue many times.

Occasionally, they would shop in the afternoons. This they did on those days when they didn't get up until after noon, when their hunger for food drove them out the door. In the boutiques, Etienne admired with great patience, pleasure even, all the selections Kat tried on and cast off. He particularly admired the very few items she purchased, carefully counting out each Franc.

At night, back at their flat, they drank *Veuve Clicquot* and played Brahms over and over on the phonograph. They ate crusty French bread with an exotic assortment of soft cheeses. Candles flickered and glowed in the room until they burned to the base and extinguished themselves. Etienne and Kat danced and kissed and

161

touched until the black sky warmed to a lavender-gray with the first hints of the new day. That afternoon they would visit Notre Dame.

The great sanctuary of Notre Dame was built of stone and marble and stained glass many centuries before Kat and Etienne stumbled through its massive doors. They knelt together, each saying their own private prayers. Kat reached over and squeezed Etienne's hand, in a gesture newly familiar and comforting to him. Women didn't typically do that to sort of thing to Etienne.

They separated at the sanctuary to wander on their own. There was much to explore in the grand historical church: the flat tombs of priests and saints long dead, embedded in the stone floor, the twelve statues of marble, immortalizing Christ's first disciples, the many carved gargoyles perched watchfully on the outer ridges and the stained glass that stretched to the ceiling, ablaze with light and color.

Etienne roamed the great structure, absorbed in history and reverence. He wasn't really aware of the time. An hour passed. Maybe less. All of a sudden, he was anxious to see Kat again, to find her, with an inexplicable sense of urgency, in this mammoth structure filled with strangers and ghosts.

He finally found her at the top of a steep, narrow staircase, a step-way of stone carved into a dark corner of the cathedral. There at the top, was a tiny cell. It housed only a crude bench of rock, with a small open-air window overlooking the *Place du Parvis* below. Sounds from below drifted upward. The plaza was lined with artists – talented and not-so-talented – selling their paintings and charcoal sketches to tourists hungry for a taste of Parisian culture, a taste they could take home and nail on the wall.

Kat stood alone at the window, the sun beaming warm light on her slender frame. She looked totally lost. Her gaze was cast far away and anxious. She looked as though she was facing bridges she didn't want to cross: bridges, perhaps, between the past and that moment, between that moment and the future.

"Kat?" Etienne had waited for her attention, but she didn't seem to know he was there.

She turned slowly, her eyes blue-green pools lit by her tears and the sunlight. "I don't want to go." She said it so quietly, he nearly missed it. He was just about to touch her, but she seemed so fragile, he hesitated. Kat drew in a quick, deep breath, and before she released it, moved through the little stone archway and onto the stairs.

Etienne listened for a minute, alone in the cell, to her rapid footsteps, until they were lost in new echoes. A trio of tourists from Germany ascended the final steps and, panting, burst through the archway. Three strangers, sweating and excited and talking all at once. Etienne left without looking back.

Then September came crashing in on them. September – cruel and cold. Unwelcome, intrusive September. Hateful September, with the ending of summer that came with it and all its ordered, immovable, inevitable expectations. September was a time of great color, change, and anticipation. To Katherine it was quieter than summer, dimmer in its hopes and prospects. The sun didn't stay as long in the sky. It was time for harvest, time for school, time for endings and beginnings. That year, the first of many, Katherine hated September.

The morning following their visit to Notre Dame, Kat and Etienne had coffee at one of their favorite cafés on the Left Bank. They were both unusually quiet, neither one wanting to say or hear what was next. They sat at an outdoor table draped in a blue-checkered cloth. Fresh cut flowers leaned out of a jam jar on the table, next to a basket of warm croissants. Kat fiddled with her coffee cup, dipping her finger in the foam that topped her coffee. She picked at the shaved chocolate sprinkled on the foam, and raised her fingers to her lips.

"We have to go back," Etienne finally said, as softly as he could. With those words, Kat heard a great betrayal. He had said it. He would go back. She hated him for that: that he would let some strange, empirical, pragmatic voice of realism override his heart. Her heart. Their heart. Whatever it was they were becoming.

"Shhh," she whispered, tears threatening to break loose. She looked away for only a moment. Then she leaned across the table, took Etienne's hand in hers, locked her eyes on his, and softly kissed him. *You are not what you thought you were. Fall now. Let go and become something else.* She sat back, drew him deep into her sad chameleon eyes, and whispered, "I would have stayed."

Etienne shoved his chair away from the table and turned away from her, closing his eyes in a useless attempt to push away his own disappointment. "*Pardon, cheri,*" he said, as he strode off to the men's room inside the café. Inside, he kicked the wall. He was angry. Angry that this hurt. Angry that he couldn't find a way to stay. When he returned to their table, minutes later, she was gone. He thought to wait for her to come back but that was ridiculous. She wasn't coming back.

Cairo 1947

Nick woke with a start from his restless dreams. The sun had fallen. He could hear laughter and conversation coming from the kitchen. Katherine was already awake, staring – from their tangled berth on the davenport – into dreams and memories of her own. They roused themselves, splashed some cold water on their faces and met Etienne on the verandah for dinner.

Etienne's live-in housekeeper, Dara, laid out an elegant meal for them. They chatted casually together, old friends, letting their weightier concerns melt into the pleasure of reminiscing. Dara began a traditional Egyptian dinner with *molokhiyya*, spicy green soup made from leafy vegetables, rice and garlic.

"I say, this is rather good," exclaimed Nick. Dara looked at him, surprised that he was surprised. "I have to confess to having grown up rather finicky," Nick added, blushing. "Though the war helped me get over that. War is neither the time nor the place to be particular." Nick, having said all the wrongs things, returned to his soup.

"Life without *aysh* is not life," said Dara, as she passed Nick a plate piled high with pita bread. "This is *aysh baladi*," she explained with a smile. Nick looked up at Etienne and cast him a look of appreciation and a tiny little bit of envy.

Dara was a willowy young woman. Her round brown eyes looked out shyly behind huge, wispy lashes. Her long hair, dark and straight, was held back with a thin blue ribbon. She wore a simple linen shift for a dress, sandals and not a stitch of makeup. Katherine could not easily isolate and admire the beauty of Dara, however. Her eyes narrowed shrewdly, and she felt an ache and a longing, as she watched Etienne follow the girl's movements with great warmth and attention.

"*Aysh* also means *life* in Arabic," explained Etienne, squeezing Dara's hand. She beamed a smile back at him. Next Dara brought *moza*, roast lamb grilled and served over rice. For dessert they had *baqlawah*, a flaky pastry topped with nuts and drizzled with warm

164

honey. They finished their meal with *Reine Cleopatra*, a sweet white wine.

"Now there's someone I admire," announced Katherine. "Cleopatra the Seventh of Egypt. The last of the Ptolemies. The last Queen of the Nile."

"She was the most powerful, wealthy and ruthless woman of her time," added Etienne. "She was also the lover of the two greatest leaders of the known world, Julius Caesar and Marc Antony."

"Now *that*," said Katherine, "was something." She looked over at Nick, wishing he would respond somehow. Sometimes he could absorb the full weight of all her thoughts and emotions and not bat an eyelash. It left her feeling invisible.

The sun settled far beyond the city and the stone houses glowed a pale silver-peach in the late hours of the evening. The immense city looked soft and still. Only the distant beeping of car horns could be heard rising from the countless, winding streets.

"If you will all excuse me," said Katherine, rising, "I need to freshen up a little. It's been a very long day."

"Of course, darling," said Nick. He and Etienne rose to their feet and watched her go.

Dara rose, too. "I have things to attend to as well."

"Stay ... and relax with us for a while," said Etienne, taking her hand.

"No, no," insisted Dara. "You have much to talk about, I'm sure." She let her fingers linger between Etienne's. "I will see you later."

Etienne kissed the back of her hand and she smiled as she left the verandah, closing the tall glass doors behind her.

"It has been a long time," began Etienne.

"Too long," said Nick.

"You've done well, I hear." Etienne poured brandy. "Partner in a law firm?"

"I've done alright, I suppose," said Nick, taking the snifter and breathing in the cinnamon aroma. "But still, sometimes I wonder if being a lawyer is what I really want to be doing for the rest of my life. Defending fat cats who are as guilty as sin and as rich as God."

"What else would you do?" asked Etienne.

"I thought once of going into teaching. But the money isn't there. Still, I think I'd much rather spend my time in a classroom than a courtroom."

"Really?" said Etienne. "I couldn't get out of school fast enough. To me, teaching sounds like being sentenced to Hell for life."

"Not at all," said Nick. "I did a little stint once for a friend at NYU. It's much different than being a student, I can assure you. There are tremendous opportunities to shape young minds. For the most part, the students are very eager to learn. They're fascinating to watch, really – naïve and enthusiastic..."

"Hmmm." Etienne broke out a box of cigars. He handed one to Nick, clipping off the end and extending a match.

"There is something about being a student I miss, to tell you the truth." Nick blew a smoke ring and examined his cigar. "Things were simpler back then. Clearer. You knew exactly who you were and what you needed to do. The decisions weren't all that hard. And your fate wasn't really up to you. Yet."

"Oxford was the last great playground for us, wasn't it?" said Etienne. "Before life began in earnest."

"The whole world is your playground, Etienne."

Etienne laughed. "We had fun didn't we, *mon ami*?"

"That we did." Nick put down his cigar, feeling dizzy from the tobacco. "I've always been very grateful that Oxford brought us all together, you and me, Ben and Katherine."

The two men sat in silence for awhile, looking out over the city lights. An onlooker might see a privileged two above the throngs: dining with beautiful women, swirling fine brandy in their snifters, smoking expensive cigars. But these two men were feeling the impoverishment of loss, with a history and a gap between them.

"Archaeology must be treating you right, Etienne," Katherine announced loudly, standing just outside the verandah doors.

166

She had been wandering around, taking in all the details of Etienne's home. "Your home is beautiful," she said, sitting down at the table. She placed a small blue-patterned vase in front of Etienne. "And so is this." Katherine lit a cigarette, sat back and crossed her legs.

"*Merci*, Katherine," said Etienne. "I'm glad to have someone like you here, who can appreciate my eclectic collection of art and architecture."

"Ming?" Katherine asked, nodding at the vase.

"*Oui*," Etienne answered, almost shyly.

"My goodness," said Nick.

"It is a family home,: offered Etienne. "And I have been very fortunate in my business dealings." Etienne rose with the vase in his hands and returned it to the house. Katherine and Nick exchanged speculative glances in his absence.

"His place is amazing, Nick," whispered Katherine. "You should see the things he's collected."

"Etienne has made quite a life for himself in these ten years," remarked Nick.

"Tomorrow we will go to Garden City and pick up the other codex," said Etienne, returning to the verandah. "I'm anxious to have it in my hands."

"I'm anxious to hear more about this Miss Donatta," said Katherine, referring to the recipient name on her shipment to Garden City. "Will we meet her, Etienne?"

Etienne shifted slightly in his seat. *She knows*, he thought. *Somehow, through some seventh sense that is entirely unfathomable, Katherine always seems to know things I'd prefer to keep to myself.* "You will undoubtedly meet her," said Etienne.

"But tell me more about the codex you got from Nelson in New York," he continued, diverting the subject, and sincerely anxious to see the pages for himself. "What did it look like?"

"Very similar to the one from the museum," she said. "Many pages of yellow papyrus. A leather cover. All bound in some strange way I couldn't quite figure out. Most interesting, I thought, was the etching on the cover."

"What?" asked Etienne. "There was an etching on the cover?"

"Very creepy," said Katherine. "Some sort of rendering of a snake."

"*Sofia*," said Etienne.

"Etienne, it was a snake. A serpent," said Katherine. "The devil incarnate. It's a very bad sign."

"No," corrected Etienne. "To the Gnostics the serpent represented *Sofia*, which means *wisdom*."

"The serpent is the Devil," insisted Katherine, pointing her cigarette at him.

"Not to the Gnostics. They believed that the god who ruled the Garden of Eden was a demi-god. This god, self-proclaimed as jealous and vengeful, forbade Adam and Eve the knowledge of good and evil, thereby keeping them forever ignorant and enslaved. The Gnostics believed, basically, that God had a mother. A higher spiritual being. It is this being they worshipped. And Sofia, or Wisdom, came in the image of a serpent to enlighten Adam and Eve with knowledge. Remember, Katherine, where the apple came from: the Tree of Knowledge."

"Sometimes I swear, Etienne," exclaimed Katherine, stubbing out her cigarette. "It's a wonder that you don't get struck by lightening right where you sit!"

"That's exactly what the Church wants you to think, Katherine. To fear the wrath of a jealous god. If God is the One, Katherine, and there is no other – just exactly *who* is he jealous of?"

Katherine, in a moment not typical of her, had nothing to say. So she changed the subject. "Etienne, I have to tell you something that you may not like. Please tell me you forgive me, in advance."

"Oh, God, Katherine, what?" asked Etienne.

"Promise me," she insisted. "Promise me you won't yell."

"*Cheri*, I want you to listen to your own heart. What does it say? All I've ever wanted from you was to see you do all you are capable of. I want to see you happy. Not hurt, not ever, least of all by me." Etienne recited the words as if they were a prayer, a ritual offering, a promise he had made many times before. "Tell me, what have you done?"

168

"Well, it's like this," began Katherine. "I wanted some assurance that I would indeed get the Knife of the Asps. In case something went wrong with this trade across the ocean. Which, I might remind you, it did. So before I shipped the dagger to you, I removed – very, very carefully – the first page of the manuscript."

Etienne visibly paled. "So, Katherine," he said, as calmly as he could. "You took out the first page. Did it come out easily, or did you have to tear it?"

"No, it slid right out," she said. "The papyrus is very fragile."

"Yes, I know that," said Etienne smoothly. "Now then, where is it? Do you have it with you? Or is it sill in America?"

"It's right here with me," said Katherine brightly. "I placed it inside a magazine and carried it right through Customs. Both times."

"I will be very anxious to see it," said Etienne. "Can you get it for me? *Now*, please?"

"Sure," said Katherine as she began to rise. "I put it on the dresser in the guest room, in my purse."

"Pardon me, Etienne." Dara suddenly burst onto the verandah. "There are two men at the door, in suits! They say they are from the Department of Antiquities and they look very unhappy. They are demanding to see you."

"Quick!" said Etienne, jumping up from his chair. "Head out back to the carriage house, and get in the jeep!" He threw a set of keys to Nick. "Be ready to leave fast. You, too, Dara. No time to pack. I'll meet you in the alley in a few minutes."

They stood up in amazement and watched Etienne stroll casually into the house, sipping his brandy, acting for all the world like nothing was wrong. Nick helped Katherine and Dara scramble over the stone wall, wishing he was back with Etienne, facing the danger head on. They crept down the short embankment leading to the grounds below. Dara led the way as they ran quietly across the lower terrace to the carriage house. Darkness had fallen, which made their way difficult, but in turn, helped cloak them from sight.

It was ten minutes before Etienne came racing around the side of the house, with his satchel strung across his chest. Nick had pushed the jeep out of the carriage house and perched it on top of the winding slope that led to the city below. Katherine and Dara were tucked together in the back seat, holding hands.

Together, Etienne and Nick gave the jeep the little nudge it needed to start it rolling down the hill. Nick was suddenly very grateful for Etienne's strategic choice in his residence on higher ground. Etienne hopped into the passenger seat and handed Katherine her purse with a sideways grin. It was not until they reached the bottom, a twisty quarter-mile later, that Nick fired up the engine and they sped off into the city.

Etienne pulled a small golden figure from his jacket pocket, and handed it to Katherine in the back seat. It was a beautiful golden snake, coiled tight, with eyes of bright green emeralds.

"What's this for?" she asked, leaning forward and accepting the exotic gift.

"It's something that I want you to have," said Etienne. "To remind you that you only think that snakes are bad. Because someone once told you so."

12

GARDENS OF THE PAST

Gamble everything for love, if you're a true human being.
If not, leave this gathering.

– Rumi

Etienne left two angry agents of the Egyptian government storming around the study of his home. Cato Nafarah had sent them to the Coptic Museum, and having failed there, they came to Etienne's house to collect the Gnostic codex. Etienne had assured Nafarah that he would deliver all 13 manuscripts, but apparently Nafarah was not waiting on faith.

Etienne had welcomed the agents and led them into the study to show them several papyrus scrolls that were recently given to him as a gift. A colleague of Etienne's had hired a scribe to make a replica of the Dead Sea Scrolls, which had been discovered in a cave in Qumran in 1945. Shepherd boys, searching for a stray goat, had stumbled upon a hidden cave in the Judean desert. The cave was very near to the famous Masada, the mountain refuge where a small tribe of Jews was once besieged by their Roman conquerors. The Jews ultimately took their own lives, stealing victory from the hands of their enemies. Etienne did not know whether there was a connection between the scrolls and The Masada. But he was intrigued by the coincidence.

His good friend and colleague sent the replicated copy of the scrolls to Etienne because he knew Etienne had been looking for ancient Christian documents throughout Egypt and the Middle East for years. As it turned out, the Dead Sea Scrolls were from a Jewish sect, called *The Essenes*, and not Christian at all. Though the documents were fascinating, Etienne's deeper interests were elsewhere.

While the two government agents bent over the scrolls in the study, Etienne offered to collect yet another papyrus scroll from his library down the hall. They barely looked up. Etienne closed the door

171

behind him and slipped a skeleton key into the lock. The men were trapped inside before they knew what had happened.

Etienne then ran down the hall and found Katherine's purse on top of the dresser in the guest room. He could hear the agents kicking and pounding on the study door as he grabbed his hat and satchel, and the stiletto from the vase in the foyer. He was two steps out the door before he went back in for the golden snake, and a glittering string of jewels from the bottom of his aquarium.

Following Etienne's directions, Nick drove toward the center of Cairo, where Dara's parents lived. "Who was at the door?" asked Nick, as he maneuvered the narrow streets.

"Nafarah's lackeys," said Etienne, placing the stiletto into a scabbard strapped inside his pant leg. "They wanted the manuscript."

"Did they get it?" asked Nick.

Etienne laughed. "Nafarah should have come himself."

"He must have returned from Tenerife by now," said Nick. "Furious."

"His thugs will probably trash the place," grumbled Etienne, cranky that he had to sacrifice his copy of the Dead Sea Scrolls.

They soon came into Dara's neighborhood, where dirt streets were crowded with houses built right next to one another. Nick let the jeep idle out front. Dara's parents, hearing the sound of late visitors, came outside. They huddled close together and peered at the jeep, wary of strangers in the night.

Times were dangerous in Cairo, with nationalists battling the monarchy and the British for political control. It was not uncommon for people to be dragged out of their homes in the night, never to be seen again. But Dara's father waved as he recognized Etienne and his daughter in the dim light. Etienne jumped out of the jeep and held his hand out to Dara. She looked frail and tenuous as she climbed out onto the dirt road.

"Don't worry, *mon cheri*," Etienne said softly in her ear. "Everything will be alright." Her chin trembled, just slightly, and he touched her on the cheek. "I'll be gone for a while, with my friends. But I'll be back. I promise you."

"Ma'as salama," she murmured. *"*Go in safety, Etienne.*"*

"Au revoir, mon petite cheri." Etienne turned back to Nick and Katherine. "We've got to get to Garden City, straight away."

Nick slid across the seat and Etienne took the wheel. With one last look back, he drove out of the courtyard, leaving behind an unhappy Dara, her stunned parents and a cloud of dust.

It was close to midnight when they rumbled to a stop in the circular driveway of Miss Donatta's house in Garden City, near the Nile. Miss Donatta looked charmingly rumpled when she came to the door. Her silk robe brushed the tops of her bare feet as she stepped along the cool tiles of the foyer. She should have been annoyed, but she smiled warmly when Etienne stepped forward and put his hat to his chest.

"Forgive me, *mon cheri.*" Etienne's silky accent dripped into the night and all was forgiven before the last syllable was spoken.

"Etienne." Miss Donatta reached out two sleepy arms to embrace him. "Do not tell me you've woken me up for that silly book from America," she said. Then she smiled and kissed him sweetly.

Etienne knew better than that. Miss Donatta had gone to some trouble, and considerable risk, to be the recipient of a smuggled manuscript. She would give Etienne the book at a time of her own choosing.

Miss Donatta was tall and dark and fully curved, with tousled black hair that fell to her shoulders. Her brown eyes danced brightly even through sleepy eyelids. Feature by feature, Miss Donatta was not particularly attractive. But there was an air of high drama, high cheekbones and high society that swirled around her like a dancer's veils. This, combined with an elegance that even sleep could not disguise, made Miss Donatta stunning.

Etienne turned to Katherine and Nick and merely shrugged as Miss Donatta ushered them all inside. "These are my friends from America," said Etienne, by way of an introduction. "Nick and Katherine Spencer."

Miss Donatta settled them in and poured them each a big glass of cabernet sauvignon before she curled up softly in an over-stuffed armchair. "As in Italy," she said, "wine for all occasions."

"Miss Donatta is from the Tuscany valley in northern Italy," explained Etienne. "And yes, she is as exotic and mysterious as her heritage suggests."

"*Il mio amore*, you really are too much," said Miss Donatta.

Etienne and Nick exchanged smiles. *Katherine is staring at us as if we're insipid twits*, noticed Etienne. *Which, around some women, I suppose we are.*

"Now, tell me, Etienne, what mischief are you and your friends up to so late in the night?" asked Miss Donatta.

"We need your help, *cheri*."

"I assumed as much," she replied, sipping her wine contentedly, cradling the fragile glass in her hands. Her nails were buffed long and clear and shiny and added to her understated elegance.

Over her shoulder Nick noticed a very familiar statue. It was of Isis – white alabaster, about three feet in height and one in diameter. She stood on a round marble pedestal carved with the image of three lions. Nick caught Katherine's eye and nodded toward the statue. Katherine's face broke into a great smile.

"We need a place to stay tonight," Etienne was saying. "And supplies for a road trip. And, of course, the manuscript."

"And what is wrong with your house tonight?" she asked sweetly.

"It's... uh… otherwise occupied."

"By who, may I ask?"

"Whom," corrected Etienne.

"By *whom*, then?"

"Men in suits," responded Etienne, seriously.

Nick, on the other hand, could not take his eyes off the couple. To someone who spent his days buried in legal briefs, Etienne's life seemed tremendously intriguing. The two were like brothers in college, but time had changed them. Choices had shaped them. And perhaps they were never that similar to begin with.

"Men in suits you say?" continued Miss Donatta, her rich Italian accent floating across the dimly lit room.

"Dark suits," said Etienne.

"Oooh, that bad?"

"Worse."

"Well. Enough said." Miss Donatta put down her wine glass and abruptly stood. "It's all settled then." Etienne stood up to join her. "My house is yours for tonight," stated Miss Donatta, without a hint of inconvenience.

"*Merci, mon cheri.*" Etienne stepped close to her. "Whatever would I do without you?" He took both of her slender hands in his and kissed them lightly as he looked into her eyes.

"Oh, you'd go somewhere else I suspect," smiled Miss Donatta. "And I couldn't have that, now could I?"

Etienne smiled sheepishly, as Nick watched him in utter disbelief. Nick's heart fell very low as he thought about Dara. Sometimes he really did not like Etienne at all.

"I'll make arrangements to gather whatever supplies you need by mid-morning," Miss Donatta was saying to Etienne. She turned warmly to Katherine and Nick. "I have a guest room waiting just for you at the end of the hall where you can rest and be comfortable." Miss Donatta turned back to Etienne. "And you, little rascal, are coming with me."

As Katherine and Nick made their way to the bedroom they heard Etienne speaking in a hushed voice. "You *do* have the codex, don't you?" he asked. Then they heard the light sound of Miss Donatta's playful laughter.

For Nick, it was a night of fitful dreams and unwelcome memories.

As morning broke over the city, Nick and Katherine found Etienne and Miss Donatta sipping hot coffee in her garden courtyard. They stumbled outside, groggy from the late night wine. They watched Etienne and Miss Donatta in silence for a while. Though they didn't want to interrupt, they couldn't tear themselves away.

Miss Donatta's garden was full of colorful flowers, delicate and lush. They moved in the light breeze, their varied petals releasing a heady aroma into the air. The stone garden walls were lined with bushes, trees and exotic plants, giving the sequestered garden a feeling of intimacy and abundance. Somewhere in the distance, a faint trickle of running water could be heard.

Etienne and Miss Donatta chatted quietly, intimately. Occasional lilts of their soft laughter drifted through the garden. Miss Donatta stretched out her long legs and rested her bare feet in Etienne's lap, which he gently, almost absently, caressed as they talked. Neither Nick or Katherine moved. They watched in the shared envy of people long married, until Etienne finally saw them.

Miss Donatta rose to greet her guests. "I have some clothes set aside for you, Catarina," she offered, using the Italian pronunciation of Katherine's name. "If you're going to be chasing around the Egyptian desert with Etienne, you'll need something suitable to our climate."

"Thank you," Katherine was surprised and softened by Miss Donatta's elegant and easy generosity. "That's very kind of you." *Kindness*, Katherine reminded herself, *is a luxury of the securely loved*. The eyes of the two women met, for the first time, at least in the broad light of day. In each other they found a warm respect and more than a little curiosity.

"Come with me," instructed Miss Donatta, taking Katherine's hand. "Let's take a long, hot soak before breakfast, shall we?"

"That sounds divine," said Katherine.

"There is a natural hot spring that runs through the arboretum," explained Miss Donatta. "Very beautiful, and very private. You'll adore it!"

"Ooh la la la la," crooned Etienne. He and Nick sat up in their chairs.

"You cannot come," Miss Donatta threw over her shoulder, as she led Katherine out of the courtyard.

Miss Donatta and Katherine stripped off their clothes and immersed themselves in the hot, steaming water that pooled around them. It was lovely there, dense with leaves and flowers. A splendid collection of plants and shrubs – some that Katherine could recognize and some that she could not – crowded the arboretum. The scent of freesia and spice and rich wet earth permeated the air. Indigo blue tiles framed the large pool where they soaked. The hot water was piped into the enclosure, and re-circulated constantly by a pump, quietly humming in the background. Katherine didn't dwell on those details, though. She was feeling dreamy and delightfully lost.

Miss Donatta was more in a mood to chat. "Etienne tells me you met at university."

"Yes," Katherine murmured. Her thoughts and her body were melting into heat and luxury.

"It's unusual, isn't it, for a woman to attend Oxford? Particularly back in the 30s?" Miss Donatta lit a cigarette from her case and held it high above the water. "I am very impressed."

"Don't be," answered Katherine. "I followed Ben there. I was obsessed, really. I would have done anything to get into that college."

"Ben was your lover?"

"Brother." As Katherine talked, she studied the fragile flowers surrounding her. "He was my twin. It was just the two of us, really. He was my companion, my friend, my confidant. I was 18 years old and had been accepted to Brown, when Ben decided to go to school in England. 'He has the promise of a great scholar,' they all said. And he had a college fund. He had to go. But it crushed me to be without him. I know that sounds odd, to be that close to your brother. Most girls ignore their brothers at that age, don't they? But we were different and I wasn't prepared to be alone."

"It sounds like you had a highly educated family."

"Not really. My mother thought I should skip college, find a nice boy, get married, settle down and raise a family. She drilled it in to me. But I looked at how her life turned out and it didn't seem so promising. Anyway, it was my father who insisted that Ben and I got the best education his money could buy."

"So, you passed on Brown and went to Oxford to be with your brother."

"Partly to be with him, partly to save him. At least in my own mind."

"Save him?"

"It was my job. Ben had saved me once, during a sad time in my life. I owed him this. And, frankly, I missed him."

"Save him how?" asked Miss Donatta.

"It was said, by those who supposedly knew, that my brother wasn't handling himself very well at university. He was drinking. He was womanizing. He was flunking. I took my own college fund and went to see for myself. I went, against all advice, against my mother's wailing and protesting, against every fear I might have had. I decided that I could handle the pressure for both of us."

"Did you?" asked Miss Donatta.

"I clung very tightly to Nick and Etienne during those years, for more support than they ever realized." Katherine had often thought of Nick and Etienne as the foundation upon which she had stood – to build her academic success, to repair what was broken and to reclaim Ben, as if she ever could.

"And Ben?"

Katherine looked over at Miss Donatta, who was watching her carefully. "Ben was a wild man. Much like he had been as a child, with that spark he had, but times ten. He was away from home for the first time, away from the rules. Ben seemed to operate at the center of his own universe. They called him, "King of the Fun Hogs," if that tells you anything. He lived at the center of a whirlwind of his own making. People loved him. It was hard not to. He had this great big dazzling smile. He loved everybody. And he was always *into* something, stirring something up, bringing a bunch of people along with him, conspiring and laughing the entire time. He was ... irresistible in a lot of ways. He really was."

"Sounds like we're talking about you," offered Miss Donatta. "Except maybe for all the laughter."

Katherine looked at her intently. "No," she said. "No."

"Where is Ben, now?" asked Miss Donatta.

"We lost him, during the war. He was one of those bright-eyed, brave lads charging off to defeat the Nazis. Ben hated Hitler with all his heart. Said he would die trying to kill the man, if it came to that." Katherine's eyes were moist, searching. "And, of course, it did."

"That explains the star."

Katherine looked down at the bronze star, lying against her bare, wet skin. "Ben nearly died earning this little thing." She touched it with her fingers.

178

"Many others did die that particular night. But I don't think Ben ever got over that episode. Ever. He never talked about it, but others did. 'Caught behind enemy lines,' they said. 'Bombs exploding everywhere. Dead bodies.' It was awful. Ben took the radio off the shattered body of another solider, called in reinforcements and led the squad, all half drowning, down a river to safety. He saved everybody. Everybody who could walk or be carried, at any rate." After Ben died, a year later and in other horrible circumstances, his commanding officer sent me a letter ... and the star."

Heroic or meritorious achievement. Katherine took that accolade as her own. Just for living without him. "Listen to me," she said, flushed. "I'm rambling."

"So many terrible losses," said Miss Donatta. "Such a dark time for the world."

"Yes," agreed Katherine. "Indeed."

"Where was your mother all this time?" asked Miss Donatta.

"Working," replied Katherine. "She was a secretary."

"What did your father do?"

"He left."

Miss Donatta looked over at Katherine. "I'm so sorry, Catarina."

"Don't be. Really. He came around from time to time, with gifts and kisses for all of us. It was my mother's heart he broke, over and over. Coming around, leaving again."

"It's quite a trick to love someone and not need them, isn't it?" said Miss Donatta. "Hard enough as an adult. Impossible for a child."

"Love and need – how does one separate the two?" asked Katherine.

"Recognize the difference, I suppose. Learn to make your own happiness."

"That's exactly what my father did, I think, now that you say it."

"Do you hope he was happy, at any rate?" she asked.

Katherine looked at her, stunned into silence. Considering his happiness had never occurred to her. All she ever thought about when she thought about her father was how much wreckage he'd left behind. She hadn't hoped for his happiness. She had hoped he was miserable. She delighted in his failures. She prayed he would spend every single day for the rest of his life regretting his choices.

But maybe there's a difference, thought Katherine suddenly, *between selfishness and survival.* "I suppose that's the test then, isn't it?" said Katherine. "To hope for happiness for those who have hurt you." *Even harder,* thought Katherine, *to forgive yourself for needing too deeply, for driving someone away.*

"Indeed," said Miss Donatta. "Now tell me, what was your father like?"

"Handsome." Katherine let herself remember things, things she hadn't thought of in a long time. "I thought he was handsome, anyway. And fun. He was dashing and reckless and irresponsible. But he knew things, amazing things. He made and lost more than one small fortune, but I don't think anything ever worked out exactly the way he thought it would."

"Is it difficult to talk about?"

Katherine looked straight at her. "Not at all. It's just details, the way things were."

"Your past has made you quite strong," said Miss Donatta.

"Perhaps," mused Katherine. "Or perhaps just very, very clear about what I want."

Miss Donatta blew smoke into the air and glanced sideways at Katherine. "Perhaps."

On the patio, Nick and Etienne were relaxing over coffee. "She's quite a knock out," commented Nick. "Miss Donatta, I mean."

"Yes," agreed Etienne. "Quite." He wasn't sure if Nick really meant to say that out loud.

"How'd you meet her?"

"Through an antiquities dealer in Cairo, Rasul Taj, an old friend. She's one of his most highly valued customers."

180

"She's rather beautiful," said Nick.

"Beautiful, rich and never bored," Etienne said. "I can tell you that."

"What is she like?" asked Nick, fascinated beyond his good manners.

Etienne sat back and mulled over his thoughts on the matter. "Intense," he said. "Respectful. Passionate. And occasional. Miss Donatta prefers it that way."

Nick sat back and crossed his legs. "My, my."

"She's a great collector of art and antiques," continued Etienne, "as you can tell from her home. She knows the art world better than most." Etienne smiled inside, lingering over private memories. "She embraces the highest aesthetics of anyone I've ever known," he explained, "flitting from one beautiful treasure to the next, drinking them all in. I like to think of her as an exotic hummingbird," he mused. "Delicate that way. Speeding away from anything harsh or unpleasant."

What Etienne didn't tell Nick was that he had enjoyed many profitable business dealings with Miss Donatta over the years. Upon occasion, Miss Donatta would hold things in safe keeping for Etienne or Rasul, as the Egyptian laws that govern antique dealers did not always apply to private collectors. Which came in handy from time to time.

Etienne had to split his loyalties between museums and private trade. While many of the artifacts he came across clearly belonged in a museum, museums typically could not afford to pay for them. For the most part, as long as the objects were preserved and appreciated, it was all the same to Etienne.

"While Miss Donatta has been very helpful in transactions of art and antiques," said Etienne, anxious to change the topic, "I've been more concerned with ancient manuscripts over the years."

"As I recall, you went to the University of Paris, after Oxford, to study religious archeology."

"Indeed. That is where I met a man named Henri Poirier. He became my mentor, my friend and my doctoral advisor. Poirier had heard that a group of Germans were working on a theory that there was a "source" gospel: one document from which the canonical gospels – Mathew, Mark, Luke and John – were copied. I was fascinated by this idea and started to study the similarities and differences between the four gospels of the New Testament. What I found was amazing. Eventually, through deduction, I began to re-create this source document, called 'Q', although no traces of it have ever been found. I began my thesis on the matter, establishing Q as a link between the Jewish world of Jesus and early Christianity."

"Why do they call it Q?" asked Nick.

"From the German word, *quelle*," explained Etienne, "which means 'source.' One source document, written by someone who was witness to his life, and had actually heard Jesus speak. It's not enough to re-create Q; I have to find it. Somewhere, hidden in the Middle Eastern deserts, is the original document. I'm convinced of it. In 1938, I went to Galilee, looking for it."

"How did you end up looking for these Gnostic Gospels instead?"

"Well, the war happened, for one. But before that, I had some disagreements with Poirier, my advisor. Some serious disagreements. I was so entirely disillusioned, I was willing to forget about Q for awhile. I joined the French Resistance and went to war instead, working undercover as an archaeologist for hire.

"I heard about the Gnostics when I was stationed in Cairo. The Gnostics became my new obsession. But I've not forgotten Q. I intend to find that source document, just as I'll find the Gnostic Gospels."

"What does it say, this Q gospel?" asked Nick.

"Well, I can tell you this: there's nothing in there about original sin. Or many of the factors typically associated with modern Christianity. The earliest Christians were concerned with their *relationship* to God and to each other. I believe the community that created Q were wandering ascetics, radicals of a sort, the type to question the status quo. They were preparing themselves for, and creating, a utopian society, the Kingdom of God on earth. They were not concerned with hell-fire and brimstone. And not with heaven, hell, or the holy trinity, either."

"You should meet Father Antonio," said Nick. "He'd have a thing or two to say about that."

"Who's Father Antonio?"

"A priest who flew with us from Tenerife to Cairo," said Nick. "He helped Katherine with some trouble she had at the airport, with

182

your friend, Nafarah. The priest ended up sitting next to us on the flight into Egypt. Eventually, the conversation turned to religion. I got into with him, I'm afraid. Nasty little argument. I'm not sure Katherine's entirely forgiven me for it."

Just then they heard Katherine and Miss Donatta approaching the patio, talking casually, as though they'd been friends for years. Nick and Etienne watched the two women as they crossed the courtyard, fresh from their mineral bath. Their thin silk robes wrapped around their bare legs as they strolled arm in arm through the garden. Nick and Etienne couldn't take their eyes off them, standing as they arrived at the table.

"Nick and I were just talking about religion," said Etienne. "And a certain priest."

"Oh?" replied Miss Donatta.

Nick reached across the table and smacked Etienne on the chest with the back of his hand. "Zip it up, old boy."

Etienne swatted his hand away, grinning.

"They are still little boys, no?" said Miss Donatta to Katherine, as they settled in at the table.

"They do love to argue," replied Katherine. "I remember many late nights and long, heated discussions in college. They'd sit in a pub all night, smoking cigarettes, drinking beer, debating the great issues of the day."

"It wasn't just us, Katherine," said Etienne. "If you recall, you were right there in the thick of it all."

"As I recall it," replied Katherine. "I did much more *listening* than talking. It was you – " she pointed at Etienne – "who was always stirring things up, causing trouble." Etienne sat back, looking startled.

"Your memory fails you, my dear," interjected Nick. "It was *you* who always brought something provocative to the discussion. And you certainly never backed away from a good argument."

"That's right," added Etienne. "You were constantly making outrageous statements, just to get everyone all riled up. You and Ben: two trouble-makers, setting the place on fire."

Katherine turned to Miss Donatta. "Speaking of fire," she said, changing the subject, "Might I have one of your lovely cigarettes?"

"Of course, Catarina," offered Miss Donatta. "You must try one of these." She lifted a silver case trimmed in gold accents, from the table. She opened it with the push of a delicate little gold button. "From the Balkans. They are absolutely decadent."

"Thank you," said Katherine, taking a slender, dark brown cigarette. "What an beautiful case," she remarked. "It's exquisite."

Miss Donatta had a lighter nearby, matching the case, silver trimmed in gold. Etienne picked up the lighter and raised it to Katherine's cigarette. Katherine's little finger brushed against Etienne's hand as she held the cigarette to the flame. They pretended to each other that it was not intentional.

Nick pretended, too. He pretended not to care that Etienne had usurped his own duty and privilege to light his wife's cigarette. He pretended not to notice the intimate gesture that passed between Etienne and his wife. From the outside, he looked entirely oblivious, entirely carefree. But not one second passed that Nick wasn't watching everyone, his mind always at work.

"We'd better get going soon," said Etienne.

"Not before you've had a proper breakfast!" interrupted Sidi. Miss Donatta's fussy and devoted houseman came out onto the patio. He was carrying a full tray of hot eggs, pita bread with cheese and fresh fruit. An exotic tea pot sat on his tray, with a long narrow spout and steam rising from its lid. A stack of delicate china plates rattled precariously as he walked across the stone patio.

"It is good to see you again, Monsieur Etienne." Sidi bowed slightly, setting the tray down in front of Miss Donatta.

"Likewise, old friend," said Etienne, bowing his head in return.

"This just came for you." Sidi handed Etienne a telegram on a small silver tray. Then he turned to Miss Donatta. "Supplies are ready and loaded as you instructed," he said.

"Thank you, Sidi," she replied with a slight nod of her head.

"Sidi, what would I do without you?" said Etienne.

"Oh, I suspect you'd go somewhere else," Sidi replied. "And," he added over his shoulder as he walked in a stately gait back into the house, "we couldn't have that now, could we?"

"Impudent man," Miss Donatta said, hiding a smile.

184

Etienne opened the telegram and read,

ZAFAR IS IN QINA STOP WILL LEAD YOU TO THE
SOURCE STOP 200K IN YOUR ACCOUNT AT THE BANK
OF EGYPT STOP HAPPY HUNTING END

"How the hell did Nelson know where I was?" Etienne asked, throwing the telegram on the table. "He even knows I've been looking for someone named Zafar. And how does he know where I bank? And my account number, for God's sake?"

"That is just the sort of thing he'd make sure he knew," replied Nick.

"And how do you know this man again?" asked Etienne.

Nick sighed. "I met him during the war. We were stationed together in a French village near Italy. Just a surveillance post. Nelson was a supply clerk. But God, he was a wily one. Unscrupulous to the extreme. And a very, *very* clever chap."

"That is just great," snapped Etienne. "I don't like this fellow. Not one damn bit."

"But, look," said Katherine, picking up the telegram. "Now we know where to begin."

Nelson wasn't giving them everything they needed to know, however. He had carefully doled out just a tidbit of what he knew. Nonetheless, Etienne now had the one piece of information that would lead him to the missing manuscripts. And the money to get him there. It was time to go.

True to his word, Sidi had packed the jeep with food, water, blankets, camping gear and intricate maps of the Egyptian countryside. He and Miss Donatta both knew the impetuous nature of many of Etienne's expeditions.

After breakfast, Katherine changed into loose cotton clothes of Miss Donatta's: khaki pants, cotton shirt and linen summer jacket, with a white silk scarf, straw hat and soft leather boots.

To Nick, Katherine looked as though she was about to head out on a casual drive through the Sahara looking for caribou and a ritzy hotel. "You look stunning," he said, holding her by the shoulders. "Ready for our next adventure?" She fell into his arms and let him hold her tight.

Nick sensed a gathering storm as he watched Katherine relent to customs and choices entirely out of her control. She seemed awkward in this unfamiliar land, caught up in the momentum of someone besides herself. As was typical, Nick tried to fix things for her, the best he could.

Katherine smiled up at Nick. "I was born ready."

The trio collected themselves around the jeep and said their good-byes to Miss Donatta.

"I have something for you, Catarina," Miss Donatta said. "For your journey." She handed a brown canvas knapsack to Katherine.

"Oh my," Katherine stammered. "You shouldn't have."

"Nonsense. You'll need a few things if you're going to be presentable out there in the desert. I've just tucked in a few necessities – and a luxury or two."

"I cannot thank you enough," said Katherine. "You've been tremendously gracious."

Before they left, Nick stepped forward and shook Miss Donatta's hand. "Thank you for everything," he said, shyly. She gave him a warm hug to send him on his way. Then she turned to Etienne. She handed him a round hatbox. Etienne knew it would contain the codex, and perhaps a note, written in her delicate curving script, just for him.

"Arrivadercí, il mio amore," she whispered, as she held Etienne in a tight embrace. "You be careful, and come back to me in one piece. Or I shall have your hide."

"That I shall look forward to," said Etienne. *"Au revoir."*

They drove off into the waning day, three intrepid friends, south to Qina to find the one man who could lead them to the words of the heretics.

13

FRIENDS AND ENEMIES

*I seek not strength to be greater than my brother or sister
But to fight my greatest enemy, myself.*

– Native American Tradition

Qina, Egypt

Before leaving Cairo, Etienne stopped for petrol and loaded up on the last few supplies he thought they might need: matches, extra blankets, dried food, cigarettes to bribe the locals.

Nick chatted nearby with some street boys, handing a few bills to one with outstretched hands, taking a trinket in return. The boy grinned and darted off down the street. His compatriots followed for a short distance and then gave up the chase, returning instead to pitch their wares to the travelers at the service station.

Nick returned to the jeep where Katherine was waiting. "Here, darling," he offered. "Why don't you sit in the front seat?"

"I like it back here," said Katherine from her nest in the rear of the jeep. "I can spread myself out. It's like my own private cubbyhole. Really. You sit up front with Etienne."

"Alright then."

"Nick?"

"Yes?"

"What was that?"

"What was what?"

"What you gave to those boys."

"Oh, nothing," shrugged Nick. "A couple of dollars. They're only children – and they're out here begging for money, trying to help feed their families."

One of those same boys had taken it upon himself to clean the jeep's front windows. Etienne approached, handed the boy some coins, and settled himself into the driver's seat. They waited together while the boy applied himself vigorously to his work. He'd been over-paid for washing windows. To show his appreciation, and to demonstrate that he was not the type to take advantage, he washed them twice.

"I think I recognized that other boy," continued Katherine. "The tall one. Didn't he look familiar?"

"God no," said Nick. "There are probably thousands of boys, just like him, in Cairo. Skinny, hungry, desperate. Just trying to make a few bucks, to help put food on the table. These kids don't go to school, you know. They work on the streets, every one of them." Nick looked sullen. "Here." He handed Katherine a papyrus sheet with a painting of King Tut on it, manufactured for mass production, cheap and easy. "A good profit," said Nick. "If you can get a few American dollars for it."

"My heart breaks for these children," said Katherine, carefully placing the papyrus into her knapsack. "Where are their mothers?"

"It's not their fault," offered Etienne. "Making children is sometimes all they have in a world gone mad. They feel powerless. Children give them at least a semblance of control over their own destiny." Etienne grinned and added, "Breeding is also a sign of virility in men, you know."

"That's nonsense," snapped Katherine. "Somebody has to take responsibility for bringing unwanted, un-cared-for children into a life of poverty and hunger. It *is* their fault. Their mothers should know better."

"Speaking of mothers," said Etienne, suddenly. "I never thought to ask: do you have children?"

"No," Nick replied, and left it at that.

"That is too bad," replied Etienne. He looked back at Katherine in the rear view mirror. "I always thought you'd make a wonderful mother."

Katherine's face was drawn into a scowl but her eyes, Etienne noticed, her eyes were soft. "I'm not the *mother* type," she stated, looking out the side of the jeep.

Etienne looked over his shoulder at Nick, who was watching his wife carefully. *Had Nick heard Katherine say this before?* Etienne wondered. *To new acquaintances at a dinner party, to nosy relatives at Thanksgiving, to colleagues at a business lunch in a trendy New York restaurant, to herself, at her mirror, alone?* Etienne pressed on, determined to satisfy his curiosity. "What *is* the mother type, exactly?"

Katherine forced a laugh. "Paragons of virtue, patience and self-sacrifice. I'm much too selfish to have children, I'm afraid." She carefully dusted invisible lint off her jacket and then looked up, uncompromising, unapologetic at Etienne.

"Children are whiny, bad-mannered, germ-infested, needy little monsters who suck the time and vitality out of a woman until there's nothing left of them but shattered hopes, wide hips and a face full of wrinkles. Believe me, I've seen it happen over and over again. No. It's not for me." Katherine wasn't laughing any longer. Etienne stopped pressing.

"Shall we get going?" Nick reached his arm back and squeezed Katherine's hand, as Etienne turned the key, revved the engine and pulled out into the stream of traffic.

They traveled out of the frenetic city and into the vast, barren desert beyond. It seemed strangely quiet and haunting to be surrounded by mile upon mile of nothing but sand and river. They were making their way south on a dirt road that followed the Nile to Upper Egypt, and more specifically, the Inland Empire.

"This region is mostly populated by *fellaheen*," explained Etienne. "Peasant farmers. They're among the hardest working and poorest Egyptians, organized by clans and small villages. This land is also occupied by traders and teachers, outlaws and bandits."

"Why don't they migrate to Cairo or Alexandria, where they'd have better opportunities?" asked Katherine.

"That's certainly a choice for them, if they can afford to get there and get established. But most who try end up living in the streets."

"Why?"

"What jobs can they get? With no formal education, they can only go into service, if they can get a position at all. Add to that, Cairo and Alexandria are occupied by the British. So you've got these fat cats in pith helmets and linen suits, sipping tea under the bougainvillea, while black-skinned men in turbans serve them crumpets and cucumber sandwiches. Women sit under umbrellas, snapping orders and gossiping about the antics of the Egyptian king. Bach plays on the phonograph for the wealthy and the chosen, but these Egyptians are not much more than slaves, and the rest of the country lives in squalor."

Nick kept his gaze straight ahead. *Etienne, you're such an ass,* he thought. But he smiled easily, and said, "I don't suppose little things like modern irrigation canals have helped these villages at all. Electricity, telephone lines, trains..."

"Rebels are bred in these villages," warned Etienne. "They're poor. They're angry. They're hopeless." Etienne looked in the rear view mirror at Katherine and then returned his eyes to the road. "But for the most part, they're preoccupied with feeding their families. It's hard to lead a revolution when you're slaving day and night just to get by, with a family to care for."

"A revolution?" asked Katherine, her face drawn into a look of concern.

"Britain protects Egypt, and has for 65 years," said Nick. "But now that the war is over, many of the locals want self rule, and control of the government. Which is absurd, frankly. They are unorganized, corrupt, mostly uneducated, and would make an entire mess of it. The British Empire has brought tremendous wealth to the Egyptians, in engineering, art, literature, science. You name it."

"And the sun never sets on the British Empire, now does it?" said Etienne, glancing at Nick.

Nick didn't reply.

"The British are hated by many who want them out of their country," continued Etienne, while Katherine leaned in closer to hear. "It's the perception of the Egyptians that His Majesty the King is mostly interested in controlling strategic areas, like the Suez Canal. And many consider King Farouk and his government mere puppets of the British."

"I wouldn't entirely agree with that," said Nick. "Protecting Suez and controlling it are two different things."

"Not to the Egyptians," said Etienne. "They want the British out and they want the monarchy out. *Istiqal el tam* – they demand independence. The Muslim Brotherhood, for example, is fighting for a government based totally on Islam and the teachings of the Koran. They despise those same Western influences you're so proud of, Nick. And they mean business. They're a highly organized, widespread group of fundamentalists striving to purge their country of what they consider corrupting forces. Riots, car bombings, sabotage, assassinations – none of this is beneath them. Dying for the cause of Allah is their supreme objective. They have declared *jihad* – holy war – against the British."

"You didn't tell me that," said Katherine, staring at her husband. Nick's face was a mask of stone, and she thought he looked far more angry than the least bit concerned.

"Oh, it gets worse, believe me," said Etienne. "The Young Egypt Party has formed paramilitary squads of youngsters, teenagers mostly, called The Green Shirts. They're turning them into hooligans, encouraging them to sabotage and terror. Most of these kids are desperately poor and fighting mad, easily recruited to a life of violence. Their main rival is the Wafd Party, which is the most popular in Egypt, but considered too sympathetic, or vulnerable, to the West, and far too interested in democracy. They have their own band of thugs, called The Blue Shirts. And they're all vying for power, following the way of the sword."

"How will it ever end?" asked Katherine.

Etienne shook his head. "The ruler of the Muslim Brotherhood has said it will take three generations to accomplish their plans: one to listen, one to fight, and one to win. The current generation is considered the *listeners*. Imagine what is coming."

Etienne looked over at Nick for a long moment before he continued. "We are now in the land of Muhanna," he said, "which stretches from Lybia to Afghanistan. This land is holy to the Muslims and, as infidels, we are all trespassers of the most offensive kind."

"That makes me feel so happy, Etienne," said Katherine. "Thank you very much." It came as some comfort to Katherine, as they drove into a desert of uncertainty, that Etienne was carrying a gun. *Sweet Mother of Jesus, I just hope we don't have to use it.*

Many miles of silence passed as Etienne drove the jeep past rippled waves of endless sand. The day grew hotter. To Etienne, they suddenly seemed like an odd threesome – as though fate had made a big mistake, casting them together again, here in the yawning desert. Etienne was used to his anonymity, and to disappearing in the crowds of the cities, and the emptiness of the desert. He hadn't expected to encounter Nick and Katherine here.

Or had I? he suddenly wondered. *Was this my doing all along?* Etienne broke what had become an uncomfortable stretch of silence.

"Another interesting thing, thinking about the end of the war," he began. "I think the discovery of the Gnostic Gospels may be a unique phenomenon, something the Buddhists call, *Terma.*"

"Terma?" asked Katherine.

"Remember your Tibetan studies, *cherí.*"

Katherine looked at Nick, her face flushed, but her husband showed no emotion whatsoever.

"We studied this in college," continued Etienne. "Terma is a tradition of Buddhism. You remember."

Katherine shook her head, confused.

"*Terma* means words written or spoken for the benefit of mankind, but *not yet*. Messages that the world is not ready for. Words that are hidden, until they can be understood and accepted."

"Yes..." said Katherine, brightening. "I remember the terma as treasures. Knowledge hidden, like forgotten thoughts or dreams, to be rediscovered at the right time, by those who have the mystical vision to understand."

"Yes," said Etienne. "And the discovery of terma always signals the opportunity for spiritual renewal. A new chance. *And,* the very first words from the *Gospel of Thomas* talk about the *hidden* teachings of Jesus."

"What does Tibetan Buddhism have to do with early Christian documents, in Egypt, of all places?" asked Nick.

"Nothing, technically," answered Etienne. "But mystical revelations occur in virtually every religion in the world. When the world learns of the Gnostic documents, and the truths in their words, it will launch nothing short of a mystical revelation. And a shift in the consciousness of humanity."

192

Is it possible, thought Nick, *that these books could actually add wisdom and perspective to a world sick with war? Are we ready to hear such words, now, in the shadow of our darkest violence? And if it's true for the world, could it also be at work on a personal level? Is there a new chance waiting for all of us ...*

Each person in the jeep that day, toddling south on a quiet road, was invoking a new chance, hoping they had the vision to understand what came their way and the fortitude to make it their own.

They drove in silence again, wind whipping over the open carriage of the jeep. Suddenly Etienne was seized with a desire to have a look at the codex in the hatbox from Miss Donatta. He'd been itching to dig into since she gave it to him.

At the next nameless village, Etienne pulled off the dirt highway in search of lunch. In the near distance, they saw smoke billowing from an open-air café.

"There," pointed Etienne.

"Perfect," replied Katherine. "We'll dine at an establishment that is on fire. How lovely."

Etienne grinned. "The only thing on fire is roasted lamb. You'll see." He pulled the jeep up front and hopped out. Nick and Katherine, both happy to be off the road for a spell, followed close behind.

"Wait," cautioned Etienne, taking a look at Katherine. "You'll need to wear a scarf here, at all times. The rural regions are not so forgiving as Cairo. Most women in these parts don't even show their faces."

"For crying out load," griped Katherine, wrapping one of her new scarves over her tousled brown hair. "When are these people going to come out of The Dark Ages?"

Nick smiled at the ground and ushered his wife to a shaded patio, lined with palm trees and jasmine, at the back of the restaurant.

When they'd ordered a lunch of savory lamb kebabs and kafka – a mix of cucumber, tomato and goat cheese – Etienne looked through Miss Donatta's hatbox.

Sure enough, he found a note, a linen handkerchief that smelled like her perfume, a little flask of Scotch, white cotton gloves and – wrapped in a silk shawl – the holy book written by an ostracized disciple. The *Gospel of Thomas*, penned to share the words of the living Jesus, lay in front of him.

For a moment, Etienne was overwhelmed beyond thought or speech. He exchanged looks with Katherine and Nick. Katherine gave him a knowing smile and nodded her encouragement.

Etienne reached into his satchel and took out Katherine's magazine, which held the first page of the *Gospel of Thomas*. He also withdrew his personal journal, full of notes, maps and scribblings of known Gnostic documents. These, he spread out on the table in front of him. From his journal, he pulled a separate ledger filled with curious symbols, phrases and words.

"It's the Coptic alphabet," Etienne explained. "And a simple dictionary. It helps me with the translation." Etienne spread this document on the table next to the pages of the *Gospel of Thomas*, making meticulous notes in his journal. Etienne quickly donned the gloves and opened the codex to the first papyrus page. While Katherine and Nick looked on, he began to study.

For the remainder of their lunch break, Etienne buried his head in his work, and the strange letters that arranged themselves there on the golden paper.

He confirmed that the page Katherine had torn from the codex in New York, was indeed the first page of the *Gospel of Thomas*. He read the same words that were in the photograph taken by Talib Mina, director of the Coptic Museum:

These are the hidden sayings that the living Jesus spoke and Judas Thomas the Twin recorded. And Jesus said, 'whoever discovers the interpretations of these sayings shall not taste death.'

He worked awhile longer and translated the next saying, which he read out loud to his friends, and then buried himself again in his work:

Jesus said, 'Let one who seeks not stop seeking until one finds. When one finds, one will be troubled. When one is troubled, one will marvel and will rule over all.'

"I don't understand," said Katherine. "Marvel and rule over all?"

"That's the secret, isn't it," replied Etienne. "To discover the interpretations of these sayings."

"So as to 'not taste death,'" interjected Nick. "What do you suppose that means?"

Etienne and Katherine exchanged looks. "Etienne thinks there is a spell or a formula of some sort in this book," Katherine whispered. "That will prolong life ... indefinitely."

"No he doesn't," Nick retorted. "That's pure poppycock. Tell her, Etienne."

"The day is waning," replied Etienne, collecting his documents. "It's time we got back on the road." He dropped some bills in Egyptian pounds on the table and the three walked outside in silence.

As the jeep trundled on in ever-increasing heat and wind, Katherine paused to take a look inside the knapsack Miss Donatta had given her. She found a red lipstick, matching nail polish, lavender soap, a hairbrush, a linen handkerchief, a small canteen of water, and the silver cigarette case and lighter, trimmed in gold.

Katherine was rocked to the bone. For the first time in her entire life, she longed to be more like another woman – easy, soft, running over with goodness. She closed her eyes and wondered, *Could I? Or would it break my heart entirely to try?* These are the questions Katherine asked herself on the trip to Qina that day. It surely felt as though that type of softening, that type of exposure, would utterly destroy her. Katherine had a long, hot, quiet time to think about it as they drove over six more hours to Qina to find the mysterious Zafar.

Qina, Egypt

They were all tired, grumpy and smelling rather foul as they pulled into the small town of Qina well after the sun had set. They found a small lodging post, really just a house with rooms for let. The water wasn't entirely hot, the beds were lumpy and the food was simple. But they were extremely grateful for all of it. The innkeeper sent a bottle of red wine to Katherine's room, at her request, and she kicked Nick out to go talk with Etienne. She wanted to sequester herself in solitude, cigarettes and cabernet.

   God, this place is awful, thought Katherine as she crawled into the rickety bed with her glass of wine. *I want ice cubes in my lemonade, money I don't have to calculate, the English language. I'm tired of seeing the indulgent look on everyone's faces while I fumble with their crazy language. Forget their impossible alphabet. Right now all I want to do is forget Hugo Nelson, forget Etienne, go back to New York, settle down and be a good wife. God help me, it sounds good. I want to shop for groceries in the mornings and read magazines in the afternoons. I want to walk children to school and do charity work. I want to play bridge and tennis. I want to kiss my husband at the end of each day. I want to dust shelves...*

   But secretly, in a quiet corner of her heart, Katherine really wanted something else entirely. Egypt was calling her name, asking her – if she dared – to reinvent herself.

   The next morning the three friends set out to find Zafar. It was surprisingly simple. They just asked the innkeeper. Qina was small and Zafar had just recently set up shop here. It was only a mile down a dirt road to the *Egyptian Trading Company*, but they took the jeep, as it would be safer to have it close by at all times.

   Etienne went in first. Nick and Katherine followed and they all stood inside the door, looking around. The store was filled with antiques and artifacts and everyday items, most of them dusty and tattered, chipped or worn. Others were polished and repaired, with tidy white price tags tied with red string. A ceiling fan stirred around the warm air, offering little respite from the heat.

   They found Zafar fussing over two customers, European tourists far too far off the typical tourist route. They appeared to be from the north country, well-heeled, over-dressed and bent on finding a treasure in the rattletrap little store of trinkets.

   Why would a woman, wondered Katherine, *insist on wearing fur, in a remote village in Egypt, 400 miles from civilization, in 70 degree weather at nine o'clock in the morning? Why?*

   Katherine watched the woman pick through the many shelves, carelessly picking up items, sighing in disdain and tossing them back. "Don't you have *anything* here that is worthwhile?" complained the woman to Zafar. "All I see is junk, and more junk."

Now I know, said Katherine to herself. *She's a shrill harpy with nothing better to do than to insert herself into other people's lives in an entirely arrogant and insulting manner. She is as transparent as she is useless.* Katherine rubbed her eyes and fought away a hangover of wine and cigarettes.

"How about this?" replied the storekeeper, handing a brass lamp to the woman. "This you will like. Yes?"

The woman took the lamp he handed her, and turned it over and over in her hands. "What is she looking for?" whispered Katherine to Nick. "Some engraving that says, 'unique, truly a valuable item, authentic, buy me?' Forget that the shopkeeper is already telling her that." Katherine leaned in conspiratorially toward her husband. "Maybe she's looking for some hint of corroboration from the lamp. Maybe if she rubs it a genie will come out and tell her to buy it – even though it's relatively worthless. I can see that from where I'm standing."

Nick cast a frown at his wife. She saw it, like she'd seen the same expression so many times before, and she let it glance off her. Katherine admitted she had a mean streak in her character, and she attributed it to her refusal to be a mousy housewife. In the same moment – that reminder of sorrow – she likewise justified all her rough edges.

Katherine would not have admitted, however, or even realized, that over the years she had become submersed in her own obsessions. No one ever pressed her to explain herself, to let go or to rise above the losses she found unbearable. That she had gone on living when others had died, in their bodies and in their hearts, pulled on Katherine. But she didn't know that something in her had sunk below the tide of living; had drowned, and taken her compassion with it.

For a woman with no one beside herself to worry about, to care for, the world spins solely around her own desires. Nick watched it happen so slowly, so silently and so inevitably, even he couldn't explain it. Only that it had happened, and that he loved her all the more. Because he knew the depth of her sorrow and the sources of her longing.

"Oh, just buy the lamp, for God's sake," muttered Katherine under her breath, staring at the shoppers. "Buy something, anything, and leave."

Etienne strode up to Zafar and his customers. "That is a gorgeous piece," he said, pointing to the lamp. "How much are you asking for it?"

The startled customers looked up at Etienne, and held tight to their find. Zafar narrowed his eyes. "50 Egyptian pounds," he replied.

"That is a bargain!" exclaimed Etienne. "I'll give you 75 pounds for that lamp."

"Uh, no," said Zafar. "I cannot. These fine people had it first."

"100 pounds, then."

"Well," said Zafar. "It is worth at least that, but..." He hesitated, looking to his customers. They looked at each other, nervous at the prospect of being usurped by an intruder to their bargain. The husband, not to be outdone in front of his wife, said, "Well, if it's worth 100 pounds, then that is what we'll pay for it. Happily. And 25 more to show our appreciation to you." He paused to scowl at Etienne. "For your loyalty."

"It is done," said Zafar, taking the lamp and wrapping it in newspaper. "You will be very happy with this, I assure you." The customers handed over 125 pounds cash while Etienne looked on with a combination of envy and injury stamped on his face. They took their parcel and left the store quickly, secure in their purchase and wanting to sip strong coffee and gloat over it.

"So, how much was that really worth?" asked Etienne of Zafar. "About 15 pounds?"

"It was worth exactly what they paid for it," said Zafar. "Because that is what they paid for it, that is what it is worth."

Etienne laughed. "Indeed."

"Now, how can I help *you* today, sir?" asked the shop keeper, eyeing Etienne carefully.

"Don't you remember me?" asked Etienne, removing his hat. "You sold me something at my home in Cairo, some months ago. A book ..."

"Yes!" Zafar's eyes widened. "Etienne Desonia, friend of Shadif."

Etienne cleared his throat. "I have come to ask you about the other books."

"What other books?" asked the shopkeeper, his eyes narrowing.

"Your colleague Jahib, with the patch on his eye – he told me that there were 12 other books like the one you sold to me. I have come to buy them."

"That conniving, dirty, double-dealing son of a camel's back-end!" Zafar paced angrily back and forth along the rough and dusty floor. "I should have expected as much from that sneaky, thieving, one-eyed goat!"

"You didn't know there were more books?" asked Etienne.

"I assure you, I did not. Or I would have come to you with them long ago. I see now that Jahib tried to cheat me, once I introduced him to you. And he shall pay for that, if I ever lay eyes on him again."

"Where is Jahib now?"

The storekeeper shook his head. "That is a mystery. I have not seen him for months. He usually comes nosing around, looking for opportunities. But I have not seen him, not since shortly after we went to Cairo. I hope some terrible fate has befallen him for trying to cheat me, that belly-sliding snake in the sand." Zafar stopped pacing and plunked himself down in the rickety chair behind his desk, folding his arms across his chest, a frown etched on his face.

"Were you not to share in the profits of all the books?" asked Etienne.

"We shared the money you gave us, by halves," said the shopkeeper. "I knew of no other books.

"How do you know Shadif?"

"I take him things some times. Special things. Sometimes old things like your book. Sometimes information."

"What kind of information?" asked Etienne.

"That is strictly between myself and Shadif," said Zafar. "I can say no more about it. But, I can tell you that Shadif was very curious about the book. That is when he told me your name. He said you liked old books. Jahib was with me when I went to see Shadif in Cairo. But he never told me there were more books. He was waiting for me to find a buyer. He was waiting for me to find *you*. Did he not come back to sell you the rest?"

"No, he did not," said Etienne. "I haven't heard from him since that night."

"May he rot under the desert sun forever and may his sons be wifeless and his daughters barren."

"It is clear, my friend, that you have been cheated in this matter," said Etienne. Zafar just grunted. "Perhaps I can help..." continued Etienne. Silence. Nick and Katherine stood watching Etienne at work. "Information can be very valuable to me," said Etienne, pulling out his wallet. Zafar eyed him sideways, leaning forward. "Where did Jahib get the book that you brought to me in Cairo?"

"Ah," began Zafar, sitting back, putting his hands together as if in prayer. "If there are many more of these books, as you suggest, that would be very valuable information, indeed." He tapped his fingers together.

"Just how valuable, would you guess?" Etienne asked, smoothly, not moving his eyes from Zafar's.

"Oh, I would say... oh, let's see..." Zafar raised his eyes to the ceiling, calculating on his fingers. He looked straight back at Etienne. "I would say 300 Egyptian pounds for that valuable of information."

Etienne smiled. "Let's say 200 Egyptian pounds for the information. And if your source yields up more books, then 200 more – once I have the books in my hands."

Zafar paused, sizing him up. "250 up front. No less."

Etienne was making the man rich by the standards of his village. "Are you saying you know *for sure* the original source of these documents?"

"Oh, yes, yes! You won't be disappointed!"

"Very well then, 250 pounds," said Etienne. "But if I'm disappointed –"

"Oh, no, you won't be!" interrupted Zafar. "I can tell you, right now, the man who gave Jahib the old book is named Muhanna Ali al-

Samara, of al-Qasr. He is a farmer there. He lives with his mother in the village just east of here, less than an hour away. Nice, hardworking people. Here, let me write it down for you." Zafar licked the tip of his pencil and hastily scrawled out some notes on a scrap of paper. Handing this to Etienne, he then sat back, anxiously awaiting his payment.

Etienne tucked the note in his wallet, and then slowly counted out 250 Egyptian pounds, laying them deliberately on the desk in front of the storekeeper. Before he could scoop up the bills, however, Etienne firmly set his hand on top of them. He looked Zafar straight in the eye. "I don't plan on being disappointed. I mean it." Etienne then gave Zafar of the *Egyptian Trading Company* such as look as to cause Nick and Katherine to stop breathing and stare in astonishment. Such was the depth of Etienne's implicit threat, and his intention to get what he had paid for.

Zafar was unfazed. "And you won't be, my friend! And I thank you. And my family thanks you. You are a good and fair man. As am I."

Etienne moved toward the door. Nick and Katherine followed. "One way or another, I will see you again," Etienne said to Zafar.

"Ah, yes, when you come back with the balance – 250 Egyptian pounds more, yes?"

Etienne just smiled as they walked out the door into the hot morning sun.

From there, Katherine, Nick and Etienne strolled along the streets of Qina, talking, sorting out their plan, buying more supplies – food mostly, a few luxuries, cigarettes, a bottle or two of Egyptian wine.

Katherine stopped to take pictures at every opportunity: of the soft-worn buildings, the shops crowded with wares and people, mothers carrying their bare-bottomed babies astride their shoulders.

She gave money to the poor who were begging on the streets, and *baksheesh* to those who would pose for a picture. She sat for a few minutes on the dirt street and joined some children who were playing their own version of marbles with sand-colored stones. She let herself laugh, for the first time in a long time, as she tousled their hair and brushed dirt from their cheeks.

Occasionally, she would kneel down and take a picture unobserved, of a moment unfolding: the sale of a book marker to a tourist and the pleased look in a young boy's eyes; the longing in a mother's face as she sat with her children on a dirty blanket by the street, begging; the sight of two young men – friends, perhaps brothers – walking arm in arm as was their custom, momentarily unburdened.

It was just such a moment when Katherine came upon a woman selling scarves in the street. Her tiny baby was tucked in a sling on her back and slept peacefully as the mother moved in a calm rhythm to serve her customers. Dozens of brightly colored scarves, in rich and intricate textures, blew in the light breeze, creating a small oasis of color, movement and beauty in the dirty street.

Katherine bought a new scarf, then another and another, while she watched them, mother and child, on their island of self-sufficiency. When the baby woke, and gurgled or fussed, the mother simply swung the baby around, tended to his needs for food or attention, and went back to her work.

Lovely, thought Katherine, as she snapped some pictures. *I could do that*, she thought suddenly. *I don't have to become my mother.*

Katherine was seized by a new vision of herself: selling antiques in a small village, with a baby strapped to her back. Katherine let her imagination take her wherever it wanted to go. She saw simple days, of love and commerce, good deeds and sweet mothering, making her way in the world.

Chamonix comes to mind. I couldn't live in Egypt forever. But a little village in France... perhaps. Better yet, I could travel the world, not selling antiques at all, but taking pictures, telling the stories of the people I meet, from Egypt to India, France to Afghanistan. A wanderer and a storyteller. Just Nick and me and our child, travelers of a friendly world.

That she hadn't been able to have children didn't concern Katherine at the moment. That Nick wouldn't consider this plan for one split second didn't concern her, either. She was wrapped in a sweet dream and she wasn't going to worry about how to get there. For the moment, just being there was enough. Katherine held the vision in her mind for a long time – seeing it, feeling it, touching, tasting and smelling it – making it real in her heart.

If Katherine set into motion the elements of an alternate future for herself, she did not know it. Indeed she was not even aware of the possibility of such kind of magic.

Katherine suddenly looked around, startled and alone. She found Etienne purchasing fruit from a vendor, haggling over the prices, inspecting each fig, orange and mango he bought. Nick soon came jogging around a corner, catching up to them. "Where'd you guys get off to?" he asked, breathless. "You were there one moment, and then I looked up and you were gone."

"We've just been walking along," said Katherine, taking his hand. "Where have you been?"

"Nowhere," said Nick. "Hey though," he turned to Etienne. "What do you make of this Zafar fellow?"

"Well," began Etienne, "I had a pretty good idea that Zafar didn't know about the other manuscripts. But I wanted to get him riled up. I wanted him to see me as his ally. I needed information from him, and that information needs to be accurate. What I got from Zafar gave me some insight into Jahib the one-eyed bandit, the discoverer Muhanna Ali al-Samara, and even the trader, Shadif."

That Shadif was involved in this transaction troubled Etienne. He didn't entirely trust the man. Etienne suspected that Shadif was involved in the Muslim Brotherhood. Shadif was keenly interested in jewelry and artifacts that contained gems. Gems, once removed from their settings, were the easiest, most valuable commodity to smuggle into, or out of, a country. It was gems that funded underground rebellions in the Middle East and Etienne knew it. And he knew Shadif had a hatred for the British and a lust for gems.

Etienne, though he enjoyed some profitable deals with Shadif, did not like him at all, not since the moment they met. He was happy that Hugo Nelson had offered to fund the search for the Gnostic Gospels, leaving Shadif out of it and leaving the Path of the Hearts bracelet in Etienne's possession.

But now Shadif had surfaced again, in connection with Zafar. Etienne shuddered and turned his attention to Muhanna Ali al-Samara, the discoverer of the Gnostic library.

al-Qasr, Egypt

Muhanna Ali al-Samara paced a dim and gloomy cell. His eyes darted around the bare, familiar room – jumpy, alert, angry. He'd been caged here, with nothing to do but pace ... and think ... for weeks. How many weeks, he'd lost count. He had counted the early days, the days when regular visits from his brothers promised that he would soon be released.

But his brothers were fools. *What are they doing to get me out of this rat hole?* Muhanna fumed. They were lazy and stupid and had likely given up, as they were now free to sit around, idle and full of sloth, with their old brother in jail and unable to guide their work. Muhanna vowed to deal with them severely for this insufferable delay.

Then, Muhanna planned to seek his revenge on Husayn, the sheriff from Hamrah Dum. *Coward!* For nearly two years the sheriff had hounded Muhanna and his family, relentlessly, cruelly. They could hardly walk down the street of their own village without being harassed. Unofficial deputies, spies really, kept an eye on every thing they did. Muhanna couldn't possibly have sold his valuable books under such scrutiny. Surely the sheriff and his al-Yassid cousins would steal them and claim the fortune for their own. *Bastards! I will kill each and every one of them when I get out of this jail...*

And, in his lonely rantings, Muhanna swore to himself to also kill Basiliyus, the one villager who finally spoke out against him. For seven seasons the brothers al-Samara were able to squelch any talk in the village about the murder of Ahmad Ismail. *Who so richly deserved to die in the first place.* Then, many months later, the conscience of Basiliyus, the only eyewitness, overcame his fear of the brothers. And Basiliyus began to talk.

It was not long until the sheriff – imposed upon the self-ruling village by the long arm of the government – put Muhanna in this jail. *For safekeeping,* he had said with a sneer, *while he collected more evidence. Safekeeping, my eye.* Muhanna spat on the floor. The sheriff would probably let him rot in this place for the rest of his life. *No, no,* Muhanna assured himself, *my brothers will surely rescue me, they will, and I will again face Sheriff Husayn. Not in a jailhouse, but in the wide open sands of the eastern desert. There I will set things straight. Just as soon as –*

Strange voices interrupted Muhanna's visions of revenge. He heard his own name echo down the long hall. *The fat sheriff sits down there, in his smelly office, lording over all he sees. Pig.* But just beyond that office was the door and Muhanna's freedom. And in between here and there, something truly odd was happening.

"We have business with him." This was the strangest accent Muhanna had ever heard. He understood English well enough. The local teacher, Raghib, who'd been traveling the regional villages for decades, had insisted on that. But this was a very strange dialect that he heard.

Muhanna heard the sheriff mumble something. *Stupid sow! What trouble is he causing me now?* "Our business with Mr. Muhanna is *our* business." *That was a woman's voice...* Then the man with the strange accent spoke again.

What is this new mischief...? Muhanna paced, paced, paced. Steps could be heard. They were coming down the narrow hallway. They were coming for him. Muhanna stopped stone cold. *What in the name of Allah do these people want with me?* he wondered. He knew he would eventually win this round with the Sheriff and be released. His brothers would see to that. But these strangers – they were another matter entirely. Muhanna walked straight to the bars that held him, ready to meet his fate head on, whatever it was.

Etienne Desonia approached the bars. "*Salam 'alekum.*"

Muhanna's eyes narrowed, but he said nothing. He was a short, wiry man, whose face was worn and weathered from the sun. His dark eyes seemed to Etienne to hide many secrets, and stories of hunger and hardship. He wore a dirty *jallabiya*, turban and a cotton scarf around his neck, woven in threads of red and yellow. His bare feet, rough, calloused and clad in thin sandals, betrayed a hard life, a life without luxury.

"I am Etienne Desonia. Your friend Zafar sent me here. He said we could be of help to each other." Muhanna still stared at them, saying nothing at all. "We are looking for books. *Kotob.*" Etienne pantomimed the opening of a book, the turning of pages. "*Wara' el bardee.* Papyrus books." Still nothing from Muhanna. Etienne continued, "*Enta bititkallim inglizi?* Do you speak any English? *O Firakh?* Or French?"

Muhanna let out a raspy laugh. He then lay down on his cot and stared ambivalently at the ceiling, with a hint of a smirk on his dark face.

"What's so funny?" asked Nick. Etienne shrugged.

"Well, now what?" asked Katherine.

"Maybe we should try someone else," Etienne suggested, loudly.

Muhanna then spoke to the ceiling in slightly broken English. "I do not speak your English. Nor the language you call *chicken*."

"My Arabic isn't quite perfect," shrugged Etienne.

"My guess is that he doesn't want us to try someone else," suggested Nick.

"Let me handle this," said Katherine, brushing Etienne and Nick aside. "This is how I see things, my friend. We have money, cash money. Now, we can either send some of this money your way. Or we can use this money," Katherine continued, waving a wad of bills through the air, "this *cash money*, to insure that you stay in this dirt pit a good long time. So what it really comes down to, is who has the most cash on hand. And I'll bet that's me. What do you think?"

Muhanna sat up, shrugged sheepishly, and moved toward the cell door. "My English is coming back to me. Just a little."

"I thought it might," said Katherine smugly.

Etienne moved in and took over. "We are looking for some books. We hear you found books, papyrus books, near here."

"Perhaps I did. Perhaps I did not."

"Can we help you remember?" Etienne motioned to Katherine for some of her cash. She handed Etienne several bills. "Would 50 Egyptian pounds help you remember?" asked Etienne. Muhanna took the money that was held out to him and quickly stuffed it inside his tunic. "Now then," said Etienne. "Did you discover papyrus books in the desert?"

"I did," replied Muhanna.

"Books? With leather covers?"

"Yes," Muhanna nodded.

"And you are the one who found them?"

"I am."

"Was there more than one?"

"Many more."

206

"How many?"

"Many."

"Were they found in this region?"

Another nod.

"Do you know where they are?"

"Yes."

"Can you direct us to them?"

"No."

"*No?*"

"No."

"Why not?" Etienne looked troubled.

"No." Muhanna just shrugged.

"Perhaps we can entice you," suggested Etienne. He gestured toward Katherine, rubbing his fingers together. Katherine whipped out her wad of cash again, peeled off a couple of bills and reached with them toward Muhanna's cell.

"No," said Muhanna, as he backed away from the bars and crossed his arms across his chest. "No."

"*No?*" All three friends replied together.

"No."

"Okay," said Katherine. "My patience is running out. You need to come up with some whole sentences. Tell us what you want in return for the books."

"I thought you would never ask!" smiled Muhanna. "Lovely lady, I would like – more than you could know – to see the sky again. To see my family again. To cast my eyes upon the mighty Nile. To dig my hands into her fertile soil. I would want to be free from these bars that so unfairly imprison me. That is what I would want."

"You've got to be kidding!" said Nick. "We can't get you out of here. You're in jail!" Katherine and Etienne smiled at each other.

"That is the price. For this, I will take you to the books," replied Muhanna.

"Why are you in jail?" Etienne asked.

"A delicate matter, not my fault, involving a family member," Muhanna looked straight into their faces. "A family member of the sheriff, that is."

"Oh great!" snapped Katherine.

Etienne proceeded. "What matter, specifically, has caused you trouble with the sheriff?"

"Well, his wife, you see... very young, very beautiful. She came to me, saying she was sent by her husband to buy some *sabakh* for their garden, to improve the miserable soil on their land. She said she had goods to trade for such a valuable commodity."

"Yes... go on," said Etienne.

"Well, I gave her the fertilizer in all good faith that she would indeed make a fair trade. We have had trouble with the al-Yassid family in the past," said Muhanna, spitting on the floor again. "They are greedy, evil, mean-spirited dogs of the earth. But," he shrugged again, "I was willing to do this to make for good blood between us."

"Go on," said Etienne.

"Well her trade was not of material goods, as she had promised. Her trade was, well, goods of the flesh."

"You had sex with the sheriff's wife for a pile of fertilizer?" interrupted Katherine.

A broad grin widened Etienne's face. He couldn't help it.

Muhanna shrugged his shoulders and looked sheepishly from Etienne to Nick. "Well, that is not how I would prefer to put it, but she was very beautiful. And very insistent. Naturally the sheriff is extremely upset. He has used his position to create my sad circumstances." Muhanna looked them straight in the eye. "He is punishing *me*, because he cannot keep his own wife on a leash. That is what he is doing!"

Etienne gently pushed Katherine into the background.

"Well," said Etienne. "In France we have a saying, a very old tradition. It goes like this: *Il est sage de pardonner les erreurs de la passion. Il est criminel de ne jamais les permettre.*"

They all looked at him. "To forgive the mistakes of passion is wise," repeated Etienne. "To never allow them – is criminal."

"You just made that up," retorted Katherine. Etienne beamed.

"How about bail?" Nick offered. "Do they have such a thing as *bail* here?"

"We can work something out with the Sheriff," said Muhanna hopefully. "But you must let me do the talking."

"Oh, that's rich!" exclaimed Katherine. "A self-confessed sex fiend parlaying our money for who knows what? He'll probably *buy* her or something. How'd you like to have that on your heads? No thank you. I'll do the talking."

Etienne couldn't stop looking at Katherine. For the second time in his life, Etienne's heart walked straight away from him, so suddenly and so completely, he didn't have a chance to stop it. He would spend much effort – as he had those familiar, bitter-sweet years ago – fighting it, reeling it back in, letting it out a little despite himself and again drawing it back, to hide and to wait and to yearn.

"My lady," Muhanna said to Katherine. "You will not get far in this village. Here, our women understand their place, and do not step outside of it. Your voice will not be heard. Women have a voice only in matters of children and cooking."

"Oh really!" Katherine put her hands on her hips and glared at Muhanna.

"He's right," said Etienne. "I'd better make the arrangements. Nick, you back me up. And Katherine," he smiled. "You stay here with Muhanna until we get this handled."

Nick trotted off with Etienne, fearing only for Muhanna's state of mind upon their return.

14

CAVES OF DECEIT

Every blade of grass has its angel that bends over it and whispers,
grow, grow.

– The Talmud

al-Qasr, Egypt

"Your debt to us is immeasurable," said Etienne, approaching Muhanna's cell. "I hope you realize that." When Nick and Etienne returned from their encounter with the sheriff, Katherine and Muhanna were standing on opposites sides of the bars, staring at each other in silence. The sheriff loped in behind them, jingling a ring of keys with each slow step.

Etienne was reeling from the frenetic debate with the sheriff, who spoke very little

English. And Etienne was still not entirely sure why the burly, arrogant law-enforcer relented. He doubted that it was their convincing argument, their promise to steward his prisoner, or even their money. It was as though something had crossed the sheriff's mind that Etienne was not privy to, and could not possibly guess.

As for Muhanna, Etienne was convinced the man had lied to him. Fidelity was of extreme importance in this culture. Any woman caught being disloyal to her husband would be hunted down by her own family and stoned to death on the spot. The matter would be settled. *So why was Muhanna in jail? And why, for the price of 500 Egyptian pounds, was he free to go?*

For his part, Muhanna was delighted. As the sheriff unlocked his cell and returned his meager possessions, Muhanna whispered something unintelligible under his breath. The sheriff smiled with a knowing that made Etienne uneasy.

Relationships could be very complicated in the small villages that sprinkled the Egyptian countryside. They were often interwoven with a long history of feuds and vendettas, embedded through time, and hidden from the stranger's eye. Etienne kept his concerns to himself, and hoped that in securing Muhanna's release, they had not overreached their own abilities.

Muhanna directed them to his home on the outskirts of al-Qasr, separated from the rest of the village as if by some forlorn – or arrogant – choice. It was a low structure of mud and stone, built square and angular. The mud bricks were forged from clay from the Nile and baked hard in the sun. Dried reeds had collected haphazardly around the perimeter of the house, with no clear purpose for being there. The open-air windows had no glass panes, but rather, rickety shutters that could be closed against the weather. A strange mixture of earth and spice hung in the air.

A low fence surrounded the home and the courtyard in front of it. A clay oven – reminiscent of a small mud hut with windows – smoldered in the courtyard. Loafs of flat, round bread lay nearby, cooling on stones. Chickens wandered the courtyard freely, along with a few goats and an occasional rooster. Sheep could be heard, restlessly bleating and shuffling behind the house.

The jeep rattled to a stop just outside the fence. Hearing noises, the woman of the house poked her head out the front door, fearful of the strange automobile. She squinted into the sunlight and called to her sons to come quickly. "Abdul, Khalifah! *Wasal bisoraa!*"

The two men came to their mother's call, and stood in front of her in the doorway, towering over the round, squat woman. Both brothers were in their late twenties, but the sun and the toil of desert life had aged them far beyond their years. Their lean, strong bodies were tensed against the possibility of the approaching, perhaps unlucky, fate.

Four people disembarked from the vehicle and moved toward the house. The sun behind them cast their shadows forward, and created four black silhouettes of the moving figures. One figure alone stood out from the rest, and could not be mistaken.

"Muhanna…" The woman took in her breath as she spoke, and her son's name came out as merely a whisper. "Muhanna!" she then called, loud and clear, her voice cracking. She ran across the courtyard, her black dress and scarf flying wildly in the wind.

211

"Muhanna!" She threw her arms around her eldest boy and wept, kissing his face. She looked deeply into his eyes, as if to make sure it was really he, and then wept and kissed him all over again.

Even his brothers held the man and cried, happy beyond speaking. They slapped Muhanna and each other on the back, and wiped the tears from their faces with the backs of their hands, grinning and crying, crying and grinning.

Katherine, Nick and Etienne stood a respectful distance apart. Eventually Muhanna himself dried tears from his own face and ushered them all inside. Together they sat in the main sitting room on a lumpy davenport, with Muhanna's mother in a chair across the room.

Electricity had not come to this part of Egypt and the room was lit with a scattering of oil lamps and candles. The floor was a combination of stone and hard-baked mud bricks. Brightly colored throw rugs, in red and blue with threads of gold – woven by Uhm Alia herself – lay on the cool floor. A scrap of papyrus hung on one wall, with Arabic words carefully penned on its rough surface. The penmanship was lovely, artful and delicate – out of place in the plain, stone home. The words, Etienne noted, were some of the ninety-nines names by which God is known in the Islamic faith. *They have made art of the name of God*, thought Etienne. The scowl that rested on his brow disappeared for a moment.

Muhanna was talking in low tones to his brothers. "*Mish aarif hiya fayn*," whispered the youngest, Abdul.

"*Ay da?*" Muhanna raised his voice, as he ushered Abdul roughly into the back of the house. The older brother followed. "*Haneamel ay!*" exclaimed Muhanna. The brothers spoke fast, in a strong regional dialect. Etienne had no idea what they were saying.

That left Katherine, Nick and Etienne alone, to shift uncomfortably under the dark stare of Muhanna's mother. Uhm Alia looked as tough as the land from which she sprang. She spoke no English, French or anything other language than her own raspy version of Arabic. A thin field of whiskers sprouted from her chin. Her dark, weathered face was made leather from the sun and she covered her hair with a black woolen scarf.

It was clear that she did not like strangers in her home, did not trust them near her family, and feared for the eternal soul of her eldest son by mere association with them. Katherine thought she just might get up and spit on their feet for all the venom seeping from her watchful eyes.

212

"Thank God for the language barrier," said Katherine. "At least we don't have to try and make small talk."

Etienne turned to Nick. "Something must be wrong," he said under his breath.

"Why are you whispering?" said Katherine. "We could call her son a dirty, rotten, sex offender – which he is, by the way – and she wouldn't understand a word of it."

A moment of uncomfortable silence fell on the room. Uhm Alia sat up straight in her chair. Nick and Etienne just stared back at her, looking guilty as sin. Katherine pressed on. "So what is going on back there?"

Muhanna, Khalifah and Abdul could still be heard arguing in hushed tones in the distant reaches of the house. Then followed a dull thud. Abdul cried out. The group in the sitting room all turned their heads in unison, Uhm Alia included, toward the back of the house.

"I have a feeling the manuscripts are not where Muhanna expected to find them," suggested Etienne grimly.

"Now what?" Nick wondered out loud. Etienne buried his head in his hands, to think.

"Well, they have to be *somewhere*," insisted Katherine. "We'll just have to find them... no problem." With that, Katherine rose and moved toward the back of the house. Uhm Alia sat up even straighter. But without further cause, she seemed bound to stay in her perch across the room. "Muhanna!" called Katherine, uncomfortably aware of his mother's posture, poised to spring at any moment should Katherine further transgress the tranquil privacy of her home.

"Katherine, do come sit down," said Nick. "We need to regroup here."

"I need a cigarette," said Katherine, as she slunk back onto the davenport.

Just then Muhanna returned to the room with Abdul. Abdul was looking a little pale, and shifted his weight uneasily as his brother spoke. There was a hint of a blue-red welt growing on his cheek.

"The manuscripts are safe," began Muhanna. "They are in the keeping of Raghib, a friend and a teacher who travels through the villages. Come back tomorrow." With that, Muhanna gave Abdul a strong shove toward the front door, whispering in Arabic. Abdul

213

scurried out the door before Muhanna had a chance to finish his sentence.

"So." Muhanna clasped his hands together. "Thank you for returning me to my family. My mother is most grateful. Until tomorrow, then."

"She doesn't look grateful," muttered Katherine.

"We would be most anxious to see the discovery site," Etienne suggested. "And since we can't see the manuscripts today, perhaps you would take us *there* instead."

"Since you're so grateful to us, that is," added Katherine.

"Oh, not today," said Muhanna quickly. "Big day. This is a big day for me and my family. You would not take a son from his mother on such a day."

"Yes, we would," offered Katherine.

"We wouldn't want to disappoint the sheriff, either," added Nick. "We promised to look after you."

"It's been a long time since I've been there," insisted Muhanna. "And Jabal al-Tarif is far from here."

"Jabal al-Tarif!" Muhanna's mother rose. "*La! La!*" She began to shake her head and gesture wildly, speaking loudly in Arabic. *No! No!*

"You see," said Muhanna, shrugging. "My mother will not abide such a thing."

"Who is in charge here?" barked Katherine. "Look, we paid good money to get you out of jail. It's time you started coughing up some results." Nick and Etienne rolled their eyes upward, as if looking for some sort of divine intervention. But these friends had a long history of supporting each other, even when one of them – usually Ben or Katherine – went too far.

"I'll tell you a secret," confessed Muhanna, seeing their resolve. "It is not safe for me to go back there. There has been trouble between our family and those of that area. The al-Yassids rule the land north and east of the Nile. The Inland Empire they call it, and they claim it as their own. Even the government cannot reach into that region. It is lawless and fierce, full of murdering thieves and vagrants. It is not safe for any of us. Even *you* would not be safe there."

The situation was beginning to become clear. Etienne had been in this region before, excavating monasteries and burial sites. The area Muhanna described was indeed secluded from the main stream of Arab culture. Clans had inhabited the Inland Empire for centuries, harboring a hostile alienation to their neighbors in nearby villages. They considered themselves a race apart, directly descended from The Prophet, Muhanna. In Etienne's experience, however, they were not necessarily dangerous. Unless, of course, one was involved in a blood feud with them. In which case, no law superseded their presumed right to exact revenge.

"So are you *personally* on bad terms with the people of the Inland Empire?" Etienne asked Muhanna, who was getting increasingly nervous.

"Bad blood," offered Muhanna, shaking his head.

"This is serious," Etienne said to Nick. "When clans feud in this area – and it appears that this is what we're dealing with – much of the transgressions are considered beyond the law. And local government is typically reluctant to interfere."

"So where does that leave us?" asked Katherine.

"We could still go, skirting the villages," suggested Etienne. "You didn't take them from a village, did you?"

"No. No," said Muhanna. "I found them below the cliffs of Jabal al-Tarif, near the river. We were digging for *sabakh* – for our crops."

"I say we go," said Nick.

"No." Muhanna flatly refused.

Etienne walked over and put his brimmed hat on Muhanna's head. "How about a disguise?"

"No."

"How about an incentive?" Katherine offered, pulling out money.

"No."

"How about a trip back to jail?" Nick threatened.

"No. No. No." Muhanna was still grumbling under his breath as he crawled under a blanket in the back seat of the jeep next to Nick. "How did I ever get into this mess?" he muttered. "I should have stayed in jail!" Muhanna silently vowed to kill his brothers – if he lived through this. While he was in jail, they had sold the ancient books for a few piasters, some cigarettes and a crate of oranges. "Stupid!"

"What was that?" asked Etienne, as he looked at Muhanna humped under the blanket.

"I was just thinking about my brothers." Muhanna popped his head out. "And how happy I am to see them again." With that, the jeep rumbled out of the courtyard, leaving Uhm Alia behind, wringing her hands and praying to the sky.

Muhanna was persuaded to come out from under his blanket for a bit, but only while they traveled where no villages or people were in sight. He was distracted though, every nerve in his body tense and alert. In this way, he told them the story of the discovery.

"My brothers and I, along with a few others from my village, went to Jabal al-Tarif one day, nearly two years ago. We were there digging in the sand for the soft, fertile soil that would help boost our crops. As we dug with our mattocks, my brother struck an object that was not a rock, and not *sabakh*. As I am the eldest, I knelt to see better, parting the sand carefully with my fingers.

"What I saw, and what I dug out with my bare hands, was an big pot, this tall, and this wide." He gestured with his arms, describing a jar that was about a meter high and 30 centimeters in diameter. "It was red, but faded and very old. I looked carefully at the top. There was a shallow bowl that made its lid, sealed with some sort of pitch, I would guess. Very beautiful, this bowl. My mother has it even now in her kitchen."

"Really?" said Etienne. "Now isn't that something…"

Muhanna went on. "I thought there might be buried treasure in the jar, and my brothers encouraged me to crack it open with my mattock. But I hesitated, for fear that a *jinn* might be hiding inside, waiting to wreak havoc on us all."

"What's a *jinn*?" asked Katherine.

"An evil spirit," explained Muhanna. "We were digging very close to burial grounds, and we did not know what spirits of the dead might be lurking about."

"Then what happened?" asked Etienne.

"Well, my brothers and my cousins prevailed upon me. Greedy they are and have a love of treasure. So I raised my mattock in the air and just as I did so, a great wind came upon us. Still I could not stop the weight of my tool once it was raised, and down it came upon the jar. The old pottery shattered instantly, and from the pieces came a creature of gold. We stood back, afraid for our lives. The gold spirit rose into the sky, shimmered brightly, and then disappeared. Just as suddenly, the wind died, and we were left in silence."

Katherine's eyes grew big. Etienne laughed. "It wasn't a *jinn* at all," he said. "What you saw were fragments of golden papyrus, crumbled to dust over the centuries, caught in the wind."

"It was a *jinn*, I tell you! And I have had nothing but trouble ever since!" exclaimed Muhanna. "Add to that, there was no treasure in the jar at all. Only old books. And those I had to share with everyone."

"You divided them up?" asked Etienne.

"At first, yes. We sat in a circle around the broken pot, and I gave each of us two books. But there were thirteen books and five of us. This did not come out right. So I had to take three books and divide them up."

"How in the hell did you do *that*?" snapped Etienne.

"Well I took the covers off and divided the pages up. That's how. I am the head of this family, and as such, am charged with the equal distribution of whatever we acquire. It is my duty."

"*C'est terrible*," Etienne exclaimed. "You shredded apart two-thousand-year-old books."

"How was I to know?" Muhanna stewed. "I was trying to be fair. It was all for nothing anyway. As we fought over who got what of the books, we decided it would be best for me to take them all, and to share the profits equally once I had sold them. So I gathered them all back up, except for the three leather covers, and tucked them inside my *jallabiya*. Then we rode home. Abdul carried the bowl, as a gift to our mother."

"Then what happened to the books?" asked Etienne.

Muhanna hesitated. "Most of them stayed in my house, hidden. One I gave to my friend Jahib, to see if he could sell it."

"Does Jahib have a patch over one eye?" asked Etienne.

"Yes! Yes, he does," said Muhanna. "Do you know him?"

"I've met him, once," said Etienne. "Did you tell him, by any chance, that there were more books?"

"Yes. Twelve more to be precise. If you count the ones that we took apart. Thirteen all together. Except for a few pages."

"What few pages?"

"Well..."

"Well?" pressed Etienne. "Tell me. What happened to a few pages?"

"Well, as we returned from our day's journey, our mother met us at the gate, with news. And with a chore for us to do. I put the books near the cook stove in our courtyard, and went off to do as she asked me."

"*Oh no,*" muttered Etienne.

"My good mother, cooking our supper for us in our absence, used some of the dry papyrus pages for... uh... kindling."

They all groaned collectively. Etienne was crestfallen at the great loss of those few fragile pages of papyrus. "Oh, Etienne, I'm so sorry," said Katherine. "I know how much these books mean to you."

"I would take it back, too, if I could," said Muhanna. "But such things are not in my hands. They are in the hands of Allah."

"Then Allah should be more bloody careful!" snapped Nick. "Perhaps He could be paying a bit more attention when things are about to go haywire. Can't He point down a bony finger, tap you on the shoulder and say, *Hey there, you sure you want to do that?*"

Katherine looked back at her husband. Nick just shrugged, knowing everyone had made mistakes wished that they could take back.

218

"So what about your mother?" asked Etienne, wanting to change the subject. "What was the great important chore your mother asked you to do?"

"That I cannot say." Muhanna crossed his arms in front of his chest and stopped talking. They pressed him for more, but he just crawled back under his blanket, and the conversation was over.

The jeep toddled along the dirt road, skirting the Nile, which flowed west before it turned north toward the Mediterranean Sea. They made a wide berth around Hamrah Dum, the walled and fortified village occupied by the al-Yassids, while Muhanna pressed himself to the floor of the rattling jeep.

They passed the peaceful village of Izbat al-Busah, and still Muhanna remained hidden from view. Nearby, Jabal al-Tarif rose like a giant monolith above the Nile toward a shapeless sky. The steep cliffs were flanked by a sloping bank of sandstone and granite – a talus – stretching out of the dry desert. The cliffs were honeycombed with caves, some of them natural, but most dug hundreds of years earlier to serve as tombs.

Though some of the entrances of these caves were just large enough for a sarcophagus to pass through, others were bigger and more elaborate. Families with the resources would dig deeper into the sandstone, creating large burial rooms for their dead. Still others had carved out small, square rooms to serve as chapels. At the back of such rooms, a shaft would be dug to inter the sarcophagus.

"Unfortunately," said Etienne, "all of these tombs have long since been looted by locals dredging artifacts to sell on the Black Market. The area is officially owned by the Egyptian Department of Antiquities. But in reality, it's controlled by neighboring villages. The government's interest is often ineffective, frequently ambivalent, and more often, just plain scared. To add to the mayhem, most of the guards patrolling the area are from the local villages." He grinned. "The foxes are guarding the hen house."

As the jeep passed from view of the last village and approached the base of the sloping talus, Etienne urged Muhanna from the floor. Muhanna looked odd with Etienne's hat pulled tight and low over his face. This he wore as a disguise to fool and fend off warring clansmen. He had removed his turban and stowed it carefully under the passenger's seat. He thought the large red scarf he wore around his neck made him look like a big, bright target on the landscape, but he was not willing to part with it.

Muhanna looked up from under the brim of his new hat just long enough to say, "Further yet," and then he hunched himself back down as if to make himself invisible. Finally, he lifted his head above the seat. "Just up here... Don't stop yet! Up a little further." The jeep crept around the natural bends and twists of the dirt road. "There!" said Muhanna, pointing to a series of boulders on the talus. Then he retreated to his huddle.

"There, *where*...exactly?" asked Etienne, his excitement growing up like a natural spring. He stopped the jeep and turned off the ignition. For a moment all they heard was the rushing wind.

"There. The broken boulder. On the slope. Now take me back."

Katherine jumped out of the jeep and tore the blanket off Muhanna. "Show us exactly where. And then we'll take you home." She paused. "I promise."

Muhanna heaved out a sigh and looked up to the heavens. He looked Katherine square in the eye and smoldered a silent challenge of wills before he crept out of the jeep. He looked over his shoulder, left and right, and headed straight toward a grouping of fallen boulders. He stopped suddenly and looked around. "In there." He pointed toward a cave with a wide opening, just topping the talus, low on the rock face of the cliff. Etienne, Katherine and Nick were scrambling up behind him when he walked straight past the boulders, not looking sideways, and began to climb the talus to the cave.

"Hey!" Etienne hollered, grabbing a lantern from the supplies. "I thought you said it was at these boulders ..."

Nick followed close behind Etienne. "Where's he going?"

Muhanna did not look back as he called over his shoulder, "The boulders are just a landmark." He pointed toward the cool, dark opening of the cave. "Up here!"

Muhanna reached the cave first, with Etienne close on his heels and Katherine and Nick just behind them. Muhanna disappeared for a moment in the cave, then poked his head out like a timid gopher, looked around, and disappeared back inside. As they followed Muhanna into the cave, no one saw the small cloud of dust that appeared, like a dainty plume, on the horizon.

They poked around the cave, quizzing Muhanna, who was becoming increasingly evasive and anxious to leave. "Well, one thing is for certain," said Etienne. "There's no indication here of recovered
220

manuscripts: no fragments of papyrus, no discarded leather coverings. The few shards of broken clay I see here are from a different era entirely, circa *yesterday*. And there's no evidence whatsoever of the *sabakh* that you were supposedly digging for." Etienne held a lantern in the darkness. "All I see here is dirt."

"You've led us on a wild goose chase, Muhanna," said Nick. "Why?"

Just then something moved in a dark corner of the cave. They heard it, rather than saw it. Then, slowly, a dark shadow began to slide across the floor. Katherine screamed. A black and deadly viper, about four feet long, slithered into the light of Etienne's lamp. Muhanna cried out and drew a knife from inside his *jallabiya*. Though no one had seen him hide it there, they were all happy enough to see him use it. Muhanna deftly leapt toward the moving snake and cut it in half with one stroke of his knife. He picked up the two dripping halves and threw them back into the corner of the cave.

Katherine watched in amazement, strangely compelled and horrified at the same time. Her eyes followed Muhanna as he casually wiped the knife on his tunic and put it back in its scabbard.

Suddenly a man's loud, throaty laughter broke into the cave. "Murder's deeds are today avenged." He spoke in a slow, cold voice. They all spun around quickly toward the entrance of the cave. A black silhouette stood like a menacing statue against the yellow sky. Three other men moved in behind their leader, swords raised and gleaming in the sunlight.

"Who are you?" asked Etienne.

"I am Abu al-Hamd, brother of Ahmad Ismail of the al-Yassid clan of Hamrah Dum." The man paused for a moment. Nobody moved. "We have been wronged," he continued. The group stepped forward into the cave. "And retribution is ours today!"

The clan looked mean and scrappy. Their tunics were stained with sand and dirt and the blood of animals. Long and scraggly beards hung to their chests, knotted with remnants of mud. Between his face and arms, each man wore more than one scar, belying a life of accepted violence. They all wore turbans of dull and grainy colors, like the crowns of Hell's princes. Dirt was worn so deeply into their hands they would never come clean. Only their swords shone clean and bright.

Muhanna shrank to the back of the cave, letting Etienne, Nick and Katherine form a barrier between himself and the angry intruders. "What's this all about?" Katherine asked, turning to square off with Muhanna. Muhanna shrugged his shoulders and tried to make himself as small as humanly possible.

Etienne took a small step forward and stretched his hands out in an open and welcoming gesture. "We have no quarrel with you, my friends," he said softly, his warm accent filling the dark cave. "We are tourists. Your land is beautiful, and we wanted to see –"

"Enough! You are intruders in a land that belongs not to you," came the response from Abu al-Hamd. "And you are fools to have aligned yourselves with a murderer!"

"No, no, you misunderstand," offered Etienne, but he was suddenly feeling that it was he himself who had misunderstood. Their safety was now in a fragile balance.

"Look..." began Katherine, stepping toward the strangers.

Etienne quickly grabbed her by the hand and pulled her back. "Please, Katherine." When she heard the intensity in Etienne's voice, she moved quietly to the back of the cave near Muhanna. Nick stood between his wife and the clansmen.

"I see your anger," Etienne said. "But we are not your enemies." Etienne motioned to Nick, who came to stand beside him. "Let us move outside where we can meet eye to eye, under the sun."

"Turn over Muhanna Ali al-Samara to us, and we will leave you in peace," demanded Abu al-Hamd. "Then leave this place and never return, or your fate will be such as your friend's."

"I am here under the authority and protection of the Egyptian Department of Antiquities, the Egyptian Royal Police, the Ministry of the Interior, the Department of Nationalization and the French government," Etienne replied calmly, listing every official organization he could think of. He flashed his international driver's license in their direction. "It is better that we talk outside, before something regretful happens."

Abu al-Hamd shifted uncertainly. He was not anxious to attract the attention of the authorities. Particularly since he had retribution on his mind. Etienne saw Abu's hesitancy and moved toward the cave's opening.

Nick turned back to Katherine. "Look for a tunnel out of here, or an adjoining cave," he whispered. He then joined Etienne outside. The four angry clansmen had backed away, just outside the cave's entrance, with Nick and Etienne forming a thin boundary between them and Muhanna and Katherine.

Etienne talked slowly and calmly, explaining his work with the Coptic Museum in Cairo, and stressing his support from the Egyptian government. The foursome was getting restless, however, squinting up at the bright sun and back to the dark entrance of the cave. They exchanged curious glances between themselves as Etienne rambled on.

Meanwhile, Katherine and Muhanna, left alone for the time being, scrambled to find a way out of the cave. Muhanna held the lantern as they ran their hands and arms along the stone walls, up and down, all through the cave, looking for even the tiniest sliver of an opening. Having no luck, Muhanna crawled down into a small tunnel which once held a sarcophagus. Katherine prayed to God that they would not find another snake, or even more terribly, that another snake would not find them, unaware. Muhanna came out of the hole, defeated.

Katherine knelt in the dirt and peered into the tunnel. There had to be a way out. She simply refused to believe that she would die there in that dark cave, half a world away from home, her flesh and bones drying to dust in the Egyptian desert. Mustering her courage, she crept into the tunnel, pushing and kicking against the dirt walls, hoping to find a weakening somewhere. Nothing. They were trapped in that cave, with absolutely no way out but through the hostile line of the al-Yassids.

As Katherine climbed back out of the tunnel, she noticed something. The lantern she was holding cast a tall shadow behind Muhanna, who had moved to the other side of the cave. His shadow crept part way up the wall, abruptly disappeared, and then reappeared further up. *There's a ridge there*, exclaimed Katherine to herself, *distorting Muhanna's shadow*. High and crooked, and almost invisible against the dark wall, sat a thin but unmistakable shelf in the high stone wall.

Moving closer, Katherine guessed it to be about ten feet above ground, and just barely wide enough to stand on. The cave wall rising above it was jutted with irregular shapes and rock formations, forming small indents and cubbyholes. "Up there," she whispered. Muhanna looked up and silently nodded his agreement.

Katherine braced herself against the wall, forming a step with her knee for Muhanna to climb up on. Muhanna quietly complied, realizing it was their best and only hope. He had to stand on Katherine's shoulders, one foot boosted further by her hands, to reach the ledge.

"I wouldn't be doing this," Katherine announced to Muhanna, pushing him up with all her strength, "if we weren't in a desperate situation."

"Of course not," said Muhanna, moving safely onto the ledge. Katherine rearranged her clothes and tried, for a singular moment, to look dignified. Muhanna lay flat on the narrow rock shelf, braced his arm around a rock jutting up from the ledge, and reached down for Katherine. The voices of the al-Yassid clan outside were getting louder and more restless.

Katherine looked to the front of the cave, seeing only the silhouettes of Nick and Etienne. The al-Yassids were beyond her line of sight. She turned the lantern down as low as she could, slowly, and placed it by the tunnel of the sarcophagus. She hoped it would draw the eyes of the al-Yassids away from them, if they should return to the cave. Then she tiptoed over to the side wall, and reached up for Muhanna.

She was surprised at the great strength Muhanna had, as he effortlessly drew her up the steep wall. *He is just full of surprises,* thought Katherine. She grasped his arm and quickly maneuvered onto the ledge.

"Thank you," she whispered.

They stood together with their backs pressed into the small nooks in the wall, their hearts beating wildly. They were almost afraid to breathe.

Abu al-Hamd could now be heard yelling. "Move aside or die where you stand!" The al-Yassid pushed his way past Nick and Etienne and stormed into the cave. His clansmen followed, swords raised. Inside the cave, Abu stopped cold. Stunned and confused, he turned around and around, scouring the cave with his eyes.

"Look outside!" he barked to the others, who looked dazedly at each other. "They must have found a tunnel leading out of here."

Abu al-Hamd was left alone. "Where are they?" he demanded, turning to Etienne and Nick, who were equally, delightedly, confused.

From out of the dark, falling as if released from the heavens, Muhanna pounced down upon his enemy. "I am here, you cowardly fool!" He wrestled Abu, kicking and hollering, to the floor. Muhanna pulled his knife out and held it to the al-Yassid's throat.

Nick looked up to see Katherine, frozen on the ledge. He held out his arms and smiled up at her. She smiled back faintly, and jumped. Nick caught her in his arms and gave her a big squeeze. "Jolly good show," he whispered.

Muhanna and Etienne were leading Abu al-Hamd out of the cave. Nick picked up the lantern and he and Katherine fell in behind them. "Stand back!" shouted Muhanna at the three clansmen as they turned to see their leader dragged outside, the sharp blade of Muhanna's knife glistening in the sunlight. "Back in the cave with you!" barked Muhanna. "Or Abu dies right here!"

The men from the al-Yassid clan surrounded Muhanna's group with startling speed. They held their swords in front of them, poised to strike, as they slowly circled their prey. "Drop that knife," rasped one of the men, stopping to stand in front of Muhanna. "Or it will be *your* blood that stains the sands this day."

Muhanna looked around. Counting only those with weapons, he saw he was vastly outnumbered. *I can kill Abu*, he reasoned, *but the other one will kill me. After that, who knows where the bloodshed will end?* Muhanna then laughed out long and loud, stunning the crowd around him. "You may indeed kill me," Muhanna said. "And all these foreigners, too." He gestured toward Katherine, Nick and Etienne. "But who will be left to bring poor Abu back to life? Can you do *that*, you murdering vagrant? Because I assure you, before I fall, Abu al-Hamd, leader of the al-Yassids, will fall with me."

The al-Yassids hesitated. This was the moment to strike, or to stand down.

"Lower your swords," offered Etienne, in a soothing voice. He slowly, deliberately removed the stiletto from the scabbard at his ankle and pointed it skyward, unthreatening. "No one needs to die here today. You have my word on that."

After exchanging tentative glances, one of the al-Yassids stepped forward. With great ceremony, and not taking his eyes from Muhanna, he placed his long sword in the belt at his side. The rest of the clan stepped back, relinquishing their position, and accepting defeat in the hope of some mercy for their leader.

"Go in that cave and stay there until we are gone," commanded Muhanna. "Do not let me see your faces again."

The al-Yassids growled their anger and humiliation at Muhanna, muttering curses under their breaths, as they moved slowly into the cave.

Etienne quickly led the way down the sloping talus. Abu al-Hamd was firmly locked in Muhanna's strong arms, his black eyes burning with hatred. Midway, Muhanna stopped and turned back. The three clansmen were peering out of the dark hole of the cave. "I should kill this cowardly scum right here on the spot!" he shouted toward the al-Yassids. "Stay out of my site, or I will do just that!"

Etienne, Nick and Katherine were already at the bottom of the talus and approaching the jeep. Just beyond the jeep, the al-Yassids had hobbled their camels to keep them from wandering, by tying one leg of each to another. Nick reached in his pocket for his Swiss army knife. Slowly approaching the camels, he knelt in the sand and cut the ropes that tethered them. The camels, being what they are, did not move far. Nick swatted them each on the rear. "Haa! Haa!" he cried, sending them darting off into the desert.

Muhanna pushed Abu-al Hamd down the slope. When they reached the jeep, Muhanna shoved his captive in the back seat and joined him there. "Drive," he commanded Etienne.

"Now wait," began Nick, sharing the front seat with Katherine.

"Drive," Muhanna repeated. "West, to the river."

Etienne started the motor and steered the jeep away from the cliffs. They shortly left the roadway, following rough trails toward the Nile. Muhanna's knife never left the base of Abu-al Hamd's throat, nor did his eyes leave the man's face.

Katherine was pale, her eyes darting from one person to another, silently asking unanswerable questions. Nick held tight to her hand, but was watching to see what Etienne would do, and how he would keep his promise to the al-Yassids for the safe passage of Abu. Etienne's face was a mask of stone.

As they approached the sandy riverbank, Muhanna ordered Etienne to stop. A dreadful moment of silence fell over the group as the jeep rumbled to a halt. Everyone turned to see what Muhanna would do.

"You killed my father," said Muhanna. "And you will die for it."

Abu sneered. "You can kill me and all my brothers, too. And still more al-Yassids will come. We will avenge my brother, Ismail, and the deaths of all al-Yassids at the hands of the al-Samara. We will not stop until the al-Samaras are no more. Your clan will evaporate in the sun and the wind, and your legacy will disappear, as we kill you one by one, until only barren woman are left behind to beg in the streets."

"And how will you do that, al-Yassid? When your heads are rolling on the ground and your hearts are in our bellies?"

"You speak big words for a little man, Muhanna. One day you will beg for your life, as your father did, crying out like a woman, whimpering on his knees."

Muhanna pulled Abu from the jeep, drug him across the sand, and threw him against a nearby palm tree. "Prepare to die, al-Yassid!"

"Don't do it, Muhanna," interrupted Etienne, as he, too, got out of the jeep. His voice was low and absolute.

Muhanna hesitated, his dark eyes darting from Etienne to Abu al-Hamd. "It will take so little effort," replied Muhanna in an eerie, hushed tone. He looked at the point of his knife pressing into Abu's skin, causing the faintest trickle of blood. "Just one little flick of my hand, and you will bleed to death where you lay, with no hope of surviving. Perhaps a crocodile will come out of the river before you draw your last breath, and will chew your arms and legs apart, while you writhe in agony. Your body will rot, here by the Nile, while the vultures peck out your eyeballs and dine on them for their supper."

Katherine closed her eyes, not wanting to see, not wanting to hear.

"Muhanna," said Etienne, approaching him softly. "There will be another time for this." Muhanna glanced over at Etienne, momentarily distracted. "You must not do this here, in front of the woman."

"What do I care what one woman sees or thinks? She is an infidel, and nothing to me."

"You must let him go," continued Etienne, in a slow rhythmic tone. "Abu al-Hamd has suffered enough injury for one day. You have broken his pride, and the spine of his will. He will take the story of

227

your triumph back to the al-Yassid clan. They will speak the name of Muhanna Ali al-Samara only in whispers, and only in the full light of day."

Muhanna stood perfectly still for what seemed like a long time. Etienne, Katherine and Nick could hear the heavy sound of his breathing, mixed with the breath of his enemy. They could hear the river softly swishing, as it flowed obliviously by. They could hear birds cawing in the far distance, busy with business of their own. They could almost hear the dark anger that flowed through the veins of these two rivals, the courage with which they faced their lives and their certain, bloody deaths.

They could not hear, however, the same dark anger that ran through their own veins—the voice inside that desired, above all, to blame; to call to task all that was made wrong in the world, to rout out the unseen enemy, to conquer it, to kill it.

Muhanna ran his knife across Abu's chin, causing a thick line of blood to emerge and begin running onto the man's neck and clothing. Abu did not budge. "Get out of here!" Muhanna then ordered, shoving Abu into the sand. "And never let me see your ugly face again. Or mine will be the last face you see on this earth."

As Abu knelt in the sand, hate and bitterness smoldered in his eyes. His throat was streaked with blood. He did not look away from Muhanna, but stared continually at him with an expression so dark and menacing it scared Katherine where she sat.

Etienne escorted Muhanna back to the jeep. Without a moment's delay, Etienne fired up the ignition and turned the jeep around in a blur, kicking up sand and rocks. They headed southeast along the Nile at top speed. "Abu's friends will have rounded up their camels by now," he said. "They'll be determined to hunt us down." They all rode in silence for miles, hearing only the wind and Muhanna's heavy breathing. Great, long sighs came from the small man, and sometimes a low grunting sound, as he sat still and hard in the back seat. No one dared to speak.

Etienne sped toward al-Qasr. He knew they were vulnerable to attack as long as they stayed in the wide-open desert. On the distant horizon, the sky was turning brown. Muhanna saw it first. "We must drive to shelter," he said to Etienne, leaning forward. "Quickly." No one else had noticed the gathering storm. Now they all looked out at the thin, dark strip where the desert met the sky. It was growing. Fast.

"*Khamis*," explained Muhanna. "Wind that grows out of the parched desert to the west."

Etienne sped east. "Perhaps we can outrun the storm and make it to Izbat al-Busah," he shouted, driving like a mad man. It was only a few minutes before a strong, hot wind was whipping through the jeep. Soon the sand would follow.

"Just keep driving!" yelled Muhanna over the din. "We cannot stop here!"

Etienne put the jeep into low gear and pressed the gas pedal to the floor. "Cover your faces with whatever you can!" he hollered, pulling a handkerchief out of his pocket. Muhanna found the hat that he'd been wearing as a disguise, and returned it to Etienne. He helped Etienne secure the handkerchief around his face, using the hat to hold it in place.

Then Muhanna took off the red scarf and wrapped it around his own head and face. Katherine did the same with the white scarf Miss Donatta had given her, and Nick used Muhanna's turban, wrapping it many times around his head, and knotting it below his chin.

Etienne dropped the jeep into a low gully, onto the hard-baked sand of a dry river bed. Such arroyos were created by the yearly flooding of the Nile, leaving behind sunken paths winding through the dunes. While the deep riverbed couldn't shield them from the squall, it provided a firm road to drive on.

Sand soon surrounded the jeep and obscured everything in sight. Nick held tight to Katherine and she buried her head in his chest. They were engulfed in a violent storm of wind and sand. Katherine couldn't hear Nick or Etienne or even the jeep, only the howling, angry wind. She couldn't tell if the jeep was moving fast or slow, or even at all. Sand rained down upon her and whipped through her scarf. It covered her hair and face and clothes. It raked across her skin and scraped her eyes. It filled her ears and nose. She thought she was surely going to suffocate. She might have thought to scream over the din for help, but it would have been useless. It would have only filled her mouth with sand, and no one would have heard her.

The storm lasted an interminable ten minutes. Then, as suddenly as it came upon them, the wind began to subside. Etienne was still moving the jeep forward. They had somehow stayed on the arroyo – and had moved against the storm to the other side. It saved their lives. They could see the *khamis* – the dark band of air and earth – moving steadily beyond them. In what direction they could not say.

Etienne rolled to a stop as they choked and gagged and spat sand out of their mouths. They looked more like sand creatures than humans, with grit clinging to their hair and clothes. Their skin, where exposed, was bitten red from with abrasions. They were dirty and wretched, disheveled from their waists to the top of their heads.

"Don't rub your eyes!" commanded Etienne, getting out of the jeep. "You'll make it worse." He groped through half-opened eyes in the back of the jeep until he found a canteen. "Here," he said. "I'll rinse the sand from your eyes. Then let them water on their own. What ever you do, *do not rub them*. Katherine, you first."

Katherine laid on her back across the hood of the jeep, with her knees bent and her head hanging off the side. Etienne brushed the hair from her face and began to gently splash water across her eyes. "Ow," she cried. "It hurts. It hurts!"

Nick stumbled over, half blind himself, and held her head in his hands. "Shhh," he said calmly. "I know. It'll be over in a minute. You're almost through. Hang on. Hang on."

"The scarf was too thin," Etienne said to Nick. "She got the worst of it."

Finally, blinking, Katherine was able to open her eyes. She saw the blurred and miserable images of her friends, covered in sand and grit. Muhanna went next, then Nick. They kept filling the canteen from one of the two large canisters of water they carried in the jeep. Finally Nick rinsed the sand from Etienne's eyes, and half their water was gone.

They all looked around to orient themselves to the land. They were totally muddled and shocked. And they were lost. The Nile, the only distinguishable landmark in rows and rows of sand dunes, had disappeared.

"Let's get out of here before the wind returns," said Etienne. "Or the al-Yassids find us."

They climbed back into the jeep and Etienne pulled a compass from the glove compartment. "I do not know which direction we were heading during the storm," he said. "But we couldn't have come very far." He handed the compass to Nick. "Guide us south and east, to al-Qasr. We'll have to follow these gullies, or else we'll get stuck in the sand."

"What happens if that happens?" asked Katherine.

"We die." Etienne looked up at the sun falling from the sky and fired up the jeep. They drove for several hours, wending their way from one gully to another while the sun fell nearer and nearer toward the horizon. Dusk began to settle on the land and it began to get cold. On and on they drove, slowly, through ripples of sand with no road in sight.

Just before dark, they saw a faint shadow rise from the land, and a sand-packed road leading toward it. Etienne gunned the engine and drove the jeep out of the gully and up onto the road. Rising in the distance, in ghostly ruins, they saw a crumbling stone building.

"There," said Etienne, pointing. "We'll go there. And you my friend," he added, turning to Muhanna. "You have a lot of damn explaining to do."

15

MEMORIES IN THE DISTANCE

Do not turn away Your face from my heart's dark secrets,
but burn them till they are alight with Your fire.

– Rabindranath Tagore

Basilica of St. Pachomius

"We know you lied." Safely ensconced inside the ruins of a crumbling monastery, Nick dropped the last load of supplies from the jeep into a jumbled pile. Then he turned to face Muhanna.

"Me?" Muhanna shrugged, making himself busy by wrapping his turban carefully around his head.

"Yes," said Nick, staring at the small man. "You."

"My business is my business." Muhanna glared back at Nick. "And not yours."

"You bloody well owe us an explanation," snapped Nick. There are rules in life and, according to Nick, people should abide by them. Nick knew just the same that Muhanna was in the habit of following his own set of rules, ungoverned by what others might think was right or wrong.

But a lawyer learns how to read people, what to say and what not to say, when and how to extract information. Nick sized up his subject. *Softening leads to softening.*

"I know you've been wronged, Muhanna. And your family has been wronged. Perhaps you can think of a way we can help set things to right."

Muhanna then launched into a tirade, listing the many injustices served up to him by the al-Yassids. For good measure, he added up the wrongs of the Egyptian monarchy, the British, pagan intruders, and the shifting sands of fate.

Nick listened with the face of compassion, shock and righteous indignation on Muhanna's behalf. He knew the conversation would eventually wind its way back to the caves of Jabal al-Tarif.

Etienne, meanwhile, was busy getting his bearings. Sprawling across an acre of sand, the basilica matched the color of the land upon which it was built. A dozen different rooms could be discerned, though all that was left of most of them were causeways, corners and crumbling stone. A giant cupola, a domed cap, which once stood above the entrance, lay in a half-covered heap in the sand.

Great walls rose up toward the sky. Though some parts of the structure were still covered, most of the roof had long since caved in. Fallen columns lay like random pick-up-sticks in the sand. *This structure must have been enormous at one time,* thought Etienne. They appeared to have landed in the skeleton of a once-great sanctuary. Light played in the exposed interior, and shadows filled the corners where high standing walls still blocked out the sun. Broken stone blocks formed makeshift tables and chairs. And the great cliff of Jabal al-Tarif loomed far in the background.

Etienne studied one of the maps Sidi had tucked into the glove compartment. Based on their approximate location when the storm hit, and the short distance they had traveled through it, he concluded that they were at the ruins of the Basilica of St. Pachomius. This monastery, built in the early years after the crucifixion, had housed Christian monks for centuries. *Perhaps,* thought Etienne, *even Gnostic Christians.*

The Basilica of St. Pachomius was still operating in 367 A.D. when Athanasius, the Arch Bishop of Alexandria, published the notorious *Lenten Letter.* This document, translated into Coptic and read in all the regional monasteries of the time, marked the beginning of the end for the Gnostics.

In this treatise, Athanasius had denounced all the written documents he considered heretical. The gospels of Thomas and Philip and the *Book of Truth* were among them. Soon after, those books and many others, disappeared entirely. Athanasius' list had provided religious leaders with the impetus they longed for to destroy the writings of the Gnostics.

Etienne looked around. This crumbling structure held memories of such times and buried secrets from the past. *What*

233

happened here, he wondered, *centuries ago, in the shadow of Jabal al-Tarif? Could the jar have been taken from this monastery and hidden in the sands of the nearby cliffs? Had the monks been under attack and in a hurry to save what they could in the time they had? Did most of them die for their efforts and their convictions?*

I may never know, he thought sadly. *So much is buried in the grains of time and memory.* He looked over at Katherine. Etienne took a pencil and traced the road from the monastery back to al-Qasr. They would return there tomorrow.

Katherine was busy across the open room, laying out blankets and sleeping bags for the night. They had decided to hold up in the basilica until the storm, and the al-Yassids, had calmed. They had enough food, supplies and blankets to tide them over for days, and once the night had passed they could assess their safety and their next move.

Etienne wandered over to Nick and Muhanna, now sitting conspiratorially in a corner of the sanctuary. He heard Nick speaking in hushed tones. "So it was to boost your crops, and your family's lot in life, that brought you to the cave to dig for fertile soil. So close to the land of the al-Yassids ... very brave of you, I must say." Muhanna sat up very straight, but kept a serious expression on his face. Sensing Etienne's presence, Nick spoke louder. "It was courage that took you there, Muhanna. Courage and great insight." Muhanna nodded solemnly, recalling his directive from Allah.

"Well, I'll tell you one thing for sure," said Etienne, approaching. "Whatever you were there for, there's no way any manuscripts were found in that cave." Nick and Muhanna looked up at Etienne. "For one, no one in their right mind would be digging for soil inside a cave." Etienne sat among the rubble next to the two men. "For two, the few scraps of pottery we did find were probably from a looter's water jug ... about a week ago."

"This is what surprises me, Muhanna," said Nick. "That someone of your character and authority would have to lie to us."

"My memory is not so good," complained Muhanna. "This whole thing has been very unhappy for me!" Muhanna crossed his arms and looked away.

"I do beg your pardon." Katherine came over to the bramble of fallen stones where the men were gathered. "Aren't we overlooking one small detail?" All three men looked over at her. "While you gentlemen are sitting around chatting about a few broken scraps of clay, I'm over here wondering about the murder."

"Right-o," said Nick. He and Etienne looked at each other. Katherine crossed her arms, waiting for an explanation. "Well, it seems that Muhanna's family is involved in a feud," Nick began. "Very common in these parts."

"The al-Yassid brothers told us their story back at the cliffs," explained Etienne. Muhanna could be heard grumbling under his breath. "From *their* point of view, that is," added Etienne.

"And?" Katherine rested her hands on her hips.

"You see," said Etienne. "It turns out that Muhanna's father killed someone from the al-Yassid clan. As these things happen, he beheaded the uncle of the man we met at the cave, Abu al-Hamd. At the time, Muhanna's father was patrolling the irrigation equipment on the perimeter of his land. He killed this uncle, whom he took to be a thief.

"Of course, Abu al-Hamd's family couldn't just let that go. So they, in turn, killed Muhanna's father. You see?"

Katherine stared back at them in disbelief.

"My brothers and I did the only thing we could do under the circumstances," broke in Muhanna.

"Do tell," snapped Katherine.

"At the direction of our mother, we found Abu al-Hamd's stupid, lazy brother, Ismail."

"Who just happens to be the son of the sheriff," interjected Etienne. "As the al-Yassids explain it, the poor fellow had fallen asleep by the side of the road. He'd come to al-Qasr to buy honey, apparently, and decided to take an unfortunate nap before walking back to his home in Hamra Dum."

"Molasses," interjected Nick. Etienne looked over at him. "It was molasses," Nick insisted.

"I was molasses," said Muhanna.

"Anyway," continued Etienne. "When Muhanna and his brothers came upon the sleeping Ismail –"

"We fell upon him, hacked him from limb to limb, and devoured his heart between us!" Muhanna proclaimed.

"It's all very normal for this culture, Katherine," offered Etienne.

"Simple, really," added Nick. "Not a big deal."

"Not a big deal," said Katherine. "Not a big deal." She started to walk away from the men, but then turned and stomped back. "I just can't believe you, Nick. What has gotten into you? That killing people is suddenly 'not a big deal'."

I am truly grateful that in Britain, thought Nick, *and even in America, people are entirely more civilized than they are in these renegade villages.* Still, it seemed to Nick as though the desert itself had changed the landscapes inside him. He was able to accept, without flinching, the violent laws of this untamed land. *We all seem to be playing beyond the rules now.*

"Well, Katherine," began Nick in his own defense, "for one thing, I'm far more keen on the manuscripts, and finding out what happened to them, than I am in worrying about Muhanna's family business."

"Is that right?" snapped Katherine.

"It is not for me," said Nick, "or you for that matter, to judge another culture; a culture that we can no sooner understand than we can bloody understand what set the earth to spinning. So why don't you just let it go?"

"Just let it go?" said Katherine. "We're running around the desert with an ax murderer, who has a warring clan of thugs chasing him, and us, bent on killing him and anyone who gets in their way, and you suggest that I just *let it go?*"

"*Yes,*" said all the men in unison.

"Where does the sheriff's wife come into all this?" asked Katherine, never willing to be told what to do by one man, let alone three.

Muhanna shrugged. "I lied."

"I expected better of you," stated Katherine, and she turned on her heel and strode across the sand. Each man assumed she was talking to him.

"You know, there's something about this murder that's curious," observed Nick, turning back to Muhanna. "Given that you killed the sheriff's son, I'm surprised he *ever* let you out of jail. I'm surprised, in fact, that he didn't kill you on the spot."

"I was under his protection, naturally," said Muhanna. "All he could do was collect evidence against me while he held me in that rat hole." Muhanna shrugged, cocking his head to one side. "Which, of course, there was none."

"No evidence?" asked Nick. "It sounds like everyone knows you did it."

"My brothers came to visit me during the long, dreadful months I was in jail," explained Muhanna proudly. "They said no one who knew anything was talking." Muhanna scowled. "Everyone hates the sheriff in my village. And my brothers can be ... well," he shrugged. "My brothers are my brothers."

"Why does everyone hate the sheriff?" asked Etienne.

"He was appointed to our village by the government," replied Muhanna. "They came in and set up a district police station in al-Qasr, replacing our own *umdah* with this al-Yassid vermin." Muhanna spat sat in the sand.

"*Umdah?*" asked Nick. "What is that?"

"The Headman of our village," explained Muhanna. "It was to him we answered. He was all we needed."

Etienne studied Muhanna. He knew that the Egyptian government, though iron-fisted, was somewhat naïve in arbitrarily posting lawmen in remote regions of which they knew little.

"That still doesn't explain why the sheriff let you go," said Nick. "Unless it was simply for the money we gave him."

"No," said Etienne, fixing his gaze on Muhanna. "It wasn't the money at all. The sheriff knew that his relatives could exact a much swifter justice than the law could. They just needed Muhanna to be out in the open again."

The smug expression on Muhanna's face turned to one of fear.

Later that afternoon, sitting in the rubble of the stone monastery, Muhanna was persuaded to speak of the books, and they began to unravel the mystery of the missing manuscripts. Etienne handed Muhanna his diary, and on a blank page, Muhanna drew the shape of the jar he had found. It was tall and slightly rounded, with four handles at the top. He also drew the bowl, and the configuration of the boulders, which he confessed was the actual discovery site.

"I don't suppose your mother would sell that bowl?" asked Etienne. "For a fair price?"

"My mother has become very attached to the bowl," said Muhanna. "But I will ask her. Perhaps she will look favorably on my new friends."

I wonder how far Etienne will go, thought Nick, *one way or another, to have that little bowl.*

Katherine joined their conversation when she brought over steaming bowls of soup and thick bread.

"*Merci*, Katherine," said Etienne, as he happily took his bowl.

"Thank you, my darling." Nick smiled at her. "You make a charming camp hostess."

Katherine scowled and held out a bowl for Muhanna. She then sat down to join them.

"So," Etienne resumed, "what happened to the manuscripts once you brought them home?"

"I sold one to Jahib Adam," said Muhanna. "The man with one eye. But well, then the trouble began. When I was taken away, my family hid the others."

"That explains why Jahib didn't return to Cairo with the rest of the manuscripts," said Etienne. "He couldn't get to them while Muhanna was in jail."

"The one thing this doesn't explain, however, is why the manuscripts weren't at your house when we got there," said Nick. They all looked at Muhanna.

"Oh," he replied, shifting uncomfortably. "Well, it seems that my brothers grew a little restless." Muhanna laughed uneasily. "You're not going to believe this."

"Try us," suggested Etienne.

"Well, just a few days ago, my little brother, Abdul, gave one book to the teacher, Raghib, to determine its value. But he promised to get it right back!"

"What about the others?" asked Nick.

"Well, that," Muhanna began, "is where Khalifah comes in."

"Who's Khalifah?" asked Etienne.

"My middle brother. Dumb as an ox, but very big." Muhanna flexed his muscles in demonstration.

"Does Khalifah have the rest?" asked Etienne, already knowing that it was too much to hope for.

"Not exactly."

"*Not exactly?*" asked Nick.

"Well, it seems that Khalifah sold them a few weeks ago, to Jahib, after all."

"Oh, dandy! That's just *dandy!*" Nick ran his hands through his hair. "And Jahib has disappeared," he said, summing up their predicament.

"Well, we'll just go find him, that's all," suggested Katherine. "How hard can it be?" Everyone fell silent, wending their own imaginary paths that would take them through the dangers of the desert to the one-eyed bandit.

"Alright then," said Nick, breaking the silence. "Tomorrow we return to al-Qasr, drop off Muhanna, and go find Jahib."

"It's not that simple," said Etienne. "Jahib could be in Cairo, looking for me, for all we know. He may very have been in Cairo while I was being held by the authorities over the matter of the Knife."

"What knife?" asked Muhanna.

"Never you mind," snapped Nick. "You have enough problems on your hands as it is."

"I'm thinking I could be helpful to you," said Muhanna, rubbing his hands together. "Maybe I shouldn't go back to al-Qasr just yet."

"You're more trouble to us than help, Muhanna," said Nick. "By far."

"You will be surprised at how helpful I can be," offered Muhanna.

"Forget it," retorted Nick.

"Stop it, you two," said Etienne, wearily. *Merde.* You're making my head spin. Let's sit on all this for now, and make our plans tomorrow." They finished their soup in the silence of their own concerns.

After dinner, Muhanna found the east entrance of the monastery and went outside to pray. Katherine and Nick wandered to the west side, to see the last of the day sink into the desert sand. Etienne stayed inside and arranged himself in a pile with his diary, the fragile manuscript from Miss Donatta, and the light of a little lantern.

The sky was orange. All orange. Not just a deepening ribbon on the horizon of a fading blue sky. A sky of entire orange. It took Katherine's breath away. She and Nick were sitting outside the monastery, putting the rabble and mayhem of the day into perspective. For just a little while, they were 'KatanNick' again. They talked the talk of married people. The talk of little things inside of bigger things. Little truths, little lies.

"You were marvelous," said Nick, speaking of the incident in the cave. "I wouldn't have believed it myself if I wasn't there. My wife planning a surprise attack from the ledge of a cave. Outstanding!" He kissed his wife on the forehead.

"You didn't know we were hiding there, did you, did you?" she asked, gloating insufferably.

"No," said Nick. "Etienne and I were looking at each other, rather mystified. That is, until Muhanna came screaming like a banshee down from the darkness."

"Muhanna is very strange," said Katherine. "Frightening in a way. There is much to him that we have no idea about."

"You don't act frightened of him."

"Do you know he is unbelievably strong? He pulled me up to that ledge like I was a sack of sugar."

"You are a sack of sugar," said Nick. "Sweet, irresistible, bad for you."

Katherine laughed. They didn't talk more about Muhanna, lest they find themselves in a disagreement over the finer points of blood feuds. Something Nick and Katherine had trained themselves keenly on were the warning signs of an impending fight, and ways to maneuver clear of it.

"I'm so glad you came with me to Egypt," Katherine admitted. "I don't know what I'd be doing without you."

"Is this what you were expecting when you decided to come here?"

"Not even close."

"Etienne has gotten us into quite an adventure, hasn't he?"

"Leave it to Etienne," she said, perhaps a little too wistfully.

"It's good to see him again," offered Nick.

"After 10 years he's no more sensible than he was in school," said Katherine. "He's still a spoiled, irreverent scoundrel." They left that conversation alone, too. Nick would have been willing to listen, curious, if Katherine had had more to share on the matter. But she didn't.

"I'd very much like to go back to Cairo, tomorrow," Katherine suggested. "Maybe we can find this one-eyed bandit who has the rest of the manuscripts."

"Yes," agreed Nick. "Let's go back to Cairo."

Katherine noticed with some degree of curiosity that Nick was getting increasingly excited about the recovery of the books. If she had let herself, she could have been delighted to watch him from a bemused and supportive distance. It was unsettling to her, however, to see aspects of her husband that she didn't thoroughly, completely and predictably understand.

There were little things, like the way he would run his hands through his hair, causing it to stick up every which way. That he would do such a gesture in the first place was remarkable for Nick. That he wouldn't smooth his hair back into place after he'd done it, was entirely outrageous.

Then there were the bigger things. Like his absolute nonchalance about Muhanna murdering someone. And his relentless pursuit to unravel the fate of the manuscripts – like a prosecuting attorney honing in on a hapless, guilty, defendant. If Katherine had put all these details together at once, and looked at them carefully, she might have seen a different picture of Nick. But maybe she only saw, would ever want to see, the Nick of her imagination.

Their married life had always been a calm one. Nick was the ballast and the center of that calm. Never over-reacting, seldom reacting to much at all, he was always the logical voice of reason. Katherine sometimes hated that. Sometimes she wanted to scream her head off until he screamed back. She simply could not imagine Nick Spencer losing control of himself. But Nick was changing, right in front of her eyes.

Just then, they were startled by Etienne's voice. When he came rushing out of the monastery the sun had all but disappeared. "You have got to hear this!" Setting down his lamp, Etienne wedged himself comfortably between Katherine and Nick in the sand. "From what I could decipher so far, the book we got from Nelson is definitely attributed to Thomas."

"Is it the real thing?" asked Nick.

"Based upon everything I've seen and know about these codices, yes. Absolutely. Yes."

"Are you talking about Doubting Thomas? The *disciple*?" Katherine asked.

"Exactly," replied Etienne. "The one who challenged Jesus to prove who he was. And in this book, Thomas is called *The Twin* – because his learning had become equivalent to that of Jesus."

"That's impossible," interjected Katherine.

Etienne continued as if he hadn't heard her. "Thomas relates a series of statements in this document, all attributed to the 'Living Jesus.' Each entry is preceded by the phrase, *Jesus said*." Etienne grinned. "We have the *Gospel of Thomas*!"

"There's no such thing," Katherine countered.

"There is now," claimed Etienne. "This is one of the many documents contemporary of Matthew, Mark, and Luke, that was purposefully *omitted* from the Bible. And here's one reason why.

Listen to this!" Etienne opened his dairy and began to read his translations under the bright, humming light of the lantern.

"Jesus said, 'If your leaders say to you, look the kingdom is in heaven, then the birds of heaven will precede you. If they say to you, it is in the sea, then the fish will precede you. Rather the kingdom is inside you and it is outside you. When you know yourself then you will be known and you will know that you are children of the living Father. But if you do not know yourself, then you will dwell in poverty and you are poverty."

"Astonishing!" said Nick.

"There's more! There's more!" added Etienne, reading on.

"Jesus said, 'If you bring forth what is within you, what you bring forth will save you. If you do not bring forth what is within you, what you do not bring forth will destroy you."

The three friends glanced between each other for a few moments.

"That implies that the path to salvation – and damnation – resides *within* each individual," said Nick.

"Yes!" exclaimed Etienne. "The heretics speak for themselves. Finally." Etienne rubbed his eyes, his voice nearly breaking. "Finally."

"Well done, my friend." Nick rested his hand on Etienne's shoulder. "Well done."

"The *Gospel of Thomas* is just the beginning," said Etienne, recovering his composure. "As I looked through the codex, I was able to confirm that it's not just *one* manuscript, but several, each attributed to a different person. Further back in the book is a document called The *Apocalypse of Peter*. I've only translated a little piece of it."

"What does it say?" Katherine's skepticism could not overcome her curiosity.

"It is a serious attack on the rulers of the Church." Etienne held his diary to the light. "Listen:

The risen Christ tells to Peter that those who name themselves Bishop, and also deacon, as if they received their authority from God, are in reality waterless canals. Although they do not understand the mystery, they boast that the mystery of truth belongs to them alone."

"My word," said Nick. "Some people are going to be very unhappy to hear this."

"Are you *sure* that's what it said?" asked Katherine. Nick and Etienne looked over at her. "Well it's just so, so... nevermind." Katherine shifted in the sand and lit a cigarette.

"Now you see why they were so hated!" exclaimed Etienne.

"And feared, I should think," added Nick.

"Well, you aren't going to be very popular if this gets published," said Katherine.

"It's not about notoriety, Katherine," said Etienne seriously. "It's about history."

"And culture," added Nick.

"And indoctrination," continued Etienne.

"And, of course, Hugo Nelson," said Nick.

Etienne did not say anything, but he looked hard at his friend. Nick stared out at the empty horizon. "Well, I guess I'll get back to it.' Etienne stood up. He lingered for just a moment longer, tracing the toe of his boot in the sand. Then he walked back into the monastery.

"He hates that you want to give the books to Nelson," said Katherine, taking a drag of her cigarette.

"I know." Nick hadn't needed Katherine to tell him that. And he was more than slightly annoyed that she had set herself up as Etienne's advocate. But he said nothing more.

Another silence fell over them. It was dark now. The last rays of light had abandoned the eastern bank of the Nile. In the darkness, with only a trace of wind, they couldn't see the coming storm.

There was a chill in the air when Etienne woke up the next morning. He built a small campfire, and then went outside to clear his head and get his mind ready for the coming day. Muhanna was kneeling to the east, praying to his God. Etienne gave him ample distance and watched the sun rise with his back against the monastery wall.

Inside the monastery, Katherine was pacing the sand floor in a sour disposition. She woke craving a hot bath, a full-length mirror, and running water to brush her teeth. *And what on God's green earth am I supposed to use for a commode?* She wandered to a deserted corner of the crumbling structure, far away from the main room where they made camp, and dug a discreet hole with a little camp shovel. *God, I hope I don't see a damn snake,* she grumbled to herself. *This is not the time to need help.*

Returning to the camp, Katherine puttered around doing little chores, while Nick slept, Muhanna prayed, and Etienne did whatever it was he did in the mornings. Katherine put coffee grounds from a tin that Miss Donatta had provided into a stained and dented coffee pot. She added water to the pot and set it in the corner of the campfire.

Then she folded up all the bedding, except for Nick's, put away the dishes from the previous night, and set a makeshift table for breakfast. Then she walked around in circles for a few minutes until the coffee was percolating. She filled two cups and went outside.

"Morning," said Katherine, interrupting Etienne's thoughts. She handed him hot coffee in a blue tin cup. "I thought you could use this."

"Please sit," he offered. "Join me."

"It's brisk out," she said, pulling out a cigarette. "Mind if I smoke?"

"Not at all," he said, engaging in the polite conversation of two people not entirely comfortable with each other. "It won't warm up for another few hours. By noon it will feel as though we're in the hottest heat of the afternoon. By afternoon, the desert will swelter like the inside of an oven."

Katherine smiled and watched Muhanna as she smoked her Lucky Strike. He was chanting something low, which she couldn't hear, and repeatedly pressed his forehead to the ground.

"Nick still asleep?" Etienne asked.

"Yes, poor man. He was up half the night, pacing around. He didn't sleep much."

"A lot is happening," suggested Etienne.

"Yes." Katherine took a long, slow drag of her cigarette. She nestled into the warm sand, and soaked up the stillness of the morning. She held her cigarette casually, absently, between her slender fingers. Her nails were long and polished bright red, and like Katherine herself, were totally out of place in Egypt. Her dark hair was typically coifed in perfect curls, drawn neatly off her face. But here, in the desert, she let it tumble recklessly around her cheeks and shoulders. She didn't see her own beauty. And she didn't see that Etienne was watching her; watching her carefully.

Odd, thought Etienne *how time travels in circles, when we think in our heads that it runs straight. Here we are, ten years from Paris, in the desert sands of Upper Egypt.*

"You still know how to show a girl a good time, anyway." Katherine wrapped her arms around her knees.

"Not quite like Paris is it, Kat?"

Katherine caught her breath. "Nobody calls me Kat any more, Etienne. I'm all grown up." Though Katherine had wanted some company, she was starting to think that she should have stuck her own forehead to the ground and prayed in humility to God. Instead she was letting herself wander down a path where she didn't belong.

She stole glances at Etienne's profile, handsome and aloof, casual against the ancient crumbling stones. Etienne looked strangely at home in this barren landscape. His dark hair fell nearly to his shoulders and looked perfectly disarrayed.

Katherine pushed against the delicious memories that tempted her. But it seemed as though a very loud and persistent voice had woken up inside of her, muscled its way into her brain, and taken up residence there. She turned her face to the sun, but it seemed far away, as it rose in no great hurry over the barren desert.

The ruins of the basilica stood dead and cold behind them. But a warm breeze had begun to blow, and it settled in around them. They relaxed into the silence and the soft sand of the morning. Eventually Etienne spoke again. "You didn't say good-bye," he said, remembering their parting one, long-time-ago summer. "In Paris, I mean."

"You didn't say 'let's stay'," she countered.

"I didn't know how."

"I know."

"So you left," he said, more to the sky than to her.

"You left me no choice."

"*Mon cherí*, you were young and beautiful and perfect. You had the world in your hands."

"You broke my heart," she accused.

Etienne offered a crooked smile. "I only bent your heart. It was mine that broke."

Katherine smiled back at him, a small, stirring smile. They both drifted off in silence to a shared memory from long ago. Ten years later, the memory of leaving Paris still stung them both. For a long while, it seemed like there was nothing they could say to each other. Katherine wiped away a runaway tear from her cheek, nonchalantly, as though she was wiping away a grain of sand.

"Why were you crying?" he asked. Then, embarrassed by his own question, but unable to let it go, he looked away. "I was just wondering what it was that made you cry."

"Was I?" Katherine nestled deeper into her summer jacket, as if it could shield her somehow. Etienne had seen her eyes like that, many years before, in Paris, when the tears and the light mixed in her eyes, and they blazed a bright blue-green.

"I was just thinking about school." Katherine spoke slowly. "I was thinking how crazy it all was. And how simple and sane it all seems now, with these many years to soften the memories. Sometimes I wish I could go back."

"Would you make different choices?" Etienne was digging, and he knew it; he was looking for something that years of excavating ancient ruins across the globe had never offered up to him.

Katherine was silent for a long time. Etienne wondered if she might actually deliver the answer he was looking for. Then he wondered if she had roamed, in her mind, beyond his question to other secret realms—realms to which he would not be invited. When she finally spoke, it was with a thoughtfulness that surprised him.

"I could no sooner have made different choices than I could re-shape my bones." Her expression was warm and tender. "I was driven, like you and Nick and Ben, and all of us back then, by who I was and who I would become. Nick was my destiny. I always knew that."

"Always?"

"Well, I forgot once. But I suppose you know that better than anyone."

"I suppose I do." It was gratifying for both of them, in some way, to talk about the past, to recount, and to say out loud, what had happened all those years ago. But Etienne couldn't let his question go. "I was just wondering, Kat, why you were crying." Katherine looked over at him. "That day at Notre Dame, I mean. What made you cry that day, before we went back to England?"

"Was I crying? I don't remember."

"From the outside, Kat, no one would ever know how fragile you are."

"Years of careful practice." Katherine was closing Etienne's narrow window of opportunity to cross back over the bridge to where her heart was.

"So long that I imagine even you don't know it anymore. How deeply sensitive, I mean. But I know. I know where it hurts, and I know where you're afraid."

Katherine winced. "What you know about me, Etienne," she said, shoving her cigarette in the sand, "you could write on the head of a pin." The moment it was out of her mouth, she regretted it. She saw the hurt on his face. She couldn't take back her words, and part of her didn't want to. She wanted to be angry and stay angry. But she couldn't do that, either. All she could do was offer up the truth.

"I'm sorry, Etienne," she whispered. "I was crying in Paris because I was sad. All I remember now of Notre Dame is the dead people buried in the floor, and the extraordinary stained glass, and feeling unbearably sad."

Etienne stayed silent, patiently waiting. "Sad because time was racing into the future and I didn't want to go." Katherine looked over the horizon at the rays of light playing in the desert sand. "I would have stayed, you know. In Paris." She spoke so softly he barely heard her. "If you'd asked me to."

248

Etienne turned to her. He wanted so badly to make her understand. "I wonder to this day if I meant it. When I said we had to go back. Or if I would have stayed if you'd only asked." He turned back to the empty desert. Katherine lit another cigarette and passed it to him. They shared this one thing in the Egyptian morning, beyond their memories of Paris.

Etienne finally spoke again. "I wonder Kat," he said. "If you asked me again. Today. Would I stay this time?"

"You're asking me to consider the un-considerable, Etienne." *He's tempting me, that cad, to think that things could have been different all this time. Could be different still.*

"You're being rather cruel, you know?" she said. The memories of it all came back to life, and Katherine stood face to face with feelings she'd built a life around forgetting. "Why does fate twist your life inside and out?" she asked, bitterly, to no one in particular. "Why aren't you rewarded for your sacrifices instead of tempted by them? Why does God have to taunt you like that? That's what I want to know."

"What I want to know, Katherine," Etienne responded, "is *would you stay*, if I asked you to?"

Katherine flicked her cigarette far across the sand, sending red embers flying. "That's not a question I get to answer." She held her jacket close around her body and walked back into the confines of the dead monastery.

16

PILLARS OF THE SOUL

…when you move amidst the world of sense
from both attachment and aversion freed,
there comes the peace in which all sorrows end,
and you live in the wisdom of the Self.

– The Bhagavad Gita

"I still say we go straight to Cairo." Nick pushed the map aside, letting it fall off the stone slab they were using as a table. He and Etienne had sat with Muhanna for the better part of an hour trying to agree on a plan. They rehashed the events at the cliff, the discovery, the murder of Ahmad Ismail, the murder of Muhanna's father. They debated the prospects of waiting in al-Qasr, exploring Qina, or returning to Cairo. Katherine eventually gave up on them and made breakfast.

On they talked. They speculated over the al-Yassids, and what they might be up to. Were they laying in wait? Regrouping? Hunkering down and licking their wounds? What would be the safest route to travel? What would be the most expeditious? The most likely place to find Jahib – the one-eyed bandit who'd gone missing? And what fate may have befallen him?

"Jahib, and the books, can be more easily traced if we begin in al-Qasr," insisted Etienne. "I've done this sort of thing before, you know."

"I'd rather not go back there just now," interjected Muhanna.

"Then we are at an impasse." Nick threw the cold dregs of his coffee from its tin cup onto the sand floor.

"This is ridiculous," said Katherine, coming over and collecting the map from the ground. "Can't three grown men work this out? I'd really, *really* like to leave this place. Soon." They ignored her.

"*Soon*, Nick." Katherine stomped off to do the breakfast dishes.

"We know that there is one book that Abu gave to the teacher, Raghib," Nick said. "At least we should get that one before we go running off to Cairo."

"It could take some time to get that back..." Muhanna said.

"Now what?" snapped Nick.

"Raghib travels through the villages, teaching, as I told you. He may not be in al-Qasr again for days. Weeks perhaps."

"And you just forgot to mention that yesterday?" Nick snapped again, his hair standing up in all directions. "Well," he sighed. "All the more reason to go to Cairo directly."

"Yes, let's avoid al-Qasr altogether for now," added Muhanna.

The sudden sound of an engine broke into their argument. "Was that the jeep?" asked Etienne, jumping up.

"*Oh, no!*" Nick ran from the basilica out to the sandy road, followed closely by Etienne and Muhanna. They arrived just in time to catch a wake of sand in their faces.

"Katherine! Come back!" Nick shouted, louder than he thought he could. "Come back!" He knew Katherine heard him. She just didn't look back. Nick stood there, flanked by Etienne and Muhanna, as they watched the jeep disappear into the desert, until it could only be recognized by its trailing veil of dust.

Nick stormed back into the monastery. Etienne and Muhanna stood in silence and watched him march around the room, kicking up sand. Nick began throwing whatever was available and unbreakable – a canteen, a fork, a saucepan, a stone – across the room.

"She does this, you know. Just takes off." Nick finally stood still in the open room. "Bloody hell." Then he turned his back and began gathering up the things he had thrown, carefully replacing them all, except for the stone, which he let be.

"Perhaps this might explain things." Muhanna walked over to the corner where the supplies were gathered. The dirty breakfast dishes lay in a heap near the cook stove. He picked up a note, carefully propped up between a coffee mug and a bowl gathering flies.

Nick snatched it out of Muhanna's hand and read out loud,

Tired of being camp maid. Just thought I'd drop into
al-Qasr to take some photographs and do some
shopping while you old hens figure out a plan.

Back soon. –K.

P.S. You do the dishes.

"She's kidding, right?" asked Etienne. Nick didn't bother to answer. "She's a pain in the ass! You know that, don't you?" fumed Etienne.

"Yes, I know that, Etienne. You're not helping!"

"Don't yell at me," retorted Etienne.

They glared at each other. Nick finally shook his head in defeat. "I'm worried about her."

"You should be," snapped Etienne. "This is not a game. If she goes snooping around for those manuscripts ... who knows what might happen."

"We must go then," said Muhanna, collecting a canteen.

"Where?" asked Etienne.

"To al-Qasr," stated Muhanna.

"You said you didn't want to go back there," stated Nick.

"Allah commands, and I go," replied Muhanna.

"On foot?" asked Etienne, already feeling the intense heat of the day.

"Right now?" asked Nick.

"It's only a desert," said Muhanna. He shrugged his shoulders and walked out of the crumbled ruins of the monastery into the rippling sea of sand.

al- Qasr, Egypt

Katherine was in a foul mood and determined to stay that way until she had exacted some sort of retribution. Retribution from whom,
252

she did not know. God, she supposed. The Universe. Fate. Etienne. Nick. Ben. She'd look almost anywhere for it, as long as it wasn't inward.

Following the rough markings Etienne had made on the map, Katherine found the main roadway that led to the Nile and into al-Qasr. She drove like a madwoman, with no posted speeds, no road signs, and virtually no other travelers in the dry and lawless land.

The last thing she heard, as she drove the jeep away from the monastery, was Nick calling her name. *Come back! Come back!* Nick's words replayed themselves over and over in her mind. Katherine forced her thoughts to the books. She wanted to finish this crazy chase for manuscripts and get back to civilization.

Comebackcomebackcomeback... The words repeated themselves so incessantly they became all one word. Like *KatanNick* had become all one word. Katherine wanted to shout the words out loud, to absolve herself of them. But she didn't. Instead she let them rattle around in her head, until the pale gray ghost of a memory came in and took hold of her.

Katherine could see it plainly, as though the memory was a movie reel, taken from a sealed vault and played in front of her eyes.

In a yellow print dress and green corduroy pinafore, a girl stood with her head pressed to the living room window – the big window that her mother kept spotless with vinegar and crumpled-up newspaper. She was a thin figure, no longer a child, not yet a woman. She held her hands against her chest, clasped together as if in some sort of distracted prayer. Her elbows were tucked in close to her body. From this solitary perch, Katherine watched her father back the baby blue Edsel out of the driveway and onto the street. A quick backward turn, a grinding of gears, then straight ahead, and away. He didn't even look back. Not once.

Comebackcomebackcomeback. Katherine had thought if she stayed there long enough, and if she said the magic words enough, he would come back. Was it an hour? Two? Only half of one? She didn't know. But she did know that it was her mother who pulled her away from the window, and broke the spell Katherine was casting to bring her father home.

"Come away from that window now, dear. Your forehead is going to get cold." Katherine's mother had said this as if it made perfect sense. The way someone would say something out loud in their sleep, or in a dream. Her mother pulled Katherine away from her sentinel post. She put her hands around Katherine's head, as she would to check her temperature. It was a *mother* thing to do, though it had taken Katherine years to realize that. It was as though this sort of distracted mothering was the first, or best, or only thing a woman, whose husband has just left her, could do.

"See? What did I tell you? Cold as ice." Katherine's mother took away her hands and wrapped them in her apron, as if to warm a chill passed from child to mother. She sighed and moved to the built-in shelves against the living room wall, fussing over glass figurines, books and photographs with a bright red dust cloth. Had she looked up from the random, aimless work, or looked back as she busied her way mechanically toward the kitchen, she might have noticed that Katherine's eyes were following her. And that it was her eyes that were cold. Cold as ice.

Young Katherine watched this absurd woman, this woman she used to recognize as her mother. No, not even recognize – this was the woman she used to *notice* in her father's shadow. Then, finished with the business of her mother, Katherine turned back to the window.

Throughout the afternoon, she stood there like a young soldier who has accepted with gravity the depth and importance, the sacred trust, of a duty never asked for or expected. She could hear her mother pass behind her from time to time, clicking her tongue, or sighing, or just breathing. They were both beginning the long, hopeful, hollow process of waiting for someone who has just barely left and is never coming back.

Her mother finally pulled her away for good, at dinner time. Some combination of anger and relief filled Katherine at that moment. She was weary and bored, and didn't want to have to blame herself for quitting. Something important was happening. Dinner, as Katherine recalled. It was something very important to her mother, at any rate. Katherine obeyed, like she was raised to, and sat down to a meal she didn't want and couldn't eat.

What Katherine did remember was hating her mother – for driving her father away, for pulling her away from the window too soon, for the red dust cloth in her apron pocket. Katherine secretly swore to God that night, over pork chops and green beans, that she would have a maid when she grew up. And she would never, ever dust bookshelves.

The village of al-Qasr appeared in front of Katherine, a mirage suddenly made solid in the nowhere of the desert. Relief washed over her. *A mind can lose itself in the desert*, she thought, *where there are no markers, no distractions, no obligations.*

A collection of low, mud-brick buildings marked the perimeter of the village. Their colors were soft and muted, scrubbed pale from torrents of sand and wind. The collective looked quiet, protected, interspersed with palm trees that stood like breezy, sleepy sentinels. It was mid morning, and sun was beating down with unrelenting heat. Katherine slowed the jeep and made her way cautiously into the heart of the quiet village.

She parked near the center of al-Qasr, where an open market marked the hub of activity and the central place of gathering. Katherine took a quick inventory: a well, a mosque, a potter spinning clay, *a butcher, a baker, a candlestick maker. This place,* she thought, *is entirely self-contained, in the middle of nowhere.*

Three women cleaning clothes in the street glanced up at her, curious, but not pausing in their work. They whispered amongst themselves and returned to the tasks before them. The clanging of a bell around the neck of an ox startled Katherine as it passed her, guided only by a big stick wielded by a small boy. Katherine turned her attention to the situation at hand. With nothing tangible to accomplish, she decided to wander.

She knew Nick was going to be furious. He had every right to be. But it was too late to fuss over that. She could have turned straight back around and returned to the basilica. She knew she should have. But having come this far, and still feeling the residue of an unnamed anger, the lure of the people kept her there. Taking photographs seemed to ground her, remind her of something she needed to know – though she could never say exactly what that was.

The people of the village were of a distant and mysterious world. They seemed so poor, on one hand, and simple. And yet, through the lens of her camera, she could see contentment, joy even, in some of their faces. Others looked hard, resilient, like the land they tilled. Still others seemed as though a darkness hung over their thoughts, in a constant state of silent restlessness. Perhaps it was because their lot in life found them in a poor village instead of a city of opportunity. Perhaps it was because lands on the Nile had been used like chattel for the pleasure of conquerors for thousands of years, from the Romans to the Turks to the British. Perhaps these few had inherited, through the generations, the hostility of their ancestors, the hostility that comes with powerlessness.

Having nearly exhausted the two rolls of film that she had in her knapsack, Katherine was feeling more at ease. She decided to search around for the Coptic church. It stood to reason that the local priest might know something about the Gnostic manuscripts. *If I can bring back some important information,* thought Katherine, *or one of the books even...* Katherine had learned early, from her visiting father, that gifts and surprises buy forgiveness. She had also decided to head straight back to the monastery after her visit to the church, and apologize profusely.

"Hello," Katherine said to a woman carrying a reed bowl full of oranges. "Do you happen to know –" The woman looked startled. She shook her head, skirting as far around Katherine as the narrow dirt street would allow.

"What?" Katherine wondered out loud, gesturing helplessly with her hands. *"What?"* Then she approached a man. "Maybe you can help me," she began.

"Yes, yes," he replied eagerly, looking her up and down with a gap-toothed smile.

"Can you tell me where the –" The man took Katherine by the hand and began leading her off the main street into a dirty alley. "Hey wait," she said, stopping in her tracks. "You're not listening to me."

"Come. This way," the man insisted. "I can help you."

"No," said Katherine, pulling her hand free. "You completely don't understand me." The man looked at her, unperturbed. "No," she repeated. Then, remembering a little bit of the Arabic she had learned, she said, *"La. La."*

The man smiled condescendingly. "La, la, la, la, la," he sing-songed. Katherine quickly returned to the street, looking over her shoulder as she scuttled along, trying her best not to run. The man merely shrugged his shoulders and walked off in the opposite direction.

In Katherine's haste to get back to the main street, she ran straight into a young man carrying a large basket full of bread. She toppled them both over, scattering bread across the road.

"'Assif, 'assif," the young man said, before he noticed that Katherine was a foreigner. "Sorry, so sorry," he added, in a faltering English.

"No, no, it was my fault," said Katherine. She helped the young man gather his bread, brushing off the dust as best she could. He looked mildly distressed as he re-filled his basket. "Let me pay you for your bread," Katherine offered.

"No to worry," said the young man. "Is only little dirt." Together they reassembled his basket, and he lifted it to his back.

"You speak English," stated Katherine.

"Leetle bit. We have teacher to come here who teaches."

"Please," said Katherine, holding out a few American dollar bills. "I insist."

"Thank you, lady," responded the young man, looking carefully at the strange money. "How many breads you like?" His dark eyes were soft, innocent. Katherine would have liked to have known him better, to have learned his story, to have heard about his family, his hopes, his sorrows.

"No bread," she said. "The money is for your trouble."

"My *trouble*?"

"The mess I made." Katherine pointed. "The soiled bread."

"I have no trouble," he responded. He shifted his feet nervously. "I cannot to take."

"Can I take your picture, then?" she asked, holding up her camera.

This he understood to be a fair trade. The young man stood up straight and proud and smiled into her lens. "Tell me your name," Katherine said, behind the camera. "Aziz," he replied. "And your father's name?" she asked.

He looked away, far past the street he stood on, as if into a memory. That was the picture she wanted, and she took it, and Aziz would never know the great gift he had given her in return for a few American dollars. "We have the same name," he said. "My father and I. We are both Aziz."

"Thank you, Aziz."

"*Shokran*. It is to be my pleasure."

"I was wondering," said Katherine. "Can you tell me where the Coptic church is?"

"Oh, yes. Come with me." Katherine hesitated. "It's okay," he said. "It's here." He gestured for her to follow. They walked to the end of the street, and rounded the corner. "Here," he pointed in the distance. "It is here." He gestured down the long, dirt road.

Katherine squinted into the sunlight. All she could see were two rows of simple, stone buildings, flat and square, unmarked and wind-blown. There was nothing, no cross, or stained glass, no gothic carvings, no steeple to indicate which building might be the church. "I don't see it," stammered Katherine. "They all look the same."

"Look again," said Aziz, guiding her eyes about two city blocks down the road.

Pale peach in color, and battered through centuries of wind and sand, stood a stone structure, flanked by homes and shops and sheds. It finally stood out on the landscape by virtue of its one distinguishing feature: it was built in the shape of a cross.

"Thank you," said Katherine, breaking into a smile. "Thank you very much."

"'*Afwan, al-affu,*" he replied. "You are welcomed."

She watched him return to the main street, the bread strapped to his back. As he reached the corner, he turned back. "Good-bye, lady," he called, waving. "No *troubles* to you."

Katherine passed through the front doors on the west side of the church and entered a world that was dim and cool and still.

"Hello?" she called tentatively. A cold chill ran up her spine. She pushed away the sudden longing she felt for Nick. "Hello?"

The church was dead quiet. Inside, it looked like any other traditional Christian church, though poorer. She made her way in silence to the far east end of the building where the altar stood, nearest to the rising sun. Walking down the main isle, Katherine noticed many columns supporting the roof, all painted in chipped and fading colors. *These people take their religion seriously,* she thought, noting the care and detail that was taken in painting the sanctuary.

Nearing, Katherine could see it was the apostles who adorned the pillars, each one immediately recognizable by a defining icon, theirs alone. She nodded to Saint Jerome, standing always with a lion, Saint Stephen, struck through with arrows, Saint Peter, holding – as is his charge – the keys to the gates of heaven and earth. Moving further, Katherine came upon the figure of Saint Paul, brandishing a sword, the symbol of his beheading, waging war on behalf of Christianity. She then moved to James, carrying his pilgrim's staff, awarded to him for being the first disciple to go forth and preach the gospel.

Thomas, next, was Katherine's favorite. Besides being the doubtful skeptic to Christ's resurrection, Thomas carried a builder's rule. Legend was told that Thomas – bidden by Jesus in a vision – went to India to build a palace for the king there. In response, the king of India gave Thomas a large some of money for the project. Later, the king learned that the disciple had given all his money to the poor. First enraged, the king eventually came to understand that his palace was not of brick and mortar, but built in the kingdom of heaven on his earthy charity.

On she moved down the aisle. Bartholomew, who carries the enormous knife by which he was flayed. Andrew, who is painted with the transverse cross, his choice in execution so as not to be crucified in the manner of his beloved Lord. Matthew, Simon...

They were all watching her, reminding her of her sins, offering her some holy degree of protection, rooted deeper in her than she could possibly explain. She stepped off her path to touch the painting of the Archangel Michael, drawing her fingers along his enormous wings. Finally, she came to stand before paintings of Christ the King and the Ever Virgin Mary on wooden screens flanking the altar. *Who are you?* she heard herself ask silently. *Who are you?*

As Katherine's eyes grew accustomed to the light, she noticed that the high altar didn't look right. There was a prayer book lying open on the floor; a small challis was tipped on its side; long, tapered candles were broken and scattered about; shattered remnants of eggs crunched under her feet. "What happened here?" she wondered out loud, stepping more carefully.

"The priest has gone."

Katherine spun around and found herself looking in the face of a slender, old man, holding a straw broom. He had entered the sanctuary from the inner chamber, behind the altar. His eyes were deep and tired. His frame was slightly bent. *Years of kneeling before God will do that to a person,* thought Katherine. The words popped into her head, like so many others did, before she had a chance to stop them. Sarcasm was familiar, hers alone, like an icon painted on the pillars of her soul.

"They took him away," said the old man, sadly.

"Who took him?" asked Katherine. She motioned the man to the first row of wooden pews and they sat together in the cool stillness of the sanctuary.

"I do not know. He was here, and then he was gone."

"It looks like they made a mess," Katherine said.

"A mess?" The old man studied Katherine's face for her meaning. Katherine gestured at the altar and the scattered things. "Yes," the man agreed. "A *mess*. Everything is a mess."

"What is this?" asked Katherine, stooping to pick up the smashed half of an eggshell.

The man took the fragile casing in trembling hands. "It is the egg of an ostrich, here to remind us how ceaselessly the creature guards and protects its unborn, and the life from lifelessness. It is with similar vigilance that we are told to mind the matters of God. Ever mindful. Ever mindful..." The man's thoughts wandered off. He shuffled to the altar and gently replaced the broken eggshell.

"Did you see who did this?" asked Katherine, looking around the church.

"It was late. Too dark to see. Only the candles of the altar were lit. Father Mhand likes to come in here alone at the nighttime. I think he likes best to talk to God, here, alone, at night."

"Were you here, too?"

"No, I was at home. Next door." The man took a great deal of time stooping over to pick up a lamp. He dusted it carefully on his sleeve, and placed it in a niche carved into the wall. "I take care of the church," he continued. "And I take care of Father Mhand. Except this time. I was not here to help. When I heard noises from my home, I came right away into the church, from back there." He pointed to a small side door near the back of the church. "I only saw them leaving out the front doors. Three of them, with Father Mhand." The caretaker bowed his head.

"Well, if you were here, you probably would have been taken away, too." Katherine touched him gently on his arm. "Did you contact the authorities?"

"They are looking into it, they said."

"What is your name?"

"Taya," came the soft reply. "I am the caretaker here. I take care of the church. And I take care of Father Mhand."

"Yes, I know," said Katherine, as warmly as she could. "And I'm sure Father Mhand will come back soon. I'm sure everything will be alright." But she was not sure at all.

"I must go now. I have to clean the rectory. It, too, is a *mess*," said the sad caretaker.

"Good-bye, Taya," said Katherine. "And, *really*, everything is going to be alright."

"Good-bye, kind lady. God bless you."

Katherine walked out of the dimly lit church onto the street, pausing momentarily as her eyes slowly adjusted to the stark light. She reached in her bag for a cigarette. *Alright, indeed*, she said to herself. *I'm getting out of here.* Katherine looked up and saw the silhouette of a familiar figure standing against the bright sunlight.

"Hello Katherine," came the rich Italian voice.

"Father Antonio! What are *you* doing here?" The priest was dressed in street clothes, and looked so different, he barely resembled the man she had met in Tenerife.

"Looking for you." Father Antonio took the cigarette from her hand and threw it on the ground.

"Hey," stammered Katherine.

He then grabbed her by the arm and started pulling her away from the church. "I need your help with something."

Katherine struggled against his grasp. "What are you *doing*?"

They rounded a corner to an alleyway, as Father Antonio led her away from the street. There, two young men, with guns, were waiting. They appeared to Katherine to be Italian, and taking their orders from Father Antonio.

261

"Get your dirty paws off me!" Katherine demanded, wriggling free. She faced the priest. "What's this all about?"

"I feel we parted too quickly at the airport in Cairo," said Father Antonio.

It occurred to Katherine to be afraid, but what came out of her instead was anger. "Your friends are pointing guns at me," she snapped.

"Yes."

"What are you *thinking*?" Katherine began to back away. "You're a priest for Christ's sake. Priests don't drag people into dark alleys, And they don't associate with men with guns. I'm leaving."

"No," stated Father Antonio. "You are not," He nodded to one of the young men. As Katherine turned to run back out into the street, he came around and blocked her way.

She turned back to Father Antonio. "This is unforgivable!" she yelled.

"Too bad," came the cold reply. He yanked Katherine's knapsack off her back, and began rummaging through it.

"What are you looking for?" demanded Katherine.

The priest looked up at her contemptuously, without saying a word, and returned to his work. Not finding what he wanted, he threw the knapsack back at her. "Let's take a ride." Father Antonio closed his hand around her arm so tightly it made her wince. The group moved down the alley and back out into the street.

"I can't, really," protested Katherine. "Nick is expecting me. In fact, he and Etienne are probably looking for me right now."

"I don't think so, my dear."

"Yes, they are. I told them I would meet them in the village square a half an hour ago. Nick must be worried sick by now. I'm never late."

"Have you always found it so easy to lie?"

"No, really. I'm always on time."

"We know you came into al-Qasr alone, Katherine. Please do not lie to me again. I cannot tolerate deception." Just then they reached
262

Etienne's jeep. "The keys," ordered Father Antonio, holding out his hand.

"What?"

"Give me the keys."

"Oh," said Katherine, rummaging around her pockets. "Well … I know they're in here somewhere." *What could they do?* she thought. *Gun me down in broad daylight? Not likely. Then again, this is al-Qasr.* "Well, where the devil are they?" she continued. "They were here just a minute ago."

"Find them, Mrs. Spencer. *Now.*"

"Are you really a priest, or was all that just a big fat lie?"

"Katherine, give me the keys. Or we will shoot you in the hands and feet, and find them ourselves."

"Are you here to inflict the wounds of Christ on everybody?" asked Katherine. "Or just me?" Father Antonio's gunmen looked at him, almost as if they, too, wanted to hear the answer.

In the quiet moment of distraction, Katherine withdrew the keys from her pocket, pitched them into the air with all her might, and ran as fast as she could in the opposite direction. She did not get far.

17

A GREAT RUCKUS OF CHICKENS AND MEN

Believe nothing, no matter where you read it, or who said it,
no matter if I have said it, unless it agrees with your own reason
and your own common sense.

– Gautama Buddha

The Desert Beyond the Basilica

It seemed as though they had been walking all day, although in fact it had only been a couple of hours. The basilica was about 10 miles from al-Qasr, according to Etienne's best guess, and the sand – soft and stinging hot – made their going slow. Nick, Etienne and Muhanna saw nothing but sand and scrub for miles and miles, as far as their eyes or imaginations could travel.

Occasionally they would cross paths with a creature of the desert—a snake or a scorpion, but the desert inhabitants seemed indifferent to this clumsy collection of intruders. As the sun reached its apex in the sky, their best hope was to reach the main road along the Nile and flag down a driver. It needed to happen soon. They were totally out of water.

"Katherine has really done it this time," complained Etienne. "We could, seriously, die out here in this desert, miles away from anywhere."

Nick had experienced many occasions when Katherine lost her temper and threw something of a fit. He typically ignored it, except when she physically removed herself from the place where they were, be it the kitchen, a restaurant, or the bedroom. Then he would go get her. He would put her arm around her, and apologize for whatever it was she thought he'd done to wrong her, and let her yell at him for a few minutes. Then it would be over. And all would be well again. But this time she really put them in a fix.

Nick wondered if Etienne's presence had something to do with her dramatic exit. And the last thing he wanted to hear was Etienne complaining about it. As if he didn't already know.

"Your wife is out of control," Etienne muttered as he trudged along in the sand.

"She's just very strong-willed," said Nick.

"No," said Muhanna. "She's totally out of control."

"When I want your advice, I'll ask for it," Nick barked, hot, tired and annoyed. "Who made you two the local experts on women anyway? I don't see either of *you* married."

"Women in my village know their place," said Muhanna.

"Women in your village have no teeth," retorted Nick.

"When I pick a woman, she will be beautiful, accommodating and wealthy," countered Muhanna.

"When you *find* a woman beautiful, accommodating and wealthy, you'll be the chap in the funny little hat carrying her bags at the local hotel."

"You know nothing," muttered Muhanna. "At least our women don't steal jeeps and give a lot of back talk."

"There's something to be said about that," snapped Etienne. "Katherine has really gone too far this time."

"You're one to talk," Nick snapped back. "She didn't go too far for you in Paris, now did she?"

"What are you griping about?" countered Etienne. "She chose you."

"You never should have taken her to Paris."

"You never should have left her behind."

"You're a selfish, self-centered, self-absorbed womanizer. You didn't love her. You used her, like you use everyone!"

"At least I don't hide behind my books and eyeglasses, waiting for life to come to me, powerless to do anything about it."

Nick stopped walking. "Oh, I guess I should be more like you – callous, selfish and arrogant."

Etienne faced his old friend. "Wouldn't hurt. At least you would have a mind of your own."

Nick's right hand came up faster than either of them realized, and caught Etienne on the left side of his chin, knocking him backwards. Etienne's startled look changed to one of anger. He dropped his head and charged Nick, catching him in the stomach with his shoulder, sending them both careening to the ground.

Muhanna patiently watched the spectacle unfold, as the two men rose from the ground and began to fight. Angry words gave way to fists and shoves as they vented their anger and helplessness. For the next few minutes, neither of them spoke nor thought nor cared, as they grappled with a history larger than themselves.

They struggled, throwing blows and sand, blinding themselves to everything but their rage. Through bleary, sand-scraped eyes, Nick saw Etienne stagger toward him, fists raised. Etienne jabbed at Nick, landing a blow just above his cheek. Nick grabbed Etienne by the lapels and flung him as hard as he could across the sand. Etienne took equal hold of Nick's shirt, however, and they both went tumbling down a steep sand dune, 20 yards, to the hard ground below.

Gasping and choking, with sand in their throats and ears and eyes, they finally fell apart, and lay panting in the sand under the steaming hot sun. Tired and hurting, their anger spent, Etienne and Nick looked at each other, each equally matched and equally uninterested in continuing. Etienne dabbed at a bloody lip and Nick was feeling the tender start of a black eye.

"Look!" said Etienne after a few minutes of silence as they recovered their breath, and some semblance of their dignity. "Here comes a car!"

They stood up and started hollering and waving. "Hello! Hello! Over here! Help!" They had landed just a few yards from the road, having come upon it quite by accident in their fall down the sand dune.

A green Chevrolet sedan rolled to a stop. Nick and Etienne were never so happy to see an American-made car in their lives. A young man climbed out of the driver's seat and came toward them with a serious expression. "Nicholas Spencer?" he asked. "Etienne Desonia?"

"Yes!" exclaimed Nick. "How did you know?"

"Katherine," he answered. "She said you were stranded at the ruins of a basilica near here. We came to get you."

"Thank God," Nick said. He and Etienne began looking around for Muhanna, but he was nowhere in sight. "We need to get to al-Qasr, straight away," said Nick to the driver.

"You'll be going to Nag Hammadi," the man said, pulling out a gun and pointing it in their faces. "Or Katherine will die."

Nag Hammadi, Egypt

They drove to Nag Hammadi in a tense silence, which only Nick broke from time to time in his despair. Neither he nor Etienne had felt so entirely helpless, or so far away from Katherine, ever.

"Where the devil is she?" demanded Nick. "What on earth do you want with her? She's done nothing!"

From the passenger seat, a second man held a gun on Nick and Etienne. Had there been only the driver, they might have thought to try and overpower him, take his gun, and switch the advantage to their side. But with two of them, both armed, it was futile. The best they could do was to wait and see where they were going, and to whom these men were answerable. For their part, the driver and his companion were not talking.

Nag Hammadi, only a few miles from al-Qasr, was a small city compared to Cairo, but by far the largest in the region, with about 50,000 inhabitants. Nick and Etienne were blindfolded as they neared the edge of town and rode the rest of the way in darkness. They could hear the call of vendors, the bleating of goats, the rumble of carts, and honking of cars – all the sounds of a bustling city center. Eventually, they left those sounds behind. Then, all they could hear was the soft swishing of the Nile floating nearby, and an occasional automobile.

Etienne's poor manners got the best of him, and he could stay silent no longer. "This is going to be fun, Nick," he whispered, loud enough for their captors to hear. "These guys have no idea what they're in for." Etienne heard Nick sigh in what sounded like a weak, hopeful smile. "We'll get Katherine back," said Etienne. "And these rat bastards are going to regret the day they ever laid their hands on her, or laid their beady eyes on us."

Etienne felt a sharp blow to his cheek, as the man in the passenger seat struck him with the butt of his gun. Etienne was rocked to the side, and he slammed into the car door. Blood and saliva pooled in his mouth from a dislodged tooth. He spit the blood, and the tooth, on the floor of the Chevrolet.

"You alright?" asked Nick.

"Round One goes to the bad guys," Etienne said, wiping his mouth on his sleeve. "But this fight is just beginning."

The car slowed, turned a corner, then immediately another corner, and then stopped. Nick and Etienne were pulled from the back seat and shoved along a gravel path, up a few steps, and through a door. Their blindfolds were then removed, and they found themselves in a small house, in a sparse, rundown neighborhood.

They had entered through the back door into a kitchen. The smell of mold hung in the air and the yellow linoleum was chipped and peeling at the corners. A few dirty plates had been left in the sink, which drew the same few flies that hovered over a bowl of bread and fruit. A green table and four metal chairs sat at one end of the room. There were no other signs of comfort or luxury. Nick and Etienne could clearly see that this was the abode of men who hadn't been there long, and didn't plan on settling in.

Out the back kitchen window they could also see the Nile in the distance and Etienne's jeep parked in the gravel driveway. With a renewed sense of confidence, Etienne looked over at Nick and winked. "Round Two," he whispered. Nick smiled back.

Nick and Etienne were led into a living room. All the shades were drawn down. Dust rose through the few shafts of sunlight that broke though the windows. An empty bookcase, a table, and a few pieces of old furniture sat here and there, looking almost forlorn, like crumbling statues in an abandoned garden. The room gave the feeling that it was not part of this earth, but rather, a dark portal to futility.

Someone suddenly turned on a lamp, spreading a weak, yellow light across the room. A man was in the corner, waiting for them. He sat casually in a chair of unraveling rose-colored upholstery. His face was tilted upwards, a sublime smile on his face. A revolver was strapped to his waist. He slowly stood and walked forward, sizing up his captives. He nodded silently to the two armed men.

Nick and Etienne were immediately frisked from head to toe. Nick ignored the man who patted him down, but his eyes smoldered on their leader. Etienne growled audibly as the stiletto that he carried, strapped to his leg, was confiscated.

Nick shook off the gunman and stepped forward. He stood face to face with the man from the chair. "What the hell are *you* doing here?" he demanded. "And tell me where Katherine is. *Right now.*"

"You know this man?" Etienne asked.

"Father Antonio," said Nick. "The priest from Tenerife. The one I quarreled with on the airplane."

The priest laughed. "An ill-advised gesture. As I'm sure you are now beginning to realize. Your arrogance and your stupidity have betrayed you."

"Where's my wife, you lying son of a bitch!" barked Nick.

"You watch your language!" retorted the priest, his voice rising.

"What do you want?" Etienne asked of the priest, trying to calm a quickly escalating fight. "Why have you brought us here?"

"You have something that I want, very badly. And when I have the Gnostic codices, you can have Katherine back."

Etienne was just about to ask, *What Gnostic codices?* when Nick broke in. "You want the codices?" he asked, furious. "So badly that you would kidnap a woman for them? Are you out of your bloody mind?"

"Hardly," scoffed Father Antonio.

Etienne knew kidnapping was the least a fanatic would do to get what he wanted.

"I want to see Katherine. Now," insisted Nick.

"And I want this!" said Father Antonio, grabbing the satchel off Etienne's shoulder. The priest withdrew the two codices and took them to a nearby table.

"Who is this person?" Etienne asked Nick.

"Some asshole, fanatical, scum of the earth," spat Nick.

"Watch yourself, boy," threatened the priest, turning from the books he was studying.

"Oh, now it's not 'my son this' and 'my son that'? You're not the wise and watchful, kind and benevolent shepherd of the human soul any more?" said Nick. "Kiss my ass!"

Father Antonio's face turned bright red. "You have no idea what you've gotten yourself into, do you?" The priest momentarily thought back to his parish in Fiumicino. His flock was as devoted to him as he was devoted to God. They trusted him. They, and many others, were counting on him. *And this fresh, ignorant upstart from America has the audacity to challenge me! What does he know? He knows nothing of the peace and purpose and righteousness of the path of God. Nothing. And yet he pretends to know all! With his arrogance and condescending intellect. In his fancy clothes and modern attitude. With his vile swear words.*

"One day you will understand," said Father Antonio smoothly. "One day you will *all* know the consequences of your sins. On the Day of Judgment." He paused. "But that is in God's hands." The priest began to pace the room, talking more to himself than to anyone else. "What is in my hands is another matter all together. Gnostics indeed! As if anyone could ever truly comprehend God. It is ridiculous!" He suddenly charged up to Nick. "And *you* are ridiculous!"

"Now that you have the codices," suggested Etienne, interrupting. "Just give us Katherine and we'll be on our way."

"But I don't have all the codices, now do I?" said Father Antonio, turning to Etienne.

"You have all the ones I know of," said Etienne flatly. "If there are more, it's news to me. And where they might be, I have no idea."

"It is not going to help you *at all* to lie to me," replied Father Antonio calmly.

"What is your interest in these manuscripts?" asked Etienne. "Just for the record."

"I am charged by God with the mission to recover all thirteen of the books of the heretics, to gather them together in one place, and to light a blaze of fire upon them to purify the world of their evil words."

"And I suppose you think you're going straight to heaven for this?" asked Nick.

"I do this for the glory of God, not for my reward in heaven."

"As if God is *so fragile* that the mere presence of some books would undermine His divine authority and tumble His holy empire," snapped Nick. "You think God is so totally helpless and inane that He would send the likes of *you* to rescue humanity? You weak, idiotic, jackass! Is that what you think? Tell me, Antonio, priest of the lame and the asinine – if God is so great, then why is He so bloody scared of a few old books?"

"God is afraid of *nothing!*" cried the priest. "It is you, *you* who should be afraid!"

"The only thing I'm afraid of is that *I* won't be the one to send you straight to Hell!" yelled Nick.

Just then a loud knock came on the front door, then another. "*Aloo! Aloo!*" cried a voice from beyond the door. "*Aloo!* Anybody home?" The doorknob began to turn. Everybody froze where they stood. *Funny*, thought Étienne, *how kidnappers would be so unconcerned about their own safety that they didn't even bother to lock their front door.*

A woman, draped head to toe in black, poked her head inside the door, just as Father Antonio gestured at one of the men. "Ronaldo, get rid of her!" he snapped. The priest led Nick and Étienne back into the kitchen.

"*Firakh, Firakh?*" asked the woman, shoving two hapless, live chickens in the gunman's face. "I have very fine chickens for sale. Grain fed! Good price!"

"No," said Ronaldo, at the door. "We don't want any."

The woman shoved her foot in the door jam, just as Ronaldo meant to close it on her. "Wait, wait," said the woman in a strong voice. "You don't understand. I have raised these chickens myself, since baby chicks. You will not find any finer."

"No!" insisted Ronaldo. "We are really not interested!" The other gunman moved to the door to help.

"Ah, *you* might understand the value of such fine chickens," the woman continued. "I can tell you, these are two of the finest chickens you'll ever have the pleasure to eat."

"No!" insisted Ronaldo. "I told you, we do not want your chickens!"

"Perhaps your friend would?"

"Scram lady," snapped the second man, Mario. "And take your chickens with you."

Suddenly there was a new commotion outside on the street. The halting hoofs of several camels could be heard. A number of voices began to cry out. The woman looked back over her shoulder and, with surprising determination, threw the two chickens into the house. "Eye, yie, yie!" she screamed, following the chickens into the living room, banging the door shut behind her.

A great ruckus of chickens and men followed. Skirts flying and veil askew, the woman chased the fleeing chickens around the room. Ronaldo and Mario, rifles slung over their shoulders, chased the woman and the chickens, but they couldn't seem to get a firm grip on any of them.

"Ronaldo!" Father Antonio barked at his second-in-command from the kitchen door. Ronaldo turned his attention to the priest. "Get in here and cover these two men. If they move one inch, shoot them." Ronaldo held his gun on Nick and Etienne, and they all watched the unfolding commotion together, from the kitchen door.

Father Antonio then strode to the center of the room, and withdrew his gun. "Mario," said the priest calmly. "Lock the front door." Ignoring the chickens, Father Antonio moved to intercept the woman, pinning her into a corner. The woman was still bent over, arms outstretched, and crying, "Eye yie yie," as she came face to face with the barrel of Father Antonio's gun. As she straightened up and clumsily rearranged her skirt, her veil fell to the ground. "I can explain this..." began Muhanna Ali al-Samara of al-Qasr.

"I can hardly wait," said Father Antonio coldly. The priest took hold of Muhanna's shoulder, and shoved him roughly into a large bedroom that adjoined the main living area. "You two," said Father Antonio, returning to the kitchen. "Get in here." Ronald escorted Nick and Etienne, accompanied by Mario, into the bedroom. Father Antonio slammed the door shut.

Muhanna, Katherine and a Coptic priest were sitting like an obedient row of ducks on a rickety old bed. Across from them, in another chair, a quiet, rigid hulk of a man sat as their guard and sentinel to their fate. *That makes four,* counted Etienne to himself: *The priest, the two men from the Chevrolet—Mario and Ronaldo – and this guy.* Etienne sized them up, looking closely at their eyes, their postures, their attitudes and bearing. *Can we take them?* he wondered. *Outnumbered and with no weapons? Could we possibly…?*

Nick's relief at seeing Katherine was so palpable, even Father Antonio's gun-toting crew felt it. The sentiment was entirely lost on Father Antonio, however, who shoved Etienne roughly into a nearby chair. Nick joined his wife on the bed and held her hands tightly, as if to never let go.

"I'm so sorry," she whispered, her voice breaking. It was then that Nick noticed something wrong. He took his wife's face in his hands and studied her carefully. A red welt rose on the surface of her pale skin, high on her cheek. A tender bruise could be seen growing around the crimson mark. Her mouth, too, red and swollen on one side, betrayed the marks of violence.

"You bastard!" raged Nick as he flung himself with unexpected force across the room at Father Antonio. The Catholic priest slammed against the wall and slid to the floor. Nick reached down and grabbed the man by the shirt, pulling him to his feet.

Nick would wonder later, *Did I feel them first? Or hear them?* He had the unmistakable understanding, however, that rifles were pressed to his back, cocked and ready to rip through his body. For a moment, Nick considered trading his life for revenge. It would be so easy to drive the butt of his hand into the priest's nose, sending splinters of bone and cartilage into the brain of the man who had done harm to his wife. *One brief moment of revenge...*

"Nick!" Katherine cried out.

Nick dropped Father Antonio to the ground.

Ronaldo rushed to help the priest to his feet. Father Antonio shook him off and strode up to Nick. "For that, *my boy*, you will pay dearly. *Dearly*." Father Antonio withdrew his gun and pressed the barrel against Nick's temple. He stared at Nick for many moments, waiting to see a tremor of discomfort. It was a look Father Antonio had come to know well, in the discipline of his followers. But it did not come from Nick Spencer.

Nick's face was as fixed and angry as it had ever been. It took all the will in the priest's possession not to shoot Nick in the head, but rather – as his God commanded – to turn the other cheek. He could not resist, however, striking Nick with the butt of his gun.

The force of the blow caused Nick to stumble backwards, nearly knocking him off his feet. But Nick regained his balance quickly and – even as a trickle of blood ran down his forehead and into his eye – continued to stare, unblinking, at the furious priest.

It was in moments such as this that Father Antonio longed most to hear the voice of God whisper in his ear. His mother had heard it; of that he was sure. The grace of God was with her always. Father Antonio knew the Word of God intimately, and lived and taught all His commandments. He loved his Lord with all his heart and soul. Fervently he prayed to feel the direct touch of God on his heart, His voice in his ear. *Soon*, thought Father Antonio, *I will be worthy*. The priest, resolute, turned his immediate attention to Muhanna. "Who are you?" he demanded.

Muhanna shrugged. "I was just trying to sell some chickens. I do not know these people."

"Unfortunate timing for you, then," said Father Antonio. "You can be our guest with the others until we get a few matters cleared up. And you can die with them if it comes to that."

"Wait a min –" began Muhanna.

"Shut up," snapped Father Antonio. "I know you are the friend of these people. I am not stupid." He turned his back on Muhanna and walked over to Etienne. "Now then, about the rest of the manuscripts. Find the other 11, or I will kill Katherine. That is the deal."

"I don't know where they are," stated Etienne. "I have no idea where to even *begin* looking. Or even if there *are* any more."

"For the love of God, please don't lie to me. I cannot tell you how much I despise that," hissed Father Antonio. "You will find the books and turn them over to me, or Katherine will die. It's as simple as that."

"Okay," said Etienne, in his most condescendingly logical tone. "Let me get this straight. You would kill this innocent woman for documents that I don't have, can't get, and that, as far as I know, don't even exist. Have I got that right?"

"They do exist. I know it. And you know it," fumed Father Antonio.

"So, help me out with something," Etienne said. They all turned to him. "I understand that you want the Gnostic manuscripts. I understand that you are a man willing to murder for what he wants. I understand that you are a little fanatical and unrealistic. I also understand that you have orders coming from somewhere above you. What I don't understand is ..." Etienne paused.

"What?" snapped Father Antonio.

274

"Who's *this* fellow?" Etienne pointed toward the Coptic priest. Sitting quietly, the Coptic Priest now sat up straight, as if woken from a daydream. His robes were disheveled and his round black hat askew on his head.

"He's walking information, that's what he is," retorted Father Antonio.

"I said *who*," countered Etienne. "Not *what*. He is a *person,* if you had not thought to notice."

"My name is Father Mhand," the Coptic priest said gently. "From al-Qasr." Father Mhand was thin, with almond eyes in a soft, wrinkled face. Shocks of thick white hair stood straight out from under his hat.

"The bastards ransacked his church and dragged him off in the middle of the night," added Katherine angrily. She held the priest's hand, gently covering his pale, tissue-thin skin with the warmth of her touch.

"Hurting women and priests, that's what they do.... they're cowards and bullies, playing a petty, unjust, cruel game." Katherine smoldered a hateful glare at Father Antonio while she spoke.

"Cruel? Perhaps. Unjust? No. Petty? My dear, *you have no idea,"* responded Father Antonio.

"You're mean, and you're small, and you're *petty*," Katherine spit the words out of her mouth.

"I work under the authority of God, the authority of the Church, and the authority of the Archbishop of Rome himself!" retorted Father Antonio.

"Bullshit," said Katherine.

"My dear, you go too far!" said Father Antonio, making a move toward her.

"Wait," shouted Nick, stretching his arm in front of Katherine. Father Antonio pulled up short. "There is something of a very sensitive nature that I need to clear up before we go any further..."

Now everyone in the room turned to look at Nick. "I just have this one burning question, just this one thing I just can't let go of until I have an honest answer..." rambled Nick. Everyone sat waiting. Nick took a long pause.

"Get on with it!" snapped Father Antonio. "My patience is gone."

"Well..." said Nick, turning to Muhanna. "How did you ever find us?"

"Ah," said Muhanna, very pleased with himself. "I was hiding behind a sand dune, listening, when you were taken away in the big black car. And I have friends in Nag Hammadi. They told me that there were strangers in town, buying guns and bullets. The locals do not like strangers. And they are most hateful of strangers with guns." Muhanna smoldered a glare at Father Antonio. Then he turned to Etienne. "But they liked your jeep. Most unusual. And they followed it. I was able to borrow the truck of a friend, who sells chickens, and I ... found these clothes ... and then I came to find you.

"Then," continued Muhanna. "I found this!" He pulled a white cloth from the waistband of his long black skirt. It was Katherine's scarf. Handing it to Nick, he then produced another small item from his skirt pocket. "And this!" He held up an earring and dangled it, letting it twinkle brightly in a shaft of sunlight.

"You dropped them on purpose?" asked Nick.

"Well...yes... I had to," said Katherine.

"Brilliant!" said Nick. "My wife is brilliant."

"Thank you!" said Katherine, putting on her earring. Nick then handed Katherine her scarf, and in a gesture so slight than no one noticed, he passed it near his face to inhale, for one brief moment, the scent of her skin.

"Enough!" shouted Father Antonio. "No one cares about your stupid earring!"

"I do," Katherine and Nick said in unison.

"It is time for you to leave," said Father Antonio, looking at Nick and Etienne. "Ronaldo and Mario will accompany you on your journey. Bring back the 11 manuscripts to me, by the year's end. That gives you more than a month. In the mean time, Mrs. Spencer, Father Mhand, and the Arab will stay with me."

"Excuse me," interrupted Father Mhand, dabbing his forehead with a handkerchief. Though the priest was old and thin, his stature suggested a youthful vigor. It might have been suggested that he was hiding a surprising history of mischievous exploits—the kind that is inevitable for rambunctious, inventive street children. But even more compelling was the look of grace that sat constantly upon the old man's face. To pinpoint its source would have been impossible. It was easy to understand, however, that across the many years this man had come to know, without question, the love and compassion of his God. It was to this quiet man that everyone now turned their attention.

"I say," said Father Mhand. "Does anyone else smell smoke?" They all started to look around and sniff the air. The distinct smell of smoke began to infiltrate the room. Ronaldo opened the bedroom door.

"Fire!" he yelled. They all saw, through the open door, flames and smoke curling around the back wall of the house.

"Ronaldo!" commanded Father Antonio. "Get out there and stop that fire!" Ronaldo ran out of the room with a look of overwhelmed defeat already set on his face. The man posted as guard in the bedroom rose and moved to the doorway. He watched Ronaldo, his compatriot, run out into the blazing room, and he feared for him. He didn't see Muhanna move, like lightening, off the bed.

Muhanna threw his veil around the guard's head, nearly choking the life out of him. He wrestled the big man to the ground, as the guard flailed his arms, gasping for breath. Sitting on top of the guard as if he was a wrestled calf, Muhanna took the veil and tied the man's hands and feet together. Muhanna tucked the guard's gun in the waistband of his long skirt, and stood over him, his legs spread and his arms crossed in pride.

Seizing the opportunity, Etienne sharply elbowed the other armed man, Mario, in the ribs, and grabbed his gun as the man hunched over in pain. With surprising deftness, Nick joined in and threw Mario to the ground. He removed the man's belt, and tied his hands behind his back.

These men are obviously not professional gunmen, thought Etienne. *Or things would have turned out quite differently, and someone would probably be dead by now.*

"Enough!" shouted Father Antonio. In the confusion, he had grabbed Katherine and was holding a gun to her head. The room suddenly became very quiet. Katherine was breathing in shallow, raspy bursts, her heart pounding so hard she thought it might beat right out of her chest. The barrel of the gun felt cold and unforgiving against her forehead.

Nick rose from the ground, where he was kneeling over Mario. "Don't you do it," he said to Father Antonio. "If you hurt her –"

"What?" scoffed Father Antonio. "What will you do?" He laughed in Nick's face. "Why don't you just drop your gun and move over there – to the far wall."

Etienne slowly stepped forward, between Nick and Katherine, and leveled his gun at Father Antonio. "Let her go," he said. "Or I will kill you where you stand."

Etienne was rolling the dice in a dangerous game, betting that Father Antonio would not be able to assassinate Katherine in cold blood. The priest, he reasoned, needed Katherine alive to play his game of kidnapping and blackmail. Etienne also knew that, if he had to, he would shoot Father Antonio on the spot.

The priest glared back at Etienne with cold eyes. Father Antonio's face showed no emotion other than hatred, and perhaps a regretful determination. It was not a look that might be interpreted as remotely compassionate or forgiving. He did not falter for even a moment, even with the barrel of Etienne's gun in his face, a blazing fire at his back, and a wandering chicken at his feet.

For a long time it seemed as though nobody even breathed, except for Katherine. She was trembling so deeply, and panting so heavily, Etienne thought she might just collapse onto the floor.

There was a sudden and loud pounding on the front door, as if a small army was kicking at it from the outside. The door, cracking loose from its lock, swung open on its hinges and slammed against the wall. Four men burst into the living room and a thundering voice rang out. "I am Abu al-Hamd, of the family of al-Yassid! Turn over Muhanna Ali al-Samara to me!"

Father Antonio, startled at the intrusion, involuntarily moved his gun away from Katherine's head. Just a little. Just enough. Nick charged the priest in a split second, chopping at the hand that held his gun. The weapon scuttled across the floor and landed under the bed. Nick reached one foot behind Father Antonio and kicked the priest's legs out from underneath him, dropping them both unceremoniously to the ground. Then Nick went for the gun.

Father Antonio cried out in rage and threw himself upon Nick's back, sending Nick sprawling, face down, across the floor. The priest wrapped his hands around Nick's neck, dug in his fingers, and began to squeeze. Arrows of pain shot through Nick's head as he struggled to breath. Nick tried to push himself onto his knees, knowing that if Father Antonio kept the higher ground, he would surely be strangled to death. The priest's strength and persistence prevailed, however, as Nick mind and vision began to blur from a lack of oxygen.

With one arm outstretched and the other holding a gun, Etienne grabbed Father Antonio by the scruff of his collar. He pulled the priest off Nick and sent him careening like a rag doll across the room. Nick snatched the gun from under the bed and sat there for a moment, rubbing his bruised throat and catching his breath.

The Coptic priest, who was dazed through most of the commotion, suddenly stood up from the bed. He scooped up the stray chicken and made his way calmly to the bedroom window. He raised the blinds and fiddled with the latch, one-handed, until it unlocked. He gave the window jam a quick rap with his hand to loosen it up, and slid the window open. "This is the way," he said to anyone who was listening. With that, the Coptic priest crawled, with the chicken, out the window and dropped a few feet to the ground below.

Etienne put his hand on Nick's shoulder. "You alright?" Nick nodded and rose to his feet. Etienne moved across the room to where Katherine was standing like a pale statue. "Ready, Cinderella?" he asked.

"Take me away from here," she said weakly. Etienne put her knapsack in her arms and he and Nick helped her out the window. Muhanna followed closely behind. Etienne then ran into the living room to recover his satchel and the manuscripts. Ronaldo had his back to Etienne, busy with the fire and the al-Yassids, and Etienne returned to the bedroom unnoticed.

He found Nick standing in the center of the bedroom, a gun pointed at Father Antonio's face. "Leave us alone," Nick said coldly to the priest. "The next time I see you, will be the day you die. No question."

"It's time to go, Nick," said Etienne softly. Nick and Etienne took one last look at the fallen men, and jumped out the open window to the ground below.

"This way," said Etienne, as they made their way to the back of the house. They all piled quickly into Etienne's jeep as the house continued to fill with smoke, fire and confusion.

"No keys," Muhanna noticed dejectedly.

"No problem," responded Etienne, smiling. He reached under the front seat and drew up a jingling set of keys. "I always keep a spare set. Because you just never know."

"Let's get out of here," said Nick, looking over his shoulder. Etienne fired up the engine and sped away. Only a spray of dust and a few chicken feathers remained in their wake. Confusion reigned in the house behind them, as the al-Yassid clan met up with the men from Italy.

Just as they were leaving the outskirts of Nag Hammadi, Katherine suddenly looked around. Her arms were wrapped around the frail bones of the Coptic priest when she sat straight up in her seat and yelled, *"Stop!"*

Etienne slammed on the brakes, skidding to a halt on the dirt road. "What? What is it?"

Katherine jumped out of the jeep and ran back a dozen yards. She looked around, bent over, picked something up from the ground, and returned to the jeep. "My other earring," she proudly announced, holding it up for all to see. She smiled and Nick kissed her sweetly on the cheek. *She'll be okay,* Nick thought. *The worst is behind us.*

"Back to the basilica?" asked Etienne.

"Back to the basilica," agreed Nick, his arm locked silently in Katherine's. Her earrings dangled softly against her skin as Etienne drove the jeep toward the eastern desert.

As if it was the cause of all the trouble, Nick put the gun he took from Father Antonio into the glove box. He slammed the little door shut, in the vain hope that it could contain any danger yet to come.

18

THE SEARCH FOR GOD AND GLORY

*Abandon the search for God and the creation and other matters of a
similar sort. Look for him by taking yourself as the starting point.
Learn who it is within you who makes everything his own and says,
'My God, my mind, my thought, my soul, my body.' Learn the sources
of sorrow, joy, love, hate... If you carefully investigate these matters,
you will find Him in yourself.*

– Gnostic Gospel of Truth, 28:16-17

Basilica of St. Pachomius

"What's for dinner?" asked Muhanna rubbing his hands together.
He had wiggled out of the black dress he had stolen, and was
adjusting his *jallabiya* with a fair amount of vanity. "I'm starving." He
looked directly at Katherine with an expectant look on his face.

Nick jumped up. "We'll make dinner tonight," he said quickly.
"Won't we, Etienne?"

"Sure. Uh, sure we will."

Nick and Etienne rummaged through the supplies. They would
not again make the mistake of letting Katherine do all the cooking and
cleaning and organizing while they sat around making plans. No
matter how reasonable that seemed to be. "We're out of food,"
announced Nick. They both looked over at Katherine, helpless.

Katherine eyed Father Mhand's chicken clucking around the
sand floor. The good priest scooped up the hapless bird. "I'll go
without," he said.

"No need, Father," laughed Katherine. "There's plenty of food.
You just have to be smart enough to recognize a noodle when you see
it." Katherine crouched beside the campfire that Etienne had built in
the middle of the open room. She stirred a pot of boiling water, and

slowly added coils of dried pasta. She set Nick to cutting potatoes, onions and sun-dried tomatoes into little pieces on a slab of rock.

"Etienne, you're excused," said Katherine, as he fumbled with a clove of garlic. She smiled at him. "Read to us from your book."

"No, I can do this," Etienne insisted, crinkling his brow and bending close over the small herb with his Swiss army knife.

"Go on," Nick said. "We'll finish this." Nick poured dates into a bowl made of reeds, and nudged Etienne away.

"It's not as though I can't cut a clove of garlic, you know," insisted Etienne. But his book drew him to surrender the point.

Katherine sprinkled the vegetables into the steaming pot, while Father Mhand moved close to Etienne to hear the ancient words. Muhanna saw that the sun had set in the sky, and moved to the eastern wall to pray. Kneeling on his prayer scarf, he bent over and over, rhythmically chanting in a low, melodic voice.

Etienne had stolen every possible moment over the past few days to translate *The Gospel of Thomas*. Totally transfixed, he would flip back and forth between the manuscript, the Coptic alphabet, his notes, and the blank pages of his diary. There, on clean white pages, he meticulously penned the words that revealed themselves to him.

"Here's what the next passage says," began Etienne. The fire danced in the background, casting a strange light in the early evening. The tones emanating from Muhanna floated through the air and mixed with the crackling fire, making Etienne's words sound like an incantation. "This is from the *Gospel of Thomas*," he began.

"Jesus said, know what is in front of your face, and what is hidden from you will be disclosed to you. For there is nothing hidden that will not be revealed.

His followers asked him, and said to him, 'Do you want us to fast? How should we pray? Should we give to charity? What diet should we observe?'

Jesus said, 'Do not lie, and do not do what you hate, because all things are disclosed before heaven. For there is nothing hidden that will not be revealed, and there is nothing covered that will remain undisclosed.'"

"The Holy Bible says the same." Everyone looked over at Father Mhand, sitting quietly, his hands folded in his lap. *"For there is nothing covered that shall not be revealed; neither hid, that shall not be known.* Luke, Chapter 12, verse 2." Father Mhand smiled. "The Gospels according to Saint Matthew and Saint Mark have virtually identical verses as well."

"Really?" asked Katherine, looking up from the fire.

Muhanna's voice rose in the darkening night. *"Bismi Allahi alrrahmani alrraheemi. Alhamdu lillahi rabbi alAAalameena. Alrrahmani alrraheemi. Maliki yawmi alddeeni. Iyyaka naAAbudu wa-iyyaka nastaAAeenu. Ihdina alssirata almustaqeema. Sirata allatheena anAAamta AAalayhim ghayri almaghdoobi AAalayhim wala alddalleena."* Whether he was praying for forgiveness, for vengeance, or for a safe return to his home, or something else altogether, was between he and Allah, his God.

Father Mhand raised his face to the sounds, and then turned back to Katherine. "Indeed," he continued. "Matthew says, *Fear them not, therefore: for there is nothing covered that shall not be revealed; or hid, that shall not be known.* Chapter 10, verse 26."

"Do you know the entire Bible by heart?" asked Katherine.

Muhanna, having finished his prayers, wrapped his scarf around his neck and slowly, quietly, came to join the others.

"More or less, I suppose I do," replied Father Mhand. "Except for Deuteronomy. I never fully understood Deuteronomy. Too many rules, I think. And too many curses."

"That's incredible," exclaimed Katherine, beaming a smile at him.

"It goes with the job," shrugged the old priest. "And I've had many years to read. And to think."

"What do you suppose it means?" Nick asked, as he cut slices of cheese with his knife. He was eating a slice or two as he went, directly from the blade, something that Katherine found as astonishing as someone knowing the entire Bible by heart.

"Well," began Father Mhand. "Perhaps it means that one day, in the Kingdom of Heaven, all will be revealed to us. Because we are all naked before God. Every hair on our head is counted."

"Why do we have to wait until we get to heaven?" asked Katherine. "Why can't we know everything now?"

"Our journey on earth is about the learning, I should think," said Etienne. "We are not meant to know."

"Indeed," remarked Father Mhand. "It is one thing to discover truths on our journey through life. Quite another to understand them; to make them our own. Knowledge does not always lead to wisdom."

"You only have to look at Hiroshima to realize that," said Nick. Nobody spoke in response but rather, looked at Nick with expressions ranging from sorrow to skepticism.

Katherine spooned pasta and broth generously into bowls, sprinkling cheese strips on top. Nick added a thick wedge of bread to each bowl, and moved to Katherine's side to help serve the steaming soup. "I always say the wrong things, don't I?" he whispered.

"Yes darling," she smiled. "But someone has to."

"*Merci*," said Etienne taking the bowl from Nick's outstretched hands. Then he turned his attention to Father Mhand. "Can you tell us why Father Antonio ransacked your church?"

"Because I had a manuscript," he replied, distracted with his bowl of dinner.

"You *did*?" exclaimed Nick, looking at Etienne.

"Yes... just like the one you have here."

"That's remarkable news!" said Etienne. "Were you able to translate it?"

"Some of it, yes. But it was not long before a man came and took it."

"Father Antonio?" asked Etienne.

"No," replied the priest. "Not him."

"One of the others in his gang? Ronaldo? Mario?"

"No. This man was different," explained Father Mhand. "He said he was with the Egyptian government. And that the book belonged to him."

"What was his name?" pressed Etienne.

"His name was odd to me. I cannot remember it exactly. And he spoke with a very strange voice." Father Mhand pointed to Etienne. "Like you."

"He was French?"

"Yes, perhaps that's it." The old priest shook his head. "I cannot exactly remember."

"Did he show you any identification?" asked Etienne.

"Identification?"

"A card, with the seal of Egypt on it, perhaps?"

"No, no. Nothing like that."

"Whoever took the book probably lied to get it," Nick said.

Etienne shuddered. "Do you remember what the book said?" he asked. "Do you remember, perhaps, who the author was?"

"I only read a little, but it was very intriguing," began Father Mhand. "It was called *The Dialogue of the Savior.*"

"Fascinating!" exclaimed Etienne. "What did it say?"

"Well, let's see here," said Father Mhand. "If I recall correctly, what I read there talked much about ignorance, and self-destruction. Yes, that was it. One must understand the mysteries of the self and of the elements of the universe, or one is bound for annihilation."

"The elements of the universe?" asked Katherine.

Father Mhand set down his bowl. "This is what I remember:

If one does not understand how the fire came to be, he will burn in it, because he does not know his root. If one does not first understand the water, he does not know anything.... If one does not understand how the wind that blows came to be, he will run with it. If one does not understand how the body that he wears came to be, he will perish with it... Whoever does not understand how he came will not understand how he will go..."

Father Mhand picked up his bowl and began to eat. "You see," he smiled at Etienne. "I remember the important things."

"You memorized all that?" asked Katherine.

"It's what priests do, my dear," replied Father Mhand humbly. "Among other things, of course."

Etienne shook his head, amazed. "Where did you get the book in the first place?" he asked.

"Khalifah," the priest replied. "Muhanna's brother. He sold it to me."

"He shall pay for that," muttered Muhanna.

"Will you try to remember the name of the man who came and took the book?" insisted Etienne. "It's very important."

"For you, I will try to remember. Because you say it is important. But my friend, perhaps these things, these truths, as your book says, will be revealed to you. If you will only believe."

After dinner, Nick sat down with Muhanna and Father Mhand and they began a lively discussion about the books they had seen. Nick barely nodded as Katherine kissed him on the forehead. "I'm going to wander outside," she said.

"Mmmm," was Nick's reply.

Katherine found Eitenne leaning against the western wall, watching the sun begin its descent from the day. "Mind if I join you?" she asked, as she nestled herself in the sand. "This place isn't so bad, you know," she said in his silence. "For a fixer-upper, that is. I could get used to it. A few curtains maybe. Running water. *Walls*. It could be very cozy."

Etienne's soft laugh drifted across the evening air. Then he turned to her. "I'm glad you're okay, Kat. But, please, *please*, don't do anything like that again."

"Are you my knight in shining armor now?" She rested her cheek upon her arms, and smiled playfully.

"Just don't make me rescue you again, *cherí*."

"Will Father Antonio be back, do you suppose?"

Etienne searched the sky. "*Oui.*" They let the truth settle on them in silence. After a while, Etienne spoke. "Can I ask you something terribly personal, Katherine?"

Katherine sat up straight. "Something that is absolutely none of your business?"

"*Oui.* Those are the only questions worth asking a woman." Etienne grinned.

"Fire away then," replied Katherine. "Just know, I may not answer."

"I just always thought you loved children. And I was wondering why you and Nick..."

"I do love children," interrupted Katherine, wrapping her jacket close around her slender body. "Other people's children."

"Why is that?" pressed Etienne.

Katherine lit a cigarette. "Well..." she said, looking Etienne straight in the eye. "Because they're whiny, snot-nosed, self-centered little brats, for one thing. And for two, the last thing I want to do is spend my days and nights changing diapers, wiping noses, and spooning baby food down the throat of someone who doesn't want to eat. Forget the fact that they throw up, throw tantrums and throw every plan you ever had for yourself down the toilet.

"Then, after all that, after you've spent the best years of your life looking after them, making sacrifices, gotten yourself old and gray and wrinkled worrying yourself sick about them, they become teenagers and hate you for everything you did or ever will do."

"Oh," said Etienne. "I see." He looked at her closely with an expression of concern on his face. She read it as she read everyone else's expression to whom she had given that speech: as shock and indignation that a woman could be so heartless.

Katherine finished her cigarette and lit another one before she spoke again. "It's so beautiful out here," she said, not looking at Etienne, but out across the desert plain.

"God."

"What?"

"I've heard it said that *God is beauty,*" said Etienne softly.

"Oh."

"Your old friend Francis of Assisi said it."

"What do you suppose he meant?"

"Well, I guess he was saying that God is everywhere, Katherine," said Etienne. "Wherever you find beauty, you find God. All around you, inside of you and outside of you."

"It's just not true for me," said Katherine. "God feels separate. Entirely separate from me. And certainly not concerned with my little life."

"The mystics taught that everything is in God and God is in everything," explained Etienne. "That means the sunsets we see, the water we drink, the food we eat, the camels, the flowers, the bugs. In Father Antonio, Nick, Muhanna, me. And in *you*, Katherine."

"I know a nun, Sister Helen Eloise," said Katherine, "who would rap your knuckles with a ruler if she heard you say that."

"You went to parochial school?" asked Etienne.

"For eight long, miserable years. I learned the rules early. Don't talk back. Don't ask for anything for yourself, *ever*. Don't question authority – neither God's nor the nuns'. Don't be too big, don't be too smart. Wear a uniform to keep you level with the other sheep in the flock. And of course I learned that that I'm a born sinner – going straight to Hell someday if I don't fix what's wrong with me. Which is pretty much everything."

"Do you believe in God?"

"Well, at some point I suppose I realized that the nuns were selling us all a bill of goods. Between science and nature, the Creation story didn't add up. But when I asked about that, I was sent straight to the back of the room to kneel on rice. That's about when I started suspecting that Hell was right here on earth."

"The Gnostics say that it is *heaven* that is right here on earth, all around us, and that we don't see it," offered Etienne.

"The God I was taught about is *out there* somewhere," replied Katherine, looking to the sky. "Up there, I guess. In heaven. Where ever that is. A wrathful God, vengeful, keeping track of everything I do. Somewhere out there... watching... ready to smack my hands with a cosmic ruler."

288

"There was a woman in the thirteenth century – you would've liked her, I think – Mechtild of Magdeburg. She was ... ahead of her time. She said that the day of her spiritual awakening was the day she saw, and knew that she saw, all things in God and God in all things."

"Sounds nice," said Katherine, searching the horizon. "But I can't see it that way."

"You don't have to believe that you can," offered Etienne. "You just have to stop believing that you cannot. Set aside your disbelief for a moment, Kat, and let all you see out here settle in on you, as real and true and part of who you are. Part of who God is."

For a long time, Katherine remained still, trying to make Etienne's words real for herself. "No," she said finally, lifting up her head. "It's all very separate. I am not the desert and the desert is not God. They are all *separate*."

"I wish I could take back every thing that religion has taught you," said Etienne softly, "and teach you instead how to fall in love with a flower. And then... with yourself."

"Self-love is blasphemy," Katherine retorted.

"And *that* is the cruelest deception ever perpetrated on humankind," said Etienne with a hint of anger. "It's called Original Sin, and it is the invention of one man. One man whose struggle against his own sexual desires led him to believe that we all came here bent, broken, stained with sin. His name was Augustine. He was a powerful Roman bishop. And he was wrong." Softening, Etienne added, "And I'm sorry that you have it wired up that way in your head. Because it is just not so."

Katherine sank down next to him in the sand. "Come here," he offered, stretching out his arm. "Listen. You are hugged by the arms of the mystery of God."

"Stop with the quotes, will you please?" She offered him a weak smile.

"Hildegaard of Bingen said that. Another woman you would have liked. She was an abbottess back in the Middle Ages who composed religious music. I always like to think of her as a petite German woman who could beat up any priest she didn't like."

That made Katherine laugh. "You are hugged by the arms of the mystery of God," Katherine repeated. "I like that." She rested her head on Etienne's shoulder as they watched the sun dip slowly below the dunes. Finally the dark and the chill and the guilt of their intimacy drove them indoors.

Nick was still talking with Muhanna and Father Mhand about the manuscripts and what might have happened to them. "Join us, join us!" said the Coptic priest. They sat around the light of a small lantern and Katherine and Etienne joined their circle. Katherine took special care to sit close to her husband.

"Will you read to us more from your book?" asked Father Mhand. "Please?"

"Of course." Etienne took the *Gospel of Thomas* from his satchel, and the priest moved the lantern close to him to illuminate the book.

Katherine took more pictures that night: of Etienne totally lost in his book, of the good priest reciting from the Bible, his face aglow from some inner rapture, and of Nick and Muhanna, their faces upturned, hearing words they didn't believe, but couldn't ignore. Katherine felt lucky that evening, momentarily blessed, to be part of that amazing circle of men.

The next morning they agreed to return to Cairo. "I'm glad to be leaving this place," said Katherine, throwing a duffel bag into the jeep.

"Me as well," said Etienne, carrying a box of supplies. "We'll be in Cairo by dinner – if all goes well."

"I'm just beginning to like this place," said Muhanna, with two sleeping bags tucked under his arms.

"What I want most right now is a long, hot, soapy bath!" Katherine said, pushing the hair out of her face.

"Ooo la la la la," grinned Etienne.

Nick watched Katherine laugh from the entrance to the great stone building. "Are we all set?" he asked, moving toward the jeep.

"It's going to be a tight fit, but I think we're ready," said Etienne.

"Where's Father Mhand?" asked Nick.

"I think he's looking for his chicken," said Katherine, smiling with a suprising tenderness.

"Here we are," said Father Mhand cheerfully. The bird was tucked contentedly under his arm as he stepped out of the monastery into the open desert.

"Let's go then," instructed Nick. "Tally ho."

Etienne climbed in behind the wheel, with Katherine in the passenger seat. Nick, Muhanna and Father Mhand squeezed themselves into the back seat with the chicken. "Father, we'll drop you and Muhanna off in al-Qasr," said Etienne. "Then we must head straight to Cairo."

"That is a bad idea," said Muhanna. "I should go with you."

"I would like to go as well," said Father Mhand.

"Yes! We could both be a great help to you," insisted Muhanna.

"Trouble follows you wherever you go, Muhanna," replied Etienne.

"If Jahib is in Cairo selling my books," said Muhanna. "I can find him. I know I can."

"No," insisted Nick. "You'd only gum things up."

"I would not," stated Muhanna, crossing his arms.

"Have you ever been to Cairo?" asked Etienne.

"*I* have," offered Father Mhand.

"*Oui, oui,*" sighed Etienne. "We shall go to Cairo... together."

Cairo

The great city cloistered around the river Nile in dense and muted building blocks of time. This place had compelled adventurers, speculators, scholars, armies, tradesmen, craftsmen and peasants alike for thousands and thousands of years. It had once been a center of great learning, progressive thinking and cultural diversity. Cairo: a city that seeped into the imaginations and dreams of people all over the world. Cairo: the City of the Thousand and One Nights.

In its shadow loomed the three pyramids of Giza, ancient and startling contrasts against the enormous modern city. They stood in pale, soft golden stone. Older and more staggering than the imagination could grasp, the pyramids were ancient sentinels reminding modern man of the ability to create perfection.

Cairo's mystique lay in the marriage of old and new, religion and intellect, wealth and poverty in their extremes, the common and the extraordinary. Domed mosques shared space with towering hotels, office buildings, and clap-trap tenements. Through it all, the Nile meandered silently, endlessly by, an attendant observer of all that had been built up around her—the source of desert life.

Goats, carts, bicycles, pedestrians, vendors and cars all jostled for space in the narrow streets of Old Cairo. Cobbled alleys and shaded courtyards were surrounded with Christian monuments, modern mosques and one ancient synagogue.

It was here, in this extremely traditional, religious sector, that they had visited the Coptic Museum only a few days before. A goat, piled high with wares for sale, tossed a tired glance at the dusty jeep threading its way through the busy crowd. The merchant who held the goat's tether did not concern himself for a moment with this jeep, or its curious load of travelers, supplies and a lone chicken.

Etienne turned off the narrow street and onto the Corniche el-Nil, which flanked the river. From there they drove north, into the lush, curved streets of Garden City. This wealthy suburb of Cairo was dotted with world embassies, consulates and cultural centers. It was also peppered with upscale places to shop, sleep and dine.

"We should be safe here," said Etienne, pulling up in front of Katherine and Nick's hotel. Turbaned doorman in starched red tunics, braided in gold, waited like sentinels at the brass doors. One of the doormen – the towering, gentle Sudanese – surveyed the jeep carefully, resting his eyes on Katherine.

Katherine waved brightly at the doorman, who nodded back solemnly. "I cannot *wait* for a hot bath and a long nap," she said, jumping from the car.

Katherine pulled out one of the scarves that she'd purchased in al-Qsar and handed it to the doorman. "For your daughter," she said, handing him the colorful, folded textile.

"And I won't take no for an answer," she quipped, just as he started to protest. Then she slid through the door and made her way to the lobby elevator.

"What about the chicken?" asked Nick, turning to Father Mhand, who was wresting his way out of the back seat of the jeep.

"Well my friend," said Father Mhand to the chicken nestled in his arms. "I'm afraid we must part our ways. I must put you back into the hands of God." The priest stepped from the jeep and crossed the busy Cairo street. Curious, Etienne followed. Katherine came too, with her camera, while Nick made arrangements with the bellman.

A young boy sat on the dirty curb, a box of matchbooks for sale by his side. His clothes and face were stained with the dirt of the streets. He was small and thin, tucked snugly into a dingy tweed suitcoat, traded for at a local shop, cheap and second-hand. His black hair was parted and combed neatly to the side, with little wisps curling at his ears. He wore a little flowered shirt, probably a girl's, under his suitcoat. His trousers, wrinkled and worn, fell noticeably short of his shoes.

Father Mhand sat next to him, his old bones struggling toward the curb. "Hello," he said. Then the priest spoke in Arabic. *"Salam 'alekum."* Katherine and Etienne stood at a discreet distance and watched. Katherine caught the conversation in pictures, engraving the boy and the priest forever in her memory.

"Wa 'alekum es salam," answered the boy. His big black eyes followed the movements of the chicken.

"You have matches for sale?" asked the priest, pointing.

The boy's face broke into a broad grin, stretching across his face and pushing against his high round cheeks. The tips of those cheeks were rosy on his dark skin, as was his little, flat nose. His eyes fell on the priest, serious and hopeful. A little red reminder of an uneasy life escaped from his eyebrow, a cut now softened into a welt, almost healed, not yet invisible.

"Yes, I do," he answered. He lifted his wares and extended them to Father Mhand, pulling a matchbook out of the box with fingers stained with the same dirt and time of the streets.

"I have no money," said the priest solemnly.

"Oh," said the boy. Reluctantly, he set the box back down on the curb.

"Would you like a chicken?" he asked the boy.

The boy gazed past the chicken and straight at Father Mhand. "You are Christian?"

"Yes."

"Is this your chicken?"

"Yes," replied the priest. "This chicken and I are friends."

"What would I do with a chicken?" asked the boy.

"Perhaps you could sell it, for money."

"Then what would happen to the chicken?"

"It would be killed, for a meal, most likely."

"You would kill your friend, the chicken?"

"I cannot keep her with me any longer."

"Maybe the chicken will be *my* friend," suggested the boy.

"Maybe she will."

"I will keep your chicken for you," said the boy seriously. "I will not kill her for a meal."

"Perhaps."

"Maybe she will lay eggs for me. And I can sell *those* for a meal."

"You will need a rooster for that, I'm afraid."

"Then I will ask Allah for a rooster, too."

"You asked Allah for a chicken?" asked the priest, intrigued.

"I prayed to Allah for help. And he brought me you. And now my chicken."

"Indeed, indeed," smiled the priest.

The boy thumbed carefully through his cardboard box and picked out just the right collection of matchbooks. He handed them gravely to the old priest. Father Mhand placed the chicken in the boy's arms, and patted them both on the head with a whispered blessing. He crossed back over the street, away from the hungry boy, clutching the book of matches in his hand.

After they all had a hot soak and a bit of a rest, they joined up on the outdoor patio of a nearby restaurant. Except for Katherine. She stayed in her room, with a bottle of chilled wine and a special assignment from Etienne.

Across the street an old woman, draped from head to ankle in layers of black, sat cross-legged in the courtyard of a mosque. Her callused feet, dirty and bare, pushed her knees up around her elbows as she bent over her book. Her head was stooped low over *The Koran*, the holy book of Islam, her face buried deep, her fingers tracing the words she knew by heart.

The little matchbox boy lingered on the sidewalk nearby. He had trailed Father Mhand to this place without saying a word. The chicken was tied with a shank of thin rope, and followed the little boy, obediently, wherever he went.

Muhanna sulked at the table, listening restlessly to Father Mhand. "You must put an end to this feud, Muhanna," said the Coptic priest, "and stop the endless killing." The priest bent over the table, leaning in close to Muhanna. "I know well the laws of Islam, as well as the laws of the desert. The laws of revenge that you follow do not supersede the holy laws."

He continued as Muhanna stared past him with a bored look on his face. "The Koran clearly states, *he who kills by design shall burn in Hell forever. He shall incur the wrath of God, who will lay His curse on him and prepare him for a woeful scourge.*"

"*Al Quran*," retorted Muhanna, using the Islamic title of the holy book, "also says God is forgiving and merciful."

"Muhanna," pressed the priest, "the words are quite clear. Killing is forbidden by God."

"You are leaving out words!" insisted Muhanna. "*Al Quran* says killing is forbidden by God, *except* for a just cause. It allows for punishment – *for murder or other villainy in the land.*"

"Are you Allah's agent of vengeance, Muhanna? Are you sure Allah has chosen *you* to police the land with your hatred and retaliation?"

"Yes."

Father Mhand pressed on. *"Whoever kills a human being shall be looked upon as though he had killed all mankind; and whoever saves a human life shall be regarded as though he had saved all mankind."*

Muhanna crossed his arms over his chest and slunk deeper into his seat. "An eye for an eye," he stated bluntly, reciting the very little he knew of the Christian Bible. "A tooth for a tooth." He slammed his hand on the table, suddenly impressed with himself.

"Turn the other cheek," quoted the priest, dabbing invisible sweat from his forehead. "In the New Testament Jesus teaches us to forgive, and to hold up our cheek to the one who has smited the other."

"Your Bible says two opposite things, then," replied Muhanna, triumphant. "And therefore cannot be trusted." Father Mhand sighed.

Suddenly, they heard the call to prayer, announced by the muezzin from the tall slender tower on top of a nearby mosque. His call, low and long, floated over the city streets, and people began to move in his direction. This he did five times a day. And five times a day, the Muslims performed their cycle of prayers to express their absolute humility and the sovereignty of God.

"I must be going," said Muhanna quickly jumping up from his seat. "There is no God but Allah, and He demands my attention now." Father Mhand nodded his respect, as Muhanna scurried across the street.

The Father sighed again. "I wonder what your Gnostics would have to say about that."

"That the Bible can't be trusted?" asked Nick.

"They would probably agree," said Etienne. "And speaking of *gnosis*, listen to this." Etienne pulled the diary out of his satchel, anxious to share his most recent translations. Etienne had been penning the words from the papyrus into his diary, writing tiny notes to himself in the margins. Nick and Father Mhand leaned in toward Etienne, a gesture of genuine interest, and respect for the work he had done.

296

"Several sayings in the *Gospel of Thomas* seem to be connected," Etienne began. "Although they are not necessarily written in order. Here's an example:

Jesus said, 'I have thrown fire upon the world, and look, I am watching it until it blazes.'

...And then this one," said Etienne, turning the page.

"Jesus said, 'Perhaps people think that I have come to impose peace upon the world. They do not know that I have come to impose conflicts upon the earth: fire, sword, war. For there will be five in a house: There will be three against two and two against three, father against son and son against father, and they will stand alone.'

This is followed later," continued Etienne, "by another saying, seemingly related:

Jesus said, 'If two make peace with each other within a single house, they will say to the mountain, Move from here, and it will move.'"

They sat in silence for a moment in the buzzing foreground of the restaurant. Father Mhand finally spoke.

"Think not that I am come to send peace on earth: I came not to send peace, but a sword. For I am come to set a variance against his father, and the daughter against her mother, and the daughter in law against her mother in law. And a man's foes shall be they of his own household.

And ye shall be betrayed both by parents, and brethren, and kinsfolks, and friends; and some of you shall they cause to be put to death. And ye shall be hated of all men for my name's sake. But there shall not a hair of your head perish. In your patience possess ye your souls."

"From the Bible?" asked Nick.

"Matthew, Chapter 10. Luke, Chapter 21," said Father Mhand.

"*Fantastique!*" said Etienne. "It seems God intends the purification of the world through the fire of conflict."

"The similarities are absolutely intriguing," said Nick.

"You have worked hard on this," stated Father Mhand, putting his hand on Etienne's shoulder.

"Huh? Oh, yes, I suppose I have. This is a very important book, Father."

"Remember to rest, Etienne. And digest what you have learned."

"What's that?" asked Etienne vaguely, his attention absorbed by the Gnostic manuscript.

"Let me offer you yet another saying," said Father Mhand. "An ancient Dzogchen saying," Etienne looked at him blankly. "As a bee seeks nectar from all kinds of flowers," recited Father Mhand, "seek teachings everywhere. Like a deer that finds a quiet place to graze, seek seclusion to digest all you have gathered..."

"*Oui, oui*, well said." Etienne turned to Nick. "Our immediate problem is to find the one-eyed outlaw, Jahib." Father Mhand sat back in his chair.

"It's likely that he is right here in Cairo, looking for you," said Nick, taking a sip from a cup of strong tea.

"Well, we cannot return to my house just yet," said Etienne. "Even the Coptic Museum may not be safe for us."

"So, now what?" asked Nick.

Etienne smiled broadly. "Miss Donatta." Nick grinned into his tea cup. "It's already set up," said Etienne. "Miss Donatta has arranged a meeting for us at Rasul Taj's antique store, downtown, tomorrow at noon. Not much goes on in Cairo in this business that Rasul does not know about. He'll also do some extra sniffing around in the mean time."

"What about Muhanna and Father Mhand?" asked Nick. "We should return them to al-Qasr."

"Not just yet, my friend," said Etienne.

298

"Muhanna is a liability," complained Nick. "Every time we turn around, some one who is trying to kill him, is trying to kill us."

Etienne laughed. "Yes, you have a point there. But the laws in Cairo are much more strict than the laws of the open desert. And until we have Jahib and the books, Muhanna may be very useful to us."

Nick squirmed just a little in his seat. "Etienne, I've been thinking... once we recover all the manuscripts –"

"I'm turning them over to the government."

"You're *what*?"

"I made a deal with Cato Nafarah. Nick, I did it to keep Katherine out of jail for the rest of her born days. Smuggling artifacts into America is serious business to the Egyptian government."

"Yes, but –"

"Frankly, I offered him the Knife of the Asps, too. It was all part of the deal."

"Have you forgotten that you promised Nelson all thirteen manuscripts in return for a million dollars?" Nick snapped. "Have you entirely forgotten that? Or have you just lost your mind? Nelson is a tremendously powerful person, Etienne. He's not going to sit back and let you double-cross him. What? You think he's just going to hand over the Knife and the money, shrug and say, 'Oh well, keep the manuscripts, what do I care'? You can't imagine that he'd offer up that much money, plus the treasure of the Knife, if he didn't really, *really* want those books."

"Oh, he'll get the manuscripts alright," said Etienne. "He and I will exchange the Knife of the Asps for the books. You and Katherine will get the million dollars, previously wired into the Swiss account."

"What about Nafarah? If you've promised the books, and the Knife, to him?"

"He's invited to the exchange party."

"You can't be serious."

"*Oui.*"

"After Nelson hands over the bank account number, we'll make the swap. Just then, Cato Nafarah will appear and arrest us both on the spot for piracy against the state. Only I – having made good on my deal with Nafarah – will go free."

"You'll make an enemy of Hugo Nelson."

"Nelson will rot in an Egyptian jail for the rest of his miserable days."

"Oh Jesus, Etienne. You truly have lost your mind."

"I think my plan is rather brilliant."

"And what do you get out all this, Etienne?"

"Photographs."

"Photographs?"

"As we speak, Katherine is taking photographs of the *Gospel of Thomas* in your hotel room."

You've conspired behind my back, with my wife, thought Nick bitterly. "Well," he said. "You've thought of everything haven't you?"

"*Oui,*" said Etienne, but deep in his gut, he wondered. And he worried. *So many things could go wrong. So many little things that I just cannot imagine, or plan for, no matter how careful I am.* "We'll take pictures of each page, in succession, as we find the manuscripts," Etienne explained. "I'll then use photographs to translate the documents from the ancient Coptic into English. I'll get a complete translation, the Government gets their artifacts, Nelson gets what he deserves, and you and Katherine get rich."

"This is not about money, Etienne!" said Nick.

"Oh, no?" said Etienne. "It's not about the million dollars you'll get if you turn over the manuscripts?"

"God no." Nick looked as though the weight of the world rested upon his shoulders at that moment.

"I'm trying to do the right thing, Nick."

"How can you say that, when I know in your heart that you want to be *the one and only person* to translate them?"

"That's not fair," snapped Etienne.

Nick leaned back in his chair. "Isn't it?"

"You know that I can translate these documents better than almost anybody."

"Yes, well, *almost*, I'm sure," said Nick, with a subtle insult that slapped Etienne's pride. "What you fail to admit is your egotistical desire to single-handedly serve up the translations to the global academic world, with your signature emblazoned in immortality!"

"You exaggerate!" retorted Etienne. "Besides, my intentions are not self-serving, profit-mongering, greedy claims for my pocketbook!"

"Are you so sure of that? Are you so sure that you are different? You are an arrogant self-righteous bastard, Etienne, if ever I have ever seen one!"

"One would have the glory, the other would have the spoils." Father Mhand's quiet voice interrupted their heated argument. "You argue over that which belongs not to you," Father Mhand continued. "Not in possession, nor in philosophy."

"Stay out of this!" Nick and Etienne snapped in unison at the priest.

"I am afraid that you are attracting a good deal of attention to yourselves, my angry friends," said Father Mhand. He put his hands gently on top of theirs. "Put your bitterness aside for now, and let us leave this place, before the entire city knows your business."

Nick looked around, as if realizing for the first time that he was in a public place. "You're right, good Father, of course," said Nick. He looked straight at Etienne. "We'll settle this business later."

"Nelson will have those books over my dead body," Etienne said, trying to get in the last word before giving up the fight.

Nick smiled disarmingly. "Did I forget to mention that you're stubborn as well?"

"I mean it, Nick," growled Etienne.

"Yes, I think you do," said Nick softly, getting up from the table. "Let's just hope it doesn't come to that."

Etienne threw a handful of bills on the table to pay their bill, and collected his satchel as they all moved together onto the sidewalk.

"Who *are* you?" Etienne asked, as they headed back to their hotel on the plaza. Nick looked at him. "I don't know you anymore."

"No, you do not," Nick responded. He turned his gaze away from his friend, and looked far into a far distant realm as they strode in silence down the street.

19

WHAT LIES WITHIN THE TRUTH

It was to manifest the truth
that I've created the heavens and the earth
and all that lies between them.

– The Koran 46:1

Opera Square, Garden City, Cairo

"**W**ell, my dear man," said Miss Donatta to Etienne. "You have gotten yourself involved in some very sticky business." Nick, Katherine, Muhanna and Father Mhand all went together to Garden City with Etienne, to meet the antique dealer, Rasul Taj.

Miss Donatta had dashed into Rasul's upscale store moments after they arrived. She was wearing a stunning purple dress with contrasting red hat, gloves, purse and shoes, as though she just stepped off the cover of French *Vogue*. In her elegantly gloved hands she carried a large shopping bag. Miss Donatta took her time removing her hat and gloves before she settled herself into a comfortable chair. "The government is very curious about the manuscripts," she said, when she finally got around to it.

"Word around town is that they want to seal them until their value – and their message – can be determined," added Rasul. The antique dealer was a bulky man, who looked like he enjoyed his fair share of rich food, fine wine, many women and all manner of general debauchery. He also had a stunning collection of lapis lazuli jewelry.

They all collected around a table in the back of the long narrow store. Columns of artifacts – vases, statues, jewelry cases, books, furniture, cookware, wooden figurines, stone carvings and every sort of pottery imaginable – were lined up like a small, still army, protecting the gathering from being viewed from the street.

Etienne withdrew the *Gospel of Thomas* from his satchel and put on the thin cotton gloves he used to protect the fragile book. They all gathered close around to observe. "Yes, yes," said Rasul, excitedly, leaning over Etienne's shoulder. "And where did you come across this?"

"Two traders – peasants really – from al-Qasr brought it to my door. Nearly a year ago. This is part of what I believe is a Gnostic library."

"Do you know how many there are, all together?" asked Rasul.

"Thirteen," said Etienne.

"What a collection this will be!" Rasul clapped his hands together.

"We only have two," said Etienne. "There are 11 more still to find."

"Make that ten," said Miss Donatta, in a suspiciously coy manner. She drew a bundle out of her shopping bag, all wrapped in newspaper. Katherine couldn't take her eyes off Miss Donatta as she slowly revealed her surprise. The others were intent on the package, but Katherine was focused on the woman. She was graceful and wealthy, generous and smart, and apparently very shrewd.

When a woman is attracted to a man, realized Katherine, *it is for entirely different reasons than when a woman is drawn to a woman. With a man, love comes for reasons of intimacy and strength and security. With a woman, it's for genuine admiration. Perhaps some envy too,* admitted Katherine. *And the compelling, disturbing realization that someone else has become everything you have failed to be.*

"I was shopping in a little book store in the market," said Miss Donatta. "When I found this..." She pulled back the newspaper and exposed a dusty papyrus manuscript, bound in leather.

Nick shot an astonished glance at Miss Donatta, but quickly turned his attention to the book. "Where on earth did you get this?"

"The great market of Khan el-Khalili," answered Miss Donatta. "It is a wonderful open-air bazaar where you can buy anything imaginable. It's been part of Cairo for as long as anyone can remember."

"Which shop, specifically, did you find it in?" asked Etienne.

"Just a little shop I visit from time to time. They sell books, papyrus, paperweights, some trinkets for the tourists. Occasionally they come across some real treasures, though – first editions, poetry, some rare books, and – this."

Etienne turned away from her, distracted by the new manuscript. He focused himself entirely on the first golden page in front of him.

"Miss Donatta," began Nick. "Will you take us back there?"

"I could," said Miss Donatta. "But it wouldn't make any difference. I spoke with the shopkeeper extensively. He swore this was the only book he had."

"Perhaps he could tell us where he came upon it..." pressed Nick.

"Nikoli," said Miss Donatta softly. "This man prefers to be anonymous in matters such as these. He trusts me. I rely on that trust. And I trust him in return."

"Listen to this!" Etienne interrupted. "The title, as I read it, is *The Gospel of Mary*."

"Mary *who*?" asked Miss Donatta and Katherine.

Etienne looked back and forth between them. "Mary of Magdala, of course."

"You are telling us that there is a holy gospel according to Mary Magdalene?" asked Katherine.

"Well, yes," said Etienne. "This is not a new discovery. A document of the same title was discovered years ago; it was purchased by a German fellow in Cairo in 1896, and taken to Berlin. The fascinating point will be to compare the two manuscripts."

"Mary Magdalene?" Katherine asked again. "The prostitute?"

"Not all scholars agree that she was ever a prostitute," said Etienne. "But yes, *that* Mary Magdalene. In Gnostic tradition, Mary Magdalene was equal – even superior – to the twelve disciples. It is in the Gospel of Mary that we see the birth of the strife between the Gnostics and the Orthodox Christians: Mary tells the other disciples that she has seen Jesus in a vision, and has spoken to him and received his counsel. She assures them that in their quest to spread His word, they will feel the continual presence of the Savior and need not fear those who oppose them. Her words are profound and comforting. After the crucifixion, you see, the disciples had become fearful for their lives.

"But Peter and Andrew denounce Mary, saying the savior wouldn't favor a woman over them. It is Levi who speaks up on Mary's behalf, calling Peter notoriously hot tempered, and asking him if the Savior made her worthy, who was he to reject her?

"From this discussion, the disciples go forth and preach the word of Jesus. They've taken courage from her words, and her strength in standing up to Peter. She had challenged his authority, and just so, they would challenge the authority of what they considered the illegitimate power of the Orthodox church.

"Levi claimed that their Lord did love Mary of Magdala more. And the Gnostics came to believe that encounters of Jesus through inner visions were more authentic and profound than the experiences of the twelve disciples, and most certainly more legitimate than the bishops and priests who claimed to be their successors."

"We must find the other codices," said Nick.

"I hear that one has left the country," offered Rasul, his dark eyes, as round as his stature, looked very sad. "I understand it's been smuggled to Belgium, and currently in possession of the Jung Institute."

"*Merde*," said Etienne. "How did that happen?"

"Well, that is a story in itself," remarked Rasul. "I heard, through various channels, that a distinguished religious historian at Urtrecht in the Netherlands, named Gilles Quispel –"

"*Oui*, I know Professor Quispel, somewhat," interrupted Etienne. "Brilliant mind. Very insightful. But, well, somewhat scatter-brained, you might say."

"Yes, very, it seems," continued Rasul. "Quispel got word of a codex through a contact of his in Cairo, apparently some traveling history teacher in Upper Egypt."

"Raghib!" said Father Mhand, looking over at Muhanna. Muhanna's eyes had narrowed and he was staring darkly off to the side.

My books have all slipped through my fingers, thought Muhanna ruefully.

306

"You know this history teacher?" asked Miss Donatta.

"Muhanna does," answered Etienne. "Please, go on about Quispel."

"Well, Quispel immediately went to the Jung Institute and convinced them to buy it. Carl Jung, the noted psychiatrist, was very anxious to have the codex. So Quispel took a train to Brussels to receive the book from a hired courier."

"Jung has been interested in Gnosticism since the early 1900s," added Etienne. "He considers the Gnostics to be early psychologists, or so he has said. He believes the Gnostics were doing the work of the soul through the healing of the mind and the emotions."

"Well," said Nick, "that makes perfect sense, doesn't it?" They all looked over at him. "Based on what Etienne has read to us, I mean. About finding out what makes you tick inside – your hopes and fears – and when you get really clear, you see that God has been inside you all along."

Katherine gazed at her husband with a mixture of pride, envy, and total astonishment. *He's speaking academically, of course... Isn't he?* She sat in the shadow of his revelation, wondering who that man was across the table, while the others seemed to take his statements all in stride. *Does everybody know something that I don't?*

"How did they get Jung's codex out of Egypt?" Etienne asked Rasul. "You can't just walk into The Netherlands with an Egyptian artifact under your arm."

"It seems you can," replied Rasul. "At least in this case." He pulled his chair conspiratorially closer to the table. "First of all, the codex was smuggled out of Egypt in a shipment of cotton from Cairo to Alexandria to Paris. From there, Quispel arranged to have it hand-delivered to him in a cafe in Brussels.

"But Quispel missed his train," continued Rasul. "He arrived in Brussels two hours late, because he stepped off the train in the wrong city and missed his connection. Much to his relief, however, when he did show up in Brussels, somewhat frazzled, the courier was still there, patiently waiting for him. And he promptly handed over the codex."

"Then how did Quispel get the text over the boarder and into Zurich?" asked Etienne.

"Apparently he just told the truth," laughed Rasul. "When the customs official questioned him about his package, Quispel just said it was an old manuscript. Apparently the customs man just made a vague gesture of indifference and let him pass. It is through a colleague of mine in Zurich that I have heard all this," explained Rasul. "He has confirmed that the Jung Institute is currently in possession of one of these mysterious codices – which he has identified as *The Gospel of Truth*."

"Well, at least it is sure to be published," remarked Etienne, hopeful if somewhat dejected. "That means there are only nine left for us to find."

"Rumor has it that an archaeologist has possession of another codex. But he is no longer in Cairo," offered Miss Donatta. "The last I heard he was headed back to the Valley of the Kings, where he is there in the south, excavating an ancient tomb."

"Who is it?" asked Etienne. "Do you know him?"

"You are not going to like this, *mio amore*," said Miss Donatta softly, touching his hand.

"What?" demanded Etienne. "Who is it?"

"*Dottore* Henri Poirier," she answered, meeting Etienne's eyes.

"Poirier!" Father Mhand looked startled. "That is the name! The very name of the man who came to my church. It is Poirier I gave the book to."

Etienne's head dropped to his chest.

"Who's this Poirier fellow?" asked Katherine, her eyes intent on Etienne. Etienne looked away, unwilling, or perhaps unable, to explain. There settled on them all a few, long, uncomfortable moments of silence.

"Does Poirier have all that remains of the codices?" asked Etienne finally, looking up at Miss Donatta with surprisingly tired eyes.

Miss Donatta looked at Rasul and they smiled broadly at Etienne. Rasul hefted his burly weight from the large oak chair, and moved with a fixed determination to a closet in the back wall of the store.

Miss Donatta took Etienne's hands in hers. *"Mio amore,"* she began. "This is not the game of children. What you are dealing with is perhaps the most valuable – and the most dangerous – collection of writings to be revealed in our time. *If* they are what we all suspect, that is. The government wants them. Black Marketeers want them, and the Coptic Museum here in Cairo has already claimed cultural rights to them. We have also heard that there are private, perhaps religious, extremists who are determined to destroy them."

"Yes," said Katherine, contemptuously. "I can vouch for that."

Just then, Rasul returned to the table with a large bundle wrapped in brown paper, which he placed carefully in its center. Etienne nearly jumped out of his seat, his eyes fixed on the package. Everyone leaned forward in tense anticipation.

"From the fourth century, to the cliffs of Jabal al-Tarif..." murmured Rasul mysteriously, as he slowly, delicately unwrapped the papers. "And from there, to Cairo, and into our very hands."

There, in a small antique shop in the heart of Cairo, 1,600 years after they were penned, lay parcels and pieces of eight leather-bound books framing ancient, fragile pages of papyrus leaves, carrying the message of a long-extinct band of ostracized, renegade Christians.

"Oh, Mother of God," whispered Etienne. He reached tenderly, almost shyly, toward the codices. He lifted the top manuscript with great care, cradling it in his hands. He leaned over the codex and gingerly opened its soft leather cover, his fingers hovering over the strange writing.

"It's Coptic," he said, looking up at all the faces staring intently at him. "Definitely, it's Coptic. And the binding is identical to the one we already have." Etienne turned to Rasul, a combination of relief and awe overtaking him. "Where did you get them?" he whispered, his voice full of emotion.

Rasul nodded knowingly at Etienne and dabbed his own eyes with a handkerchief. "A man from al-Qasr," he explained when he recovered himself. "Jahib was his name."

"The one-eyed outlaw," said Nick.

"A scruffy character," continued Rasul. "He probably bought them in a neighboring village for a song. But I was not asking questions. The Coptic Museum had already contacted me. The director there explained to me the value of the codices, and suspected that you might resurface, Etienne, sometime soon in my store. And he was obviously correct in his assumptions. What neither of us could have guessed, however, was that the codices would be delivered into my hands before you arrived."

Etienne, meanwhile, was buried in the words on the golden pages. "*The Apocryphon of John*," he read out loud, after a few minutes of translating. He laid aside the book with extreme care and then reached for another. He noticed several covers were missing, leaving the brittle papyrus exposed. Etienne shot a look at Muhanna, but quickly returned to his work.

"Apocryphon?" inquired Katherine. "What does apocryphon mean?"

"Translated literally, Apocryphon, means a *secret book*," answered Etienne.

"*Secret book*," marveled Nick. "The *Gospel of Thomas* identified itself as *the secret words* that Jesus spoke."

"Why were these books kept secret?" asked Miss Donatta.

"The Gnostics felt that only enlightened individuals, those with *gnosis* – personal experience of the Divine – should be privy to these writings," offered Etienne. "Listen to this:

Jesus said, 'Write down my teachings and keep them in a safe place. Cursed be everyone who will exchange these words for a gift, or for food, or for drink, or for clothing, or for any other such personal thing.'"

Like a million dollars? thought Katherine.

"These books are cursed!" exclaimed Miss Donatta.

"Surely you don't believe in curses," said Nick.

"It might be typical of such a group, ostracized as the Gnostics were, to put such a warning in their library," offered Etienne.

"Still, I don't like it, Etienne," said Miss Donatta. "I worry for you."

"You cannot sell these books, Etienne," said Rasul gravely. The group exchanged nervous looks with each other while a wall clock ticked away the time through their silence.

"You must donate the collection to a museum," pressed Miss Donatta.

Etienne did not look convinced. Katherine, sensing an argument, got up and wandered to the front of the store. She was thrilled for Etienne, to have recovered nearly all of the lost codices. But she was also strangely sad. Or am I annoyed? she wondered. This all seems so easy for Etienne. Katherine sighed. Maybe I should just go home. Let these people sort it all out.

Part of Katherine wished, in a tiny, quiet voice, that Rasul had never come across that cache of books. She looked around for an ashtray, feeling anxious and distantly upset. She decided to step outside for a quick cigarette. Her heart leapt to her throat as she went to the glass doors.

"Nick! Etienne!" Katherine cried, hurrying back to the table where everyone was gathered. "Nafarah is right across the street!"

"Hurry! Hide the books!" said Nick, coming to his feet.

Etienne instinctively reached for the Gospel of Thomas, as if it were a favored child, wrapped it quickly in its cloth, and put it in his satchel. "Katherine, Nick, go to the front of the store and slow them down!"

"Who is Nafarah?" asked Rasul, coming to his feet.

"An agent from the government," said Etienne, hastily. "He has been hounding me for years, like a hungry dog. If I'd done half the things he suspects me of doing, I'd be dead." Etienne tore off the white gloves. "Or very wealthy." He put the gloves in the satchel, and looked around desperately for a hiding place.

Rasul tenderly scooped up the remaining books and handed them to Miss Donatta. "Pass these up to me," he instructed. He then pushed his chair to a standing bookcase in the corner of the room. Climbing onto the chair, and with one deft stroke of his arm, the squat man pushed aside a series of dusty books.

Behind the tall books, Rasul released a false panel, which slid open and disappeared behind an adjacent shelf. A deep, dark cupboard spread out behind the bookcase, extending far back into the wall. The hidden cabinet was easily deep enough to hide the Gnostic manuscripts. It was big enough, in fact, and tested to be true, to hide a whole person, should the need arise.

At the front of the store, Nick and Katherine watched Nafarah give what appeared to be last-minute instructions to two other men. One of the men was Kassab, the Egyptian agent who had visited Katherine in New York. All three men suddenly turned and moved across the street.

Miss Donatta, meanwhile, with the help of Father Mhand, passed the bulky package of manuscripts up to Rasul, who carefully slid them into the hidden cupboard. "Etienne, your bag, if you please," said Rasul, looking over his shoulder. Etienne passed his satchel up to the cunning antique dealer.

Rasul placed the bag inside the cupboard, quietly closed the panel, and replaced the scattered books. Rasul then took one book from the shelf and laid it down flat. Opening the cover, he revealed many pages cut thick and deep, creating a small, makeshift container. From this container, Rasul pinched out a small handful of a fine, gray substance. Rasul closed the book with his other hand, and replaced it on the shelf, just as the tinkle of the bell on the front door chimed the entrance of visitors.

Nick and Katherine could be heard talking, their voices mixed with the impatient demands of the intruders. Rasul quickly sprinkled the curious substance around the shelf and books and then, to everyone's astonishment, he blew on it. The gray powder rose in the air and, in settling, covered his fingerprints. The result created the illusion of a thin veil of dust on a long-undisturbed shelf of ratty old books.

"What is that stuff?" asked Etienne.

"Bird feathers," whispered Rasul. "So finely minced as to resemble a powder. Or … dust." The man beamed, but not for long.

"Move aside!" the voice of Nafarah rang through the store.

"Well, why on earth wouldn't we?" came Katherine's voice. "I just wanted to mention that little business in Tenerife. And make it clear that the United States of America is going to have something to say about it."

Rasul jumped off his chair with the grace of a gazelle, and seated himself calmly back at the table. Etienne had grabbed some vases from a nearby shelf, and everyone sat around the table feigning interest in the pottery.

"You are an inconsequential woman," muttered Nafarah, as he and his associates moved past Katherine and Nick, leaving them no choice but to follow or be left behind. The Egyptians, their determination penetrating the very air in the room, quickly made their way to the back of Rasul 's store. Etienne looked bored. Katherine took a seat at the table next to him, her eyes contemptuously following Cato Nafarah's every move. Nick came to stand behind Miss Donatta, who was chatting casually with Rasul about her comparative collection of porcelain from the Ptolemy Dynasty. Muhanna's eyes darted warily around the room. Father Mhand pulled out his handkerchief and blew his nose.

"May I help you?" asked Rasul in a calm, welcoming voice.

"What an interesting collection of friends you entertain, Mr. Taj," said Nafarah. He was turning a gold coin through his fingers as he spoke.

"Customers is the more appropriate term," smiled Rasul. "At least, if Allah smiles on me today. But how is it that I can be of service to you gentlemen?"

"Let me introduce myself," breathed Nafarah, as Kassab and the other man looked suspiciously around the room. "My name is Cato Nafarah, field agent for the Egyptian Department of Antiquities. And I am very interested in some manuscripts which have recently come into your possession."

"Ah yes, you must mean the Egyptian scrolls of Tanis. Although I have had them for only a few days, and have not yet fully appraised them, I would be happy to pass them on to Your Excellency for a very fair price," offered Rasul, as he moved toward the front of the store. With his back to Nafarah, Rasul drew several scrolls from a wicker basket. He proudly held the scrolls out to the tall Egyptian.

Nafarah smiled as he approached Rasul. "And you will sell these to me for a very fair price?" he began. Nafarah returned the coin to his pocket.

Rasul suspected by the look of the man – the obvious physical strength hidden beneath his fine clothes, the calm cadence of his voice, the intensity of his stare – that his cold brown eyes hid a history of meanness. Étienne knew it to be true.

"Well, yes, of course," said Rasul, beginning to show the first strains of discomfort under Nafarah's menacing stare. "Anyone with the government is, of course, a valued–"

Nafarah abruptly swept the back of his hand across the scrolls, sending them flying across the room to lay scattered upon the rough wooden floor. Rasul rubbed his hands, humbled, and looked away from everyone's staring eyes. "That is what I think of your scrolls of Tanis!" stormed Nafarah. He then nodded coldly to his two associates, who began searching the store.

"And when I find what I do want," continued Nafarah, "I will take them under the authority of the Egyptian government and you, little man, will spend the rest of your trading career behind the walls of a prison."

Was it the way he casually adjusted his cuff links as he spoke? Or the cold monotone with which he delivered his words? There was something in his voice, so detached, and so intensely certain, that everyone in the room realized with frightening clarity that Cato Nafarah would induldge in any cruelty to get what he wanted.

Kassab and his colleague assaulted the store in their search, knocking over and breaking whatever was in their way. Rasul, entirely miserable, moved along behind them, rescuing whatever fragile pieces he could. The damage to his property, and to his own elegant spirit, would be inestimable.

"Excuse me," offered Etienne, stepping forward. "I am afraid there has been a grave misunderstanding." Nafarah turned to fix his steely stare squarely on Etienne. Not flinching a bit, Etienne continued.

"I said I would recover the documents that you are looking for … The Gnostic Gospels …" Nafarah's eyes narrowed in a dark, smoldering glare. Etienne continued. "And I will. One was in my possession earlier. Unfortunately, when I went to the Coptic Museum here in Cairo, where I had it secured in my office, it was gone. Stolen. I suspect by religious zealots. We have been looking for it ever since, but," shrugged Etienne, "with no luck so far."

"Really?" asked Nafarah sarcastically.

314

"Réelllement," Etienne responded sincerely, in his softest tone of voice.

"And Mrs. Spencer? She came along, too, to help?" asked Nafarah slyly. Katherine felt as though her face must have turned bright screaming red, just hearing the cold way he said her name.

"Leave her out of this," snapped Nick, stepping forward. "She is not involved with this at all."

"Oh, no?" taunted Nafarah. "She is not, perhaps, trying to recover the Knife of the Asps, pirated from Egypt, and unexpectedly missing from her warehouse in America?"

Katherine struggled to appear calm. "I've already told your associate, Mr. Kassab here, I don't know anything about this Knife of the Asps."

"So it's just a coincidence that you're here in Egypt with Etienne Desonia, who you said you had no further business with. Is that right?" He didn't give Katherine time to answer. "And you haven't borrowed from investors to keep your antique store from bankruptcy?" Nafarah sneered at Katherine. "I wonder, Mrs. Spencer, just how desperate you've become. Just how far you will go..."

"You are way out of line, Nafarah!" shot Nick.

"I could arrest you all on the spot!" Nafarah spat back.

"I beg your pardon," interjected Miss Donatta indignantly.

Nafarah laughed dryly. "Miss Maria Donatta, of the northern provinces of Italy, I presume."

Miss Donatta held out her hand. Nafarah rejected it. "Are you not the same Miss Donatta currently living in Garden City? Currently living, I believe, in a luxurious house purchased by the sale of rare artifacts, many of which were illegally obtained through the underhanded trading of our Mr. Taj here?"

How does he know so much? they each wondered silently.

"It is my job, and my responsibility, to be aware of all activities involving the cultural treasures of Egypt," said Nafarah smugly, by way of an intuitive answer to their collective amazement. "It is, in fact, my sacred trust. A trust you have all challenged." Nafarah again began rolling a coin deftly through his fingers. "But the sands of deceit are shifting beneath you – all of you. And you will eventually suffocate, breath by tortured breath."

No one spoke as the tall man strode casually around the room, his command swelling. "Those who travel above our laws inevitably find the threads of their lives unraveling around them." Nafarah sneered. "Our prisons, you may find, are not as luxurious as the lifestyles and accommodations you are currently enjoying."

Miss Donatta paled ever so slightly, but pointed back a long red fingernail in return. "I do not think you mean to threaten us, Mr. Nafarah. It would not suit you, I should imagine, to be held accountable for thinly-veiled threats to a de facto ambassador to your country. Particularly one who enjoys a special invitation to Egypt, and the private company of Prime Minister Pasha."

Etienne looked at her, cocking an eyebrow in a gesture of surprise. Nokrashi Pasha was the notorious leader of Egypt, known for his ruthlessness and his unquestioned power. Was she making this up? he wondered. But the stifled manner in which Nafarah backed down indicated that he might know a truth about the allusive Miss Donatta that even Etienne was not privy to.

Nafarah looked at his agents, who shrugged futilely, having uncovered no sign of the manuscripts in Rasul's store. "Nothing?" said Nafarah in a low voice, moving toward his men.

"We found no papyrus books," admitted Kassab. "Nothing at all out of the ordinary."

"They are here," insisted Nafarah. "And we are not leaving until we find them. I don't care if we have to tear this entire store down brick by brick." Father Mhand's eyes drifted involuntarily to the dusty shelf of books. Nafarah caught the priest's expression and moved to the bookcase in the corner of the room. He began to examine it carefully, treading his finger through the dust. He rubbed the fine powder between his fingers and scowled.

"We did notice one unusual thing," Kassab piped in, unhappy that his boss was taking it upon himself to double-check his meticulous work. "While we didn't find the books, we also did not find one other thing that should be here, and is not." Everyone turned to Kassab. Etienne set his jaw and braced for the worst. "We did not find Monsieur Desonia's valise," continued Kassab. "I have never seen him without it. And I have seen him many times."

A broad smirk spread across Nafarah's face. "So, Monsieur Desonia, what is this news? Have you brought yourself here without your treasured satchel?" How many treasures have been pirated from the hands of Egypt and carried in that satchel? fumed Nafarah silently. He motioned to his second agent. The man withdrew a pistol from his side and aimed it at Etienne. Someday, thought Nafarah, Etienne and his nasty little satchel will belong to me. "I have grown so tired of your games," Nafarah said in a voice slowly dripping with venom. "Tell me where the satchel is." Nafarah reached over and took the agent's arm in his hand. He swiveled it until the gun was pointed directly at Katherine. "Tell me right now."

"It's at the hotel," protested Etienne.

"You left your bag behind at the hotel?" scoffed Nafarah. "Hardly."

Etienne paused, deciding how much to reveal, knowing that a lie, hidden inside a truth, can be mistaken for the truth itself. "I have an artifact in the satchel," admitted Etienne. "It is a snake, a solid gold replica from the collected treasures of Ramesses II. This figurine is in the satchel, and the satchel is locked in a safe at the Shepheard's hotel."

"A replica, you say?"

"I assure you," said Etienne. "It is a replica."

"Why is it, Monsieur Desonia, that I don't believe you?" asked Nafarah mockingly.

"Whether you believe it or not," replied Etienne, "does not change the truth. It is a replica, I tell you. A damned expensive one, but a replica nonetheless."

Nafarah's mind seemed to move in another direction, as though he was trying to recapture an important thought that he had touched on before, but had slipped from his grasp. "So this replica is in a safe, you say?"

"Yes, at the Shepheard's Hotel," repeated Etienne emphatically.

Kassab stepped forward. "Speaking of safes," he said to Nafarah. "We found no safe here on the premises," he said. "Which, too, is unusual."

Nafarah sighed. "Lower your gun," he said to the agent. Nafarah turned to Rasul without saying another word.

"I hide my safe," admitted Rasul. "Not from Your Excellency, of course, but from marauders who are known to break into fine stores such as this." Rasul looked as though someone had raked sandpaper over his heartstrings. "I have ... much to protect."

"Where is the safe?" demanded Kassab.

"It is here," sighed Rasul in resignation. "Follow me."

Kassab followed the suddenly bent and shuffling storekeeper to a closet at very back of the store. The door had been flung open and stacks of boxes sat in the darkness. Rasul pulled a string overhead and a bare light bulb glowed to life. Kassab pushed the man aside and began hauling out the boxes with the help of the other agent. Soon they emptied the entire closet. Together they all saw a closet full of absolutely nothing.

"Here." Rasul stepped in and pressed his hands firmly against the back wall. It sprung open, from hinges and lines so imperceptible as to resemble the dark grain of the wood itself. Behind the wall sat a safe, as short and square as the man who owned it.

"Empty it," commanded Nafarah. Miss Donatta feared for her friend Rasul and her heart broke for his losses.

Rasul turned the dial to a five-digit combination, which he cloaked as subtly as he could by pressing his face nearly to the door of the safe as he spun the enormous dial. With a hand that shook only in the slightest, he swung open the thick metal door. In the glaring light of the bare bulb, stacks and stacks of paper money shone alluringly from the top shelf of the safe.

The bottom two shelves were empty, waiting for the nightly storage of Rasul's most precious items of jewelry and beads and stone. From the top shelf, Kassab extracted a moneybox, which rattled with the heavy sound of coins. He moved with the box to the nearby table as everyone followed.

"Allow me, please," offered Rasul, producing a set of keys, just as Kassab was taking aim at the padlock with a gun. Kassab snatched the keys and opened the moneybox. Not surprising, the box contained a scattering of coins, from Egyptian piasters to English pounds. It also contained various oddities, such as few buttons, a stray key, a pink ribbon, an empty money clip and some pencils. The box contained nothing of great value to anyone except Rasul Taj. Kassab swept the box and it contents off the table sending them clattering to the floor.

Rasul sighed deeply and turned back to the safe. "Perhaps, I can ease your disappointment, Your Excellency, with some offerings to our benevolent government..." Rasul took a stack of bills and held them loosely in his hands.

"Mister Taj," snapped Nafarah impatiently. "I don't know who you've been dealing with, or who you think you're dealing with today. But I am a servant of the people of Egypt, not a thief." Nafarah leaned in so close to Rasul that the shopkeeper could feel the heat of Nafarah's breath on his face. "You keep your money for yourself," said Nafarah slowly. If the other two agents of the government felt a pang of disappointment, they kept it entirely to themselves. "When you do come across the manuscripts of the Gnostics," continued Nafarah, "and I'm confident you will, I trust you will turn them over to me. Immediately."

"Of course," offered Rasul, too happy to be seeing Nafarah leave his store to pretend to argue his innocence. "Of course I will."

"We have a little errand to run at the Shepheard's Hotel," smirked Nafarah. No one else said a word as the Egyptian agents made their way to the front door. But before he left, Nafarah turned back ominously and added, "I see you. I know what you do. All of you. All of the time." Nafarah turned on his heel and his two associates – guns shadowed darkly through the outline of their suit coats – fell in closely behind him. In a swift moment, they were out the door and gone. The room was silent for a few extremely tense moments.

"Well," began Miss Donatta, brightly. "I must take my leave as well." She delicately put on her red gloves, as she prepared for a hasty exit. "It has been a thrill as always." She kissed Etienne on each cheek. "You must call me, mio amore, when you resolve this messy business."

Miss Donatta turned to Rasul and shook his hand formally. "Mr. Taj, it has been a pleasure seeing you again. But I do not expect that we shall have further business to discuss in the immediate future." She waved at the rest of them, sitting again at the table. "Arrivaderci. And good luck to you all."

"Thank you, mon cheri," said Etienne walking with her to the door. "For all you have done for me. I shall miss you."

"Oh, I don't suspect that I have seen the last of you, Etienne," she responded coyly. "You are much too often in trouble to stay away for very long." She smiled. "Besides, without you, what would I do for fun?"

"I imagine the Prime Minister might have something to say about that."

"You are naughty, Etienne!" Miss Donatta said. But she leaned forward and kissed him below his ear. "But that is what I adore about you."

Etienne kissed her on the mouth, and the hint of a tear threatened to spill from behind her eyes. He pulled away and gazed upon the strong features of her lovely, upturned face. "Take care of yourself, mio amore," she whispered.

"Au revoir, mon cherí..."

Miss Donatta turned and stepped from the store.

"You must take these books from here," Rasul said to Etienne when he returned to the back of the room. "They have attracted much too much interest to be of any value to me."

"Yes, but how can we do that, my friend, without Nafarah pouncing on us like a rabid, mongrel dog?" asked Etienne.

"You are going south from here, I presume?" asked Rasul. "To the Valley of the Kings?"

"You know me too well, my friend," replied Etienne.

Rasul smiled slyly. "I will arrange for a delivery of artworks through a variety of channels to the ultimate destination of the Luxor Museum, care of Doctor Etienne Desonia."

Rasul went to the stack of boxes from the empty closet and picked out a dusty traveling chest. "Hidden in a sealed compartment of this special chest," said Rasul, as he threw back the lid, "you will find your precious documents. But my friend," Rasul put his hand on Etienne's shoulder. "I fear that this may not be safe for some time yet." Etienne cocked an eyebrow over his broadening grin. "Within the week, then, look in Luxor for your delivery," said Rasul. "And be careful, Etienne. This is bigger than I think you understand."

320

"I will, Rasul," said Etienne warmly. "And thank you."

"Safe travels to you all," said the shopkeeper, bowing his good-byes. *"Ma'as salama."*

Nick shook Rasul's hand. "Thank you Mr. Taj. We are very grateful for your help. You have no idea."

Muhanna, they discovered, had a peculiar gift for making himself little, quiet and almost invisible. They found him wedged in between a shelf of silver flatware and a mannequin adorned in heavily beaded robes. "Let's be on our way," said Etienne, grabbing Muhanna by the collar.

"We're going to the Valley of the Kings?" asked Katherine.

"We're going to find Henri Poirier," said Etienne.

"Poirier was your doctoral advisor at the University of Paris, wasn't he?" asked Nick, as they exited Rasul's store onto Opera Square. "The one you had a falling-out with."

"Oui," answered Etienne softly. "But that is a story for another day."

20

THE PRICE TO PAY

My debts are large, my failures great, my shame secret and heavy;
yet when I come to ask for my good,
I quake in fear lest my prayer be granted.

— Rabindranath Tagore

Valley of the Kings

R ed hills sloped and pitched under a pale blue sky. The air was dry and thick. Heat radiated in billowing sheets from the sand. *El-Qurn*, the highest peak in the valley, loomed powerful and ominous over the necropolis. Its perfectly triangular summit resembled a symbolic pyramid rising from the earth. This was a place of death and history, one of the most fascinating and mysterious places on earth: The Valley of the Kings. Etienne drove the jeep downhill, along a narrow ribbon of road to the base of the valley. The company was quiet that late afternoon, and the soft rumblings of the jeep were the only sounds to echo off the high red walls.

Generations of ancient pharaohs were sprinkled in mammoth temples beneath the dry land – buried, lost, mostly forgotten. Thousands of years of sand had blown through this valley, obscuring every human thing underneath strata upon strata of new earth. A recent flood and subsequent landslide, however, had unearthed a massive new burial sight. Archaeologists from around the world had gathered in a collaborative – albeit competitive – effort to excavate the newly discovered temple. A buzzing hive of workers could be seen scattered all across the eastern slope of the valley.

"How will we ever find Henri Poirier?" asked Nick from the back seat. "This area is huge."

Follow the stench, Etienne thought grimly. "He'll find us," said Etienne. "We just need to find the local watering hole."

"Now that you suggest it," quipped Katherine, "a nice little cocktail sounds rather refreshing."

Etienne pulled the jeep into the base camp near the digging site. Such camps were set up in haste, but afforded all the essential luxuries worthy of archaeologists on the cusp of greatness. This little collection of tents became a village of its own – a small oasis in the desolate land – that would fold up and disappear as quickly as it had arrived.

Operating at the center of the camp was a large mess hall, contracted out to restaurateurs from the nearby city of Luxor. In the supply tent one could purchase anything from candy bars and aspirin, to yesterday's international newspapers, to a woman to keep company with for the night. The infirmary was nearby and fully prepared to treat sunstroke, dehydration, scorpion bites, and the poison of any of the 34 species of venomous snakes common to the region. And, at the heart of this makeshift town, there sat a cantina.

Nick, Katherine and Etienne stepped up to the long wooden bar and were immediately greeted by the bartender – a short, plump man who fussed like a rat king around his tented empire. Muhanna and Father Mhand joined them somewhat tentatively, feeling both fascinated and guilty. They took up seats at the bar, though, and looked around expectantly.

"I'd like a double vodka gibson, on the rocks," ordered Katherine politely, wiggling onto her barstool. "With cocktail onions—three please." She dropped her knapsack on the floor. The bartender stared at her with a blank look on his face.

Etienne interceded. "How about tall cold beers. Muhanna?"

"I will say, no," replied the Muslim. "It is against God's laws, the drinking of alcohol."

"Father Mhand?" asked Etienne.

"I think I will," replied the priest. "The God of Abraham is more tolerant on this matter than the God of Islam. Or perhaps, He is more forgiving. Scratch that," he added. "They are one and the same." He paused. "Yes, I'll have a beer."

"Four beers, then," ordered Etienne. "A one sarsaparilla."

"What kind of bar can't make a simple little martini?" whispered Katherine as the bar keeper scampered to pour the golden ale into glasses.

"Truth be told," said Father Mhand, dabbing his forehead, "I have never tasted beer before." He took a shy little sip. "Oh my, that's quite good isn't it?" He took another sip.

Muhanna drank his soda with great enthusiasm, pushing the empty glass to the edge of the bar and pointing to it for a refill. The bartender appeared immediately with a new glass, fizzing over at the top.

"So, Katherine," said Etienne, not looking directly at her. "Would this be a good time to tell us all about your financial difficulties?"

Everyone turned to look at Katherine. She crossed her legs, locked her fingers around one knee, and leaned back on the tall bar stool. "Actually, Etienne, I think this is the perfect time for your to mind your own business," she said lightly.

"Katherine isn't in debt," announced Nick. "Nafarah was wrong about all that."

"Was he?" asked Etienne.

"He was just trying to intimidate us, there in Rasul's store," Nick explained.

"Is that *your* story, Katherine?" asked Etienne.

Katherine leaned forward and took a slow drink from her mug of beer. "My story is rather more dismal, I'm afraid," she said.

"What?" Nick stared at her. "What story? What are you talking about?"

"You really don't want to know."

"Oh, I really *do* want to know," said Nick. "I really should know, don't you think?"

"Yes, I think we all should," added Etienne.

"What the hell business is it of yours?" snapped Katherine.

"Katherine, I've made a very tricky deal with Cato Nafarah – on your behalf, I might add. If he knows something about you and your motivations for selling the Knife of the Asps, don't you think I deserve to know?"

"No. You don't."

"Yes," insisted Etienne. "I do."

"Fine," she snapped. She didn't look at Nick, or Etienne, but drew the silver cigarette case from her knapsack and slowly, with great intention, put a cigarette to her lips and lit the end. She blew a gray haze of smoke over the bar. "Let me tell you something about the retail business," she began. "You need capital to make it work. Lots of it. It's not like selling cookies at the charity bake sale. You need to be committed for the long haul, and have the reserves to back you up. My pockets were never deep enough to make that happen. I was constantly dipping into my reserves, spending just a little more money each month than I brought in."

She looked over at her husband. "Nick. Let me just apologize in advance. What I'm going to say is going to make you angry. And I am truly very sorry."

"What?" Nick's face was suddenly hot. "What is it?"

Katherine began talking, fast, as though once she started, she needed to get it all out and over with. "Inventory is outrageously expensive," she began. "And no one is going to come into a store that looks sparse and poor. In this business, you have to look extravagant, as though everything most precious in the world is right there, inside your door. Inventory, insurance, payroll, rent – Fifth Avenue is not cheap, believe me – it all adds up."

Katherine tapped her cigarette against the lip of the ashtray and watched the spent ashes fall away.

"And..?" asked Nick, sitting silent as a stone.

"*The Silver Butterfly* was going under. And I thought if I could make one big sale, one solid deal, I could get on top of things for good."

"And..?"

Katherine took another long drink of her beer. "Two years ago, I borrowed money to buy a particularly rare and unusual collection of coins, from the Byzantine Empire. I had a buyer all lined up, and would have made a large commission on the sale – a very large commission. But the buyer backed out at the last minute, and now I'm stuck with 25,000 dollars of eleventh century gold coins that nobody wants."

"You borrowed money?" asked Nick.

"Yes. I did."

"How much money?"

"Much," she said quietly, looking at her husband square in the face.

Nick stood up and paced back and forth behind her. "Whatever made you think of such a thing? Let alone act on it! Katherine, have you gone totally mad?"

"Please don't treat me like a child, Nick. Do sit down, for God's sake."

Nick stopped pacing. "I will not sit down! You have absolutely astonished me, Katherine. I cannot *tell* you how disappointed I am."

"Oh, stop talking, will you?" muttered Katherine. "The money from Nelson will set everything to right. And then some."

The room seemed to disappear around Nick. He suddenly couldn't hear the many voices in conversation, the occasional bursts of raucous laughter, the tinkling of ice in glasses. They were all muted and transparent against the incessant throbbing in his head.

"Nick, don't worry," insisted Katherine. "I'll work it out. I will. Trust me."

"Trust you? Trust you?" Nick shook his head as if to shake away a descending veil of fog. "How can you possibly say that? Are you daft? Etienne has no intention of giving the manuscripts to Nelson. Do you realize that? There's not a chance in hell that we're going to walk out of this deal with any money. We'll be lucky if we walk out of it with our lives!"

"Nick —"

Etienne spoke up. "We'll get the money from Nelson, believe me. I have it all worked out."

"You're just a regular saint, aren't you Etienne?" snapped Nick. "It's just like you to try to insinuate yourself as the hero in all this. When you're the one who started it all."

"I was only offering to help."

"Well don't, damn it," snapped Nick. He turned to square off with Katherine. "You *lied* to me. Why?"

"You wouldn't understand."

"Wouldn't understand? Wouldn't understand? What about this wouldn't I understand? You didn't tell me because you knew I *would* understand. And you knew I wouldn't stand for it!"

"All right then. I knew you wouldn't stand for it. Does that make you feel better?"

"Look at you, Katherine. Look at what you've done. At who you've become. I don't even know you all of a sudden. Do you? Do you even know yourself any more?"

"I know exactly who I am. And what I'm doing."

"Is this – when you were little – all you ever hoped and dreamed you would become? Is it?"

"Really, Nick, it's not that bad."

"Not that bad." Nick repeated, incredulously. "A smuggler. A liar. A thief. *Not that bad?*"

"Get off your high horse, Nick. I am sick to death of this. I will hear no more of this from you."

"Believe me, my dear, I've only just begun."

Father Mhand and Muhanna looked on, transfixed. The argument had drawn little attention from the noisy bar, but these two felt like interlopers into a tender and private affair.

The company of strangers was not stopping Katherine. "Aren't you superior?" she snapped. "Why don't you come down here in the squalor with the rest of us. Struggle for something. Need something that you cannot ever have. Earn something. Just once. Then you look me in the eye and tell me I'm no good."

"Earn something? By God, Katherine. I have *earned* my life. All of it. I've worked bloody hard for what I have. For everything—my education, my career, my home. I simply never suspected that I had to earn *you*. And earn you over and over and over."

"That's not what I meant."

"If accepting all this rot about lying and borrowing money – if that is what it takes to earn your regard, well by God, no thank you, my dear. No thank you very much indeed!"

"I did it for *us*, Nick. Maybe you could find some gratitude in that self-righteous heart of yours."

"*For us*? Oh, poppycock! You did it for yourself. Everything you do is to serve the greater glory of Katherine Spencer. Name one selfless thing you've ever done."

Katherine was silent. She stubbed out her cigarette and crossed her arms over her chest.

"There aren't any, are there?" pressed Nick. "You've been clawing your way through life as long as I've known you. Trying to make up for the sins of the father."

Etienne interjected. "That's enough, Nick."

"Shut up." Nick didn't even look at him.

Katherine looked at her husband as if he was the devil. Then she turned her back on him and walked out of the cantina.

"You went too far, Nick," said Etienne.

"Etienne, you have no right to an opinion here. I'd appreciate it if you'd just butt the hell out."

"Well then," Etienne replied as he stood up to go find Katherine. "I certainly hope you, at least, feel good about all this."

"No," replied Nick, though Etienne was already gone. "I feel dreadful." Father Mhand moved slowly to Nick's side. Nick turned to him. "But that doesn't mean I'm wrong, Father. Though I was wrong to say it out loud."

"The truth slices one to the bone, doesn't it?" said Father Mhand. "Wherever one is most fragile."

"Yes, it does," conceded Nick, not angry for the first time in a long time.

"The sword has two edges to it, yes?" the priest continued. "Here you've wounded yourself. Perhaps the most." Father Mhand laid his soft, wrinkled hand on Nick's arm.

"But this truth," he continued, "this very important thing, must be heard and – one prays – accepted and reconciled. It is a gift, this thing called Truth. Though neither of you recognize it, it is a good thing that you have given your beloved, and yourself, this day." Father Mhand patted Nick on the knee and rose slowly to his feet. "Now you must wrap your sword in garlands, my friend, and let her know that she is still loved."

Etienne and Katherine returned some time later. What they spoke of, whether she cried, how Etienne comforted her, Nick did not care to consider. "I apologize, Katherine," he said as she sat up at the bar. "I went too far. Forgive me." Katherine let Nick hold her in his arms for a moment, giving temporary absolution to them both.

"I'm sorry, too," Katherine whispered. Though there was a hollowness in her voice, as though the depth of her regret was overshadowed by the depth of the hurt and shame she felt.

Nick heard the silence of her blame, and knew it well for what it was. He would be the guilty one. In the only defense he knew, Nick hunkered down someplace deep and angry and private – a place where he kept himself free from the burdens of outward expression. Everything about his posture and attitude had closed down, as though the lights in a tall building all flickered at the same moment and went out.

Katherine saw the retreat and instantly, intuitively knew that her husband would be absent for a long time. It was a form of abandonment she had come to accept. When he came back, that would be the time for more words. But until then, a gulf of silence would separate them, as if he'd just driven away in a baby blue Edsel. Reacting, as she had so many times, Katherine stole away to her own private refuge. There, in the meanderings of her imagination, she plotted her escape from all the unhappy consequences she'd brought upon herself.

Etienne turned his attention to the bartender and let Katherine and Nick sit in stony silence while Muhanna and Father Mhand looked on, enjoying nothing more of this whole episode than the taste of cold drinks. "Another round, *s'il vous plait*," said Etienne. "For everyone."

"And a shot of whiskey," added Katherine. If anyone looked at her with curiosity or judgment – for anything – she didn't care to acknowledge it.

"So," Etienne asked the bartender, who was setting fresh mugs on the counter. "What do you hear about the dig?" The bar man looked at Etienne through narrowed eyes. Etienne pushed a twenty-pound note across the bar.

"Oh, all good things!" exclaimed the little man as he scooped up the bill and put it in his pocket. "They have broken though to the antechamber, guarded – it is rumored – by four ancient goddesses molded from solid gold. Very exciting! Soon they will find the burial chamber." The beer kept coming as did the money and the information, with an occasional shot of whiskey for Katherine.

"I say," said Father Mhand, after three cold glasses of beer. "I'm feeling quite strange. I think I may very well be sick."

"The latrine is just outside a ways," offered the barman hastily. "To the left, as you exit."

"Very undignified," said Father Mhand, as he stumbled toward the door. He turned back and, clearing his throat, addressed the crowded, noisy bar. "But God invented sin so He could have the pleasure of forgiving us, and we could know the fullness of His grace." Everyone looked up from their drinks and their conversations and stared at him. The Coptic priest looked confused momentarily, then smiled and wobbled out the door.

Nick reached out and gave Katherine's hand a squeeze. He mouthed the words, *I'm sorry,* feeling hopeful somehow from Father Mhand's words. Katherine returned a weak smile.

After about ten minutes the Coptic Priest returned, looking pale and blurry-eyed. He stumbled up to the bar, holding onto Muhanna to steady himself. "I'm going to bed," he announced. "If anyone needs me, I'll be in the jeep."

Muhanna drew himself up from that bar and puffed out his chest. "I will take you to Luxor," he boasted. "In the jeep."

"Like hell," said Nick. "You probably don't even know how to drive."

"Yes, I do," insisted Muhanna. "I drove the chicken truck to Nag Hammadi, now didn't I?"

"I'll drive you both back to the hotel myself," Etienne said, sighing.

"No, no, I can do it," said Muhanna.

"I'll take them," offered Nick, standing up. "You wait here for Poirier." He looked at his wife. "Katherine?"

"I'll stay," she said after a moment. She reached over and squeezed his hand. "We'll work this out. I promise."

Nick gave her a small, sad smile, but didn't answer. He kissed his wife on the top of her head, mostly as a gesture to help himself forgive her.

Katherine smiled up at her husband, breaking the tension. "Could I ask you to pick up a teensy little bottle of vermouth and some cocktail onions on your way back?"

"Behave," he whispered. He took the keys from Etienne and nudged Muhanna off his barstool. "I'll return as soon as I can." Nick ushered Muhanna and Father Mhand through the door, passing several dusty archaeologists on their way in for refreshment and self-congratulations.

Etienne and Katherine watched them leave, and then turned back to the bar. Etienne leaned over to Katherine. "Well, my dear, I'll tell you this. There's a little green-eyed snake that can solve your financial problems – if all else fails."

"That was a gift, Etienne. I couldn't possibly –"

"Yes, you could. If you had to."

"I won't have to. I'll work it out."

"Of course you will." Etienne touched her on the arm. "If anyone can do such a thing, it is you."

Katherine drew another cigarette from her case. Etienne reached for the lighter and lit her cigarette. "Nick is angry now," said Katherine, straightening in her seat. "But he really is having the time of his life. I'm glad we came here."

"As am I," said Etienne. Katherine averted her eyes, so Etienne turned his attention back to the bartender. "Tell me, have you heard of a man on this dig named Poirier? Henri Poirier?"

"Poirier... Poirier... No. No. I don't believe so."

"Curiosity killed the cat, you know."

Katherine and Etienne turned to the man who had spoken. He sported a thin, dark mustache and was leaning casually against the far end of the bar.

"Henri Poirier," said Etienne. "Isn't it always the *dog* that says that?"

"Whiskeys for my friends," ordered Henri, as he sidled up to the bar next to Katherine. "On me."

"And isn't that same dog just licking his chops?" Etienne added under his breath.

"So what brings you to the Valley of the Kings, Etienne?" asked Henri.

"Why, *you* do, Henri."

"You flatter me, dear boy."

"Don't get ahead of yourself."

Henri raised his whiskey in a toast. "Welcome, both of you, to the Valley of the Kings." His eyes lingered on Katherine. She sipped the strong liquid but kept her eyes on Etienne.

"So, Henri, how's the dig going?" asked Etienne, while he stared straight ahead, not looking at the man.

"Now, what dig would that be?"

"I understand they found another burial site on the eastern slope," said Etienne into his drink.

"I could not care less," said Henri. "Barman! Another round of whiskey! And a beer for me." He slammed a wad of bills on the counter. The barman refilled their glasses and, smiling, left the bottle behind. The drunker they got, the finer with him. Nobody here had far to travel. And many would return early the next day for the solution that was both the poison and the remedy: cold beer. "What happens on the eastern dig is of no consequence to me whatsoever," Henri continued.

"Is that a fact?" asked Etienne, finally turning to face him.

"I'm working on something bigger." Henri's smirk mixed with a sense of something darker, something akin to contempt. "Something bigger than these idiots could possibly imagine." He downed his second whiskey in one long draw. "Now why don't you tell me, Etienne," continued Henri, "what brought you here. And with such stunning company." Again he turned his gaze to Katherine. She stared straight back at him.

"As I said, I came to find you," Etienne answered calmly.

"Well, I can't imagine why. But I'm very impressed with the company you're keeping these days," said Henri. "And you," he reached across Katherine and pointed his finger hard into Etienne's chest. "You should be very impressed – with me."

"Frankly, Henri, you offend me," said Etienne flatly.

"Yes," smiled Henri. "But you are a person of rare sensitivities."

"And you are a person of rare bastardry." Etienne was drunker than he realized.

"Bastardry? Now you're making up words, my boy."

"You can use it if you care to," offered Etienne. "Not that you wouldn't just take anything you wanted, anyway. Whether you owned it or discovered it or – I don't know, say, researched and wrote it for yourself – or not."

"Whatever are you rambling about?" said Henri, splashing another shot of whiskey in his glass. "I swear, Etienne, you've changed."

"Time will do that to a person, I suppose."

"You're a bitter man, Etienne."

"And you're a thief."

Henri laughed hard. He threw back his drink and let the burn of it simmer down his throat. Then he brought the empty glass down hard on the bar. "Watch yourself, my boy," he said.

Etienne stared at him for a long time. "I heard you were in al-Qasr recently," he said finally, with a tone much lighter than he felt.

"My, my," said Henri. "You do get around, don't you?"

"I do."

"It seems that, once again, we have a shared interest," said Henri.

"We do."

"As in anything from antiquity, there are many different pieces to the whole puzzle, aren't there?" said Henri.

"And you have one of those puzzle pieces, don't you?" replied Etienne.

"Indeed. As do *you*, if my information is correct."

"Oh, your information is always correct, Henri. Isn't it?"

"Nearly always."

"Then we understand each other well enough."

Henri laughed into his beer. "What is it you came here for? Exactly?"

"I came to make a trade," said Etienne.

"I don't suppose you came all the way to this valley to give me *your* codex?" said Henri.

"Codices," Etienne replied.

"So." Henri sounded genuinely surprised. "You have more than one?"

"I do," said Etienne. "Many more. And as I have the lion's share, perhaps you'd like to give me the one you took from Father Mhand."

"Father Mhand?"

"The priest in al-Qasr you stole the codex from."

"I did no such thing!" said Henri.

"Rot." Katherine had been quiet all this time. But no more.

"The lady speaks," smirked Henri, turning. "And what do you know of this, my dear?"

"We've spoken with Father Mhand," she said.

"I do not know this Father Mhand of yours," shrugged Henri.

"Yes, you do," said Katherine, spinning the ice in her whiskey with a long red fingernail.

"I'm afraid you are mistaken," insisted Henri.

"Perhaps you'll join us in Luxor for lunch tomorrow," Etienne offered. "I have a new friend I'd like you to meet. An older gentleman – white hair, black cassock. Big cross around his neck."

"Is that so?" said Henri, shifting ever so slightly in his seat. Etienne lifted a glass of beer to his mouth, concealing a smile. "You know, Etienne," began Henri. "I am working on the most fascinating theory."

"So I heard," Etienne lied.

"Perhaps you'd like to have a look," said Henri. "I could use a second opinion."

"Is that so?"

"You could take a look at the dig site, tell me what you think, and I could perhaps find this manuscript for you."

"Perhaps?"

"Perhaps."

Etienne cleared his throat. "And I suppose once you *found* this manuscript, you'd sell it to me for a very reasonable price."

"Something like that," conceded Henri smugly.

"So what's this dig you're so proud of?" Etienne asked.

"It's a little site, across the valley. Just me and a handful of workers, quietly digging. Faint inscriptions in a plundered, deserted tomb captured my attention long after my other colleagues had abandoned it to explore newer, more popular sights."

"What are you looking for?"

"Something everybody else has missed, or forgot, or never thought to look for," said Henri smugly.

"Such as?"

Henri looked over his shoulder and lowered his voice. "A sub-chamber, reached by a secret staircase carved into the ground."

"And you think there is such a secret staircase where you are digging?" Etienne asked.

"When you see the landscape, you will understand. You see, funerary temples were typically built with adjoining chambers connected through intricate series of tunnels, side by side. In this particular section of land, though, where a large gully drops suddenly into the earth, a secret chamber could, quite possibly, be supported from above."

"And what do you expect to find in this hidden chamber that everyone else has missed?"

Henri smiled. "A renegade..."

"Hello there." Nick stepped up to the bar, and stood beside Etienne.

"I'll look at your dig, Henri," Etienne announced, standing up and strapping his satchel over his shoulder. "And you will give the manuscript to me."

Henri threw back the last of his whiskey. "Fair enough," he said. "I have bigger fish to fry."

Etienne was full of doubt, though, as he and his friends walked to the canvas door of the cantina and out into the dark night. *It can't be this easy,* thought Etienne. *Henri will pull another card out of his sleeve before this is over.*

Striding toward the jeep, Katherine touched Etienne on the shoulder. "Why do you hate him so much?"

"Who says I hate him?"

"Every word you said in there tells me that you hate him," she said. "Who is this fellow anyway?"

Etienne looked up at the blanket of stars and sighed deeply, as if he had literally forgotten to breathe. "Henri Poirier was my advisor at the University of Paris," he confessed. "He was a great teacher and my confidant. My friend, even." Etienne began walking faster, and Katherine and Nick had to hurry to keep up. "I was conducting extensive research on the gaps between early Christianity and Judaism. Henri sent me on an assignment in Galilee, claiming there could be

336

further links to my work in the Middle East. While I was gone, Henri published my research under his own name."

"Son of a bitch," said Nick.

"Oh, Etienne," said Katherine. "You must've been devastated."

They reached the jeep and Etienne pulled himself into the driver's seat. "Henri Poirier was my greatest teacher," he said. "He taught me hate. *Et vengeance.*" Etienne revved the engine and pulled out of the tented village. "And what it's like to never forgive."

21

A HEART'S WEIGHT

*For the word of God is living and active, sharper than any two-edged
sword, piercing to the division of soul and of spirit, of joints and of
marrow, and discerning the thoughts and intentions of the heart.*

– The Holy Bible, Hebrews 4:12

Morning broke. Clouds rolled up above the dry, sloping hills—
bright red clouds, underscored with gold turning to silver turning
to white. Dawn lit the sacred land, as it had time and again through the
millennia, unconcerned with witnesses and travelers and their
desperate purposes. This particular morning, two rivals came to claim
their spoils from the land and from each other. Henri Poirier and
Etienne Desonia stood at the entrance to KV12.

Archaeologists labeled each site in the region according to its
chronological discovery, preceded by the letters KV, to designate
King's Valley. "This particular tomb was found early, excavated and
forgotten," explained Henri. "It was assumed to belong to a relatively
insignificant, if royal, woman – with no artifacts left to unearth, no
hieroglyphs worth remembering." Henri pointed west. "It was just
across this valley, at KV62, that the sensational tomb of King
Tutankhamun was discovered in 1922. A most remarkable find!
Unfortunately," Henri stroked his mustache, "the two chaps involved
died shortly after."

"There were rumors of a curse," said Etienne.

Henri laughed loud, throwing his head back. "Yes, indeed there
were! The curse of a mosquito bite, for one."

"There is something to be said about not disturbing the dead,"
said Etienne, his face hot with embarrassment.

Henri's laughter tricked to a self-conscious chuckle before it
subsided altogether. "And if I remember," he mused, "that is what
338

compels *you* to dig, doesn't it, Etienne? Tempting the forces of darkness. Daring evil to touch you. Surviving it, over and over."

"*Que ridicule*," snapped Etienne. "Let's get on with this, shall we?"

They stood in silence for a moment at the doorway of the tomb. Henri gestured with his arm. "Come inside," he said. "I've been supervising this project for months." They walked along a narrow passage, supported by heavy wooden beams. "After the lengthy process of procuring funding for an extended excavation, that is. I have my contacts in the Egyptian government, of course, but they accused me of following 'unsound logic'. Idiots. Fortunately, my contacts with private collectors run deeper. I got the money all right. And now, I am on the verge of an extraordinary discovery. I can feel it."

"Is that right?"

"But something in this temple is alluding me. I am missing something, and it tugs at the back of my brain, but I am quite unable to grasp it."

"What is it, Henri, that you expect to find in this abandoned tomb?"

"A set of stairs. And a burial chamber below it."

"Yes, Henri, I understand that. But *who* do you expect to find there?"

"You always were an impatient one," said Henri. "Come with me."

A half dozen men were already inside the temple, hired from nearby Luxor. They worked to the rhythm of traditional chants – as their ancestors had done before them – scraping the floors and walls washed hard over thousands of years of floods and baking sun. Etienne wondered if, in fact, the blood of the men who built this temple – all those centuries ago – might run through the veins of these same men. *Their work, their legacy,* thought Etienne, *becomes as enduring as the monuments around them.*

Etienne looked around him. The walls of the temple were inscribed with hundreds of symbols relating the *Egyptian Book of the Dead*. This inscription provided instructions to the deceased, guiding the god-king through the afterlife, where he would reign forever, providing rule and order to the universe.

Etienne moved carefully, his boots treading slowly over the hard sacred ground. Occasionally he would stop and study a particular prayer or incantation. In the air, he traced the hieroglyphic shapes with his fingers, murmuring the ancient words as he went.

"May Ra give glory and power and truth-speaking... Oh, all ye gods of the House of the Soul, who weigh heaven and earth in balance... the earth becomes light at his birth each day, he proceeds until he reaches the place he was yesterday... Let my name be called out ... Let there be prepared for me a seat in the Boat of the Sun on the day the god sails... Let me be received in the presence of Osiris in the Land of Truth Speaking..."

When Henri urged him forward, Etienne would hold his fingers several inches from the wall as he moved along, as if his hands alone could stay there, and read and read and read.

From the long tunnel, they entered the antechamber, which opened up broadly and suddenly. This room was designed to house the king's many material possessions. It also kept the internal organs of the pharaoh, preserved and sealed in canopic jars to ensure the rebirth of the physical body.

The Egyptians believed that the pharaoh's *kas*, or spirit, would continue to exist after the death of the body. And that the king could continue to exist in his funerary temple or travel on to join the gods. Thus mummification was perfected, and thus the king's worldly goods were also buried with him.

Typically this room would be guarded by statues and icons of the Egyptian Gods – Osiris, God of the underworld, the mother-goddess Isis and the Sun God, Ra – to protect and guide the king. It would also be stocked with food and supplies to aid the pharaoh on his journey through the afterlife.

In KV12, the antechamber was empty, either looted long ago by ancient grave robbers, or possibly never occupied at all. Beyond the antechamber would typically be the burial chamber, where the sarcophagus would lay, interring the king deep within several coffins.

No such room had ever been discovered in KV12. Most archaeologists concluded that the tomb had been abandoned before it was completed. Consequently, it had never been thoroughly excavated. The scientists turned their thoughts, and their resources, elsewhere.

340

Henri ushered Etienne out of the antechamber and down along another long tunnel, his lantern swaying wildly. There, in a narrow passage, lit only by the light of a few gas lanterns, read a fascinating story:

The pharaoh was led through a traditional burial rite, in accordance with the *Book of the Dead*, by the jackal-headed god, Anubus. The pictures Henri and Etienne gazed upon depicted the scene of the Last Judgement. There, the pharaoh's heart was weighed against a feather.

The goddess, Maat, personification of the physical and moral laws of the universe, presided over the ceremony. If the sins of the pharaoh's heart weighed no more than a feather, it was proof that he led a moral life, and could pass into the afterlife and live forever. If not, the beast Amam, whose name means, "the devourer," was waiting beneath the scales to consume the pharaoh's heart, denying his ascent into eternity.

Etienne and Henri followed the story with their eyes, both knowing it well. "Ever see one of these scenes where the pharaoh *flunks* the test?" asked Henri, smirking.

"Of course not, Henri," replied Etienne quietly, wanting to hold the moment in silence.

Next in the painted story came Thoth, the god of wisdom, who recorded the results of the judgement. The pharaoh, having passed the test, was then escorted to Osiris, resurrected creator of all things, supreme judge of the dead and ruler of the underworld.

Henri flashed his lantern close to the wall. "The deceased has never been identified," he said. Etienne looked closer. A woman was making an offering of wine to Osiris. "The odd thing about these hieroglyphics," said Henri, "is the seeming secrecy of the ceremony itself. Only two people stand in attendance. See? And the moon is painted, not the sun. See these lines here. I believe they're part of the double crown of upper and lower Egypt. The rest is chipped away."

"It's possible," said Etienne. "But very few women claimed ever claimed the title of pharaoh. The last one being Cleopatra of the Ptolemies. But she was buried in Alexandria."

"Exactly," said Henri. "And here, look close." He pulled a magnifying glass from his jacket pocket. "Look at that face, that most unusual face."

The relief, 3,300 years old, was worn and blotched. But Etienne could see that the face was very long, with huge almond-shaped eyes and thick full lips. The body was soft looking, protruding at the chest and belly. *"Fantastique – "* Etienne began.

"Yes!" Henri laughed. "This is not a woman at all!" he exclaimed. "This is a man, a pharaoh. And the scribe who created this particular burial story reveals his identity. "You are staring," announced Henri, "at the dead painted face of Akhenaton, the heretic king."

Etienne leaned again into the wall, studying the figure. "My God, Henri!" he said. "I believe you are right."

"The burial place of Akhenaton has been a great mystery – and a great challenge – compelling archaeologists worldwide, for centuries." Henri gestured dramatically, something Etienne had never seen.

Akhenaton was a pharaoh of the New Kingdom, in 1350 b.c., thought to be the father of young Tutankhamun, or King Tut. Akhenaton was an intriguing figure. Etienne wanted to reach out and touch him, but he just looked up and stared at his profile. Etienne had seen statues and other renderings of Akhenaton in the Egyptian museum in Cairo. Never in Egyptian history was a pharaoh so strangely depicted, with dramatic, almost feminine features of face and body.

The heretic Akhenaton had rejected the entire pantheon of Egyptian gods that had been worshipped for centuries. Akhenaton favored the Sun god, Ra, the source of all life, and worshipped only him. While he had many followers, much of the Egyptian people simply could not accept his radical, sweeping changes, and Akhenaton was thought to have met a violent and untimely end.

Upon Akhenaton's death, Tutankhamun took the throne and, under the supervision of priests from the old order, the much-beloved boy King restored Egypt to its former traditions. Still, Akhenaton remained one of the most enigmatic and compelling characters in Egyptian history, advocating monotheism a millennia before modern religion.

"Yours is a fascinating theory, Henri," Etienne admitted. "But Akhenaton had moved the capitol of Egypt from Thebes to Amarna, where he constructed a great city. Why wouldn't Akhenaton have been buried there, in his city of the sun?"

"If you were burying a pharaoh, who ruled during the New Kingdom, you would put him where?" asked Henri. Etienne said nothing. "Where? *Where?*" pressed Henri. "*Here!* In the Valley of the Kings, the most sacred land in Egypt!"

"Yes, perhaps..."

"Here it is!" exclaimed Henri with great excitement. "This is what I want you to see!" Henri pointed to a wall relief. "This section here," he explained, "was previously covered with a thin layer of caked-on dirt. No one even knew it was here. I came upon it entirely by accident myself."

"How was that?" asked Etienne.

"I fell upon it. Literally. I stumbled on a random stone laying in the pathway. My lantern scraped the wall as I tripped, and a huge chunk of dried sand chipped off and fell to the ground. There on the wall, I discovered these carvings. But it was not a random accident," added Henri. "It was destiny."

Etienne approached the carvings on the wall that told the story of the pharaoh's burial. "Here is the clue that everyone else missed! And the proof that this is, in fact, the burial place of Akhenaton... Take a look." Henri handed Etienne the magnifying glass and held a gas lantern close to the wall.

Etienne studied the hieroglyphs from top to bottom, copying each symbol into his journal, fully aware and awed that the words were etched 33 centuries before he was born. Henri leaned in close and together they huddled over the ancient writing, losing their own tempestuous past in the far more distant history of this particular god-king.

"Fascinating," said Etienne. "Here's the moon god, Khons, with his hawk head. That surprises me."

Henri grinned broadly. "Now you've got it!" he said. "This king was buried in secret, under the cover of night. *Why?* To protect his grave from his enemies, of course! People hated him so fiercely they would have desecrated his remains. Another clue. Which is why this tomb was abandoned so quickly. With no identity inscribed in the tomb, archaeologists considered it unimportant. When, in fact, it was the most important!"

"Is this your only evidence?"

Henri scowled. "No, my boy. Read this." He pointed to a faint inscription under the depiction of the funerary procession, a singular footnote.

Etienne held up the magnifying glass, and began to read. *"We go..."* he began.

"No, no," interrupted Henri. *"We come..."*

"We come here," continued Etienne, scribing and translating into his journal with care. Etienne hesitated. *"... in mask of..."* Henri was leaning in so close that Etienne could smell his breath, which was getting heavier with each passing moment. "I can't quite make it out," said Etienne, stepping back from the wall.

Henri moved in. *"We come here,"* he read, *"in mask and silence, and forever here, so the Great One can forever rest."*

"Say that again," said Etienne.

"We come here, in mask and silence, and forever here, so the Great One can forever rest," boasted Henri, turning back to his former student.

"I must say, Henri, this is exciting!" If Etienne felt the sting of jealousy, he would not admit it. "I'm tremendously impressed."

"Come, let me show you the progress we've made on the lower stairs." Henri led Etienne further down the dark passageway, holding the lamp well in front of him. One never knew when a stray cobra, silent and deadly, might wander through.

"Here. Here we found the first traces of a lower chamber. See this line here?" Henri pointed to a foot-long indentation in the stone ground, swept clear of sand and debris by a worker's stiff brush.

"Further on down, here," continued Henri, "we picked up the line again." They approached several workers, picking gently at the hardened earth.

Etienne stood at a discreet distance. Henri was intently fingering his meticulous black mustache while local workers chipped carefully at the caked mud floors. Henri was looking, searching, virtually *willing* the pencil-thin indentation that would reveal evidence of a lower chamber beneath the temple's hard-trodden floor. Henri bent over the workers. They shifted slightly in their rhythmic tasks.

"Easy there!" barked Henri at one of the men. "Give me that trowel." Henri bent over and began to demonstrate what the worker already knew perfectly well.

Etienne picked up a nearby lantern, and returned to the hall where the funerary procession was carved. Etienne studied the engravings again for a long, long time. The lantern hummed indifferently on the ground as Etienne made notes in his journal. Finally, Etienne sat back against the opposite wall, folded his arms across his knees and buried his head there.

"I say there, my boy," Henri came up beside him. "Is everything alright?"

"Fine, fine," said Etienne, not looking up at Henri.

"What is it then?"

Etienne rose from the ground and dusted off his pants. "Nothing, Henri. It's nothing."

"Tell me, Etienne. I know you well enough –"

"Really Henri, let it go."

"I will not let it go! Tell me –"

"You've made an astonishing discovery, Henri—a significant one. I offer you my congratulations." Etienne turned to leave the temple.

"Wait! Tell me what you think you've found," pressed Henri. He grabbed Etienne by the arm. "Tell me –"

"*Again,*" blurted Etienne, wresting loose his arm. "It says *again.*"

"What?"

Etienne sighed deeply and stepped up to the inscription on the wall. "... And so we go *again* – not *here*, but *again* – in mask and silence."

"That's not right!" insisted Henri.

"Look." Etienne pointed to the definitive symbols. "They are not coming here, but *going again.*"

"No –"

"And this line, here." Etienne pointed. "And ever again, *until* – not *so* he can forever rest – but rather, *until* the Great One forever rests."

"No, no, you're wrong," said Henri. "It says *here*. We come *here*."

Etienne held out his journal where he had transcribed the hieroglyphics. *We go again, in mask and silence, and forever again, until the Great One can forever rest.*

"Henri, they were removing Akhenaton *from* this temple, and taking his remains elsewhere." Etienne looked at the man who he had hated and despised and plotted against for years. His rival now seemed vulnerable – plainly human, and not of the monstrous proportions in Etienne's mind. "You are searching for an empty tomb, Henri."

"He is here, I tell you!" shouted Henri. "And you are wrong!"

"Still, Henri, you have found something magnificent. And if you do find your stairs in the floor, they may lead to unbelievably extraordinary artifacts."

"Jealousy has clouded your eyes, Etienne."

"No, Henri. It has not." Etienne shook his head as he walked out of the long tunnel and into the fresh clear air. *But this one time,* Etienne said to himself, *I almost wish you were right.*

Valley of the Kings

Despite their argument, Henri sent a courier to the hotel in Luxor inviting Etienne and his friends to dinner. Etienne would have liked to have refused, but Henri still had the last missing piece of the Gnostic library. So they accepted. Father Mhand and Muhanna had opted to stay at the hotel, where the good priest was still recovering from three glasses of beer the night before.

The sky met the land in a muted curtain of spun gold, resting softly on the hard, dry hills. The sand glowed bright and warm in the twilight of the day. Henri had pitched a large tent and made his camp only a few miles from his dig, where the steep valley walls leveled briefly to a plateau that overlooked the entire region.

Etienne, Katherine and Nick drove out to the plateau, and parked the jeep a hundred or so yards from Henri's camp, opting to walk over the last, bumpiest parts of the dirt road. As the sun, compelled by night, fell behind the red hills, Henri hosted a simple, hearty meal around a blazing campfire. The night chill would soon set upon them, and they sat close in an intimate gathering of body and thought. They ate well, told many stories, and drank from a seemingly endless supply of imported scotch whiskey.

As the evening wore on, Henri forced a tainted optimism into the discussion. He began to talk incessantly about the heretic king, Akhenaton, and his own impending discovery. But feelings of grave and unendurable disappointment kept seeping into his heart, and his thoughts became dark and bitter. Etienne had told Katherine and Nick what had happened between he and Henri in the temple, and of Henri's refusal to believe Etienne's interpretation of the inscriptions. But Etienne did not discuss his differing opinion over dinner. He let Henri do the talking.

"Akhenaton was a brilliant, tortured man," Henri boasted, loud. "Totally unappreciated. He knew, back before astronomy was invented, that the sun was the source of all life. As scientists, we know today that he was absolutely right. And as the source, Akhenaton reasoned that the sun *only* was the creator, and the ruling god."

Henri took a long draw on his chipped tin cup. "He was an extraordinary man," he droned on, throwing back more drink. Henri poured whiskey from the bottle into everyone's cup, splashing much into the sand. "*Human*. He was an extraordinary human being."

"He was also a horrible tyrant," said Etienne flatly. "Akhenaton forced his beliefs on the masses, desecrating temples and statues of the other, long-revered, gods." Etienne threw the last few sips of his drink onto the ground. "With an absolute intolerance for differing views."

"What happened to him, in the end?" asked Katherine, setting her own cup in the sand, her eyes on Etienne.

Henri stared at her through a whiskey haze, his head dipping from its own weight. He stared a long time. "Nobody knows," he finally said, emptying his cup. "Suddenly, he was just gone. And his successors, and their high priests, wanted to eradicate the heretic from the people's memory. All known records of Akhenaton's life, and death, were destroyed. The only surviving documents were found a thousand years after his reign on earth."

Only the fire crackled an acknowledgment. Henri filled his cup again in the silence. "You see," said Henri, sullen, bitter. "Fate interferes with all of us. She lands her spiteful gaze upon you, and you obey. You must concede *absolutely* to her will."

"That's a woman for you," Nick offered, laughing that make-believe laugh that never makes anyone as comfortable as it intends.

"Hey now," said Katherine, laughing with Nick to lighten the tension.

"Tell me Katherine," said Henri. "Does it give you women *pleasure* to toy with men? Must you constantly meddle in our lives? Is it out of *spite* that you do it? Or are you merely bored?"

"I say now," interrupted Nick. "You're going too far."

"Too far? Too far?" slurred Henri. "What do *you* know? What could you *possibly* know?"

"I know you've had a lot to drink, for one thing," said Nick, still trying to sound jocular. "I also know you're very close to a bloody lip, old boy."

"Perhaps we should return to the hotel," suggested Katherine, getting up from her stool.

"Now, now, you're not going to run off so fast are you?" Henri grabbed Katherine by the wrist. "Not very gracious of you, my dear."

"Ow!" Katherine pulled against him. "Let go!" Nick rose immediately to his feet.

"I'm not boring you, am I?" Henri bent Katherine's wrist, hard, and forced her back into her seat.

Etienne stood up and intercepted Nick. "Henri," he stated calmly. Henri turned to face Etienne, still holding tight to Katherine. Without another word, Etienne raised his booted foot and kicked Henri in the chest. The impact sent both Henri and Katherine sprawling onto the sand. Etienne picked Katherine up with one swift movement, positioning himself between her and Henri. Nick rushed to her side and put his arm around her. She shrugged him off.

"You are a horrible man!" Katherine spat the words at Henri, still on his back on the ground. She returned to Nick's side. "Let's go," she said. Nick wrapped her slender frame in his arms.

Henri was struggling to his feet when Etienne laid his heavy boot on the man's chest, pinning him to the sand. "Not so fast."

"Get off me, you cad!" hissed Henri.

"Cad?" Etienne pressed harder with his boot. "Cad?" Henri struggled against him, but the weight of the whiskey and the boot rendered him useless.

"Go to hell!" hissed Henri.

"I say, Henri," said Etienne with his arms crossed casually. "Would this be a good time to discuss that codex?"

Henri laughed. He laughed and laughed, right into the dirt and sand. "Etienne," he said. "You'll get that codex over my dead body."

"*Tres bien*," said Etienne. "Have it your way." He reached down and grabbed Henri by the lapels of his leather jacket. Yanking him to his feet in a single motion, Etienne then swung hard with the back of his hand, striking Henri on the face. Henri careened back into the sand. Etienne loomed over him while Katherine and Nick watched the startling spectacle unfold, transfixed to where they stood.

Henri pushed against the ground with his fists, and struggled to his side. "I'm not dead yet, my boy," he said, breathing heavily, leaning against one arm. He wiped the blood from his mouth.

Etienne advanced. He did not see the thin silver blade as he reached again for Henri. Katherine and Nick did. "Etienne!" screamed Katherine.

Henri rose to his knee, and thrust a knife into Etienne's flesh. Etienne, shock stamped on his face, fell forward upon Henri. Henri pushed Etienne away and pulled the knife from his rival's body. Katherine and Nick watched their friend fall by the fire, his hands stained red at his side. "The price you pay, Etienne, is always too high," said Henri, staggering to his feet.

"Oh my God! Nick, get the jeep!" Katherine rushed over and knelt beside Etienne. "Etienne, are you alright?" she asked, pulling the white silk scarf from around her neck. She pressed the thin fabric to Etienne's side. It was soaked with blood in a matter of seconds.

"Please tell me you're alright," demanded Katherine. Etienne looked at her, confused, his eyes drawn into a glazed scowl. "You'll be okay, Etienne," said Katherine. "Nick's coming right back. You'll be okay." But she was trembling from bone to bone.

349

Etienne clasped a bloody hand over hers and tried to speak. His voice came out a faint, raspy whisper. "Kat," he said. "Kat, listen to me."

"I'm right here, Etienne," she said, bending close to him. "I'm right here."

"In my satchel, there's a b—," But the rest of his words slurred into nothingness as his head rolled to the side and he lost consciousness.

"Come back," said Katherine, shaking him lightly. "Etienne, I'm right here. Come back to me."

This is not the game of children, Miss Donatta had warned. *This may not be safe,* Rasul had said. But, in her heart, Katherine hadn't really believed them. She somehow thought they were all above true harm. *How could this be happening to us?* If she'd stopped to consider it, she would have realized she was casting all the blame on the God she'd long abandoned.

"Etienne, please come back." Over and over Katherine said it, as much to herself as to him as she cradled his head in her lap. She was still saying it, and straining her eyes into the night, when Nick returned with the jeep. Her hands and clothes were wet with blood. Henri had disappeared into his tent. Nick let the jeep idle and came to Etienne's side. "Come back. Come back." Katherine was almost chanting. Etienne was still and silent and startlingly pale. *"Come back."*

Nick knelt by Etienne and touched Katherine's bloody hands. She lifted them. Etienne's hand fell limp to the ground. Nick pulled the away stained scarf and examined the wound.

Etienne was losing a lot of blood. The knife sliced deeply into the fleshy side of Etienne's abdomen, and might have reached his stomach or kidneys. *This is bad,* thought Nick. "We must move him very carefully," said Nick. He replaced Katherine's blood-soaked scarf with his own clean handkerchief and placed Etienne's limp hands on top of it. "I'll be right back," Nick said to Katherine. "Press hard on the wound. You must slow the bleeding. Do you understand?" Nick looked at his wife, shock carved into her face. "Katherine, look at me. Do you understand?"

"Oh my God, oh my God," was all she said in response. But she pressed the full weight of her hands and arms against the bleeding wound.

Nick stood up and strode into Henri's tent. Henri was half passed out from scotch, laying face down on his cot, mumbling something under his breath. He rolled over when Nick approached. "I'll take that codex now," said Nick. "Right now. This second." It had been a long time since Nick had pointed a gun in a man's face. Not since the war had he even handled a gun, until he came to Egypt. But Nick had put the gun he took from Father Antonio into the glove box of the jeep, and when he pulled the jeep up to the campsite, he couldn't help thinking of it. And of the codex.

"Go to hell," said Henri.

Nick released the safety on the 7mm Beretta semi-automatic and pressed it to Henri's head. "I want the codex now," he said, with a detached calmness. "Or I will shoot you where you lay, and take it for myself, if I have to tear apart this entire tent."

Henri looked at Nick, squinting as if in disbelief, or perhaps by then he was merely seeing double. But he got up from his bed and stumbled over to a traveling chest in the corner of the tent. Nick accompanied him step by step, the barrel of his gun pressed to Henri's ear. Henri hit his head on a mirror that dangled from a pole supporting the tent, and still Nick kept the gun fixed to its position. Rummaging through the chest, barely able to stand up without swaying, Henri finally pulled out a thin box tied with a string.

"Show me," demanded Nick. Henri swayed toward him as he fumbled with the cover. In one unbelievably quick motion, Henri dropped the box and swung his arm around, knocking the pistol out of Nick's hand. It flew across the tent and, for one stunned moment, the two men just stared at each other. The gleaming weapon lay near the cot, a prize for the taking. They both raced toward it, kicking and pushing at each other as they scrambled across the floor. The whiskey finally got the better of Henri, however, and he found himself splayed out on his back with the gun in his face.

Nick kicked Henri in the stomach to immobilize him. Then, still aiming the gun in his direction, Nick crossed the tent and picked up the box. "Show me," Nick demanded, returning to Henri. Breathing heavily, Henri drew himself up to a sitting position. Taking the box, he broke the string and lifted the lid. With reluctant, shaking hands, he pulled back a soft cloth and revealed a papyrus manuscript with a leather cover—just like the ones Nick had already seen. Nick took the box with one hand and, with the other, smacked Henri on the temple with the butt of his gun. It didn't take much. Henri toppled over in a defeated, drunken heap.

Nick hurried outside and put the box in the front seat of the jeep. Then he rushed to Etienne's side. "Katherine, you take his feet," he said. Nick placed his arms under Etienne's torso. "Etienne... Etienne? Can you hear me?" Etienne was as still as death. *This is not good*, thought Nick grimly. *Maybe I shouldn't have waited. Even for one second.* Katherine and Nick struggled to carry Etienne across the thick, uneven sand. They loaded him clumsily into the back seat of the jeep, and wrapped a blanket close around him.

"There's a hospital in Luxor," said Nick, settling Katherine into the back seat next to Etienne. "We'll be there in no time. Just hold on tight." Nick spun sand high into the air as they raced away from Henri's darkening camp. In the rear view mirror Nick saw the fire spit its ashes into the clear, cold night.

22

CAPTURE AND CONSEQUENCE

This is the way to slip through to your inner most home:
close your eyes, and surrender.

– Rumi

Winter Palace Hotel, Luxor

It was near dawn when Nick and Katherine left the hospital with Etienne and drove to their hotel. A seemingly endless conclave of birds was flying on the dim eastern horizon. It seemed as though the entire species had all risen together and joined in a mass exodus to somewhere else. The disquieted birds just kept coming and coming.

"I can do this on my own, you know," insisted Etienne, as his friends helped him out of the jeep.

"Rubbish," said Nick. He and Katherine each held on to one of Etienne's arms as they walked him into the hotel and down the hall to his room. "When the morphine wears off, you'll be wishing we'd carried you on our backs the entire way. Believe me."

Father Mhand, hearing their early morning commotion, opened the door to his room and popped his head out. His white hair was sticking up in all directions. "My Lord in heaven," he said. "What has happened?"

"Etienne's been hurt," said Katherine.

"I'm fine," stated Etienne.

"Well, if you call a stab wound and 25 stitches *fine*," said Nick. "Then I suppose you're just swell." Though Henri's blade had missed Etienne's vital organs, the wound was still deep and an infection alone could easily kill him.

Father Mhand followed them to Etienne's room and Katherine recounted the story for him. "You should contact the authorities," insisted the priest, bending over Etienne. "A serious crime has been committed." Father Mhand sat beside Etienne on the soft bed. "And you are very lucky to be alive."

Etienne struggled to sit up, groaning. "No." He winced. "No police." A stain of blood seeped to the surface of Etienne's bandaged waist. He fell back on the bed.

Nick paced the room. "This is bad, Etienne. I think Father Mhand is right. We should contact the authorities."

"I said, *no.*"

"I agree with Etienne." Katherine stood at the window, overlooking the Nile.

"I cannot understand you, Katherine," said Nick, looking across the room at his wife.

"What?" Katherine turned from the window.

"Nothing," said Nick, shaking his head.

"What?" she demanded.

"*Nothing.*"

"Will you people please leave my room?" Etienne turned on his side, away from Katherine. "I need some rest."

"Of course you do," offered Father Mhand. "You go to sleep now. We'll check in on you later."

"Is there anything you need?" asked Katherine. Nick walked out of the room. Katherine followed her husband down the hallway to their suite. "What's bothering you?" she asked as she closed the door.

"What's bothering me?" he asked.

"You know, darling, you have the most annoying habit of repeating things that you've just heard perfectly well."

"I just can't believe that you asked it. What's bothering me, indeed! Good God, Katherine. Etienne has been stabbed, feuding clansmen are hunting us down like dogs, religious fanatics are trying to kill us, the Egyptian government is watching every move we make—ready to throw us in prison at the least provocation, and

354

Etienne has promised the manuscripts to both Hugo Nelson and Cato Nafarah. You've broken the law, lied to me and incurred debts that we apparently can't pay back. And you ask what is *bothering* me? What is *not* bothering me, for Christ's sake!"

"I have a solution, Nick. You'll be proud of me." She pulled him to the davenport in their room and held his hands while she spoke.

"I'm terribly regretful of things, really I am. Sometimes you take one small step down a path, and it doesn't seem so bad. Then you take another step, and before you realize it, you're way down a road you never really intended to be on. But it seems impossible to get off of it. Do you understand?"

"No," snapped Nick, though he understood perfectly.

"Nick, I kept getting further and further in, and I'd made promises. Surely you can understand that."

"Why didn't you just come to me and tell me what was happening?"

"Nick, *The Silver Butterfly* is the one and only thing that's ever been mine. Just mine. I wanted to do it on my own."

"Well, you made a bloody mess of it, my dear."

"Yes, well, if you could stop being angry for two seconds about all that, I could tell you how I'm going to fix it."

"I'm listening."

"The Egyptian shipment from Etienne carried many other artifacts, all legitimate, all very valuable," said Katherine. "Eugene is selling those pieces even as we speak."

"And that will cover your debt?"

"Yes. Well, maybe. If not, Etienne has generously allowed that I sell the golden snake, as well."

"Fine. Sell that too."

"I will." She sat, waiting for Nick's approval, his consent, his acknowledgment that she had rectified her sins, paid her penance. "Combined," she went on, "these items will pay back the investors and put the business back on solid ground."

"And you will have nothing to do with Hugo Nelson, or Etienne again? Ever? Katherine, look at me."

She looked at her husband square in the face. "I promise." Even as she said it, she wondered if she was lying.

The Winter Palace Hotel in Luxor was located on the East Bank, on the Corniche, one of the three main, and only named, streets in Luxor. The Nile slid silently by, the life blood of this enduring and mysterious civilization. The hotel itself was a grand old structure, Victorian in architecture and appointments. Built in 1886 to attract wealthy European travelers, the imposing, cream-colored building stood out against a landscape of more traditional, mid-eastern structures.

Two enormous curving staircases, with lush burgundy carpeting, led to the main entrance from opposite sides. A columned portico jutted out majestically from the second floor of the building. Two additional stories rose above the entrance, tapering to a scalloped façade, with British, French and Egyptian flags blowing lightly in the breeze above.

Inside the lobby hung a crystal chandelier, which was nothing short of breathtaking. To the right, a sitting room welcomed guests with a blazing fire in its hearth. High-backed leather chairs and plush sofas gave ease to weary voyagers. Shelves upon shelves of books lined the walls. Nick spent as many hours as he could in that sitting room, talking with travelers and traders, reading, sitting alone, thinking.

The Winter Palace could as easily have been in London as in Luxor, and for one brief moment, the first time Nick saw it, he felt a longing, an enormous wave of homesickness. A desire to be young again. And innocent.

Their rooms were charming and spacious, with high ceilings and windows that faced the Nile. Each was uniquely appointed in rich fabrics, elegant furnishings, and bedding so soft it seemed to claim the weary travelers in a resplendent cocoon. It was said that the famous archaeologist Howard Carter was staying at the Winter Palace when he discovered the extraordinary tomb of King Tut. Nick couldn't help but wonder, *which room? Was it my room? And will some of his fortune, for good or for bad, rub off on me?*

356

Katherine and Nick had a corner room on the second floor of the hotel. French doors led to two adjacent balconies, one facing the Nile, the other overlooking the Luxor Temple. This massive temple complex was large enough to house a village, and looked strikingly graceful on the landscape. The entrance was marked with one remaining obelisk, an enormous column made of pink granite, its square sides tapering to a once gilded point. Three, of what originally was six, imposing statues of the Pharaoh Ramses II guarded the entrance.

Near the Luxor Temple, the Nile floated slowly by on its timeless journey. Beyond the river, stretching to the west, were tremendous archaeological complexes. For thousands and thousands of years, dynasties grew and faded in this region. Lands were lost and gained in bloody conquests, and enormous strides were made in art and architecture.

The labor and lives of countless men and women rested to the west. Nick had been mesmerized with the thought of it all: the Valley of the Queens, the Tombs of the Nobles, the extraordinary Temple of Hatshepsut at Deir al-Bahri. And beyond these, the Valley of the Kings.

But Katherine wasn't thinking about any of that as she brushed her dark hair in the mirror. She was wrapped in a long, indigo dressing gown made of silk, which she had purchased at the marketplace the previous morning. She had also bought lotions and soaps and oils. And toothpaste. An excessively long hot bath, a nap, a light snack in her room, and Katherine was beginning to feel like herself again. She had even repaired her shiny red nails with Miss Donatta's polish.

As satisfying as these indulgences were, Katherine still fumed all morning about Etienne. *He is reckless, and irresponsible. He could have gotten us all killed. He provoked Henri Poirier on purpose, and had enjoyed it.*

Katherine threw her hairbrush on the dressing table and sat back in her chair, resting her bare feet on an open drawer of the vanity bureau. She looked out the window and sat there for a long time, trying to put all the recent events in order in her head. The landscape soon drew her to daydreaming, however. Its otherworldly images lingering around the corners of her imagination.

It was beautiful in Luxor, hot and dry and muted, like a page out of lost time. Katherine looked out beyond their balcony and watched the river slip by. *Fallucas*, sail boats, glided along the water.

There must have been 20 or 30 just outside her window, their triangular white sails like nimble butterflies dancing across the water.

Nick had not stayed long after their argument. He left rather abruptly, wanting, he said, to explore as many of the monuments as possible while they were in Luxor. He said he would be gone all day. Katherine was just as happy to have the day to herself, to give them both a break.

"Bon jour."

Katherine spun around. Etienne stood in her room. She was not aware that she had left the door unlocked. Or perhaps Nick had neglected to lock it when he left.

"You startled me!" she said. Etienne said nothing, but stood in the doorway, his strong shirtless chest rising above the white gauze of his bandages.

"Are you alright?" Katherine rose from her chair. They stood across the room from each other. Still Etienne said nothing. "Etienne? What is it?"

"You are like me," he said softly.

"What do you mean? Come in here. Sit down." They sat together on the long davenport, which was covered in soft yellow damask.

Etienne took time to gather his thoughts, and when he was ready he looked over at Katherine and began to speak. "Nick has spent his whole life in academia, then inside the sanctuary of a white-collar courtroom. He has no real understanding of how the real world works. It saddens me to see him judge you, to make you think you were bad."

"Nick is just idealistic," said Katherine. "He holds himself, and others, to a higher standard."

"No, Katherine, he holds us to an impossible standard. For him it works, because he is protected from life as it is – in its ugliness, its strife and its cruelties. He even spent the war behind a desk. Since then, he has built an entire compound of legal briefs and wealthy clients to protect himself. But the real test, Katherine, is in the real world. Nick has never gone there. His naiveté has made him arrogant, and simple."

"You have no idea what Nick did in the war," said Katherine. "You really don't. I barely know... He also has a good heart," she

358

continued. "And a natural generosity. Something neither you or I could ever have, or even ever understand."

"As I said, you and I are the same." Etienne leaned in– crossing a bridge of time and space and propriety – and kissed her on the mouth. Katherine said nothing. Her face was on fire; her heart was pounding in her chest. She felt his kiss all through her body. "*Je t'aime*," he whispered.

"Etienne, stop this."

"I love you, Katherine."

"This isn't right."

"Ask yourself, Katherine, in your heart." He entwined his fingers in hers. "Only your head says its wrong."

"What are you saying?"

"I'm saying that you belong with me." He moved his hand to her cheek.

"Don't touch me like that." Katherine put her hand on his bare chest to push him away. "I might take you seriously."

He put his hand on top of hers. "I love you. Seriously."

Katherine paused for a long moment, looking into his face. His expression was soft as he gazed back at her. "But you don't love like other people," she said. Katherine rose and stormed the room, walking in circles, her eyes fixed on the floor as she talked. "You love a bird the same as a sunset, the same as your work, the relics you find, the tombs you dig up; the same as any of the dozens of women you have loved and left behind. It's all the same to you."

"No –"

Katherine stopped pacing and looked straight at him. "I won't be left behind, Etienne. I will not. Not ever."

"Katherine –"

"It's not *human* to love that way, Etienne. It's not fair. The rest of us love with all our hearts. We risk pain and loss and disappointment. You talk about Nick staying safe, but it's *you*. You're always safe. Nothing touches you. And everything touches you. And it's all the same to you!" Katherine walked to the French doors and looked out over the Nile. "Everything and nothing."

Etienne crossed the room and stood behind her. "I don't want to be safe anymore, Katherine. I want to be with you."

"I don't believe you."

"Katherine, you're not listening –"

"You live without feeling."

"Come here." He took hold of her shoulders and gently turned her around to face him.

"I don't love you," she insisted. He touched his hand to her face, brushing back the hair from her temple.

"*Je t'aime, mon cherí. Je t'aime.*"

"I don't –" she started. He pulled her into his arms.

"Shhh." He held her tight and buried his face in her hair.

"I don't love you..." Katherine's voice was suddenly mixed with tears. She pressed her face to the warm bare skin of his chest. He held her there a long time.

"Damn," she said softly, pulling herself away. Katherine stepped back slowly and said, with great struggle, "I cannot do this." She turned abruptly and escaped into the bathroom, her dressing gown swirling around her bare legs.

Etienne sat on the bed and held his head in his hands.

Five minutes later, Katherine swept out of the bathroom, her hair clipped back, her eyes soft with the remnants of moisture, in the way only crying can make them. She brushed past Etienne as if he was not there and walked to a chair, collecting her freshly laundered clothes. Etienne stood up and followed her.

"You're right," he said, touching her shoulder and turning her around to face him. "I don't love the way other people do. But I do love *you*. And it's more real to me than everything else combined – all the treasures and the mysteries and the women. And it won't go away." He paused. "It won't go away."

"Until when, Etienne? It won't go away until *when*?" Katherine turned her back to him and gathered up more clothes.

360

"Until forever. *Forever*, dammit!" Etienne took the bundle of clothes out of her arms and threw them to the floor.

Katherine looked down at the heap of clothes and then back at her former lover. "There is sorrow in this world, Etienne, that brings people to their knees. It can crush the life out of you. And you, you skip blithely through it all. Unscathed, even from the damage you've participated in; callous to the wreckage you've left behind."

"Please don't. Please don't *do* that."

"Do what?" she snapped.

"Don't try so hard to make me hate you."

A cloud passed over her face. Etienne could see in her eyes that she was preparing to fire another barrage of words at him, to sting him, to wound him irreparably. *I can take it,* he thought. *This time I will ride it out.* So he waited for the storm, watching her face. He let it build. And he watched it pass. She said nothing.

"Love me, Katherine. Love me." Etienne pulled Katherine to him and kissed her, firm and unremitting. He kissed her beyond the nails she dug into his skin, beyond vague, murmured protests, beyond his own fears, until he felt her soften in his arms.

Katherine's anger dissolved and she surrendered to her longing. She had waited, in secret even to herself, ten years for Etienne to kiss her like that again. She held his face in her hands and kissed him back.

Katherine closed her eyes and let her whole world become the scent of Etienne, the feel of his skin, the sound of his breath.

Etienne kissed her mouth, her face, her neck; his hands gripped the soft silk of her robe. She smelled so good; she was so small and slender in his arms. Her skin felt like the softest thing imaginable.

Etienne led her to the chaise, where they sat and wrapped their arms around each other. They wanted to linger, to expand this time, these kisses, into forever.

When Katherine opened her eyes some time later, she saw blood. "Oh, my God!" she exclaimed, sitting up. Etienne's blood had soaked through his bandages, onto him, onto her robe, onto the chaise. "What did we do?"

"It's okay." He held her hands. "Katherine, it's okay. It doesn't hurt."

Katherine jumped up and ran barefoot down the hall to Etienne's room. She returned a minute later with fresh bandages and antiseptic. He stood over the bathroom sink and Katherine washed the blood off him, carefully dabbing his stitches with a towel. With shaking hands, she poured half a bottle of hydrogen peroxide on the wound.

"I'm so sorry," she said. "I'm so sorry."

"I think that's enough," said Etienne, pushing back the brown bottle of medicine. "It's clean."

"It'll be clean when I say it's clean." Katherine poured the rest of the bottle over the tender incision. Then she wrapped a new dressing around his waist, bending her head to his chest as she reached her arms around and around him with the shrinking roll of white gauze.

He kissed her forehead and got up. "I'm not sorry," he said, as he picked the bloodstained towel from the floor. Katherine rose up next to him. She looked as though she had something to say, but no words to say it. "Now what happens?" he asked.

"I don't know," she said, turning to the sink.

"I should leave," he said. But Etienne didn't move.

"Yes."

"Well then..."

Katherine buried her face in that wonderful hollow, the soft warm space, where his shoulder met his neck. "Go," she whispered.

"Alright then." Etienne walked to the door and opened it. "*Je t'aime,*" he said, turning back. "I love you."

Saying nothing, Katherine let him walk out the door, closing it slowly behind him. Time began to tick away. Katherine knew that if four seconds became five, and she didn't speak, then five seconds would become six and six would become forever. She turned away from the door. Then suddenly, as if someone else was doing it for her, she turned back.

"Wait!" Katherine threw open the door and ran out into the hall. "Wait. Come back a minute." She took his hand and walked him back into the room. But neither one knew what – between heaven and hell, between yes and no, between indulgence and restraint – to say. Katherine finally spoke. "Kiss me that way again, before you go."

"What way?"

"Like it's the last and only kiss on earth, for all time."

"*Oui.*" Etienne took her face in his hands.

"Just one more time," she whispered. They kissed each other tenderly, deeply, as the afternoon sun streamed through the window, lighting a heap of freshly laundered clothes scattered on the floor.

"My, my." Nick stood in the doorway, his arms folded across his chest. "What have we got here?"

Nick gave Etienne a look that left no doubt that it was time for him to leave, and that there was no room for discussion.

Etienne was silently relieved at Nick's arrival. Now they could not, none of them, pretend that what happened didn't happen. When he left, he cast Katherine a long, intimate look that she supposedly understood, and Nick supposedly did not.

Etienne limped back to his room, leaving Nick and Katherine to sort out what belonged only in the realm of a husband and a wife. But he wished he hadn't. He sat alone all evening and into the night, wondering what was happening, wishing he had stayed, wishing he had claimed her, right there, in front of Nick. He waited and waited, hoping in vain that she would come to him.

There are nights, filled with terrible hours, that seem as though they'll last forever. Nick had thought that he and his wife would never fight like that again, and that the light of day would never come. He began his march through those awful hours by asking the most painful question of all: "Do you love him?"

"Oh, for crying out loud Nick. It was just a stupid kiss."

"There's no such thing as *just a kiss*, stupid or otherwise."

"Really, you're making too much of this." The lies just rolled off her lips.

"Just tell me why, Katherine. Why did you have to do *the one thing t*hat could ruin us?"

She lit a Lucky Strike and sat quietly for a long time, holding the cigarette in so absent a way, Nick thought she actually might drop it on the floor.

"I don't know, Nick. I simply do not know."

"You bloody well do too know!" he snapped. "Just tell me the dammed truth for a change."

Nick wished he could crawl inside her head, see the truth, feel it for one terrible, unbearable moment, and have it be done with. He sat down in a chair, placed his hands on the armrests, and waited.

When she spoke she did not look at her husband, but stared only at her own hand, tracing the striped fabric of the davenport where she sat. "Nick, I don't like who I've become lately. And I know I've done some crazy things. But with Etienne I feel accepted – with all my faults. I'm a better person when I'm with him."

"Well naturally," snapped Nick. "It's easy to be your best when you're flitting around Paris without a care in the world, least of all about me. Or when you're on some great adventure in Egypt, instead of living real life, with real people, back home. Reality isn't always thrilling Katherine. Not even with Etienne."

She looked at the ceiling, as if she hadn't heard him. "I want to be messy and flawed. I want to make mistakes and have it be all right. Etienne ... I don't know ... he calls to a much deeper part of me. A part that wants, well ..." she said it so softly, "...*more.*"

Nick crossed his legs, one over the other. "He'll leave you Katherine. He will."

"I know who Etienne is, Nick. Believe me. And I've fought it. And I'm tired. And I don't know what to do."

"You think I haven't seen this coming, ever since we got here? Please don't insult me by pretending that this is all so bloody hard for you."

"Okay, mister tough man," snapped Katherine, stubbing out her cigarette. "You want the truth? I want you *both*. That's the real

364

truth. I don't want to have to choose. I want to be like men are: they have their wives and their lovers both. And everyone just looks the other way. The men slap each other on the back, and the women, the women just bear it. Over and over and over.

"Could you do that? Do you have that kind of strength? To watch the person you love with all your heart walk out the door, time after time. To re-heat his dinners for him. To wait. To spend your nights and weekends alone, knowing he is with someone else. My mother did it. Could you? Women suffer through it all the time. So why can't *I* be like a man? Why can't I have you both? And let *you* bear it?"

Nick sighed. "Even you, Katherine, can't have both. Not even you."

Katherine paused for a moment, knowing the inferno of truth would scar them both forever. *No more secrets. No more lies.* She blurted out her words. "I think I love him."

Nick looked at his wife with a pain in his eyes that seemed as though it sprang from the deepest vein of his lifeblood.

Katherine looked at Nick square in the eye, her voice softening. "And I'm so very sorry that that hurts."

"You never stopped loving him, did you? Not since that one summer."

"Yes, I did," she insisted. "I put that summer and those feelings behind me. And I looked only ahead of me. Of us."

"But not really." In his bitterness, Nick was speaking only to himself.

Katherine held her ground. "Etienne became part of the past."

"Until just a few months ago."

She sighed deeply. "When Etienne called on the telephone, asking me to put this deal together for him, it was as though something in me woke up. Something I stopped listening to forever ago. And that voice was as real and strong as it was when I buried it. I've been fighting and denying it ever since I picked up that telephone."

"Go then," Nick said flatly. "Go to your beloved Etienne."

Katherine held a pillow to her chest, suddenly faced with a moment that was bigger than she was. "I don't know what to do."

"Well, you damn well better figure it out," snapped Nick.

She looked up at him through eyes that were focused on the past. "I can't go back to the way things were," she said. "I can't go back to being invisible."

Nick just shook his head. "I'm not your father, Katherine," he snapped. "Stop blaming me. Jesus, how much does a person need to do to fill you up? I tell you, it's exhausting. Nothing, *nothing* is ever enough for you.

Nick knew he was wounding her, and it pained him. He had tried for so long to protect her. And he, like so many, had fed his own heart off of hers – her energy and enthusiasm and uncompromising demands of life. The last thing he had ever wanted to do was to hurt her. And there he was, crushing her heart in his hands, and he could not stop.

Nick ran his hands through his hair. "Will you please look around and see all the love that's around you? And always has been?" She said nothing, but continued to withdraw into herself, shutting him further and further out. Her silence made him louder.

"You know what will happen, Katherine? I'll tell you what: Etienne will not be enough for you either, eventually. You're going to walk down that same road forever, even though it loops you 'round and 'round. Soon enough your hunger will rise up. It will devour Etienne, and your love, and everything you thought was so important."

Having emptied his heart and his anger, having uncovered things that were buried for years, and having brought them into the bright glaring spotlight of words, Nick fell silent.

Katherine curled her feet underneath her and laid her head on a pillow. There was nothing she could think of to say. Drained, weary, too spent to even ask a word from her, Nick rose from his chair. "I'm going to bed," he muttered.

At the bathroom door, he turned back to her. "I guess, in the end, I'll just wait with my hat in my hand like some idiot, for you to decide." She looked up at him, her eyes vacant, looking as exhausted as he felt. "But hurry it up, will you?" he added, leaving the room. "This is killing me."

The air was still and heavy the next day as they drove to the Luxor museum. No one was talking. No one was listening to anything more than the steady whirring of the jeep and their own private rumblings.

Etienne drove fast. What he was driving toward, or away from, was his alone to tell. That morning, he had insisted that he was well enough to leave the hotel—though everyone knew he needed more time to recover. He said he felt an urgency to get to the Luxor Museum and retrieve the traveling chest sent by Rasul Taj.

Once Etienne had the manuscripts from Rasul, he was planning on finding Henri Poirier to claim the last remaining book. Henri owed him, as far as Etienne figured. And he was sure Henri knew it, too. By the time Henri recovered from what promised to be a raging hangover, he would certainly regret how things had gone. But Etienne would worry about that later. The task at hand was to recover the traveling case from the museum and the eight manuscripts hidden inside.

Nick, keeping the secret of Henri's manuscript to himself, had urged against going to the Luxor Museum. "It's too early," he insisted. "We must wait until things calm down a little."

"Always playing it safe," muttered Etienne in response. He did not look at Nick, but held tight to the sharp pain in his side. "When I have all the remaining books, we'll return to Cairo to photograph them. After that, we'll contact Hugo Nelson."

"But —" Nick began.

"No discussion." Etienne turned his face away and sped through the city streets.

The Luxor Museum was housed in a small building on the Corniche. Etienne pulled the jeep to a stop directly in front and stepped out carefully. The others followed, except for Nick.

"I'm not going in." Nick sat back in his seat and crossed his arms.

"Suit yourself." Etienne shrugged and pulled his satchel over his shoulder.

"Anyone who would try to cheat Hugo Nelson," snapped Nick, loudly, "knowing full well the danger he'd be putting his so-called friends in, is a —"

"A what?" snapped Etienne. Nick turned his head away. "A *what*, Nick?"

Nick stepped out of the jeep and faced Etienne directly. "A self-serving, arrogant son-of-a-bitch, that's what!" Katherine, Muhanna and Father Mhand looked nervously at each other.

"Nick, you are the most insipid, boring, endlessly dull and monotonous human being I know," said Etienne. "So shut up, will you?"

Father Mhand stepped forward. "I will remind you, my two angry friends, of something we learned at the basilica just a few days ago. Perhaps it will help you to hear it again."

"What?" Etienne and Nick turned in unified frustration to the priest.

"From your *Gospel of Thomas*," continued Father Mhand, slowly and calmly, *"And Jesus said, 'If two make peace with each other within a single house, they will say to the mountain, Move from here, and it will move.'"*

"I thought the mountain parable was about faith," interrupted Katherine, anxious to divert the confrontation between Etienne and Nick. *"If your faith is no greater than that of a mustard seed, you can say to the mountain, 'move from here to there,' and it will."*

"On that day," added Muhanna, *"the heaven will shake and reel, and the mountains move and pass away. On that day, woe betide the unbelievers, who now divert themselves with vain disputes."* Everyone fell silent for a moment. "From *al Quran*," added Muhanna.

"You can compare religious sayings all you like," said Nick bitterly. "You..." he pointed into Etienne's face, "... are still an asshole."

"Why don't you *think* for a minute, you self-righteous bastard!" snapped Etienne. "Where will the documents be the safest? With you? With Hugo Nelson? Better yet, what do you suppose Father Antonio would do with them? Use your head, Nick. The safest place for all the manuscripts is with the government."

"I don't agree!" yelled Nick. "At all!"

"You are just going to have to trust me, Nick. I know what I'm doing."

"Trust you? Like I trusted you alone for five minutes with my wife?" No one said a word. Everyone shifted nervously around the two men as they squared off, launching ice-cold daggers at each other from their eyes.

Etienne finally spoke. "I'm going inside for the manuscripts. You do as you please."

Nick hesitated. He could have taken hold of Katherine right then and there, rented a car and left Etienne, and his manuscripts, in Luxor. They could have left the whole messy business behind them. They could have gone back to New York and started over. It sounded so easy.

Etienne disappeared through the museum doors, with Father Mhand and Muhanna shuffling in behind him. Nick took Katherine by the arm and led her into the building. He wondered, though, why he didn't walk away with his wife. Why he didn't just walk away? And he wondered what ever would have happened if he had. *These are the moments,* he thought, *rare and distant, that change your life; so distant that you don't recognize them for the mistakes they are.*

The air was cool inside the Luxor Museum, the lighting dim. The building housed jewelry, pottery, furniture and statues from various dynasties of the Middle and New Kingdoms, dating as far back as 1436 B.C. A cow-goddess from King Tutankhamun's tomb greeted the unhappy group as they entered the main room. They stood nervously for a few minutes, witnessed only by relics from the long dead past. Shortly, the museum's curator, Aboudi, came shuffling around a corner. Etienne stepped forward and greeted the keeper of the artifacts. The others hovered in the background.

"I am Etienne Desonia, of the Coptic Museum in Cairo. I wonder if my colleagues and I might have a word with you."

"Yes, yes, of course," said Aboudi, bowing politely. "I have been expecting you."

"You have?"

"I have something here in your name. It came only yesterday." Etienne looked around the room. "Come, come." Aboudi led him by the arm. "My office is back here." They obligingly followed Aboudi into the back corner of the museum, walking single file and in complete silence.

They all crowded together into Aboudi's small office. Nick kept his hand on Katherine's arm and kept them both as far away from Etienne as he could. Rasul's traveling chest sat on a corner table, dusty and alluring. Etienne walked automatically to it and reached out his hands.

"Not so fast." The small office door closed behind them. They heard the tumbler of the lock click over. Cato Nafarah stood inside, a smirk covering his brown face. Kassab, and the other gunman they had seen in Rasul's store, stepped into the room from behind a closet door. Their hands were on the guns they had belted at their waists. The museum curator shrugged, guilty and embarrassed, into Etienne's face.

"Any reason you didn't have these delivered directly to me, Etienne?" asked Nafarah coolly. "As you promised?" The Egyptian official leaned against the solid desk in the middle of the room. Etienne's group simultaneously released a collective moan of dread. This was the worst possible thing that could have happened in that particular moment, and they all knew it. The rift between Etienne and Nick threatened the end of their unity, and they were suddenly facing an unforgiving enemy, trapped within a mausoleum of lives gone by.

Light filtered through the office windows in dreary streaks, illuminating invisible pockets of dust in the air. The room smelled stale and old, with lingering memories of cigarettes and homemade sandwiches. *This is a miserable little place to accept defeat*, thought Etienne. He saw his comrades looking at him, expectant, hopeful, doomed.

"Search their bags," commanded Nafarah. Kassab took Katherine's knapsack and splayed the contents across the desk, rifling through her cosmetics, pocketbook, cigarette case. The other man did not move or flinch the entire time, but kept vigil over all of them with his gun.

"Where you are going," Nafarah said, picking up Katherine and Nick's passports, "you won't be needing these." He tucked them inside his jacket pocket. Then he turned his attention to a bulky item, wrapped in tissue paper. "Well now, where did you steal this little treasure?" sneered Nafarah, unwrapping the golden, green-eyed snake.

"That's mine," said Katherine, stepping forward.

"Not any more," said Nafarah, holding the green-eyed snake up to a shaft of sunlight. Its gold body glinted in the light, eyes ablaze. Nafarah handed the coiled snake to Kassab, who placed it in the traveling chest from Rasul. Etienne stared at the floor. Katherine looked like she was about to cry. Instead she stepped to the table and carefully returned each precious item to her knapsack.

"Look in Etienne's bag," said Nafarah. Kassab took Etienne's satchel and pulled out his diary and the two heavy codices wrapped in cloth. He then dropped the satchel carelessly onto the floor. Nafarah took the diary first and flipped through it. "This might make for some very interesting reading," he said, and he started to hand it to Kassab.

"Wait," he said, as his eyes were drawn to an open page. Nafarah studied the page carefully, and then snapped the book closed. "Search the bag again," he demanded, showing Kassab the page. Kassab splayed everything in Etienne's satchel onto the table and rummaged through it. But he found nothing there of further interest. Kassab shrugged his shoulders futilely. "Then search *him*," instructed Nafarah, nodding at Etienne.

"I have to decline," said Etienne coolly. Nafarah cocked an amused eyebrow in Etienne's direction. "I've been injured, as you can see." Etienne raised his shirt to reveal the bandage around his waist, and the few spot of blood that had seeped to the surface.

"Ouch," said Nafarah. "That must hurt."

"*Oui*," said Etienne.

"Too bad," replied Nafarah, nodding at Kassab to proceed. "Though I'm sure that will make for an interesting story," he added. "When we get around to it."

Under Etienne's angry stare Kassab patted him down, cautious of his wound, but thorough nonetheless. A smile broke over Kassab's face, and he reached into Etienne's pants' pocket and withdrew a small bundle wrapped in a handkerchief.

Unfolding the crisp white linen, Kassab held up a silver bracelet, with seven stunning jewels of seven different colors. The room seemed to shrink. Every single person leaned forward to gaze at the jewels. "You shouldn't have drawn a picture of it, Etienne," smirked Nafarah. "But your vanity made you do it, didn't it? You couldn't just keep it in silence, could you?"

"That is colored glass and paste, if you must know," said Etienne. "Take it if you want. But you will be pegged as a fool when you serve this up to your masters."

"A fool?" sneered Nafarah. "A fool?" he laughed out loud. "I know what this is. This alone, Etienne Desonia, will put you in front of a firing squad."

"Oh, don't be so sure," snapped Etienne. "When you learn where I found it, you'll die of embarrassment. Worse, you'll probably be demoted to desk duty, where you'll be filing paperwork for Monsieur Kassab here." Etienne turned to Kassab, who shifted uneasily.

Kassab knew that bringing a false artifact forward to their superiors would be disastrous to their careers. And Kassab, with a wife and seven children to feed, needed this government job. Plenty of people, equally as qualified, were starving in the streets of Cairo these days. "You'd like to crack the whip over Nafarah, wouldn't you?" taunted Etienne. "Well, you just might very well have your chance."

"Do you honestly think, Etienne," retorted Nafarah, "that after 20 years in the field, I don't recognize a precious stone when I see one? Do you assume that I'm just going to hand this back to you?" Nafarah shook his head and put the bracelet in his other suit pocket. "Etienne Desonia, in the company of these witnesses, and under the authority of the Egyptian Department of Antiquities, I'm placing you under arrest. You'll accompany me to Cairo, where you'll be held in confinement until you confess where you found this." Nafarah was nearly glowing. "And you will confess. Then you'll be stood up in front of a firing squad and executed for egregious and repeated acts of piracy against the state of Egypt."

Etienne's face was a stone mask. Beneath that mask, however, anger seethed.

"Now then." Nafarah turned his attention to the codices. "Let's have a look at these." As he began to unwrap the cloth that protected the *Gospel of Thomas*, Etienne dropped his head to his chest.

"What is this?" Nafarah demanded.

Etienne looked up. Instead of papyrus manuscripts, there lay two thick encyclopedias, the kind he'd noticed earlier on a shelf in the sitting room of their hotel. *Someone must have slipped into my room and stolen the books while I was sleeping, drugged from the morphine. But who? Father Antonio? Henri?* Then Etienne saw the look on Nick's face. Kind of a grin, but not: rather a look of arrogant impatience.

Nafarah, disappointed and angry, walked over to the traveling chest from Rasul. The eight manuscripts were laying on top of a jumbled pile of clothing. Nafarah lifted out a leather codex. "Care to explain these?" he asked. He flipped open the cover.

"Careful," said Etienne. "You know those manuscripts have a curse on them, don't you?" Much to Etienne's pleasure, Nafarah instinctively put the book back in the chest. "Much like the discovery of King Tutankhamun, in 1922," continued Etienne. "Within 10 years, more than 20 people associated with that discovery were dead."

"Rubbish!" snapped Nafarah. But he stepped away from the chest. He knew the mysterious deaths associated with the discovery of King Tut were not rubbish at all, but the absolute truth. "You're all under arrest!" he said. "For illegal possession of artifacts of the state."

Nick stepped forward. "As you can clearly see, we're not in possession of any codices," he said calmly. "Artifacts of Egypt, or otherwise."

"You are if I say you are," smirked Nafarah. "Arrest them all," he said to Kassab.

"Let my friends go," said Etienne, his voice rising. "They are not responsible –"

"Responsible? *Responsible?*" Nafarah taunted them. "You are all responsible!" He crossed his arms over his chest. Shiny onyx cufflinks peeked out from under the sleeve of his crisp black suit. A starched white handkerchief was folded precisely into his lapel pocket. "My only question is whether to execute you all, or let your bones dry to dust in a filthy prison for the rest of your sorry lives."

The museum curator paled. "You made no mention of –I" Nafarah turned and glared in Aboudi's small, round face. "–of ..." Aboudi trailed off weakly under Nafarah's intolerant stare.

"As I was saying," Nafarah paused as he turned back to them. "Shall I kill you all for crimes against the state?" He paused again. "Or shall I throw you into prison and let you ponder your sins under the harsh discipline of our jail masters?" He casually adjusted his cuffs. "So many choices..."

Katherine stepped forward, a strange combination of fear and adrenaline propelling her, and making her bold. "You cannot do either, Mr. Nafarah, and you know it. You are just trying to frighten us."

"Is that right?" Nafarah looked at Kassab. Kassab smiled back. "Now, Mrs. Spencer, what makes you think that I cannot do whatever I please with criminals?"

"For one, we're not criminals. We are simply tourists who have come across some relics. What will you charge us with? Buying old books? For two, Nick and I are Americans. Our government will not take lightly any injury done to innocent tourists."

"You are not innocent tourists!" Nafarah slammed his hand on the desk as he drew himself up to his full height and towered over her. "You are not innocent. You have been warned and warned and warned. And my patience is up."

"Perhaps I can help." Muhanna stepped forward and spoke softly to Nafarah. "It is I, Muhanna Ali al-Samara, who discovered the books that you want." Nafarah stared down at the little Muslim man. "Perhaps if I take you to where I found them, and you could find more, that would make for good blood between us, and you could find it in your heart to forgive us."

Nafarah sat back down on the desk. "There are more codices?"

Muhanna shrugged. "I truly do not know. But we know of three other books, hidden back in the caves where I found them, near my home in al-Qasr. Very near to Nag Hammadi." *What is a little fib*, Muhanna asked silently of Allah, *when it might provide us a fair chance to escape injustice?*

"You told me that you had only one codex, and that it was stolen – by religious zealots – if I recall," mused Nafarah.

Nafarah's body might never be found in those caves. "Yes, well, we did have a run-in with some very nasty people from Italy, I can tell you that," said Muhanna.

"And the codex? Was it stolen – or not?"

"Well, we may have been confused about that."

"Really?"

"Really."

"Are you confused now?"

Muhanna gazed up at Nafarah, his big brown eyes unflinching. "No."

374

"What about the codex Henri Poirier gave you?"

Muhanna shrugged again. "Henri Poirier gave us no codex."

"You lie and you lie!" Nafarah grabbed him by the collar of his *jallabiya* and twisted the cloth against his neck. Muhanna gasped for air. Nafarah slowly, steadily wrung the fabric tighter and tighter. He hated Muhanna, for no other crime than being one of Egypt's perpetually poor. Muhanna's eyes rolled back into their sockets.

Everyone stood helplessly by, looking at each other and the weapons Kassab and the gunman had aimed at them. The color drained from Muhanna's face and his limbs started to jerk as the last of his breath was being choked out of him. Time hung in that room hopelessly, as death approached on its quiet, steady path.

"Stop!" shout Nick, interrupting the terrible spectacle. "I have the codex from Henri Poirier. *I have the codex!* Muhanna knew nothing about it."

Nafarah held Muhanna in place a moment longer – longer than they thought he could possibly endure. Then he released the struggling man, who fell into a heap on the floor. A moment of pure stillness, and then Muhanna drew in a giant, dry gasp of air. His friends nearly wept from relief. Katherine moved to his side and helped him sit up. Muhanna slowly began to catch his breath, in short raspy gulps. "I have the codex," repeated Nick.

"Well now. We're finally making some progress. Perhaps you could hand it over to me, and I may find some leniency – for you at least." Nafarah steely eyes wandered from Nick to Etienne.

"I do not have it with me," confessed Nick. Nafarah folded his arms again across his chest. "I took it yesterday to Deir al-Bahri and hid it in the Temple of Hatshepsut."

"You did?" interrupted Etienne. "What gave you the right –?"

"Silence!" Nafarah stood up. "You." He pointed at Father Mhand. "You are to stay here." He looked into the eyes of the gunman. "If we are not back in three hours, kill the Christian priest."

The gunman smiled. Nafarah looked around the room. "The rest of you are coming with me. We will get this book at Deir al-Bahri. Tomorrow, we will return to this cave of yours near al-Qasr. And you will give me the three codices you have hidden there. And if there are more in the cave, then all the better for me."

Nafarah and Kassab escorted them out into the hot, bright glare of the midday sun. Kassab put the suitcase from Rasul Taj in the trunk of the Cadillac. Father Mhand remained behind, locked in Aboudi's small office, the gun and the Egyptian who carried it, his only company. Nafarah handed the museum curator a handful of folded paper money as they left the museum steps.

Nick, Katherine, Muhanna and Etienne crowded into the back of Nafarah's long black car. They spoke not a word to each other. Kassab drove the dusty road to Deir al-Bahri, while Nafarah, from the passenger seat, pointed a gun at them the entire time. Nick sat silent as a stone, staring across the many waves of sand that loomed for miles around them.

23

THE LONG ROAD BACK

... it is in the giving that we receive;
It is in the pardoning that we are pardoned;
It is in dying to the self that we are born to eternal life.

– from the Prayer of St. Francis

Deir al-Bahri, outside Luxor

The grand, architectural spectacle of Hatshepsut's Temple rose as if half by nature and half by labor from the desert plain. It dominated the landscape as the black Cadillac rounded the last series of sand dunes into the bottom of the valley. Hatshepsut's Temple merged in a series of terraces with the sheer limestone cliffs of the Theban Mountain behind it.

Built in the New Kingdom, when Egypt was at the peak of its military power, Hatshepsut dedicated this temple to her father, Tuthmosis I. The massive funerary complex was cut partly from the mountain rock and was partly freestanding, with two levels of columned buildings separated by three lavish terraces. A ramp sloped from the sandy ground to the highest terrace. Tourists flocked to this site, one of the most stunning monuments of ancient Egypt.

Nafarah ushered his captives through the meandering crowd, with a firm grip on Nick's shoulder. Kassab followed behind with Muhanna, Katherine and Etienne, his hand resting on his hip, inside his jacket and just above his gun. Nick led the way up the wide ramp to the second colonnade. As they passed the lower terrace they could see delicate reliefs and exquisite carvings that told the stories of Hatshepsut's reign. Tragically, every figure of the woman ruler had been chiseled from the walls, leaving only her shadow behind.

As they entered the central court, Etienne began to speak. "Hatshepsut rose to power amid a bitter and vengeful controversy," he explained. "Following the death of Tuthmosis I, almost 2,500 years ago, the Pharaoh's daughter, Hatshepsut, and his grandson, Tuthmosis III, fought over the right to the throne. The formidable Hatshepsut eventually won the struggle and declared herself Pharaoh. She was the first woman ever in the history of Egypt to rule as king." He winked at Katherine. It did not ease the tension in her face.

"Hatshepsut ruled for 20 years, and for Egypt it was a time of peace and growth. It is not known how she died – whether by natural causes or at the hands of her enemies, led by Tuthmosis III."

As they walked solemnly through the central court, they saw the wall carvings that depicted Hatshepsut's 'divine' birth, her coronation and her life. The carvings were many, and detailed with images of Egyptian life and bounty from the Nile. The 2,500-year old colors of red and yellow and blue, though fading, still hinted at a time of glory, pageantry and extraordinary wealth. Each and every image of the woman king, however, had been scraped from the temple, picked away by a mason's sharp tools and obliterated.

"Why?" asked Katherine as she touched the wall briefly. "What was the point of this?"

"*Vengeance*," answered Etienne. "She had made Tuthmosis III wait 20 years to ascend the throne of Egypt, and he insisted on his revenge."

"Move along," growled Kassab.

They picked up their pace, but Etienne continued. "Her image has only been heightened by the petty and destructive acts of her rival. Tuthmosis III has gone down in history as a weak and vague and vengeful ruler, who led his country only to war. She, however, is remembered for more than the building of this great monument. She is remembered for her tremendous power, her vision, her genius. And for her courage. She will never be forgotten."

At the end of his story, through fearful eyes, Katherine smiled briefly at Etienne.

They finally reached a narrow archway in the back of the central chamber. A sign, suspended from a rope across the entrance, read, CLOSED. Nick reached for a torch burning in a sconce, which was intended just for show, on the stone wall near the door of the chapel. A museum employee quickly moved to intercept him. "I say there," he began. "That area is off limits to vis–." He said no more. Nafarah reached inside his jacket pocket and pulled out his identification. He flashed it in the face of the startled employee as he pulled back his suit coat to reveal his silver gun. The museum employee nodded without a word and scurried to the far side of the colonnade.

Nick led the way inside the Chapel of Hathor. The room was filled with hieroglyphics and delicate carvings, all devoted to the daughter of Ra, the falcon-headed sun god who was the god of creation. Hathor was the goddess of joy and love, shown in the carvings with cow horns on her head. Between the horns sat a disk, representing the sun. In ancient Egypt, Hathor was known as the protector of women and travelers. Nick knew this when he picked this particular place in the temple.

"Where's the codex?" demanded Nafarah.

Nick placed the torch in a sconce on the inside wall of the chapel and moved to a large, rectangular altar in the back of the room. The altar was imposing, made of solid, pink granite and, other than minor chipping along its edges, not a crack or divot could be found on it. Nick hoisted himself up and sat irreverently on the ancient block, which served in its day as a place of offerings and sacrifices. Above the altar, an undamaged figure of Hatshepsut worshipped the cow-goddess, Hathor. Somehow the enemies of the woman king had overlooked, or spared, this particular chapel.

"Let them go," said Nick, folding his hands carefully in his lap. "And I will give you the codex."

Nafarah laughed in his face. "Just give it to me."

"No."

Nafarah withdrew his gun and leveled it at Nick. Katherine's breath caught in her throat and she started, instinctively, to move toward her husband. Nick held out his arm to stop her. "I know where Muhanna's cave is," he said to Nafarah, taking up the thread of Muhanna's fib. "I know where the *Gospel of Thomas* and the other two books are hidden. And I alone can lead you to the manuscript in this temple. Let my wife and my friends leave."

Nafarah cocked his pistol. "I will not ask again."

"Katherine, leave this place, *now*," instructed Nick, with a tone as calm and commanding as if he himself was holding the gun to Nafarah's head. "Etienne – take her out of here."

Kassab pulled out his gun to stop them, but neither Etienne nor Katherine had moved, transfixed by the confrontation. Their eyes darted between Nick and Nafarah fearing that the Egyptian would simply lose all restraint in his mounting anger and frustration, and shoot Nick dead. *It would only take one split second,* thought Etienne. *One tiny little amount of pressure on the trigger...*

Nafarah spoke over the top of his gun with deadly certainty. "I will tear down every stone of this temple if I have to, but I will find that codex. And your dying will go much easier if you cooperate with me."

Nick was silent. It was as though nobody dared to breathe, as fear and anticipation grew larger than the room they occupied. Katherine's face was pale and ghostly in the flickering light of the chapel. *Is this our fate?* she wondered desperately. *To die in this disfigured temple? To lose Nick forever in a moment of stubbornness and rage?* "Please don't shoot." Her voice came out as barely a whisper. "Please."

"I *will* shoot you," breathed Nafarah in response, who hadn't, for even a second, taken his eyes off Nick.

"You will shoot us all in the end," snapped Nick impatiently. "Or worse, put us in prison. What have we to gain?" Nick rose from the altar. "Find the codex yourself. We're leaving."

He brushed past Nafarah and reached for Katherine's arm. For a moment, Nick thought they actually might walk themselves out the door. Then, an ice-cold hand grabbed his neck and pulled him back. Nafarah threw Nick against the altar. The impact brought Nick to his knees. He groaned as waves of pain rippled down his back and through his legs. He felt weak and sick as he struggled to stand up, his bones pounding. Katherine, her face a mask of worry, moved to help him. He stood up, leaning against the altar, his wife at his side.

"This is my promise to you, thief," spat Nafarah. "When the codices are mine – each and every one of them – you shall go free, all of you." He looked around the crowded room. "Except Etienne Desonia. He is an enemy of the state and will stay in my custody. The rest of you shall go free. Muhanna Ali al-Samara, you will go back to your village and forget all that you have seen. And you two –" He pointed his gun between Katherine and Nick. "You will go straight back to America and never, *ever* come back to this land."

"Take his offer, Nick," said Etienne bluntly. "*Now.* Take Katherine and Muhanna and go."

380

Nick considered Nafarah's words carefully. Then he looked down at the floor and shook his head. "Etienne was once my friend. That's not true any more." Somewhere between longing and shame, Katherine and Etienne exchanged glances. Nick looked straight up at Nafarah. "But Etienne will come with me. And we will leave Egypt, together."

They all stood in silence and tense anticipation, waiting for Nafarah to respond. Nick didn't take his eyes from Nafarah's, but stared at him with a grim resolution that reached far back beyond this one confrontation and left no room for compromise. After a silence so thick and wearing that Katherine thought she couldn't stand another second of it, Nafarah lowered his gun. "I accept," he said.

Nick didn't entirely believe him, but there was nothing more he could do for the moment. So he stared at Nafarah a few moments longer, as if to ratify the agreement in both of their minds. Slowly, in a fair amount of physical pain, Nick knelt before the pink granite altar. The giant block of stone was supported about five inches above the ground by four granite bricks, one at each corner. Nick reached his arm far underneath, and withdrew a thin box – the box that Henri had given him. He sat back on his haunches and handed the codex up to Nafarah. The blaze of the torch danced on the chapel walls and Hatshepsut worshipped in the golden ribbons of its glow. *We have lost another codex,* thought Nick. *And Nelson is going to be furious.*

As they descended the long ramp to the lower terrace, Nafarah issued orders. "We will sleep in Luxor tonight. Tomorrow morning we will go to al-Qasr, and from there to the caves." He held the codex in his hands and spoke with great confidence. "I will shoot anyone on the spot who tries to escape. This, I promise you."

That is the one promise I believe, thought Nick. Outside, Nick breathed in the fresh, dry air of the late afternoon. He walked slowly away from Nafarah and the group, to where lush myrrh trees once stood, surrounded by garden beds of colorful and heady-scented flowers. One look back at his wife and friends, and Nick leaned over and threw up in the sand.

Luxor, Egypt

Katherine looked at her husband beyond the dark barrier she had built as if he was a complete stranger. In all their years together, she had never seen Nick like he was at the Temple of Hatshepsut. It made her wonder what Nick really did do during the war. *What duties to God and country,* she wondered, *had he experienced to make him so incredibly, unflinchingly brave?* Katherine hadn't talked much to Nick after their great fight, or even really looked him in the eyes, but she was noticing everything, as if they had both inadvertently wandered under a monocle of the soul.

Kassab drove into Luxor from Deir al-Bahri, and parked the car in front of a small stone building. "Get out," ordered Nafarah. They all tumbled out of the Cadillac weary and uncertain. There were bars on the windows of the building, and it suddenly occurred to Katherine where they were. "You don't mean to keep us in jail!" she said, instinctively backing away.

"Yes, in fact, I do." Nafarah grabbed her by the neck and pushed her toward the door. The police station was situated on a side street adjacent to the Avenue of the Sphinxes. Little remained of the once massive carvings, like so much of ancient Egypt – incomprehensibly old. Katherine found herself longing for something new and whole and safe. "I can't possibly stay in jail," she insisted.

Kassab stepped forward. "You would rather sleep between soft, cool sheets, have a hot meal, and have no worry of snakes and scorpions in the corners of your cell..."

"Frankly, yes," she admitted.

Nafarah's smirk gave Kassab permission to go further. "Very well, then," he said, taking her by the arm. "Come with me ..."

"No!" Katherine pulled away. Nick moved to her side. Etienne stepped in front of both of them.

"*Bien, bien,*" said Etienne, extending his hands. "We will stay here tonight. And tomorrow you will have the last of the codices."

Nafarah smiled and escorted them into the stone building that housed the strict and humorless authority of Luxor. Father Mhand was delivered from the Luxor Museum in good condition and fair spirits. Together they were placed under the watchful eyes of the Luxor sheriff. Nafarah, Kassab and the other gunman would rest comfortably at the nearby Nefertiti Hotel.

"Yes," said Nafarah, staring at Etienne through distant eyes. "When tomorrow's day ends, my business with you will be finished. Forever." There was a surprising note of longing in Nafarah's voice.

He strode away as they were handed over to the local police and led to their cell.

Dawn broke early in the stark cell of the Luxor jailhouse. They had not slept well, but they all slept together on cots in the same large room with its one wall of bars, safe for the time being. Katherine woke to the eastward sun burning in her eyes, and the familiar rumble of Etienne's jeep outside the barred window. She rose stiff and weary, and rubbed at the grains of sleep in her eyes. The others roused themselves as well, seeming so much less unhappy than Katherine felt.

"My kingdom for a cup of coffee," she grumbled, her brown hair tousled all around her. "I feel awful."

Muhanna went quietly to the window, making certain of his position to the east, toward Mecca. He circled to the furthest corner of the small room, and took off the sandals he'd slept in. Holding them sole to sole in his left hand, he walked barefoot to the opposite wall. He placed his sandals on the floor below the small basin and slowly washed his hands.

Facing the direction of the sun low in the sky, he unwrapped the red scarf from his neck and laid it with precision and care on the rough stone floor. Muhanna Ali al-Samara then bent to his knees and stretched his hands and arms in front of him. He bowed his head down, touching his forehead to the ground.

"Praise be to Allah," he began softly. *"Lord of the Worlds, the Beneficent, the Merciful, Owner of the Day of Judgment, Thee alone we worship; Thee alone we ask for help. Show us the straight path, the path of those whom Thou hast favoured; not the path of those who earn Thine anger nor of those who go astray."* Muhanna remained for many long minutes, rhythmically reciting the first passages of *The Koran*, the Seven of the Oft Repeated, the verses that contained within them the essence of the holy book of Islam, without which no prayer was complete.

Nick pulled Katherine aside as Etienne stepped with Father Mhand to the bars to watch the front door. "Here," said Nick, taking her hand. "Take this. It may very well save your life." He pressed a small gold key into her hand.

"What is it?" she whispered.

"The bus station on the Corniche," said Nick, barely audible. "To a locker there."

"Why?" began Katherine.

"The three missing codices are there." The jangling of keys and the voice of Cato Nafarah interrupted them. Nick put his finger to Katherine's lips. "Shhh." Katherine turned her back to the bars and slipped the key into the front pocket of her dusty khaki pants.

Nafarah stepped up to the bars and cleared his throat. "*Sabah al-kher*. Good morning."

"I am getting weary of this man," Muhanna mumbled as he brought himself to his feet. "Will we ever be rid of him?"

"Soon, soon," assured Father Mhand, helping Muhanna up. "Soon we will be home and happy, and all will be well."

"I hope you are right, Father," said Etienne. "I most sincerely hope you are right."

They collected nervously around the jeep, which Kassab had driven to the police station. Kassab was conducting a thorough search of the jeep while they stood under the warm morning sun and looked on. Kassab rifled through all their supplies and then checked under the seats for any kind of weapon. Satisfied, he gave a nod to Nafarah.

"I will let you drive yourselves," announced Nafarah, feeling benevolent after a good night's sleep and a sumptuous breakfast. He was also feeling very near to the completion of the challenge that had consumed his career. "We shall follow you. But if you try the slightest diversion," he added without humor, "I will happily gun you all down."

As the two cars wound northward along the Nile, the day passed in indifferent heat. That sun had seen many evolutions of human life and suffering under the building and destruction of numerous dynasties, one after the other, over the many centuries. It would not pause today over the drama of this small group of rivals. But the wind blew. It came up suddenly and stayed with them throughout their trip north.

"So, Nick," said Etienne, out of nowhere. "Want to tell me what you were planning to do with the codices you stole?"

The hot dry wind swirled around them, angry, unsettled.

"I was going to give them to Hugo Nelson," Nick stated flatly.

"Oh, you were, were you?"

"Yes, I was."

"I can't say I'm entirely surprised."

"No, I don't suppose so."

"So then, want to tell us all how Nelson got the Knife of the Asps from the crate I shipped to Katherine?"

"What would I know about that?" Nick asked, scowling.

"Who else *would* know, Nick?" replied Etienne. "Only four people knew where the dagger was: me, Katherine, the potter I'd hired to conceal it, and ... *you.*"

"Then why don't you ask your potter friend?"

"For one, he's not my friend. For two, I don't need to."

"And why's that?" asked Nick.

"Because I know it was you."

"Oh, that's rubbish! You're just making all this up for Katherine's benefit."

"Am I?" asked Etienne. "Or have you been in contact with Nelson all along – through a hired courier? In Cairo, al-Qasr and Luxor? Is Nelson not sending Father Antonio to find us everywhere we go? To take the manuscripts from us?"

"I think too many years in the desert have fried your brain, Etienne. Or are you so desperate to have Katherine that you'll go to this extreme? Get a hold of yourself."

"You gave up the Knife of the Asps to Hugo Nelson," continued Etienne. "And you have been fighting me this whole time to make sure Nelson gets his cache in the end. You met a messenger, the same young boy, in every city we've been to so far."

"That's true," said Katherine, feeling a sense of dread descend on her like a heavy, gray veil. "I saw the same boy as well."

"Just tell me why," said Etienne. "What has Nelson got over you?"

Nick was silent for a long time. Katherine was anxiously waiting for him to tear into Etienne, to tell him he was wrong, and conniving and cruel, to explain himself. But Nick did none of those things. He just sat there and let sound of the wind orchestrate the overture of his undoing.

"Nick?" said Katherine. "Say something. Speak up for God's sake."

Nick looked back at his wife with an expression of such longing, it rocked her to her bones. Then he began to speak. "I knew Nelson in the war, as you know. He and I were stationed for a while in Chamonix, a small village in France, bordering Italy. British intelligence was there on surveillance. So was a group of Americans, patrolling the border.

"I knew nothing of Father Antonio then, but I now suspect that Nelson did. I now believe that the priest was Nelson's contact, his courier, if you will, slipping Allied secrets to the enemy. As for this business in Egypt, I suspect that Nelson has hired Father Antonio, and the Italians, as sort of a back up plan." Nick laughed bitterly. "Nelson always has a back up plan."

Katherine felt desperation rising in her stomach. Between the episode at Hatshepsut's temple and this outrageous story, she could not recognize the man she'd known for almost 15 years. The man she'd slept with, dreamt with, cooked for, spent her days and nights and body with.

Nick went on. "We got to know each other, Nelson and I, though we were an unlikely pair: the intelligence officer and the supply clerk. Somehow though, Nelson seemed to be everywhere, know everything. We drank together, talked, argued about politics, simple stuff, innocent enough. Then I was sent back to HQ in London and didn't see him for months after that. Not until Tenerife." Nick glanced back at his wife again, the same look of longing on his face.

"What?" demanded Katherine. She felt her face grow hot and noticed that her insides had started to shake. "What happened in Tenerife?"

Nick turned his eyes forward, no longer able to look at her. "I made a mistake," he said. "One stupid, drunk, unforgivable mistake. It didn't mean anything, of course. No one should ever have been the wiser. Even I would have forgotten about it, long before now. Except for Nelson. Nelson has photographs."

"Photographs of what, exactly?" asked Katherine. Her heart was nearly pounding out of her chest in anticipation of a confession she didn't want to hear, could hardly believe, and knew was coming.

"I was set up," said Nick. "Nelson sent a woman to ..." he shook his head at the memory, increasingly unable to shake it away. "... talk and giggle. To pour me another beer and another and another. With shots of whiskey in between. To lead me to her room. To undress for me. And then to undress me. I was half out of my mind from liquor."

"You slept with someone?" The words physically hurt to say out loud.

"I'm sorry, Katherine," he said. "My God, I can't tell you how sorry I am."

"That doesn't help," she said, as if anything could.

Etienne tried to intervene. "And you suspect Nelson set you up?" he asked.

"Nelson arranged the whole sordid thing. When I returned to HQ, I received an envelope, with photographs in it. Of me and the girl. And I have been under Nelson's thumb ever since."

"Why you?" asked Etienne.

"Because I was in Intelligence. I knew things. And he was a traitor."

"And he blackmailed you?" asked Etienne, a cloud crossing his face.

"Yes."

"You gave away war secrets?" An anger, a long forgotten rage, began to rise inside Etienne.

"Yes," said Nick, flatly. "I did."

"Damn you," exclaimed Etienne under his breath. "God damn you to Hell."

"Oh, don't get so bloody self-righteous, Etienne. The intelligence I gave him was loaded – imprecise at best. Plain wrong,

387

sometimes. Or right information that was old, or half true. Nelson could accomplish very little with the secrets I gave him. And in some instances, it worked to the Allied advantage. We could anticipate Nazi movements, based on the strategic 'facts' I gave Nelson. He wasn't an entirely successful saboteur. But he didn't care – he made himself filthy stinking rich by trying. He traded information for Jewish art and gold, which he had shipped to Switzerland. After the war, he claimed a fortune, returned to America, and built an empire of power on top of that fortune."

Etienne sighed. "I understand," he said quietly. "And Nelson always had something to hold over you, didn't he?"

"I lived in fear that someday Nelson would re-appear, to collect another pound of flesh." Nick looked straight at Etienne. "That day turned out to be the day you called Katherine."

"Did you know Father Antonio was going to *kidnap* me? Push me around? Threaten me?" snapped Katherine. "Was that part of your rotten little plan?"

"No! God no," replied Nick desperately. "I was outraged. I would have killed the priest on the spot. I didn't know who he was in Tenerife, or on the airplane for that matter. It was all Nelson's doing, behind my back."

"What does Nelson plan to do with the manuscripts?" asked Etienne.

"Destroy them. He feels they'll undermine Christianity, Catholicism in particular, and an ordered society. He's truly a fanatic."

"So he called in your debt," said Etienne. "And you told him exactly where to find the dagger – in the statue of Isis."

"That's about it," said Nick flatly. "And when he takes possession of the 13 manuscripts, I will be free of my obligations to him, forever."

"But that's not going to happen now, is it?" said Etienne.

"Nope." Nick sat in a dark and stony silence after that, not looking anywhere except into the past, maybe into the future.

Katherine did the same, and everything that she considered of the then and now and would-be of her life, came from an imagination tortured with doubt. No one else in the jeep could bear to look at her, for the anguish that rose and fell on her face was private, and painful to see.

"I simply cannot *believe* you," she blurted out after they'd gone several miles in silence.

"I know you can't," replied Nick in a tone she'd never heard before. "I've been trying to live up to who you thought I was all this time, and all this time, keeping this terrible secret from you."

Their private conversations had become a court of public confession. Father Mhand, Muhanna and Etienne would become their witnesses, their silent defenders, and perhaps even their judges. In speaking out, Nick had twice broken a covenant of silence that both he and Katherine had agreed to, and comforted themselves with, for over a decade of time.

"Sometimes I thought I could actually keep this secret from you forever," continued Nick. "That you would die not knowing. Frankly, it comes as something of a relief that you know. The crown has slipped. I've committed the unforgivable. And somehow I'm still here, breathing."

It was, perhaps, the first time in Katherine's life that she had nothing to say. She thought she should be screaming or yelling or crying, but she couldn't do any of those things. All she could do was sit there, a woman betrayed, in the company of men above such betrayal. Every thing she ever thought about herself, about her place in the world, had changed in an instant.

With hands that shook like an old woman's, Katherine lit a cigarette. She suppressed an impulse to hurt Nick, to pound her fists into his body until her rage was spent. Instead, she sat back and imagined the tryst of her beloved in all its torturous variations. She never suspected such a thing, not in the least. And that made her question her own judgement. More: it brought to light a glaring hole in the armor of her security. The only defense against abandonment, Katherine had learned, was being fully aware that it was coming. Her only protection was in the naming of it, and in doing so, becoming its master.

Despair grew in Katherine for all that was lost. She felt a crushing grief for all that could never again be made whole. But she could not say a word out loud about any of it. There were no words she knew of that were big enough to wrap around her regret. Nothing on earth could fix what had been broken.

Katherine didn't know if she would ever be able to sort out her understanding of this, or reconcile the bitterness, and the trading of sins. For the time being, she just sat there smoking cigarettes, one after the next. The next few hours went by in silence.

Finally, the Nile pitched sharply to the east in a hook that resembled a giant question mark on the landscape before it flowed west into al-Qasr. There the winds settled. Soon they would be at the caves, with nothing to save them from Nafarah but the truth.

Etienne broke the silent pall inside the jeep. "Nafarah would have been wise to separate us."

"He knows we are helpless," began Katherine, in a bitter, sarcastic tone of voice, which didn't come close to matching how she felt. "What does he care? He'll shoot us all dead when we get to the caves anyway. Or have you people conveniently forgotten that there are no codices there?"

"Nafarah knows we are helpless, for now," said Etienne, calmly. His cool manner managed to heighten Katherine's anger. "But when we get to the caves, well, there are only two of them, and five of us."

"Maybe you should drop me off at my church," suggested Father Mhand.

"Me, too," added Muhanna hastily.

Etienne couldn't suppress his smile. "What about the al-Yassids?"

"Bah! We will we go on fighting and killing and fighting long after we have forgotten what began it all." Muhanna shrugged. "It is our way."

"Yes – what about the al-Yassids?" repeated Nick. "What about them?"

"As I said," began Muhanna, "We will –"

"No, no, I have an idea," said Nick. "What if we did leave Father Mhand in al-Qasr? And what if Father Mhand let slip to the sheriff that Muhanna was up at the caves? And what if the al-Yassids came to those caves while we were there?" Everyone waited in anticipation. Except for Katherine. She stared out the window, pretending to ignore him. Nick looked at the others. "Well?" he asked, goading them on.

"Well?" Muhanna raised his hands. "This does not sound like such a good idea to me."

"It may provide a useful distraction," offered Etienne.

Father Mhand nodded his head vigorously. "Yes. I will go straight to Sheriff Hussayn and tell him where you are, Muhanna. And that if he and his cousins go in haste ..."

"It's a long shot," said Etienne. "But it may just give us a chance. One little chance. Besides *this*." Etienne reached under his seat, groped around, and pulled out a revolver: small, black and loaded with bullets.

"Where did you get that?" asked Katherine. "How did they miss it when they searched the jeep?"

"I hid it really well," said Etienne with a sideways grin.

"Oh, and we always have *this*." Nick lifted his pant leg where another gun was strapped to his calf.

"You've had that the whole time?" Katherine was getting madder and madder.

"It's Father Antonio's gun," said Nick.

"Why didn't you use it yesterday?" she asked.

"I would've, if I'd had to," he said. "But I thought I'd save it for a rainy day."

Katherine didn't know when, or if, she would be able to forgive Nick. She didn't know if she wanted to. She'd spent the last five hours trying to hate him, to make him guilty for every thing that was wrong with her life, or in their marriage. But Katherine was guilty, too. She had distanced herself from her husband over the years. She had lied, stolen, and loved another. Who was the most guilty? Did it matter? Could they rise above any of it? All of it?

"Well done, Nick!" said Etienne, smiling. "The advantage is shifting," He slipped his gun deep into his pant's pocket, and settled back into his seat. "Nafarah would have been wise to separate us," he said, looking very pleased with himself, as they pulled into the dusty village of al-Qasr.

al-Qasr, Upper Egypt

Etienne parked the jeep in front of the Coptic Church in al-Qasr. The black Cadillac was crunching to a slow stop behind them on the dirt road. Taya, the caretaker of the church, rushed out to meet them. He stood humbly in the street, his head bowed as Father Mhand lifted himself from the back seat. When the Coptic priest went over to the small and bent man, and embraced him in his arms, the caretaker wept openly, his face a mask of relief, his bright blue eyes moist in the sunlight. Taya nodded his head. "Welcome home," he said, his voice cracking. He nodded again. "Welcome back home." Muhanna followed them inside the church.

Outside, Nick, Katherine and Etienne leaned casually against the jeep, as if waiting aimlessly for overdue friends. Katherine puffed on a Balkan Sobranie, examining her fingernails, annoyed that the red polish was chipping. "Lunch?" offered Etienne, as Nafarah stepped slowly out of the back seat of his car. "I'm starving."

"Shut up!" snapped Nafarah. "Where are the priest and the little man?"

"In the church," explained Nick. "Making lunch, I hope."

"Get inside," ordered Nafarah, pulling out his gun, his eyes darting up and down the quiet street. They all entered the dark cool sanctuary of the little church. Taya had restored the damage done by Father Antonio and his gang, and a rough hewn cross was again hanging over the altar. Candles warmed the room with their feathery light. A reverent stillness hung in the air.

"You can put your gun away," said Father Mhand quietly as he approached them in fresh robes. "This is a church. You will find no resistance here."

"We will eat here," ordered Nafarah, who was as hungry as the rest. "Then we will go straight to the caves. You," he pointed at Muhanna. "You will lead us there in my car. I will ride in the jeep with the others."

"Now there is some good news," mumbled Muhanna.

"Fine, fine," said Father Mhand. "Taya will make a nice lunch for us." Taya hurried to the rectory, a small building of mud bricks, behind the church.

"Kassab," instructed Nafarah. "Search them."

"Why?" said Katherine with desperation in her eyes. "What's the point?" Nick and Etienne looked at each other, trapped and guilty. Nafarah sat back in a wooden pew and rested his gun on his knee. Kassab moved to Nick first, as the gunman kept anyone from resisting with the barrel of his weapon. Nick gritted his teeth as Kassab patted him down, eventually producing the pistol strapped to his leg. Kassab held it up like an unexpected gift – a token to trade for Nafarah's approval.

"Where did he get that, I wonder?" asked Etienne. He moved to the pew and sat down next to Nafarah, as though they were allies and Nick the lone offender. Nafarah lifted his gun from his knee, clicked back the hammer and leveled it at Etienne's head. "Get up," he ordered, his voice without amusement. Etienne didn't budge from his seat, however, but stared at Nafarah with a defiant expression. *What are you going to do now, you son of a bitch?* goaded Etienne silently. Nafarah's face was drawn into an angry, hateful scowl.

Kassab intervened on his boss' behalf and grabbed Etienne roughly by the collar. He pulled Etienne from the pew and threw him against a painted column in the aisle. Etienne grinned at them both as he regained his balance. Kassab approached him with some hesitation, but within moments, he found the gun in Etienne's pocket. Another prize for his boss. Nafarah set the guns beside him on the pew and smiled.

Kassab then moved to Katherine. "Don't touch me, you dog!" she spat. Kassab hesitated.

"Search her," demanded Nafarah.

Kassab took his time. Katherine stared directly at him the whole time his hands covered her body and lingered where he desired. Etienne put his hand on Nick's arm and silently shook his head, joining him in a combined effort of restraint.

When Kassab was done, Katherine raised her hand and slapped him across the face. Kassab raised the back of his hand as if to strike her, and when he glanced at his boss for approval, Nafarah gave it. Katherine went sprawling across the stone floor.

"Search the villager," demanded Nafarah, as Nick went to his wife's side and helped her to her feet. Together they sat in a nearby pew, where Katherine collapsed in a heap, where Katherine sat in a smoldering pit of rage.

Etienne looked at Nafarah with a new and deepening anger in his eyes. *The game you've been playing is over,* raged Etienne silently. *Now, it is I who have had enough of it.*

Kassab rubbed his own reddening cheek and cast a scalding look at Katherine, even as he moved toward Muhanna. Muhanna uttered curses in Arabic under his breath as Kassab searched him with some amount of distaste. It took no time at all to produce the knife that Muhanna had secretly and silently been carrying ever since they left his home, so seemingly long ago.

"How did you miss that in Luxor?" demanded Nafarah. Kassab shrugged in embarrassment, all his good efforts washed away in one moment of failure. He hadn't searched Muhanna thoroughly back in Luxor, because in truth, the little man reminded him of his own humble beginnings as a butcher's son, and had repelled him.

"If I find one more weapon on you people," snapped Nafarah, "I'm going to use it on one of you." But there were no more weapons to be found.

"I will go help Taya prepare the lunch," said Father Mhand, walking slowly to the back of the church. Minutes later, he and Taya brought out plates of cold roasted chicken, pita bread, nuts, dates and sweet semolina cakes. They ate in silence and washed down their lunch with ceremonial wine. Taya and Father Mhand also brought out water flasks that they could take with them to the caves.

As Nafarah dabbed the last stain of grease from his lips with his cloth napkin, he stood and raised his gun. "It is time." Nafarah turned to the gunman. "You stay here, with the priest. I want no surprises from him. Do not let him leave the church."

Etienne looked at Nick helplessly.

Nick, who'd been thumbing absently through a Bible from the church pew, looked at Etienne and snapped the Bible shut. "I have to use the water closet, urgently," he said.

"Me too," added Etienne.

"Kassab, go with them," said Nafarah, narrowing his eyes. "Shoot them on the spot if they try anything funny. Anything at all."

"*Merde,*" Etienne whispered to no one but the lifeless portraits watching over them. Father Mhand would have to be very clever to somehow get word to the sheriff about their location. It was their last hope for a distraction, and only chance to take the advantage. Etienne didn't know if the old priest would be up to such a task.

Nick and Etienne used the stalls, which provided some degree of privacy from Kassab, who stood at the urinal.

"Got any toilet paper over there?" asked Nick. "I'm out over here."

"Sure," said Etienne, handing a wad of tissue under the stall.

Several seconds passed before Nick said, "Oh, never mind. Here's a roll I didn't see. You can have this back." Nick passed the handful of tissue back under the stall to Etienne.

"No, really," said Etienne. "Keep it."

"I wouldn't want to waste it, really," insisted Nick. "You use it."

"How thoughtful of you," said Etienne, rolling his eyes. But he looked twice when he took the tissue back, for it was folded neatly into fourths, instead of wadded all up, as it was when he passed it to Nick.

Etienne unfolded the tissue and saw that Nick had scribbled something on it in pencil – a pencil he snagged from the pew where he and Katherine had been sitting.

Etienne read a long string of numbers and letters:

10-33.6057234474.1SAM22.1.

"Father Mhand sure is a great fellow, isn't he?" said Nick, over the stall. "We'll have to call him when we get through all this. I imagine he has a telephone in the rectory, don't you?"

Etienne looked again. "I'm sure of it," he replied, smiling. He didn't know what the code meant, but he knew his assignment. He folded the tissue into a small square and closed his hand around it.

Kassab banged his gun of the door of the stall. "It will serve you better," he jeered, "to make less conversation and greater haste."

"What?" asked Nick and Etienne in unison.

"Get moving!" They did just that, and Kassab followed them back into the sanctuary. They gathered into a group and prepared to leave. Etienne went to Father Mhand. "Thank you for all you've done for us," he said. "We couldn't have asked for more." Etienne placed his hand in the priest's and shook it warmly.

Katherine, Nick, Muhanna and Etienne walked in single file from the church into the bright hot light of the day. Kassab escorted Muhanna to the black car. "I have always wanted to ride in one of these," said Muhanna. "May I drive it?" Kassab shoved him into the passenger seat and slammed the door behind him.

"Get in," said Nafarah, waving his gun toward the jeep. Etienne took the wheel. Katherine sat directly behind Etienne in the back seat and Nick sat next to her. Nafarah moved into the front passenger seat, his gun aimed at Etienne.

Father Mhand hurried from the church, flanked by the true and faithful Taya. The priest walked up to Kassab's car and passed a mattock through the window to Muhanna. "You'll need this, Muhanna," said the priest, winking. "If you're going digging for treasure again at Jabal al-Tarif."

Then Father Mhand approached the jeep. "Blessings to you all," he said.

"Enough!" snapped Nafarah. "We are leaving!" He raised his gun to Etienne's head. "Drive."

"They may not see tomorrow's dawn," insisted Father Mhand softly. "They have a right to be blessed."

Nafarah glared at the unwavering priest, but he lowered his weapon. "Be quick about it then."

"Etienne," said the Father Mhand, coming to the driver's side of the vehicle. "Your way lies in distant lands. Always take God with you. And never forget that He is your home. Then you will never be lost." Etienne touched Father Mhand on the arm and smiled into his wrinkled eyes.

Then the priest moved to Katherine. "Go with God," he said, laying his hand softly on her head. "In life there is always loss. It is God's way. It is how he makes us worthy of Him. May you recover that which is truly most precious to you, my dear. I think it is not where you've been looking for it."

"Thank you, Father." Katherine kissed his hand and held it to her cheek. If she survived this day, Katherine would miss the gentle priest. Besides Ben, the brother of her youth, Father Mhand was the first man that she let wholly into her heart. He would, quite possibly, be the last.

Father Mhand shuffled to the other side of the jeep. "Nicholas, I will finish for you the ancient Dzogchen saying which I began in Cairo. Listen now: *As a bee seeks nectar from all kinds of flowers, seek teachings everywhere. Like the deer who finds a quiet place to graze, seek seclusion to digest all you have gathered.*" Father Mhand winked at Nick through a warm smile, reached within the folds of his robe, and placed a gun on the floor of the jeep. *"And like a madman, beyond all limits, go wherever you please, and live like the lion, completely free of all fear."*

"I will Father," said Nick quietly. "Thank you."

"Enough already," Nafarah nudged Etienne with his gun. "Get moving!" Etienne started the engine.

"Blessings on you, too, Mr. Nafarah," said Father Mhand. "Remember that hatred will bind you forever to those you call enemy, and eventually it will destroy –"

"Get away from me." Nafarah pushed the old priest aside.

Nick tucked the gun into his leg holster while Katherine tried to look nonchalant and Etienne pulled the jeep away from the stone church. Kassab and Muhanna pulled out in front of them, and Etienne followed closely behind.

Father Mhand and Taya looked on, long after the caravan had disappeared. "God, go with them," said the elderly priest, over and over and over. When the dust settled on the horizon, only then did Father Mhand unfold the note that Etienne had pressed into his hand:

10-33.6057234474.1SAM22.1

The priest studied the configuration of numbers and letters for a few moments and then broke into a broad smile. He knew exactly what to do.

24

CAVES OF THE HEART

You said live *out* loud, *and* die *you said lightly,*
and over and over you said be.

– Rainer Maria Rilke

Jabal al-Tarif

Muhanna looked up at the cliff of Jabal al-Tarif rising against an endless blue sky. It towered over their small group – ominous, silent, enduring – holding the secrets of a thousand generations. The lowering sun cast long shadows on the valley floor in the waning hours of the afternoon.

Muhanna gazed passed the split boulders and searched the talus for a large, deep cave. He held his mattock at his side, the way he did almost two years ago, when he and his brothers first dug there. That day he had felt only the never-ending pressure of feeding his family, his hatred for the al-Yassids, and a certainty in his own, predictable future. Today he felt the breath of Allah on his face, and knew as clearly as the sky, that this day would not unfold without the imposition of God's will. *As,* he reminded himself, *every day unfolds.* He could not help, however, wonder what Allah might be planning for him today, for them all.

Nafarah came over and stood next to Muhanna. "Well?" he demanded.

Muhanna pointed. "It is there," he said. "The cave with the books." The group of six made their way up the sloping talus. Nafarah didn't even noticed the split boulders, where the books had originally been found. At that moment his gun was pressed into the flesh of Muhanna's neck.

"Just up here," said Muhanna. As they passed the boulders, Muhanna couldn't help but glance over. *Where is the jinn now?* he wondered. *Could it work some mischief on our behalf?*

Nick, meanwhile, kept stride with Muhanna and Nafarah. *What will we do?* he wondered. *What on earth will we do, when we get there, and there are no hidden books?* Together they crossed the lip of a large, dark cave.

Etienne stepped forward with two gas lanterns and a box of matchsticks. Nick struck a match across a rock, sending miniscule sparks of sulfur flying through the dark. He looked like a lord of ghosts carrying the match to the lantern. When he lit the wick, the globe radiated a flickering light among the restless group. They all looked like apparitions of Unhappy Fate, their stark faces lit unearthly and their shadows disappearing in the darkness. They shuffled in the eerie stillness, while Nick lit the second lantern. One he handed back to Etienne. One he kept. In the shadowy light, they could see that the cave had many levels, fallen rocks and chambers carved into the mountain wall. It was a tomb, an ending place that would seal the fate of those who entered there.

"So," commanded Nafarah, his voice booming against the walls. "Where are the codices?"

Muhanna hesitated. Nick swung his lantern around the cave. A particular outcropping of stone had shaped itself into somewhat of a down-pointing arrow. Just a triangular rock formation, really, but it caught Nick's immediate attention. "There," he said. "The rock points to the hiding place."

Nafarah snatched up Muhanna's mattock and shoved it at Nick. "Dig," he ordered. "I want you to find those codices. And I want you to find them *now*."

Nick handed his lantern to Muhanna and began digging in the corner of the cave. Muhanna and Etienne stood close over him, but Nafarah moved in and shoved them out of the way. "Stand back!" he barked.

Nick dug steadily with the mattock for many minutes, uncovering a wide patch of earth, while every one shifted nervously in the dim silence of the cave. Nick wondered how long he could dig, how long he could stall the inevitable, and what Nafarah would do when his patience finally ran out for good. No sound came from the cave in those long minutes, nothing but the scraping of the shovel through the packed dirt floor, and the soft sounds of earth falling from the mattock, piling upon itself.

Then Nick's tool struck something. Genuinely curious, he bent over the hole and dug in the dirt with his hands. Something indeed was buried right there, under the pointed rock. Nick traced the ages of it, and then dug underneath it, until he could loosen it from its grave. He drew out a bone, long, thin, and decaying.

"You are digging up a person, not a book!" snapped Nafarah, automatically stepping back.

"These are the bones of an animal," explained Muhanna, kneeling in the sandy dirt with his lantern. "Probably a wild goat."

"I want those codices!" snapped Nafarah. "Not a body; not an animal!"

Muhanna stood up. "I think this may be the wrong cave, after all." Nafarah turned and stared at Muhanna with eyes that seemed to burn right through him. Muhanna shifted uncomfortably, wishing he hadn't been the one to speak up. Nafarah reached inside his suit coat and pulled out his gun. Without a word, without a warning of any kind, he leveled his weapon at Muhanna and pulled the trigger.

The sound echoed on the cave walls and reverberated right through everyone standing. They stood absolutely still, in shock and fear. Muhanna dropped the lantern he was holding, a startled expression frozen on his face. The globe of the lamp shattered on a rock, spraying kerosene across the floor and onto Muhanna. Muhanna looked down at his *jallabiya* and – so slowly that he seemed to be suspended in the air – he dropped to the ground. He broke the terrible silence in the cave when he finally gasped out loud in pain. Blood stained his hands and his clothing and the dirt beneath him.

It was then that the kerosene ignited in a burst of blue flame. It rose suddenly and violently from the earth, as if the Devil himself was being announced. The fire on the dirt floor burned itself out quickly enough, but a fragment of it had found a path to Muhanna. Before anyone could move, the man was on fire.

Nick dropped the mattock, tore off his rumpled cotton jacket and threw it, and himself, on top of Muhanna. Muhanna was now overwhelmed with fear and pain, his eyes darting madly about the cave in anguished helplessness. Nick patted down the flames the best he could and smothered the rest with his weight. Nick knew it was hurting Muhanna to have 190 pounds of grown man flailing around on top of him. But the alternative – to see his friend burned alive, scarred, tortured with fire – was unutterable.

It seemed like an interminable time before Nick could completely smother all the flames. Muhanna's clothes were literally smoking. They could smell the burned cotton, and Nick prayed to whatever powers of Fate and Fortune existed in the universe that Muhanna's flesh was not singed off his bones.

"Oh my God!" cried Katherine, rushing toward them. "Muhanna!"

Nafarah stepped forward, grabbed her with one hand and threw her to the ground. Katherine stared up at Nafarah, rage rising inside her. She wanted to curse this man, to call out his cruelty for Man and God to hear, to name his sins and hold him accountable for them. But fear overcame her anger and she kept silent.

Nick took a closer look, gently pealing back Muhanna's *jallabiya* while the Muslim thrashed on the ground, his distress overtaking him. "Muhanna. Muhanna," said Nick, in a soothing voice. "Try to relax. You're going to be alright." At a glance, the flames seemed only to have singed Muhanna's clothes. His skin, red in splotches, was more irritated than actually burned. Nick found the gun wound, thankfully, in Muhanna's thigh, which was exponentially better than a chest or stomach wound. It was not a clean shot, however, and Nick could find no exit wound on the back of Muhanna's leg. The question also lingered as to whether the bullet shattered any bones, and whether Muhanna would ever be able to walk on this leg again.

That would be for a doctor to determine. Nick's triage skills were reaching their limit, but he took a handkerchief from his pocket and created a tourniquet high on Muhanna's thigh to stop the bleeding. It appeared Muhanna would survive both the fire and the gunshot, if any of them made it out of the cave at all.

Muhanna rolled on the ground, breathing very hard, moaning softy. Coming to his feet, Nick took a hold of Katherine and drew her up behind him. Never more so in her life than in that moment, did Katherine want to be back home. She craved the bright view from her squeaky clean kitchen, the comfort of her worn chair at the little Formica table and the white eyelet curtains blowing in the breeze. The common and the ordinary took on a compelling light, and a comfort, there in the dark reaches of danger.

Nafarah stuck his gun in Nick's face. "Where are the codices?"

Time is up, thought Nick grimly.

Nafarah cocked the hammer of his silver revolver. "*Where?*" he demanded. Nobody moved. "You have *one second* to tell me." Nafarah narrowed his black eyes. "One." Nafarah moved his finger to the trigger.

"Wait!" cried Katherine. "I have the codices." She stepped forward. "I have them."

"No!" said Nick. "Katherine, don't!"

Nafarah did not lower his gun, but kept it aimed at Nick's forehead. "*Where* do you have the books, you lying woman? Hidden in your pocket?"

"Yes, exactly." Katherine withdrew the golden key that Nick had given her in the Luxor jailhouse. "Here. Here are the codices. In a locker, at the bus station at Luxor. Please, please take it."

"Oh, Katherine." Nick hung his head, betrayed in the end by his wife's love.

"I'll take that key."

Everyone in the cave turned to the entrance. The bright light outside silhouetted four dark figures at the wide mouth of the cave. Nick could not help but smile. He recognized that voice completely. Katherine instinctively put the key back into her pocket.

"Who are you?" Nafarah moved the aim of his gun toward the man who spoke. "And why are you so anxious to die this day?"

Father Antonio stepped into the dimly lit cave, adjusting his eyes to the light of the one lantern. His three partners moved in behind him, guns held high, unwavering. "That key belongs to the Holy Mother Church," said Father Antonio coolly.

"That key belongs to the Egyptian Government," spat Nafarah. "And you are merely thieves, trying to steal valuable artifacts of the state. I could kill you where you stand."

"I represent the One God," countered Father Antonio. "Your Egyptian laws are not above the laws of the Church. And you will give me that key."

As they argued, Nick took Katherine's hand and led her to a low rock wall. Behind the wall the ground was sunken, built to house a sarcophagus, thousand of years before. Nick steered Katherine behind the wall, and stood in front of her, on the other side. The wall created something of a ledge, and a barrier to protect Katherine, at least partially.

Silence fell on the cave. Nafarah and Kassab were outgunned. The tension was thick and heavy, increasing with each passing moment. Father Antonio pressed further into the cave, intent on reaching Katherine. "Do not take another step," threatened Nafarah.

"You will give me that key," announced Father Antonio, as he slowly came to stand in the middle of the cave. Nafarah and Kassab simply waited. "You will not leave this cave alive," said Nafarah to the Catholic priest. "With or without that key. I will make sure of it."

As the tension escalated, the cave seemed to pulsate with the quiet. *Anything could happen,* thought Nick. *Particularly mistakes.* Father Antonio had moved to within a few feet of him, pointing his gun at Katherine. Nafarah aimed his weapon at Father Antonio. Kassab was pointing his at Etienne, who was now kneeling over Muhanna. The three other Italians were pointing nervously at anything and everything that moved. *They are the most likely,* Nick thought, *to do something really, really stupid.*

"Looks like a rainy day in Egypt," said Nick softly, as he placed his foot up on the ledge in front of Katherine. His calve was about waist-high to her.

"Antonio," said Nick loudly. "I can see that you and your colleagues have brought the most guns to this party. We will give *you* the key, happily, and you can take it with you. But you must take us four, alive, out of this cave, and set us free." Nick pointed to Katherine, Etienne and Muhanna. "Do what you will with the Egyptians."

Father Antonio felt very close to victory, and wondered in a brief flash if his mother would understand what he was about to do. "Very well, then," he said, cocking back the hammer on his pistol. He swung his weapon away from Katherine and pointed it squarely into Nafarah's face.

Nafarah sneered at the priest. "You are dreaming," he said. "None of you will leave this cave alive." Father Antonio's attention was totally directed at Nafarah for the moment, giving Katherine the small space of time she needed. *So much can happen,* thought Nick, *for right or wrong, in just seconds, in moments frozen in time.* He knew Katherine was not one to let such moments pass her by.

In the end, it all went rather quickly. Katherine grabbed the gun from Nick's leg holster. An unknown instinct told her that she must not hesitate; she must not pause to think about it. It was as though an ancestral voice, in one brief flash, was shouting a message into her ear. *Survive. Now.*

Katherine fired straight into Father Antonio's chest and a deafening clap of noise echoed through the cave. They all automatically flinched, their hearts pounding. For a one brief second they all stood still, breathing into the gradual silence. Then all hell broke loose.

The Catholic priest died where he stood, too swiftly to even be surprised. Stunned, Nafarah and Kassab momentarily lost their guard. Katherine, having started down this fatal path, was suddenly and completely immersed in it. She shot Nafarah, too. His gun was flung ten feet across the cave as the bullet hit his hand. He dropped to his knees in pain and astonishment as blood spilled onto his white monogrammed cuffs.

Etienne seized the opportunity and swung Muhanna's mattock at Kassab, knocking him, unconscious, to the ground. Then he scooped up Kassab's gun and aimed it at the startled Italians.

Muhanna crawled across the cave floor at a startling clip and picked up Nafarah's gun. He waved the gun around the cave from his position on the ground. "Don't anybody move," he shouted. "I am not in a forgiving mood."

Nick looked over at Katherine. Tears were spilling down her face. He took the gun from her shaking hands and pulled her around the rock wall beside him. Katherine looked at the dead priest and covered her face in her hands. Nick put his arm around his wife and kept her there. The gun he pointed at Nafarah.

"Drop your weapons," ordered Etienne, pressing toward Father Antonio's brethren. The three Italian conspirators, overcome, dropped their guns to the ground without hesitation. Two weapons were pointed in their faces, and their charismatic leader was lying on the dirty ground in a darkening pool of blood. In that moment they questioned not their faith or the noble wisdom of their quest, but rather, God's purpose in the taking of Father Antonio, and the leaving behind of them. They raised their hands high over their heads.

Etienne approached one of the Italians. "Ronaldo, isn't it?" The man nodded, fear and disbelief raining down on him. "You have something of mine," said Etienne. Etienne reached into a scabbard at Ronaldo's waist and removed the stiletto that had been taken from him in Nag Hammadi. He quickly tucked the knife into his belt and stepped away.

Muhanna collected up the remaining weapons and struggled to his feet. One gun he tucked into his waist belt, one he gave Etienne and two he held directly at the Italians. "Allah has smiled on me today," he said to Nafarah, over his shoulder. "And not you."

Nafarah said nothing, but glared at Muhanna, as he held tight to his injured hand. His crisp white handkerchief, serving as a bandage, was soaked red with blood.

Etienne shoved the extra gun Muhanna gave him into the back of his pants. "I'd like to get to the bottom of a few things," he said, zeroing in on Ronaldo. Ronaldo's face visibly paled. "For starters," said Etienne, "who are you working for?"

"Father Antonio," stammered the Italian. Under the gaze of no less than three guns, his astonishment at the turn of their fate escalated into fear for his life.

"No," said Etienne. "Who hired Father Antonio?"

Ronaldo paused, looking between him and his compatriots. Etienne studied him carefully. *Does he not know? Or is he just not saying? Is he perhaps protecting somebody..?* Etienne swung his gun over to one of the other Italians, named Mario, advancing until the barrel of his pistol was just inches from the man's head. He cocked back the hammer of the weapon and waited. The look on the face of Mario – utterly at the mercy of discompassionate men – was one of futility. He'd seen blood spilled too easily in that cave today, and understood that his may very well be next.

Ronaldo put his arm out, gesturing toward Etienne in an enterprise of truce. "A man from America," he confessed. "He hired us to follow you, and to take the books if we could."

"His name?" asked Etienne.

"Nelson," answered Ronaldo, the truth spilling out of him easily. "Hugo Nelson."

"How did you know where to find us?"

"We were receiving communiqués."

"From who?" Etienne voice was entirely without emotion.

Ronaldo shifted nervously. "Through a messenger who brought us reports of you: where you were, where the codices were, and where you would be going next. It was important not to lose track of you, so we had spies, just little kids, who would do anything for money. They followed you everywhere. One, who served as courier, would make contact in inconspicuous places, and he would bring back coded messages to us."

"Make contact with who?" asked Etienne.

Ronaldo looked over at Nick. Nick did not waver as the gaze of an accusing crowd turned towards him. He was the traitor among them, the one with no proud purpose, the one who engineered an intention secret and contrary to that of his fellows. Nick issued no apology or remorse. He had chosen his course carefully and regretted only the failure of his task.

"After Nag Hammadi, we thought the messages would stop coming," said Ronaldo to Nick. "And that you had realized it was Father Antonio who was receiving your reports. But the messages kept coming."

"And let me guess," added Etienne. "Nelson had sworn you all to secrecy about his involvement – at the penalty of your lives."

"*Yes.*" Ronaldo nodded emphatically. "So we were able to shadow your movements, waiting for the best opportunity to take the heretical books. Our first report led us to the basement of the Coptic Museum in Cairo. Our last report was from Luxor. Then the communications stopped, until an hour ago."

A look of understanding crossed Etienne's face as he recalled their narrow escape from the museum. "How much did Nelson pay you?" he asked, dryly.

"Fifty thousand dollars up front," said Ronaldo, looking at the ground. He seemed torn, uncomfortable that his divine mission had been tainted with the promise of money. "And another 50,000 dollars on delivery of the codices."

"Safe bet for Nelson," said Etienne, turning to Nick. "What's 100,000 dollars to insure that he gets the manuscripts in case we double crossed him? And save almost a million dollars in the process."

"Million dollars?" Ronaldo looked up.

"You were grossly under paid, I'm afraid," said Etienne wryly. Ronaldo stared in continuing disbelief at Etienne. His colleagues looked at each other with wide, frightful eyes. Etienne turned back to Nick. "If Father Antonio delivered the codices, Nelson could keep the Knife, too," he said. "His deal with us was a total lie."

"So was yours," Nick reminded him.

Etienne turned back to Ronaldo. "What was he going to do with the codices once he had them?"

"Destroy them," stated Ronaldo. "Signor Nelson hated the Gnostics – the very idea of them. Nelson is a devoted Catholic," added Ronaldo. "He's a good and righteous follower of the Holy Church."

"Nelson never followed anything or anybody in his life," said Nick. "He makes up the rules as he goes. For everybody."

"I tell you he hated that those words were ever written," insisted Ronaldo. "He told us so. He said that this was his personal holy war, against the codices. That he would do everything in his power to see them destroyed."

"The message of the Gnostic is self-accountability," Nick reasoned out loud. "Nelson couldn't live with that. It was his fanatical belief that he was directed by God to do all the terrible things he ever did – a self-proclaimed, righteous, and deserving agent of the Lord."

"He said that he had read part of one of the books," added Ronaldo. "That he knew of a way to become God's twin. And that whoever learned from the book would not ever die."

Etienne recited from the Gospel of Thomas:

"These are the hidden sayings that the living Jesus spoke and Judas Thomas the Twin recorded. And Jesus said, 'whoever discovers the interpretations of these sayings shall not taste death."

"Immortality and power," said Nick, stunned. "But if Nelson believed that the secrets of the Gnostics would make him equal with God, why did he want to destroy them?"

"To keep the secrets for himself only," said Ronaldo. "He said the books would be full of spells and chants."

"Well, he was wrong," said Etienne. "The secret of *gnosis* is not spells of immortality. It is this: to *know yourself*, at the deepest level, is to simultaneously know God. That is the secret of the Gnostics."

"Nelson didn't want to know himself," added Nick. "It is the very thing that he wants *least* to know."

"It will be his ruin, I promise you," said Etienne.

"You will kill us all," stated Ronaldo. He hung his head and waited to die.

"Not likely," said Etienne, releasing the hammer of his gun and tucking it into his waistband. "I am not in the business of murder." He looked over at Muhanna. "Keep your eyes sharp," he said, nodding toward the Italians. "I have a few more things to do."

Etienne went over to Nafarah who was leaning against the cave wall, under Nick's careful guard. Etienne reached inside of Nafarah's crisp black suit.

"I will take these," he said. He withdrew Nick and Katherine's passports and handed them to Nick. Nafarah's eyes never left Etienne, but he did not try to stop him. Etienne also wrestled the charm bracelet from Nafarah's suit pocket. "This never belonged to you," he said, as he shoved the jeweled treasure deep in his pocket. "And it never will."

"You shall regret this one day, Etienne Desonia," warned Nafarah. "If you think this is over, it is not."

"No it is not," replied Etienne. "Because we are going to finish our deal. Then, I expect that you shall be leaving me alone, forever."

"You are a thief," stated Nafarah.

"I will be taking the codices with me when I leave here," said Etienne. Nafarah smoldered a dark hateful stare at Etienne. "It is the only way I can get the Knife of the Asps for you," he explained. "Hugo Nelson has the Knife. And he wants the codices, all of them."

"And you have them all?" asked Nafarah, his eyes narrowing.

"Except for one," admitted Etienne. "Which you will find at the Jung Institute in Zurich."

408

"How did a codex get there?" snapped Nafarah.

"It was not my doing," said Etienne. "It was smuggled out of Egypt without my knowing about it."

"You're lying."

"No," sighed Etienne, weary of the battle. "I am not."

"We'll see about that," muttered Nafarah.

"I will call you in two days' time," continued Etienne, "to tell you when and where to meet me. You can arrive in time to witness Hugo Nelson trade the codices for the Knife. You can arrest us both then and there for smuggling, illegal possession of state artifacts, and whatever else you can drum up."

"You will have yourself arrested?" smirked Nafarah. "I don't think so."

"In appearance only," continued Etienne. "Having made good on my promise, and delivered to you the Gnostic manuscripts and the Knife of the Asps, I fully intend to be released. But you and I – and these good people here – will be the only ones to know that." Etienne waved his gun at the Italians. "And no one is going to be passing that information around. Isn't that right?" Father Antonio's men eagerly nodded their agreement.

"And what if I find Hugo Nelson first?" asked Nafarah. "Without your help?"

"Then you'll get the Knife, yes," answered Etienne. "But not the codices. Those, I will have."

Nafarah stood for a while sizing up the situation. "How do I know you will keep your word?" he asked.

"You do not," replied Etienne. "But try to understand my logic: We have made promises to the man who has possession of the Knife. I do not want him hounding us for the rest of our lives."

"I understand you perfectly," said Nafarah, indignation mixing with the hatred in his eyes.

"Now," said Etienne. "How will I know that you will keep your word?"

"You do not," replied Nafarah. A bitter laugh escaped him. "We will just have to trust one another."

"Well, no," said Etienne. "We don't have to go that far. If you detain me longer than five minutes, a friend of mine, Miss Donatta, will have Prime Minister Nokrashi Pasha telephoning you, demanding an explanation."

Nafarah looked down at his bloody hand. "You have a deal, Monsieur Desonia. I will await your call within two days."

"One last thing," Etienne added. "It's a personal matter. The matter of my diary ..."

"Find it on your own," spat Nafarah.

"It is in the car," said Etienne. "No?" Nafarah looked away. Etienne smiled as if this was no more difficult or nasty than a rugby match. A match where he had scored the winning goal.

Katherine stepped forward, tears stained on her face. "Let's get the hell out of here," she said.

This day had unfolded well for them, as well or better than Etienne's best hopes. But the price had been high, and Katherine had paid for part of it with coin from her soul. She came to Egypt an ambitious marauder of antiquities. But she found herself on a journey she had not expected to take. Etienne knew that she would leave Egypt with marks of change carved inside her.

Etienne nodded his agreement, taking his eyes from the woman to whom his heart was inextricably bound. Together, the companions hastened around the various men in the cave, each one beaten or fallen, and began their descent down the talus. Katherine and Nick supported Muhanna, who refused to turn his back on the cave, waving his guns as they half-carried, half-drug him down the sloping hill.

Etienne was at the Cadillac, prying open the trunk with the small shovel from the jeep. He found the suitcase inside and lifted the lid. After a quick inventory of the codices, he recovered his diary and tucked it into his satchel. Then, very carefully, he lifted the suitcase out of the trunk and packed it tightly in the far back of the jeep, with the supplies.

Nafarah moved to the cave's entrance, holding his bleeding hand in the air. "Two days, Etienne Desonia," he shouted, cold and steely. "If I do not hear from you within two days, I will hunt you down like the dog you are and shoot you on the spot."

410

"Until then, then," Etienne called across the abandoned desert. He glanced back only once before he ripped the jeep down the sandy road toward the Nile and out of Nafarah's lingering sight.

The red stain of blood on Muhanna's *jallabiya* was growing. Katherine could see that from where she was sitting, in the front seat of the jeep. "We've got to get Muhanna to a hospital," she called out over the wind that surrounded them. "He's bleeding ... badly."

Muhanna lay in the back seat, resting his head in Nick's lap. Nick held on to him, bending over to his ear, whispering words of comfort that Katherine could not hear.

Etienne looked over his shoulder at Muhanna and then back to the horizon. Even as the sun began to fall, a dark ribbon of sand was rising to meet it. Another storm was gathering to the west. "Sand storm," announced Etienne. Nick and Katherine turned their heads to look.

"Oh, no," whispered Katherine, her hands involuntarily starting to clench into fists. She shifted in her seat, anticipating the merciless, biting sand, powerless to stop the fury of the *khamis*.

"If we seek shelter, Muhanna may not make it," said Etienne grimly. "If the storm catches us, however, we will all die out here."

Muhanna had faded into a delirious haze, his fever rising at a startling rate. He was moving in and out of consciousness, and his fate would be determined without his arguments.

Nick held on to the strange and feisty man who'd become their collaborator and their friend; who had crossed the boundaries between his culture and theirs, and who had shown them some of the beauty of his beloved Islam and the spirit to survive the hardships of desert. *How can we abandon him now?* "Press forward," said Nick. "Drive as fast as you possibly can."

No, thought Katherine desperately. *I don't want to suffocate out here, my skin shredded from my face, my lungs caked solid with sand, dead and rotting in the middle of this godforsaken desert.* Katherine wanted to scream. Instead, she couched her fear in logic.

"He'll have to be okay," she argued. "None of us may survive out here, with no place to hide. What's the point of saving Muhanna from bleeding to death, only to let him suffocate in the sand?"

"We made it through last time," insisted Nick. "We'll make it through again."

Katherine turned to Etienne. The wind was rising. She expected Etienne to agree with her, to accommodate her. She was, in fact, counting on it with her life. But she hadn't earned that guarantee. Etienne would answer to no one but the voice of his own reason. It might have been otherwise, long ago, when they loved each other so wildly that logic was irrelevant.

With fear mounting in her throat, Katherine realized that she had no more influence over her fate than the delirious Muhanna. She had lost much in these untamed landscapes over the past many days. Much of what she believed, much of what anchored her, much of what shaped her image of herself.

Now I might give up that crazy, muddled life, she thought desperately, *to the shifting sands of this unforgiving desert.* She wished she had Nick's grace and selflessness in the path of impending doom. But Katherine was clinging to that mixed-up life, with hope, and regret, and promises to God in the far reaches of her heart.

While Katherine stared at him, Etienne looked only to the sky. He measured the distance of the flying wall of sand against the increasing wind and the miles yet to travel. He swerved the jeep sharply to the east. "The basilica," he stated, steering over the bumpy land. "We'll have to operate on Muhanna there."

Muhanna groaned in his darkening world of pain. Katherine relaxed visibly, though she bent over and kept her face buried in her hands for the rest of the journey – whether from fear of the *khamis*, the shame of selfishness, or the memory of the man she had killed – was hers to reconcile. Nick set his jaw against the weather and rode in silence, with Muhanna's thin, fevered body trembling in his arms.

25

A RAGING STORM

And when the storm comes,
and the mighty wind shakes the forest,
and thunder and lightening proclaim the majesty of the sky,
then let your heart say in awe, 'God moves in passion.'

– Kahlil Gibran

Basilica of St. Pachomius

The jeep sped up to the Basilica of St. Pachomius just as dusk was settling on the horizon. The wind howled overhead, and sprinklets of sand were starting to dash themselves across the land. The miniature pebbles hit the jeep with soft tinkling sounds, a sweet calling ushering in a reign of fury.

Together, Etienne and Nick carried Muhanna from the jeep and laid him in the soft sand inside the inner sanctuary. Katherine frantically rummaged through the jeep for supplies and bandages, as the first wave of sand began to pelt her. She found a first aid kit, food, water, and the black dress which Muhanna had stolen in Nag Hammadi.

She tried to bundle them all together and run with them in to the safety of the basilica. But the load was heavy and unwieldy. She dropped first one thing and then another, until she was carrying almost nothing. Overwhelmed with the futility of her effort, she left the food on the ground and ran with the medical supplies into the basilica. She set them in a heap by Muhanna.

The comfort and safety of the building was calling to her. *Stay inside. Find a small warm corner, hunker down, and wait until the storm passes. Don't go back out there. Don't go.* She looked at Nick and Etienne hunched over the struggling Muhanna and she ran back outside.

Katherine scooped up all the supplies she'd dropped and threw them recklessly into the back seat of the jeep. She hopped into the driver's seat and found Etienne's keys still in the ignition. Firing up the engine with a roar, she peeled with ferocity away from the entrance.

Grit was starting to gather in her clothes and hair. The swelling wall of sand had blocked out the remaining traces of light. Fueled by a combination of fear and bravado, Katherine drove the jeep to the furthest end of the long, crumbling building. During one of her sojourns through the relic structure she had come across a low wall, fallen over the centuries to stone and rubble. Katherine spun around the corner of the building, looking for that opening, kicking up sand for yards behind her.

When she found it, she drove some 100 feet in the opposite direction. Then she spun the jeep around and paused there, squarely facing the wall. The sand was biting into her skin now, getting in her eyes and causing her to squint and wince against the stinging pellets. Revving the engine to its extreme, Katherine raced across the sand toward a head-on collision with the fallen wall. With one deep breath and a loud cry, she catapulted herself through the scattered rubble. She rammed the jeep through the debris like a wild banshee, trying to get inside the protection of the basilica.

"Come on, come on," she yelled, willing herself through the barricade. She pressed the accelerator to the floor and did not let up.

The jeep was jostled from side to side and when Katherine hit her chin violently on the steering column, the shock of it nearly stopped her. But the jeep had a momentum of its own by then and she was able to press forward. Sharp rocks scraped and dented Etienne's coveted vehicle, and one of the tires blew, firing like a gunshot.

Katherine screamed as though she'd been startled by a snake, but the three other tires held up and carried her over the last few yards. In a cloud of falling dust, the jeep came to rest inside the shelter of the old monastery.

Katherine looked around in a sort of shocked astonishment, and for the first time in days, smiled. She made several trips though the length of the building, hauling supplies to the main sanctuary, while the storm raged beyond the walls that surrounded her.

Etienne and Nick worked quickly over Muhanna. "... hurts ... hurts!" murmured Muhanna, his head rolling from side to side. With a tourniquet on Muhanna's leg, Etienne was able to quell most of the bleeding. His skills at field triage were rough, at best, but better than Nick's. So it fell to Etienne. Nick dabbed away excess blood so Etienne could see clearly to do the delicate, intrusive work. Beads of sweat gathered on Etienne's brow. "I need more light," he said, his voice hard. "Katherine, find the flashlight. And the lantern."

In a moment of lucidity, Muhanna raised his head and exclaimed, "Stop that or I will kill you dead!" Etienne continued without pause. He gently probed the area of the wound, using hydrogen peroxide and a long pair of tweezers. "That hurts, you swine! Allah's revenge will sweep down upon you and you will know the wrath of Hell!"

"*Merde*," said Etienne. "The bullet is lodged next to his tibia."

"Are you going to take it out?" asked Nick, holding Muhanna's arms.

"No no no no no!" pleaded Muhanna. "Do not touch me anymore!"

"Do not worry, my friend," said Etienne, in a soothing voice. "No more. I am going to bandage you up now."

"Okay, okay," whispered Muhanna, his head falling back in the sand, his mind falling back into delirium.

Etienne took a deep breath. "You are going to want to bite down on this, though," he said, placing a wad of cotton in Muhanna's mouth.

It was done before anyone knew what was happening. A few quick gestures and Etienne had pulled the bullet from Muhanna's thigh. He held it up with the long tweezers and sat back on his haunches in relief.

Muhanna's gaze was half-crazed. "I hate you," he spat. His head fell back to the ground. "Thank you. Thank you, my friend."

"He will have to go to a hospital," warned Etienne. 'The wound will surely get infected out here." Etienne sewed the incision closed with a needle and thread, creating a rough wrinkle in Muhanna's swollen skin. Then he wrapped bandages firmly around Muhanna's leg, using all the gauze he had and the cloth from the white underskirt of the stolen dress.

Then he released the tourniquet. They all held their collective breath and waited to see if the stitches would hold. Muhanna's leg looked like a skinny stick tucked inside a bale of cotton, but the dressing held. While some blood leaked out, the loss was limited to a few dark splotches.

"As long as he doesn't start bleeding again," said Etienne with shaky confidence, "he should be alright." Etienne patted Muhanna gently on the shoulder. "We will keep a careful eye on you through the night, Muhanna. Rest easily. You're going to be just fine."

"*Insha Allah ...*" murmured Muhanna, as he drifted in and out of consciousness. God Willing.

Quietly, Etienne spoke to Nick and Katherine. "I don't want to move him for another day or two, until the wound starts to heal. If he goes much further into shock, we may lose him."

"We have enough supplies to hold out here at the basilica for another day," offered Katherine. "Maybe two."

"We'll stay here, then, until Muhanna is well enough to move," said Nick. "If need be, I'll drive into Nag Hammadi when the storm passes, for extra provisions ... and a doctor."

"Agreed," said Etienne.

Water was heating on a fire Katherine had built in the center of the main sanctuary. She took the little pan into a neighboring room and poured warm water over Etienne's hands. Etienne washed Muhanna's blood away with the lavender soap from Miss Donatta. This they did in silence. The room they were in was small and gloomy. Jagged walls rose high into the night, casting spectral shadows as the wind and sand blew overhead.

Perhaps this room had once been a library, thought Etienne. *A place where scribes translated and copied sacred texts. Or perhaps it was once a kitchen.* There was no way to know.

Etienne washed and dried his hands by the light of the lantern. He and Katherine made little stools of the scattered stones and rested themselves there, listening to the storm. After a few minutes, Etienne reached into his pocket and handled the spun-silver charm bracelet to Katherine. "Keep this for me, will you?" he said.

Katherine looked closely at the seven stunning jewels. They were strangely compelling, as if calling to her in some ancient language, with words she knew but couldn't quite hear. "I can't, Etienne. This is far too valuable. It makes me nervous just holding it."

"You must," he said. "It is called the "Path of the Hearts" and it won't be safe with me any more. When Nafarah takes me into custody, he will confiscate everything I own, just for spite. Including this." He closed her fingers around the bracelet. "Don't ever take it apart, Katherine. And for God's sake don't sell it, whatever you do. It's more valuable than the sum of its gems. More valuable than any of us may even realize. Which reminds me, you're going to have to hide it from Customs. Hide it well, Katherine. Swallow it whole if you have to. But don't lose possession of it. Promise me, Katherine."

"I don't know where to hide it. Etienne, you're frightening me."

"Don't be afraid. Go get your knapsack. I want to show you something."

Katherine took the lantern, leaving Etienne in the dark. She was only gone a minute before she returned and settled back in amongst the rubble, dropping her knapsack at her feet.

"How about a cigarette?" asked Etienne. Katherine thought it was a strange request, but dug through her bag and drew out the silver case from Miss Donatta. "Watch this," said Etienne, opening the lid. He dumped all the cigarettes, sitting in a tidy row, onto his lap. A decorative pattern of roses was etched into the bottom the case, underneath the cigarettes.

He looked up at Katherine. "Got a hairpin?" She looked back at him with an incredulous look on her face. Her hair was a tossed and tangled mess around her shoulders. "How about a pen, then?" he asked. She dug around the knapsack and produced a slender fountain pen.

"Watch carefully," instructed Etienne, as he lay open the case. He took the tip of the silver quill and pressed it into three different thorns on three different roses. The silver-etched plate sprung neatly open, revealing a secret chamber in the bottom of the case. Katherine gasped. Etienne tucked the bracelet inside and snapped the chamber shut. "Now you try," he said, handing her the case.

Katherine took the pen and depressed each thorn in turn. The silver panel clicked once and popped open. Katherine and Etienne smiled at each other as they closed the chamber and replaced the cigarettes.

They let more silence fill their time together. As the weight of the day began to settle in on them, neither knew what to say or even how to begin.

"Are you alright?" asked Etienne eventually.

"Considering that I just found out my husband was unfaithful to me with some bombshell in a bar?" said Katherine, not looking at him. "Or that I just killed a man?"

"It was self defense, Katherine. You must remember that. If you hadn't defended yourself, he would have killed you to get that key. I know he would have. He would've killed all of us. You. Me. Nick. Muhanna. We all owe our lives to you. Father Antonio would have shot everyone of us if he had to – to get what he wanted."

Katherine didn't reply. She was looking at a million grains of sand in the light of a lantern, nothing more.

"And about Nick," continued Etienne. "Really, it wasn't his fault and it wasn't about you. It didn't happen because he didn't love you. War does strange things to people. He was under tremendous pressure. And, remember Katherine, he didn't go looking for it."

"Well, he didn't walk away from it either, now did he?" Katherine threw the water pot against the wall. "You know what I hate? What I despise the most? It's the lies. Years of deceit. I can't stand it. I keep thinking, how many times was this secret running through his mind while he was making love to me? Or just talking with me? Or sitting silently over dinner, remembering this woman. And I sat there the whole time like an idiot, trusting him entirely. I hate the lies, Etienne. I hate all the lies he told me over the years to cover up the truth."

"You're the one who's lying. Even right now."

"What?" Katherine and Etienne spun around. Nick was standing inside the ghostly room, with his arms crossed in front of his chest.

"How many lies have you told, Katherine? Without batting an eyelash. Hundreds. I've heard you tell *hundreds* of lies. No, not hundreds of lies. One lie, a hundred times. How can you sit there and pretend that it is lies that you hate?"

"You don't know what you're talking about Nick," snapped Katherine, as Nick approached the corner where she was sitting. "So why don't you just shut the hell up."

"That's right. Never talk about it. Never tell the truth about it. You disguise your truth in lies, Katherine. You've been doing it for years."

"That's just not true," said Katherine, her voice rising.

"The truth about what?" asked Etienne.

"Go ahead, Katherine," pressed Nick. He put one foot upon a fallen stone and leaned in toward his wife. "Tell him. Tell Etienne the truth."

Katherine's face grew hot and she rose to her feet, putting some distance between she and her husband. "I don't know what you're talking about."

"Tell me, Katherine," said Etienne, soothingly. "It can't be so bad, now, can it?"

"Must you press me?" she barked, unaware that she was ringing her hands. "Can't you hear? Don't you understand? I haven't any idea what he's getting at. Just drop it, will you please?"

"Katherine, whatever it is, it is eating you up," said Etienne. "Look at you. *Cherí*, you're all tied up in knots. Can't you tell me?"

"Go ahead, Katherine," urged Nick. "Say what happened."

Katherine knew she could turn and walk away. She could leave this conversation behind her and let Nick and Etienne sort it out for themselves. She could go inside, find a place to be alone, and chase the demons away. But something compelled her to stay and fight – something akin to fury. She was not the woman she was when she first came to Egypt. A door to forsaken places had been cracked open. The depth of grief on the other side, even she didn't know.

"Have you ever had a longing," she began. "Something you desired down to your bones – something you couldn't have? Something that tore at you, little by little, day after day?"

"Yes," stated Etienne. "I have."

"Bullshit," retorted Katherine. Nick sat and watched his wife. Etienne did not back down. Katherine sighed and walked to the basilica wall. There she leaned her body of trembling bones, and there she told the story.

"I don't know what secrets sorrows you may have, Etienne. I apologize," Katherine said. "It was wrong of me to say that."

Etienne came to stand beside her, leaning with his side against the same wall. "What sorrows do you have, Katherine? I wish you'd tell me."

Katherine searched the skies for some help, as if she could draw strength or courage from the storm. She was looking for a map, some assistance, or perhaps inspiration on her way to the truth. She found none. "I can't have a baby," she quietly confessed. "I keep saying I don't want one, that they're miserable creatures. But it's not true. And it weighs on me."

"I'm so sorry, Katherine," said Etienne, studying her carefully.

"I wanted babies to love and to raise. All that was good from my family, I wanted to pass on to my children. To leave something of us behind. I think of my father, and of Ben, and all that was extraordinary about them, all those wonderful, intangible things, unique just to them … gone."

Katherine voice sounded hollow and far away. "Now we will die, my family. There will be nothing left of us." Katherine didn't mention that there were things she didn't have growing up, that she wanted to make right through her children. She knew the heart of her longing was to recreate her own history, her own story, making it right and good through her happy children. That secret, however, was more than she cared to discuss.

Etienne looked at Nick, but Nick was staring at the ground. Katherine turned her face to Etienne. "Who will love me?" she whispered. "Who will ever love me?"

"You are loved, Katherine, said Nick quietly. "You are dearly cherished."

"I would have been a good mother," she stated, only to herself.

"*Cherí*, you are young, with your whole, long, beautiful life yet to be lived. Do not give up hope that good things will come to you. Tremendous things. Things you have not yet dreamed of."

Nick ran his hands through his hair and shook his head. *She's done it again*, he thought. *She's stirred up the truth and told it as a lie.*

420

Naming it, Nick knew, saying it out loud for Etienne to hear, would make the loss real.

"Why don't you tell Etienne the rest?" said Nick, looking up at her from where he sat.

"The rest of what?" asked Etienne, with genuine concern carved on his face.

"Oh, right," snapped Katherine. "Who cares about one melodramatic woman and the children she'll never have? Let's talk about *something else*, something *important*, something *a man* would care about."

"Katherine, I care about this," offered Etienne. "I do. I'm sorry to hear it. Nothing can replace such a thing. And I know nothing can comfort the hole in your heart. Truly, I'm sorry."

"I'm tired," said Katherine, wiping a puddle of tears off her face with her hands. "I'm going to bed."

There she goes, thought Nick. *She is a master at this.* Nick grabbed her hand as she walked by. He had let the weight of the truth bear down on him. *By God, so would she.* "Tell Etienne about Ben," he said.

"Let go of me," she said, snatching away her hand. She stopped and rubbed her hand furiously, avoiding Etienne's gaze. Any hope of a graceful exit had just been taken from her. "Why are you doing this, Nick?"

"Because it's important," replied Nick calmly.

Katherine stared at him from a sarcastic distance, like he was a husband turned fiend, come to tear her heart out. "I cannot for the life of me imagine what good you think is going to come out of this. You're being cruel, Nick. And that's not like you."

"You tell it, or I tell it, but the truth is coming out."

Katherine looked between Nick and Etienne. They were pillars of stability, looking at her in calm and indulgent sympathy, while she crumbled in front of them.

Katherine took a deep breath and looked into Etienne's concerned, accepting face.

"Ben didn't die in the war. He died after the war. He came home safe, in the fall of 1945, and I thought everything was going to be okay. Everything would go back to normal. But he wasn't the same. He said he just *had* to go back. To help the refugees. To set the world to right again.

"I was so angry at him. He'd already been gone too long. I was furious. So I didn't stop him. I didn't beg him to stay. I didn't even try to talk him out of it. I just let him go. I let Ben go. And he never came back.

"Not two months had gone by when I got word that he'd died … from a bloody land mine. Blown to hell-and-gone."

Etienne's face crinkled into a mask of astonishment. Whatever he might have been expecting, this was not it. Katherine could not bear the look if it. She turned on her heel and walked out of the room.

Katherine found herself in what appeared to have been a hallway, a wide aisle scattered with stones. Katherine bent over in the cool stillness. Her heart was pounding so hard it physically hurt. She looked around the empty space in the ghostly basilica, as if looking for some comfort, a long-awaited pair of Godly arms, perhaps, to welcome her home. To welcome her back into the land of the Living and the Truthful, where the people who knew contentment resided.

But there was nothing, and nowhere to go that didn't feel dark and empty. The only sounds she heard came from the lonely *khamis*. She rose to her full height and stomped back to her husband.

Nick and Etienne were talking in hushed tones where they sat among the fallen bricks of stone.

"Are you satisfied, Nick?" she hollered. "Have you gotten whatever it is you wanted out of this?" She turned to Etienne. "And you – have you judged and decided for yourself why Ben left me, what drove him to his death?"

"Slow down, Katherine," offered Etienne gently. "You're hurting, *cheri*. Slow down and tell me about it."

"There's nothing more to tell." If Katherine had been listening, she might have realized that a small, lost part of her longed to tell the story—to be heard and forgiven and comforted.

"*Cheri,* your sorrow is in the past. It can't hurt you now."

But Katherine didn't hear him. All she heard was a jumble of sounds in the background of her escape. She had tested her limit and found herself too far beyond it. She rose and walked from the room without another word. What Nick and Etienne discussed after she left, she didn't want to know.

Katherine slept fitfully that night, while the storm continued to wail and moan and throw sand through the sky. She dreamed of snakes and guns and dark corners of time.

Nick and Etienne took turns keeping vigil over Muhanna and Katherine, in their cocoons of pain, as the night reached into morning.

26

THE WAY, THE TRUTH AND THE LIFE

You are not dead yet, it is not too late
to open your depths by plunging into them
and drink in the life
that reveals itself quietly there.

– Rainer Maria Rilke

Basilica of St. Pachomius

As if it had never happened, the storm was gone the next morning. The sky was fresh and raw and scrubbed bright blue. Waves of sand had piled themselves against the western wall of the basilica and in soft corners within the sanctuary. Other than that, the desert, in its ever-changing form, remained the same.

In the sweet warmth of the new day, it was tempting for Katherine to pretend that her episode with Nick and Etienne hadn't happened either. She spent many minutes laying in her sleeping bag fighting a sense of shame. Then she flung away her covers and hoped madly that they wouldn't mention Ben again. That they could put that storm behind them, too.

Muhanna rolled and moaned in his sleep and Katherine went to his side. He looked up at her with a face of innocence and a kind of unexpected vulnerability that unnerved her. She took his hand. *Please be okay*, she silently implored. *We cannot bear to lose you.*

"You're looking better this morning," announced Nick, standing over Katherine's shoulder. She thought for a moment he meant her. "How're you feeling?" Without words, Nick touched his wife on her back in a gesture of silent comfort and concern.

Muhanna raised his head and whispered in a raspy voice. "Terrible. I'm terrible." He held up an arm and tried to wave it around. The fabric of his *jallabiya* was singed from fire. "Revenge will ...

424

revenge w –" Muhanna's voice faded and his arm fell back to the ground. They thought he'd fallen asleep, too tired even to plot his retribution. After a few moments Muhanna opened his eyes again. "Thirsty…"

Katherine ran to the supplies for water while Nick bent over Muhanna, examining his dressing. "You're a lucky man, Muhanna Ali al-Samara," Nick said. Katherine returned with the canteen and held Muhanna's head while he drank.

Muhanna drank heartily, as if he thought this might be his only drink of the whole day. It made Katherine wonder what hardships of land and circumstance had shaped the desert farmer. *What remarkable reserves of fortitude,* she realized, *were held within this small, unlikely hero.*

"Rest now," commanded Nick, rising to his feet. "Rest and give that leg a chance to heal."

Uncomfortable, not knowing what to do next, Nick and Katherine shuffled around the sanctuary making themselves busy. They heard the jeep fire up in the distant reaches of the basilica. They looked up from their respective tasks, silently wondering the exact same thing. *What was Etienne up to now?* In a few minutes, they heard the jeep rumble to a stop in front of the basilica and they walked outside to greet him.

Etienne popped out of the jeep, wiping his hands on a dirty rag. He'd spent the morning changing the tire, cleaning sand out of the jeep's engine and moving rocks.

"You've saved our lives again, Katherine," he announced. "Though you killed one of my tires." Nick and Katherine looked at the beat-up jeep. "Fortunately, I had a spare."

"What happened here?" asked Nick, pointing to the dents and scrapes.

"Katherine went for a drive." Etienne smiled.

"I'm sorry about your jeep," stated Katherine.

"Don't be. If we'd left the jeep in the storm, it would be thoroughly caked with sand and we would be stranded here. Again." Etienne winced.

Katherine looked to the ground. *I'm tired of apologizing.*

"I don't know how you got the jeep into the basilica," Etienne said, his voice intending to encourage, to forgive. "But truly, the jeep would be ruined if you hadn't."

"Don't thank me," said Katherine. "It was just dumb luck."

"A blessing," said Etienne, looking at her carefully. "Don't you think maybe it was a blessing?"

"No, I don't."

"Why? Why can't you believe that God could look down on you and say, 'Oops, look, Katherine is in trouble.' Why can't you believe that maybe, just once in awhile, God intervenes on your behalf?"

"I don't know, Etienne," said Katherine sarcastically. "Because He doesn't exist?"

"Are you so sure of that?"

"God died in Auschwitz, with the Jews. The Nazis killed him. Or hadn't you heard?"

"You are so angry," stated Etienne.

"I am not."

"Yes. You are."

Katherine looked at Nick as though he should rise to her defense. When he didn't, she turned her back on him and launched her attack fully on Etienne.

"You're damn right I'm angry," she snapped. "Why aren't you? What's the matter with you? You should be angry; you should be *furious*. We all should be. Bad things have happened. Terrible things. And yet we walk through life, accepting the death and suffering, as if it didn't matter. As if it was all okay. Well, it's not okay."

"Slow down a minute, Katherine," offered Etienne. He looked into her eyes and saw a wall of rage behind them. There was a question to be asked. Although he already knew the answer, and the consequences, he plunged himself into the depths of Katherine's rage and asked it. "Is it the holocaust you're talking about, Katherine? Or something else?"

Katherine looked back and forth between Etienne and Nick. "What?" She scowled at Etienne as if he was the most ridiculous man on earth.

"Let's talk about Ben," said Etienne firmly.

Why can't you people have the good manners to drop this? fumed Katherine. *Why must you badger me?* "Etienne, let me tell you something. Do not tell me to slow down. You have no idea, no *idea* what's in my heart. Or even who I am, for that matter. Just ... shut up!"

"Katherine, he's trying to help you," said Nick.

"I don't need his help. Or yours for that matter. I can't believe you two. Can't you possibly begin to try to understand what it's like? To lose someone you love that much? You have no idea. You stand there so detached and superior. As if you have all the answers and I'm just some hysterical woman ranting about nothing."

"We know you're not hysterical, Katherine," offered Nick. "And we know it's not nothing. We both want you to face this. To look at your grief and your loss with your heart wide open, and let it go."

"Let it go? *Let it go?*" Katherine paused as if realizing something for the first time. "I don't want to let it go. I don't want it to be alright. You think this should be *alright*?"

"No *cherí*, it is not alright," said Etienne. "Sit down with me and tell me about it. I want to understand." Etienne took her by the hand and she let him guide her to the ground where they sat together in the sand, just like they had the first evening at the basilica, when things seemed simpler, just days ago.

Nick sat in the sand, some distance away and watched his wife. The expression on her face went from indignation to acceptance. She sighed impatiently, as if she could tell this story, get it over with, and come through it unscathed.

She began speaking in a distant monotone, telling a story that dwelled only in the most secret chambers of her heart. She didn't look at Etienne or Nick when she spoke. She looked only at the treacherous sand in front of her.

"It was last September," she began quietly. "Just an ordinary day. The war was over. We were all moving forward with our lives. We felt hopeful, new, optimistic ...

427

"Except for Ben. He was sinking. He came back from Europe different. The part of him that was so dazzling and brilliant, was gone. Just gone. It was as if someone scooped out the best of him and left him with only the bones that held him up. I kept looking for that part of him to come back, like it was sleeping or something, and if I just tried hard enough, pulled hard enough, it would wake up and come out. But his eyes had a vacancy. So... empty, so..."

Katherine's voice trailed off and it was a few moments before she spoke again, as if she needed to find another path from which to speak. "One day we were supposed to meet for lunch, but he never came. I waited at Le Cirque an for hour and he never showed up. I ordered lunch and he still didn't show up. So I ate." *I was eating chilled shrimp salad*, Katherine reminded herself silently, *and drinking iced tea while Ben was on his way back to Europe. On his way to die.*

"I ate my lunch by myself and waited. But he never came. And he never picked up his telephone, all day. I called and called. Eventually, I went to his house. It was dark outside, and cold, like summer was completely over and long gone. Even though it had been nice out just days before. That night was cold."

She continued, not wanting to finish the story, not wanting to answer the questions she knew would follow. "He'd bought this old house in Brooklyn that he was going to restore. He had this idea that he'd refurbish this ratty old house, get married to a pretty girl, find a good job, work hard, raise children, mow the lawn, put the war behind him. I hoped so too, but it didn't work out that way.

"Anyway, I took the train to his house after work that evening. I had a spare key, but the door wasn't locked." She paused, looking at the empty house in her memory. "There was a bottle of wine on the kitchen table, all gone. Everything else was tidy as a pin. I moved through the house calling his name. I went into every room. Over and over I called his name." Again she paused to stare into her memory and the pictures it laid out before her, one at a time. "And then I saw the note." Katherine recited the last words Ben had shared with her:

"My darling girl, my sister, my other self,
I have to go. There is something I must do.
We will see each other again some day. I promise. No matter what.
No matter what.
I carry you with me in my heart,
because it is safe there and full of love.
--Your Ben

"Some days, the thought occurs to me that he's not really dead. It's as if I can feel him and he's still alive, somewhere on this earth. And I want to believe it so badly." Tears welled up suddenly in her eyes. With practiced precision, she pushed them back into the darkness of her mind.

"Katherine, you could not have stopped him," insisted Nick. "No matter what. It is not your fault."

"He knew I would be broken without him," she said, as though she hadn't heard Etienne at all. She was absently fingering the bronze star that hung around her neck.

"When was the last time you saw him?" asked Etienne. Katherine looked right through him.

"The evening before. He'd been for a drive, something he said he'd come to do often. He stopped by the store at closing time and we sat in my office and talked. I had my mind on other things, I guess. I should have known, really. I've known what Ben was thinking my whole life.

"I don't even remember what we talked about. But somewhere in the conversation Ben stopped. He looked out the window and broke into a peal of laughter. A delightful burst of laughter. His eyes lit up. It was the way Ben used to laugh – you know – the way that made everyone laugh too, just to hear him. His pleasure seemed so complete, so entirely compelling. It was as if in that moment Ben saw all his sorrows fall away. It was as though suddenly he felt an abundance of something – love maybe – enough love for himself, enough love for everybody. It made me smile. His laughter sounded to me like the sound of bells chiming in my mind. It always had. I let myself think that everything was going to be okay."

Nick and Etienne listened. Perhaps if they had said something, if either one had said any simple thing at that moment, things might have gone differently. But they didn't. Something held them suspended inside Katherine's grief.

"Do you know I went to church to find a priest? Weeks before Ben died. I wanted to know how I could help him. How I could protect him from all the pain he felt. From the misery left over from that goddamn war.

"I would have saved him if I could have. I wanted to. It was my job. But no. I was told, 'You have to trust.' That's what the priest said. 'Tell your brother to surrender to the loving arms of God.' Whatever

429

the hell that means. 'Leave your brother in better hands. God will watch over him'.

"I made myself believe that no more bad things could happen to Ben. He'd gone through enough. He was blessed. He was mine. He was meant for ... for better things."

Katherine started to weep openly and she talked right through the tears, letting them come in torrents. She was talking to nobody, to everybody. "We were the same. We were part of something bigger than both of us. We knew each other's thoughts, sometimes even before we knew them ourselves. We knew what to say to each other. What the other needed. We were two halves of the same person. We were bound together forever. There is not one without the other. Darkness and light. Good and evil. Joy and sorrow. You can't have the one without the other. We rose and fell together, one mirroring the other. It was always that way. It was always supposed to be that way."

Katherine looked at Etienne with desperation in her eyes. "I'm not whole without him," she explained, half choking with sorrow. "I don't know what to do, who to be. I'd rather be where ever he is, than be here without him."

"It must be awful," said Etienne. "I'm so sorry, Katherine." He let her cry for a time and didn't touch her or interrupt or try to make her stop. When he felt she was ready to hear him, he spoke again. "*Cheri*, you must find a way to let Ben go. Let him be dead. And let yourself be alive."

Katherine drew in her breath and fought for her composure. She stared at Etienne for a long moment. "I'm not going to *let it go*," she stated, incredulously. "And don't start on me to move on with my life without him. I've heard it before." She shook her head vehemently.

"No. I don't want to *move on*. And I don't want to forget. I don't even want to stop hurting. You have no idea. If you did you wouldn't be able to sit there and cavalierly say that to me. To my face. 'Oh, just move on, Katherine. Live your life; life goes on.' *Life doesn't go on*. It's never the same. Never!"

"Katherine, my darling –" began Nick.

"Where was God when Ben needed him?" demanded Katherine. "Where was God when the Nazis were marching innocent people to the death camps? This God of yours – where was he looking?"

"You're blaming this on God?" asked Etienne.

"Yes I am," snapped Katherine.

"Etienne, let it alone," protested Nick, wiping his face with his handkerchief. He, too, was spent, and weary and had heard all that he thought he could bear. For as often as he'd wished she would talk about it, now he wished it to be over.

"God wasn't looking, that's what happened!" snapped Katherine, rising to her feet. "He turned his back on the whole damn world." She brushed the dirt and sand from her trousers.

"He cast His almighty eye from Ben's sight and he died. Because this bullshit god of yours – the one that everyone's running around trying so hard to find – *doesn't exist*. And if He does, he doesn't care. Get it? It's all a lie. A big fat goddamn lie. And you know it. And I know it. And Ben is dead because your God was *never* there, watching over him."

Katherine pointed her words at Nick and Etienne as of they were the agents of God on earth. "And no one was there to stop him. No one was there to comfort him. No one was there to give him hope."

"And no one stopped him from going," stated Etienne gently.

"Etienne, stop it," said Nick, choking through his own sorrow. "Enough now." As she spoke, Nick put his fists to his face and forced back tears of his own.

"*I* didn't stop him!" raged Katherine. "Do you get it? I wasn't watching over him. I didn't protect him when he needed me. *I was responsible!*"

"Katherine, that's just not true," said Nick, raising his stricken face to hers. "Come here," he said, gesturing for her to sit.

She held out her arm as if to ward him off. "No." Katherine looked around, seeming desperate for something, looking for some particular thing to come to her, out of nowhere.

"I want him back," she said, calm and entirely detached for a brief, frightening moment. "I want my brother *back!*" Katherine then screamed a loud guttural, indistinguishable cry, from the bottom of her entire being into the empty air.

Nick and Etienne both had tears streaming down their own faces by then, but neither moved to touch her. They feared she just might shatter into a thousand pieces right in front of their eyes.

Katherine spoke as if from a dream or a distant place, a place as far away and dark as an autumn night. "The god that abandoned both of us has left me to live alone. It's my penance to live and to remember. Every day every day every day...." Katherine's voice faded to nothing. And the tears streamed, finally, fully, out of the dark well of her heart into the warm, forgiving light of day.

The sun was soothing to her, heating her like a soft blanket. Her face was washed in tears and sorrow. She felt hollow and light and entirely wasted into nothing. She drifted down to a heap on the ground like a silk scarf tossed in the breeze. She rested there, crying softly, holding her head in her hands. Barely out loud she cried, so quietly that Nick and Etienne couldn't tell if the sounds they were hearing were her tears, or theirs.

Like a soft wind, the Breath of fall came to rest upon her. *You are not what you thought you were. Fall now. Let go and become something else. You will discover, through the flame of the fall, that you are other than you know.*

Nick finally reached for his wife, his own heart scoured and raw. She let him hold her and she held him back. Somewhere beyond time and blame, Katherine finally gave Ben over to death. He separated her no more from the life that was hers alone.

A long time they rested there, Katherine, Nick and Etienne, in their collective comfort and individual sorrow. The sun rose over them in the sky, a witness to their journey. The dark hollows of their hearts were filled, briefly, with the presence of each other and the absolute absence of anything else.

"You know," said Katherine in a voice that seemed to have come back to her from some place else. "I wish I knew what Ben was laughing at that day before he died. It haunts me. I never knew what it was he saw that seemed to make him – at least for that one moment – so completely happy."

Katherine sat up. "Maybe, Etienne, when you finally find your God, it will make you stop, like looking out a window and seeing something both unexpected and obvious. It will make your whole world stop moving, for just one instant, and your joy will be so overwhelming that you'll laugh out loud."

And then, thought Katherine, *you will die. You will be taken from the lives of everyone whoever loved you or needed you. All the laughter will die in sorrow.*

Katherine took a deep breath. No. That was a voice she didn't want to hear anymore. "And then you'll laugh out loud," repeated Katherine. "And it will sound – to those who love you – like the chiming of bells."

27

THE KEY

We choose our joys and sorrows
long before we experience them.

– Kahlil Gibran

Basilica of St. Pachomius

The next day passed with the quiet heaviness of a dream. A stillness hung over the gathering, a quiet repose that was healing, that no one wanted to break. They moved through the day slowly, tending Muhanna, talking in warm, muted tones. They ate, they explored the ruins of the basilica, they read, they slept. Evening came.

Muhanna was recovering steadily. His fever was dropping and he slept less fitfully. Every few hours, Etienne doled out little bits of morphine from the first aid kit, to keep Muhanna calm and to ease the waves of pain.

Katherine made another dinner of pasta with dried meat and bread. They were running out of food. "We'll have to leave in the morning," she announced. "Or we'll all be getting very hungry, very fast."

"Muhanna's fever is coming down," replied Etienne. "Tomorrow we leave for Nag Hammadi and the hospital there."

"Done," said Nick.

Katherine agreed. "Done."

One question, however, one request, remained silent on all of their minds throughout the dinner they ate, past the setting of the sun, and into the hour when they gathered around the fire to study nothing more than the light reflecting against the stone walls.

Etienne finally spoke it. "I would have that key," he said calmly into the night shadows. "So I can give those three books, with the others, to Cato Nafarah." Katherine was silent. "*Cherí*, I want you to listen to your heart. What does it say? You know that all I've ever wanted was to see you do all you are capable of doing. I want to see you happy. Not hurt, not ever, least of all by me. Trust yourself, Katherine, and trust me."

"Katherine, that's rubbish, and you know it," said Nick. "But whatever you think of Etienne, you must give the key to me. Darling, I have to give the books to Nelson, all of them. And Nelson must go free. But Etienne can have the Knife of the Asps, and do with it what he will."

Nick turned to Etienne. "You can tell Nafarah that I stole the books from you. Just give me one day before you contact him. I'll make the trade with Nelson over the boarder, in Palestine, and from there escape to Europe. Katherine, whatever I have done against you, I ask you to do this one last thing, for me."

Katherine stared at the wall. Nick stared back, and not hearing an answer, turned to look at the ground. This was going to be a sad moment, a moment of separation, a moment when everything that followed would be different. At least for these three troubled friends.

Katherine felt a rising anxiety over the decision she had to make. For Nick and Etienne it was about a key, and three books, simple and straightforward. But for Katherine, a tangled choice loomed under the surface. She felt the depth of Nick's longing. She felt the intensity of Etienne's desire. Two curving paths laid themselves out in her mind, winding into an unknown future. Her imagination couldn't take her very far down either road. Her destiny was concealed in a veil of clouds.

I'm a childless woman, she thought, *living in New York City, with a dead brother and a bankrupt business. I've ruined everything I've touched.* Katherine closed her eyes. *Maybe I'm not supposed to be living that life at all. Maybe my truest destiny is elsewhere. I can recreate my life, be better at it, be a better person. Just walk away ...*

Nick and Etienne were expecting an answer and she felt the time and the silence bearing down on her. The choosing of one would be the losing of the other. She opened her eyes and gazed into empty space. *How*, she wondered, *from where I started, did I ever get to here?*

Nick continued to stare at the ground. His hair was tousled, his face, stained with sweat and strife, was strong, incisive. He knew what was about to happen. Sorrow pooled behind his eyes. Etienne looked at Katherine, unswerving. She felt the weight of his wanting and reached into her pocket.

"I know you both want this," she said, holding the key in the palm of her hand. "I know what it means to you. To all of us." Etienne did not reach out his hand, but continued to gaze straight into her eyes. Nick traced his finger in the sand. His eyes followed only the little ridges he was making in the shifting grains.

"I've made a lot of mistakes," began Katherine, her voice subdued in the waning night. "It seems I'm always in over my head. You know, some days I just make things up as I go along, and everything falls into place. As though it's enough just to try, to have the intent – and the world just responds. And some days ... I do everything wrong.

"Ever since you called, Etienne, things have been different. As though there's been a quickening, somehow. It's what happens when you're around me. In the past week I've seen more about the world, you, Nick, and – God knows – myself, than I ever wanted to know. Worse, I put everyone I love in danger's way."

Katherine paused, not knowing how to tell them what she felt, what she wanted—how unfair it was to have to choose. "What I'm trying to tell you is that I don't always believe in myself," she said. "And I don't always believe in you, Nick. Especially now." He looked up at her for the first time in minutes.

The fire shifted and crackled and spit ashes into the silence.

"But I believe in us," Katherine stated, looking at Nick with renewed clarity.

No one spoke for a while as the blaze of the fire lit the dark walls of the basilica and a sea of stars kept witness overhead. "I don't know about the future," she said into the darkness. "And I don't entirely understand the past. I'm uncertain in all things, except this one." She reached over and touched Nick on the arm. "My destiny is with us." Katherine dropped the key through the night air into her husband's hand. "It always has been." Her words burned themselves into the night.

"Almost," said Etienne, turning to the far wall where the light played itself against the rough stones. "Almost always. Almost mine."

"I am sorry, Etienne," she said.

Etienne cleared his throat. "Tomorrow we go to Nag Hammadi, and drop off Muhanna. Then we will return to Cairo."

The fire continued its wild dance on the cold stone walls.

It was cold in the basilica when the sun rose over the lowest crest of the fallen walls. Muhanna had slept through the night, snoring intermittently, but lying as still as the dead. His wound did not begin to bleed again, to everyone's great relief. Katherine slept in Nick's arms all night, safer, more peaceful than she felt in a long while. Etienne did not sleep much at all.

He was leaning against the outside wall, smoking one of the Balkan cigarettes from Katherine's knapsack, when he saw a plume of sand rise in the distance. "*Merde*," he complained out loud. "What now?" Etienne flicked the cigarette through his fingertips across the sand and drew himself to his feet.

Just then Nick came outside the monastery and blinked into the morning sun. They stood side by side in silence, watching the plume grow as the vehicle came closer and closer to their meager refuge.

Nick turned to his friend. "Take this. Please," he said, pressing the small gold key into Etienne's hand.

Etienne examined the little thing very closely, touching it with his fingers. "Why?"

"Yours is the better plan," he explained. "I just wanted Katherine to choose, once and for all, and get it over with. I truly thought she'd choose you."

So did Etienne. But he kept that mistake to himself. "Nick, I promise to turn over the Swiss bank account number to you and Katherine. And Nelson will be off your back forever." Etienne put his hand on Nick's shoulder.

"One mistake shouldn't follow you your entire life. You deserve to be free of that burden, to be forgiven. Forgive yourself, my old friend and leave the past behind you, where it belongs."

437

"Is that what you'll do?" Nick asked Etienne. "Put the past behind you?"

"I've been trying to do that for years," said Etienne with his trademark grin. "Maybe I'll get it right this time."

"You know she loves you. Deep down inside, she really does. She has never stopped loving you. She told me so herself."

Etienne's smile left his face. "I think I'll keep this key," he said, "after I recover the manuscripts from Luxor. It will remind me of you and Katherine and our great adventure. Maybe it will bring me luck."

"Don't tell me you believe in magic now," said Nick, smiling.

"My friend, I've seen enough and felt enough to know there are mysteries in this world beyond my understanding. Pagan, Christian, or otherwise, the truth of one doesn't mean the lie of another."

"Whatever your talisman," offered Nick, "I hope it brings you everything you're seeking, and keeps you safe in the process."

Nick and Etienne held each other's eye for a moment. Then they pulled out their guns and turned together to face their newest guest, whomever that might be, whatever that might bring.

A dilapidated old Ford sedan jerked through the last hundred yards of its journey and sputtered to a stop in front of them. It was a long moment before the car door opened on its rusty hinges. Father Mhand slowly pulled himself from the driver's seat. "I didn't know I could drive so well," he smiled satisfactorily. "I came with important news ..."

Nick and Etienne put away their weapons and embraced Father Mhand with warmth and relief. "I am so glad you are both well," the Father beamed. "And Katherine? Is she alright?"

"Yes," said Nick. "Terribly dazed, I think. But she's okay."

"God was surely with you at the caves," said Father Mhand.

"Not so much with Muhanna, I'm afraid," Etienne explained, leading the priest into the monastery. "He was hit with a bullet, in his leg."

"Then I say Allah was definitely with him," assured Father Mhand. "Else he surely would have been hit in the heart." They found

438

Muhanna inside, leaning against the wall, wrapped in blankets, eating ravenously. Katherine moved in a constant stream between Muhanna and the supplies, feeding him one after another remaining ration.

"Well, well," said Nick, hovering over them. "You seem to be feeling much better this morning."

"Perhaps you would like to be Waitress of the Desert for awhile," grumbled Katherine, dusting off her trousers. She threw herself into Father Mhand's frail arms and held him very tightly for a long, long time.

"I killed somebody," she blurted through teary eyes. "I killed Father Antonio." She searched the priest's wrinkled face for help, for answers.

Father Mhand lifted her chin and looked directly into her eyes. "Life and death belong in the realm of God. Only He can give it and He owns it forever. Your life – he intended to spare yesterday. Father Antonio's life – he intended to take back. It was planned that way, it was written in the Book of Time, or else it would not have happened so. Forgive yourself, Katherine. God already has."

The priest held Katherine in his arms a long time, while the others stood in silence and let her weep there, for as long as it took her to spend the tears. She finally released Father Mhand, and wiped her eyes many times with the back of her hand. "How did you know we were here?" she asked.

Father Mhand sat down on a slab of stone, and dabbed his forehead. "It was God," he said. "He told me. Of course."

"Of course," smiled Etienne.

"He did," insisted the priest. "He reminded me of the basilica you spoke about one day, near the cliffs."

"*Oui*," Etienne said, nodding. "I understand."

"Thank you for making that telephone call, Father," said Nick. "It truly saved our lives."

"Ah, yes," said Father Mhand. "That was easy enough." The priest pulled a crumpled wad of toilet paper out of his pocket and read:

"10-33.6057234474.1SAM22.1"

"What does it mean?" asked Etienne. "Beyond 10-33 for *emergency* in military 10-code, that is."

"Yes," nodded Nick. "The numbers that follow aren't a code at all, just a regular old phone number. Direct to Father Antonio."

"Who I called immediately," said Father Mhand. "And the rest was simple: I told the Italian priest that he and his brothers were urgently needed at the caves of Jabal al-Tarif."

"How did you know to tell them that?" asked Katherine, incredulous.

"So David departed from there and escaped to the cave of Adullam; and when his brothers and all his father's household heard of it, they went down there to him," recited Father Mhand. "First Samuel, chapter 22, verse 1."

"That's it, exactly," said Nick, sitting beside the priest on the great stone slab. "Tell me, how did you escape Nafarah's henchman?"

"I did not," explained Father Mhand. "He just left."

"He left?" asked Etienne.

"Mr. Nafarah came to my church last evening. His hand was bandaged and bloody."

Nick looked at Katherine. He was not sure if she would ever get over what had happened in the cave, having the death of one man and the blood of another on her hands. *She was not made for such things.*

Father Mhand continued. "Mr. Nafarah stood in the doorway, angry, as he always was. With a snap of his fingers, the man who always had a gun, but never had a name, left my side. They conferred for only a moment, very quietly. Then, they simply turned and walked together out of the door." The priest dabbed his forehead again. "Oh, my, I nearly forgot," he said, suddenly sitting up straight. "I have important news for you. The most important news."

"What is it?" asked Etienne. "What has happened?"

"Today, a new nation state has been born," said the Father in a hushed tone. "The United Nations of the world has given the Jews a homeland, Israel, in the lands of Palestine."

They all sat in silence for a moment and let the news sink in. "This will surely mean war in the Arab nations," said Nick.

"What about Jerusalem?" asked Muhanna, his voice grim and raspy.

"The country has been partitioned," said Father Mhand. "With Jewish settlements scattered throughout more than half the country." He looked at Muhanna with softness, and hope. "Jerusalem is holy to both the Jews and the Arabs, Muhanna. It will be shared, belonging to neither, occupied by both."

Father Mhand held his hands out to Katherine and Nick. "Your lives are in real danger, now. There will likely be rioting, assassinations. Many blame the Americans, who have taken sides with the Jewish. You must leave this country at once. For your own safety, you must go. But perhaps not forever."

"Well, I am glad to hear about Israel, at any rate," said Katherine. "They deserve to have, finally, their Promised Land."

"Not in the holy land of The Prophet," snapped Muhanna. "Palestine is sacred. There will be no peace over this."

"I sincerely hope you are wrong, Muhanna," said Etienne, troubled. "The Jews and the Muslims must find a way to live together, in peace." Muhanna just grunted.

They gathered outside the stone walls and waded through their awkward good-byes. These were the farewells of people who had known each other for only a very short time, but for whom that period left an indelible mark on all their lives; the farewells of people not wanting to say good-bye, knowing their lives will surely move forward without each other.

Nick and Etienne helped Muhanna into the rusty Ford, tucking him in securely with several blankets, two guns and a prayer to protect him. They each took a turn to say good-bye. Nick reached inside the car and grasped the small man's arm at the elbow. "Look out for the al-Yassids," said Nick. "And watch your back. I don't want to be worrying about you."

"Worry only for them," smiled Muhanna. "I shall be fine."

"*Ma'as salama*," Etienne said, bowing. "Go in safety, Muhanna Ali al-Samara." Muhanna only smiled again, but his eyes danced as he turned his head away from Nick and Etienne.

441

Katherine approached the old car. She held her hands in front of her as if in prayer and bowed her head. *"Salam alekum,"* she said.

"And peace upon you," replied Muhanna, bowing his head in return.

Katherine then wrapped herself around Father Mhand, her mouth bent unwillingly into a frown. "Be safe," he told her, holding her face in his soft wrinkled hands. "Be safe and be happy."

"You will never know how much you mean to me." whispered, Katherine, as the tears began to burn behind her eyes. The priest's eyes sparkled in return.

Father Mhand then offered blessings to Nick and Etienne. "Always and in all things," he said to each of them, placing his hand on their shoulders, "remember the love you have for each other and the love I have for you. For when you do, God will smile upon you. That is how He sees His love reflected back to Himself. And this is the loftiest of all goals we can achieve. The most precious treasure we can find on earth."

The old priest then bent his slender frame into the old car and lurched it away from the basilica. Nick, Katherine and Etienne stood like statues in the sand and watched, until the little plume of dust that marked the car on the horizon faded into air.

Their attention was suddenly and uniformly turned overhead to the screaming roar of engines. Three United States military airplanes broke the calm of the desert ceiling. The group turned their faces to the sky and followed the war machines beyond their seeing. "B-29 Liberators," announced Nick. "They're on their way to Palestine to be sure. The UN resolution is nothing without a little muscle from America." They stood awhile and looked to the eastern horizon, following the future in their imaginations.

"God only knows what will happen in Palestine," murmured Nick.

"My word, Nick Spencer," said Etienne. "You almost sound as if you actually believe in God."

"I don't know," said Nick. "All of a sudden, I truly do not know." Katherine reached over and squeezed his hand.

"Maybe knowing that you don't know is a good beginning," mused Etienne.

"What will you do now, Etienne?" asked Katherine. "After you finish the business with Nelson and Nafarah?"

"Palestine. I will head to Palestine."

"Nothing like heading into the heart of the storm," remarked Nick.

"Why Palestine, of all places?" asked Katherine.

"Q. The source Gospel. I will find it there. Or I will find the beginnings of finding it." Etienne grinned. "If it's the last thing I do."

"I think you will indeed," said Katherine quietly.

Was that a longing I heard in her voice? Etienne wondered. He let himself imagine – one last time – he and Katherine exploring the world. He digging in the earth for hidden stories, she telling those stories with her camera. *No,* sighed Etienne. *Wanting something to be true doesn't make it so.*

"Let's get you two out of here," said Etienne. They threw the last of the supplies into the back of the jeep, and Nick and Katherine climbed in the back seat together. They all took one last look at the basilica that had protected them so well. Katherine rested her head on Nick's shoulder.

Etienne moved to the driver's side door and looked east. The breeze stirred up a skiff of sand that gathered itself into a spiral and danced across the dunes in front of them. The whirling dervish headed across the desert toward Suez and beyond. They drove north, to Cairo, as the strength of the wind gathered.

Epilogue

Journeys Onward

Whether you turn to the right or to the left,
Your ears will hear a voice behind you, saying
'this is the way; walk in it.'
— The Holy Bible, Isaiah 30:21

Cairo, Egypt

The meeting between Etienne and Hugo Nelson went off without a hitch, although not without some noise. Caught red-handed with the jeweled Knife of the Asps and 12 Gnostic codices, there was nothing Nelson could do but surrender to the authorities.

First, though, he went crazy with rage. In his anger and desperation, Nelson threatened Nafarah with everything he could think of, including a slow, excruciating death. Even as he was being hauled off indignantly in handcuffs, Nelson rattled off the names of his many powerful connections in the United States government who would see to his release. Nafarah ignored him entirely. Etienne had no doubt, however, that Nelson would sooner or later go free.

Nick had sent word from America that he was cooperating with the military, and in exchange for his own immunity, was to testify against Nelson for treason during the war. The two governments would fight over their claims against Nelson for years, until each had doled out its respective punishment. How long they would be able to keep Nelson incarcerated, Nick could not guess.

Word also came from America that Katherine and Nick had successfully obtained the Swiss bank account number and everything that came with it, including a chance to start over. Etienne telegraphed Nick back with the warning that, in the end, they had all made an enemy of Nelson, and to forever keep track of him. If Nelson were going to strike Nick where he was most vulnerable, Katherine would be his target.

Nafarah had the Knife of the Asps, which was to be displayed for a time at the Egyptian Museum in Cairo. From there, it would reside permanently in the arms of safety and luxury at the Louvre in Paris.

Nafarah would turn the Gnostic Gospels over to the Coptic Museum, eventually, once the government had ascertained their content and their value. Which would likely take decades. Nafarah was true to his word, however, and, unlocking Etienne's handcuffs, agreed to let him be – as long as he stayed within the bounds of the law, or out of Egypt entirely. Etienne fully expected to cross paths with Nafarah again someday.

For Etienne, he had more than 500 photographs of the Gnostics Gospels. He contacted UNESCO, the United Nations Educational, Scientific, and Cultural Organization, about the recent recovery of the manuscripts. They agreed to establish an international committee, including Etienne, to translate and publish them all.

Etienne returned to the village of Qina, as promised, with 250 Egyptian pounds for the storekeeper, Zafar. Their gratitude mutual, the two men agreed to do business together whenever the opportunity presented itself. It was an agreement that revolved more around information than the selling of antiques, but it suited them both. Pleased, but feeling distantly sad, Etienne made his way back to Cairo.

Etienne's immediate plans were to leave for Palestine – into a region brewing with tension and conflict – to resume his search for Q. Etienne was convinced it would be found in the land of Galilee, though he only had the vaguest idea of where to begin looking.

Etienne had come to believe, however, that once he took a firm step in the direction of his dream – if it was meant to be – the Universe would conspire in his favor, setting in motion unimaginable things that he could not possibly arrange for himself, no matter how hard he tried. He was counting on this: that Q was meant to be his, and Katherine was not. One dream he should embrace, the other he should let go.

Etienne closed up his house for the duration of his trip, with the cupboards bare, all the furniture covered with sheets, and only a lonely stillness taking occupancy. He packed a month's worth of supplies in the jeep: food, water, maps, clothing, a tent and bedroll, and a bottle of scotch for the many solitary nights ahead of him. Etienne put the house key under the door mat, just in case, and took one last look at his home. He had once thought to settle here and live a quiet life, after the war, with a wife and children. But that, too, was a dream outside his grasp.

Just as Etienne started the engine and made ready to leave east, toward Suez and Sinai, a taxicab rolled to a stop in his driveway. From the rear view mirror he saw the shape of a woman step from the cab. As she leaned forward and handed the driver his fare, he saw that she was wearing traveling clothes. Not the type of clothing a woman wears to travel in luxury, but the rugged clothes of desert travel and nights under endless starry skies. She thanked the driver and then turned to Etienne, a bright smile painted on her lips and a renegade lock of hair popping out of her chignon.

Carrying a duffel bag, she came to stand by Etienne's side. "Room for one more?" she asked. As she walked around to the passenger door, Etienne smiled and laid his hand upon his chest, touching a small golden key held there by a braided chain.

THE END

Made in the USA
San Bernardino, CA
09 June 2017